CABIN FEVER

"If you are bent on seduction, sir," Melanie said, "you'd best go back to your hammock, for I vow that you shall have no willing partner."

"But it's you, my dear Meilani, who seems bent on seduction," Ryan objected softly. "And it's you who used the bewitching ploy of the most accomplished seductress—brushing your glorious tresses . . . tresses that beg to be combed by a lover's fingers!" Ryan wound the silken strands about his hands until his fingers stroked the nape of Melanie's neck.

She felt his lips close upon her own, claiming her ever so gently, coaxing her breath away. Something kept her from moving away. . . .

Then, without warning, Ryan drew away from her and patted her shoulder mischievously. "Think well about it, blue eyes," he said.

His retreating chuckle was more than she could stand. Without looking at him, she condemned him through clenched teeth. "You are, by far, the most—the most—"

"Yes, my dear," Ryan retorted. "And I have at last met my match."

FIERY ROMANCE

CALIFORNIA CARESS (2771, $3.75)
by Rebecca Sinclair

Hope Bennett was determined to save her brother's life. And if that meant paying notorious gunslinger Drake Frazier to take his place in a fight, she'd barter her last gold nugget. But Hope soon discovered she'd have to give the handsome rattlesnake more than riches if she wanted his help. His improper demands infuriated her; even as she luxuriated in the tantalizing heat of his embrace, she refused to yield to her desires.

ARIZONA CAPTIVE (2718, $3.75)
by Laree Bryant

Logan Powers had always taken his role as a lady-killer very seriously and no woman was going to change that. Not even the breathtakingly beautiful Callie Nolan with her luxuriant black hair and startling blue eyes. Logan might have considered a lusty romp with her but it was apparent she was a lady, through and through. Hard as he tried, Logan couldn't resist wanting to take her warm slender body in his arms and hold her close to his heart forever.

DECEPTION'S EMBRACE (2720, $3.75)
by Jeanne Hansen

Terrified heiress Katrina Montgomery fled Memphis with what little she could carry and headed west, hiding in a freight car. By the time she reached Kansas City, she was feeling almost safe . . . until the handsomest man she'd ever seen entered the car and swept her into his embrace. She didn't know who he was or why he refused to let her go, but when she gazed into his eyes, she somehow knew she could trust him with her life . . . and her heart.

Available wherever paperbacks are sold, or order direct from the Publisher. Send cover price plus 50¢ per copy for mailing and handling to Zebra Books, Dept. 3156, 475 Park Avenue South, New York, N.Y. 10016. Residents of New York, New Jersey and Pennsylvania must include sales tax. DO NOT SEND CASH.

HAWAIIAN CARESS

LINDA WINDSOR

ZEBRA BOOKS
KENSINGTON PUBLISHING CORP.

ZEBRA BOOKS

are published by

Kensington Publishing Corp.
475 Park Avenue South
New York, NY 10016

First printing: October, 1990

Printed in the United States of America

Part One
Lahaina, Maui 1888 . . .

Chapter One

The rough muslin of her gown clung damply to her skin as Melanie Hammond rang the school bell dismissing class. The children of the *kula*, both native and *haole*, chattered in delight as they scampered out of the open thatched roof building toward the inviting creek. The ever-present island breeze did little to alleviate her discomfort and she found herself looking forward to joining her friends at the secluded bathing pool nearby. They would be preparing for the night's festivities. Blue eyes that had earned her the nickname *maku polu* among the islanders, or "eyes of the sea," guiltily stole a glance at the petite woman sitting at the desk near the head of the classroom.

Hair that had once been the color of Melanie's ebony tresses was now peppered with white and drawn back in a severe knot atop her head. The stern lines of her pale face, which had set many of her pupils to right in reprimand, refused to relax even though she was taking a few pleasurable moments to read verses from her Bible. Even in her quiet moments her mother appeared cross, Melanie observed sadly as she turned and started away from the *kulu*, grateful that Lydia Hammond was so absorbed in her Bible she did not give her the usual parting interrogation about where she was going and why.

Neither of her parents would approve of her going to the Frenchman's plantation, where young ladies of decent upbringing simply were not seen, especially if they knew the reason why. But Melanie was willing to risk their ire, as well as the temptations of the sinful playground notorious for sailors, where girls danced half naked and satisfied the lusty clientele's baser needs in the huts and dense thickets surrounding the isolated place her father constantly strove to have closed down.

She would risk anything to see 'Io—'Io, whom she'd grown up with and idolized as a child, like the older brother she'd never had; 'Io, who had gone away to Boston at her father's direction to attend the same seminary; 'Io, who had returned more handsome than ever and had changed, just as Melanie had in the few years he was gone.

But when they'd announced their engagement, both sets of parents had shocked them by forbidding it. Melanie had been locked in her room and forbidden to see her sweetheart again, with not a reasonable word of explanation except that their marriage was impossible. And 'Io had left Maui . . . left without saying good-bye.

Melanie's throat tightened as she recalled her anguish at the news. How she resented her father and mother for separating them! She begged Abner Hammond to tell her what terrible things he had said to drive 'Io away, but his explanation was weak and fostered more resentment. Her mother's hope that when she was old enough she would marry a planter's son, a *haole*, she vowed would never be realized. Her parents were hypocrites to profess their love of the Hawaiians and equality of all men under God, and yet deny their daughter the right to marry one.

If not by blood, Melanie was Hawaiian at heart. She knew their ways and spoke their language as though it were her own. The islanders accepted her, not as a *haole*, but as Meilani, *me maku polu*, with eyes of the sea. And at eighteen, the same age Lydia had been when she had eloped with Abner Hammond, she was certainly old enough to plan her own future and escape the endless hours of entertaining the boring suitors her mother arranged to visit the mission house.

The path leading to the waterfall where she was to meet

Nani, 'Io's younger sister and her best friend, was narrow, the low-growing tropical greenery reaching out to catch the hem of her dress as Melanie made her way toward the laughter that rose above the trees. At the break in the forest was a pool, where the dancing water cascaded from the rocky ledge above. Several nubile Hawaiian girls, Nani among them, were splashing playfully in the warm sunlight.

This was the bathing pool forbidden to the *kanes*, the men of the village, since the earliest missionaries came to the island. As Melanie unbound her hair, letting the pins drop to the crumpled heap of the shift she'd shed at her feet, she luxuriated in the bath of the sun that warmed her already-tanned skin, refusing to let the pang of remorse for the worry it caused her mother daunt her spirits. Lydia Hammond fretted constantly that her skin might stay that color forever and ruin her chances of getting a suitable husband.

But Melanie did not want the kind of man her mother considered suitable. She was going to marry 'Io. Her Hawaiian beau would not care that her skin was nearly as dark as his own. In fact, it would amuse him that she spent hours in the sun shamelessly naked. Burying her fingers in the satiny tresses that fell in a tangled mass to her hips, she lifted them away, permitting the caress of the afternoon breeze to dry the perspiration from her slender body. Her ripe breasts grew taut in anticipation of the chill of the crystal clear waters stretching before her.

As if in worship, she paid homage to the sun, stretching and reaching for the celestial orb above, seeking, absorbing its energy. Then with a wistful glance in the direction of the plantation where she would seek out her love, she blew him a kiss, her full lips pursing and spreading into a seductive smile before she dove into the cool waters at her feet in reckless abandon.

Ryan Caldwell caught his breath as the blue-eyed native girl looked straight into his glass, as though she knew he were watching. Common sense assuring him otherwise, he stood mesmerized, barely hearing what the crude Frenchman at his side was saying in his guttural speech. She had to be the most beautiful creature he had ever seen, as wild and intoxicating as the orchids that grew in the forest. Her hair was like shining black silk clinging to her lithesome body, so that the sun caught and highlighted each luscious curve. He could almost taste the sweetness of the lips that kissed him across the distance.

But it was the eyes that stirred his blood and made him acutely aware of the tightening ache in his groin. Good God, they were like sapphires . . . hot ice, filled with the promise of unsurpassed passion. She was a pagan temptress designed by Satan himself to drive a man insane with desire. Unconsciously, he moistened his dry lips with his tongue.

"So many beauties to warm the blood of you and your men, no, *mon ami?*"

Damnation, Ryan cursed silently, casting an irritated look in the direction of his host and snapping the telescope shut. He had not intended to spy on innocent maids. The idea was repulsive, as much so as paying this vermin for the delights of their youthful bodies. He had not paid for a passionate tumble in the sheets, since he was a young buck eager to learn the secrets of the upper rooms of the dockside taverns. His lean golden looks and rakish charm was all the enticement most women needed to share his bed. But he had promised his men a rewarding night in Lahaina before sailing on to Honolulu. *His* purpose for going was to meet Wilcox on business. That and to keep an eye on his men.

Still, if she were to be among the women the Frenchman provided . . . "Have you any wenches with blue eyes?"

The Frenchman grinned, revealing a smattering of yellowed teeth, and clapped a heavy hand on Ryan's shoulder. "So you liked what you saw, *mon ami.*"

"I am not your friend, sir. I have engaged your plantation to reward my men and I have asked you a simple question." Ryan's amber eyes glittered in contempt as they burned into the unwelcome hand on his person, as if it soiled him; but the Frenchman remained oblivious to the insult. He was more irritated that his interest was obvious than he was by

10

the man who perceived it and might profit from it.

The Frenchman shrugged. "Blue eyes, green . . . their mothers have known many sailors in the past. I am certain you will find what will please you, monsieur. But first, the money we discussed." The dirt-stained hand that had rested on Ryan's shoulder was now outstretched greedily.

Ryan's lips tightened into a humorless smile as he unfastened the purse he had tied to his belt and slapped it into the Frenchman's palm. "Just so my men enjoy themselves without any trouble from the authorities."

The last thing he needed was to have to bail his men out of prison for wreaking havoc in the streets. He had hoped the isolation of the plantation from town would insure that that wouldn't happen. After all, that was the benefit of dealing with the Frenchman. Who could complain about a good time, no matter how boisterous, out here in the hills? Not that he cared personally for what the prominent citizens of Lahaina thought, but businesswise, it did not pay to offend them. Transport of their sugar was a new venture for the Caldwell lines, an expansion he had fought his family to establish.

"Monsieur, the night will be theirs to spend as they wish. This is paradise, no?" Tobacco-tinted drool slipped out of the corner of the stocky man's mouth and he absently wiped it on his sleeve.

"So it appears," Ryan agreed, his thoughts returning to the vision he had just seen.

The ache in his loins increased as he replayed the softly blown kiss in his mind, and Ryan shook himself to erase the image. He had been at sea too long. Surely that was it. Even if the wench were not present tonight, he would find consolation with another once business was taken care of. Females were females, and while some possessed more charm than others, they were all much the same to him — the weaker sex that would latch onto any man fool enough to confuse desire with love. God knows his brother had paid dearly for his mistake. In fact, Ryan doubted the existence of such an intangible emotion. No woman, no matter how

11

lovely, had ever tempted him to stay in one place any longer than the time it took to tire of her, and to his mind, that was how it should be.

As the sun made its rapid descent on the orange-glazed horizon, the sound of drums and stringed instruments resounded through the trees and mingled with the boisterous voices of the seamen seated around long lengths of woven mats strewn with wooden bowls and utensils. The tantalizing scent of the roasted pig that had been steaming in the *imu,* a pit filled with hot lava rock and covered with taro leaves, filled the air, along with the other delicacies prepared for the feast. Brown-skinned island women were scattered among the guests, keeping their mugs filled with rum punch and flirtatiously offering tastes of the foods spread before them. An occasional kiss was stolen by some of the bolder seamen, which was usually received with a coy snicker and returned with the promise of more as the evening wore on.

Melanie and Nani stopped at the edge of a grove of mangoes and looked at each other for moral support. Dressed much like the other women who circulated about the grounds, they wore thick grass skirts and garlands of *leis* over a single thin shift that they were loath to give up, not being as bold as some of their friends. Although most of the island women wore skirts and blouses, instead of the traditional tapa cloth of bygone days, the Frenchman felt the grass skirts and *leis* added flavor to his entertainment. And they certainly enhanced the poetic presentation of the hula.

"Do you see him?" Nani whispered. Her voice betrayed her fear of discovery and Melanie gave her hand a squeeze of uncertain reassurance.

"No, but he will come. All we have to do is mingle." She prayed silently that the young men she had overheard had not been wrong. She was certain she had heard one of them say that he was meeting 'Io, the carver's son, along with his friends from Honolulu, here.

"But what if one of those men wants us to—?" Nani chewed her lower lip, unable to finish the suggestion.

"One step at a time, Nani," Melanie cautioned calmly, hiding the fact that that thought had crossed her mind as well. "Once we find 'Io, we can leave with him and we'll be safe."

Melanie was beginning to regret sharing her plan with Nani. Even though Nani was a sweet individual who wholeheartedly endorsed the love between her brother and Melanie, she was also one who enjoyed the strict confines of everyday life. She would have made the perfect daughter for Lydia Hammond . . . someone who would accept and obey without question.

"If you begin to feel uncomfortable, just make an excuse to leave for a minute and make your way home as quickly as you can. I promise, if I do not leave with 'Io, I will meet you there before morning."

For a moment, panic that her information was false and that 'Io might not show up at the *luau* started to rise again, but she steeled herself. He would be there. He had to come. Yet, as her eyes scanned the guests gathered around the mats, she could not find a familiar face. Without realizing it, she stepped forward into the glow of the torches that lit the clearing in the plantation yard.

"You there! *Wiki, wiki!* Carry these to the hungry gentlemen who have just arrived and make them welcome." A heavyset woman in a billowing skirt of red dyed tapa rushed over to where Melanie and Nani stood and shoved a gourd of rum punch at Melanie. "For the golden one and his men," she instructed, handing Nani two wooden cups. "Well, go on!"

A fat hand shooed Melanie and a wide-eyed Nani off in the direction of the men who had just emerged from a small shack at the edge of the clearing. Her heart pounding in her throat, Melanie forced a wide smile and rushed toward the group. As she reached them, Nani on her heels, the Frenchman and the golden one the auntie had indicated broke off their conversation abruptly and stared in open interest.

13

Melanie hesitated, words failing her under the green-eyed gaze of the golden stranger. For a moment she could have sworn she had seen a flicker of recognition on his face, but her own bold return of his appraisal quickly assured her that had she ever seen a man as devilishly handsome as the one before her, she would certainly have remembered.

"Where is your tongue, girl? Can you not see that the captain wishes to be welcomed?"

Bewilderment stirred the blue waters of her eyes as she glanced uncertainly at Nani. But Nani showed more resource than Melanie had given her credit for. After all, she was Hawaiian, and besides knowing the ways of the *haole* taught by the missionaries, she knew the hospitable ways of her people. Promptly, the younger girl placed the cups at her feet and removed one of the *leis* from her neck. To Melanie's astonishment, she placed the flowers about the neck of the older man next to the captain and planted a kiss on his bearded cheek with a bright smile.

"Aloha, kelamaku!" Welcome, sailor.

Feeling curious eyes upon her, Melanie quickly followed suit, but as she rose on tiptoe to bestow the friendly kiss, the captain turned his head so that her lips brushed his. His eyes twinkled at her sharp intake of breath, refusing to release her from their hypnotic gaze. *"Aloha,"* she whispered, mentally shaking herself into action. In the time it took to pick up the gourd, she managed to recover from the electric charge that set her senses on alert.

"Gentlemen, I shall leave you to the mademoiselles for a moment, as I have other guests arriving," the Frenchman announced, giving Melanie one more curious appraisal. "You have but to ask for anything you wish."

Melanie neither saw the meaningful look he directed at the golden-haired man now seated beside her, nor the silently spoken "blue eyes" that formed on the host's thick lips. She was intent on pouring the liquored punch into the cups that Nani held with hands steadier than her own. She chastised herself severely for her brief panic, condemning herself for nearly giving them away before they had even had a

14

hance to look for 'Io.

"What is your name?"

Melanie looked up blankly, startled by the deep baritone voice that seemed to stroke her spine, undermining her efforts to remain cool and aloof.

Mistaking her hesitation as an indication that she did not speak English, the grey-bearded man interpreted the question in broken Hawaiian, directing it at both she and Nani.

Nani answered with a shy smile. "Nani."

"Meilani," Melanie responded, tearing her eyes away to concentrate on not spilling the full cup she handed to the soft-spoken stranger.

"That's a good one, sir," the mate commented wryly. "This pretty little thing's named *beauty*," he informed his captain, pointing to Nani. "I'd say her mama knew what she was doing when she named her."

"If that were so, Amos, then all of these lovely creatures would be called Nani," the captain responded, reaching out to trace the curve of Melanie's face. "Particularly this one. Meilani," he repeated, rolling her name off his tongue in a way that sent a shiver of excitement through her in spite of the balmy evening temperature

"Ye keep talkin' like that, Cap'n, and she'll get your meanin' mighty quick," Amos remarked with a snicker. "Never know'd language to stop ye yet."

Melanie lowered her face to hide the blush rising to her cheeks. A sideways glance revealed many of the other girls putting food on the plates for the men, and she dedicated herself to the same task. Steamed taro cut in cubes and in the puddinglike state of *poi*, sweet potatoes, fresh pieces of fruit, marinated mushrooms, as well as assorted meats were spread upon the mats in abundance. Realizing that she had not eaten since early that morning, Melanie helped herself to the mushrooms, one of her favorites, as she filled the wide shallow bowl and returned to her guest.

"Thank you, Meilani," the captain said as she placed the bowl in front of him. His smile revealed even white teeth that contrasted starkly with his sun-bronzed face. Hair that curled mischievously down on his forehead was further evidence of a life spent on sea, for it was an uncommonly golden color, no doubt tinted by the sun.

"*Mahalo*," Amos prompted.

"*Mahalo*, Meilani," the captain repeated, crossing his legs so that the white material of his rolled-up trousers stretched across well-developed thighs and placing the bowl in his lap.

Melanie nodded and smiled in answer, keeping to her earlier agreement with Nani that they pretend to be ignorant of English in order to protect their identities.

"Now blamed if this ain't livin'!" Amos exclaimed, biting into a chunk of roast pork that Nani handed him. "Give that," he added in awkward Hawaiian, pointing to another type of meat. "Damned if I ain't goin' to try it all after eatin salt food day in an' out."

Melanie held back a snicker as Nani put the delicacy to his lips and turned in time to see his captain curiously tasting the same. She turned her face away to hide her amusement as the two men exchanged bemused looks, each chewing thoughtfully.

"Aha?" Amos finally asked of Nani.

" *Ilio*," Nani answered in round-eyed innocence, not daring to look at Melanie.

"Christ!" Amos exclaimed, spitting the remainder of the meat in the dirt behind him. "It's dog meat!"

Melanie could not help the amusement that escaped, despite the hand she had placed over her mouth as Amos rinsed out his mouth with the punch and spat it aside as well.

"It's really quite tasty, Amos," the golden captain commented, reaching down in his bowl for another piece. "Here, Meilani. I forgot my manners."

Melanie jerked back as he put the meat to her lips and, shaking her head mutely, pushed it back toward his own. Green eyes helds her as in brief challenge before his wide shoulders began to shake a with a chuckle. "I see, Amos, that not all Hawaiians have acquired a taste for this supreme delicacy, either," he laughed, winking mischievously at Melanie as he tossed the morsel over his shoulder.

Relieved of the momentary tension, she joined in his amusement. He was certainly one of the most fascinating men she had ever met. When she recovered her breath, she pointed at him, poking her finger playfully at the crisp mat of burnished gold revealed by the open laces of his shirt.

"What is his name?" she asked the first mate, who was just beginning to see a little humor in the situation.

"She wants to know your name," Amos interpreted, suspiciously eyeing the piece of fruit Nani handed him.

"Ryan." As Melanie nodded in acknowledgment, Ryan put his fingers to her lips. "Ryan," he said again, prompting her to repeat it.

His fingers were warm, and the way they tutored her was strangely disturbing. Melanie said the name and smiled, inadvertently contacting his fingers with each syllable. Upon realization of what she had done, she pulled back, but Ryan caught her wrist and put her hand to the bowl of food.

"Go on, Meilani. I'm anxious to see what other delicacies you have to offer me," he said softly, in a tone meant to assuage her sudden panic.

Melanie hesitated, almost afraid to go along with the golden stranger and yet compelled to do so. Here was a man who didn't fit into any of the categories she had formed in her mind of the opposite sex. He was not like the planters' sons she had met, spoiled by a life of ease and certain that she would fawn for their attentions. His hands were roughened by the elements and his eyes were speculative, as if not quite sure what she would do. Nor was he like the Frenchman and many of the men surrounding them. He certainly was not like her father, and even the category she held dear for 'Io did not exactly apply. He was beyond her experience, she concluded, and she found herself eager to know more about this particular type of man.

Her pulse beat against the side of her throat as she grasped a piece of fruit, her gaze transfixed by that of the golden captain, and raised it to his mouth. Perhaps she should have felt indignation for what he might be suggesting, and yet it excited her more than she cared to admit. Surely the eyes of the serpent in the Garden of Eden had been green and its hide golden. His white teeth nibbled at the morsel until they teased the flesh of her fingers, his tongue lapping up the sweet nectar that clung to them. Melanie watched in awe as her trembling fingers traced his lips.

" 'Io!"

Nani's exclamation broke the sensuous trance and Melanie visibly shook herself, drawing back as if bitten. Her eyes grew round in astonishment at the hot flash that enveloped her, burning her skin as the sun never had.

"Meilani!" Nani insisted, directing Melanie's shaken attention across the clearing, where a tall dark-skinned young man embraced a comrade.

" 'Io," she echoed numbly. "Oh, 'Io!" Her eyes took on a glow that rivaled the torches flickering against the velvet night as the spell was broken and the meaning of Nani's interruption sunk in.

For a moment the fair captain had distracted her, but now he need not have existed, for 'Io had her full attention. Unlike his fellow merrymakers who had donned the ancient dress for the celebration, 'Io was dressed in the white trousers of the *haole*. But he had done away with the shirt, wearing only the *lei* of *kukui* nuts against a muscular chest that rippled with every movement of his arms as he halfheartedly fell in with some impromptu dance movements to the music. Melanie felt as if her heart would burst with joy as she watched him. But when his sister rose and raced toward him, her limbs refused to move, as if stricken by the apprehension Nani had voiced earlier . . . that he might not be pleased to see her.

She closed her eyes in a brief prayer to the contrary, and when she opened them again, Nani was in his arms. She started to rise to her feet when a band of steel clamped about her wrist in restraint. Her startled glance was met with demanding inquiry from the stranger who but a moment ago had held her trapped in a warm world of golden

18

enchantment. He would understand, she thought, smiling apologetically as she gently pried his fingers away.

"Tell him I must go speak to someone for a moment, please," she explained to a completely befuddled Amos.

"She says she's got to speak to the young man and she'll be back."

The face that had reminded her of a sun-god darkened, clouded with thunder, before he released her wrist. With a less than enthusiastic smile, Ryan Caldwell let her go and observed with keen interest as she made her way through the crowd to where the tight-lipped native watched her approach. Whoever the lad was, he was not any more pleased to see the girl here than Ryan was to let her go.

Melanie could see by the angry glow in 'Io's dark eyes that she and Nani had displeased him, but she was certain that once they were alone, she could improve his humor. Hadn't she always made him laugh when he was upset with her, making him swing her about in his strong arms and shake her in loving chastisement? But as she reached him, instead of greeting her, 'Io pivoted and stalked off into the privacy of the mango grove with a jerking motion of his head for her to follow.

That was it, she reassured herself. He didn't want to call attention to her in the crowd. He had always been thoughtful of her in that way. Of course it would prove an embarrassment to her family to be recognized at the Frenchman's *luau*. But Melanie had decided 'Io was worth that risk.

"I do not know which of you is the bigger fool!" 'Io declared, spinning around to face the two girls who followed him. Even in the clothing of civilization, he was a creature of the wild, his movements like that of the winged predator, swift and sure, yet graceful. "How did you know I was here?"

"Secrets are hard to keep in the village, 'Io," Nani spoke up timidly. Her eyes glistened with hurt at her brother's outburst. "We wanted so much to see you. It has been a long time, brother."

"Do you know what could happen to you?" he demanded

19

incredulously. "Look at you! You're half naked!"

Melanie stepped forward defiantly, having endured enough of his temper. "We are dressed in the garb of our ancestors," she challenged proudly. She actually looked forward to their argument, for she anticipated the sweet reconciliation that would inevitably follow.

"*Our* ancestors, Meilani," 'Io pointed out, his voice dropping as he feasted his eyes upon her. "You are a *haole*."

Melanie stepped back as if he had slapped her. This could not be 'Io. Never had he called her a white person. The difference in their race had never been a barrier between them. She was his little blue eyes, his *maka polu li 'i*. As if recognizing his blunder, he gentled his voice. "I am only concerned for the safety of two who are very precious to me, Meilani." He motioned her to him. "You and Nani must go home at once."

But Melanie held her ground. "That is not why I came, 'Io. I am not satisfied to merely see you and go back to my lonely room again."

'Io saw the grim determination on Melanie's face and wondered how he was going to convince her to leave without a scene. There was more than one danger at the Frenchman's plantation. Not only was her honor in jeopardy, but conceivably her life should she be in the wrong place at the wrong time. If anything happened to her, he'd never forgive himself or ever be able to face Abner Hammond again. "Nani!"

"Yes, 'Io?" Nani hopped to attention, like the blue jackets that frequented the streets of Lahaina responding to their superior's command. She eagerly sought to win his approval as she waited for him to speak, but his somber attention was fixed on Melanie.

"Go to the plantation road and wait for Meilani . . . and tell Mother and Father that I am well and will see them soon, but this time it is impossible."

"Why, 'Io? Are you in trouble?"

"Just do as I say," 'Io snapped impatiently. "Please," he added, gathering his sister to him and bussing her on the

20

strength to resist such compelling temptation.

"I love you, 'Io," Melanie cried against his lips desperately, thrusting her body against his until she felt the hard evidence of his need for her.

Encouraged, she kissed him, alternately nibbling and caressing his lips. However insurmountable this barrier was that separated them, they could find a way, she thought wildly as the flame of desire began to race unchecked through her veins.

"No!"

Melanie was unprepared for the vehement thrust that sent her sprawling backwards. Blindly, she caught herself on the rough bark of a tree and tried to gather her wits. Bewildered blue eyes sought angry dark ones in the moonlight and suddenly the white heat that had consumed her turned to ice. Her hands shook visibly as she drew herself upright and crossed her arms protectively against her aching breasts. She warily eyed the man standing a few feet from her, for he was no longer her 'Io, but rather a stranger whose hostility reached across the distance between them in his voice.

"Go home, Meilani, and don't ever try to see me again!"

Surely no warrior had ever looked more formidable. His white teeth were clenched and his towering figure loomed over her in the darkness, frightening her to the core of her being. No weapon he could wield could have wounded her more than the harsh words he grated out. He looked at her as though he hated her, as if he felt nothing but contempt for the love she had offered him.

Like in a cornered animal, adrenaline began to pump its renewing life into Melanie's veins, thawing the shock of his rejection with anger born of pain. She squared her shoulders, rearranging the tumble of *leis* around her neck with a calculated calm, aware that 'Io watched the metamorphosis in wonder. Taking slow, deliberate breaths, Melanie walked toward the young man, a living example of his childhood image of Pele, goddess of the volcano. Boiling in the depths of her eyes was molten sapphire, the fury of the woman scorned.

"I am home, 'Io. It's you I send to whatever depths of hell you came from to torture me so."

When her hand lashed out, drawing its nails across his cheek, he made no effort to protect himself. He could not deny her that. He wanted a physical pain to help ease the torment he felt inside. It took all the endurance he had to watch her leave him, to let her go without telling her the truth he had promised to keep secret . . . that her father and his were one and the same.

Chapter Two

"Guns, Captain. They need to be unloaded on the beach. Our own men can pick them up there and hide them."

Ryan Caldwell listened to the proposition of the mustached gentleman seated on his left and toyed with the food Meilani had abandoned. His appetite had merely been whetted . . . and it was not for food. Although he gave the ridiculously uniformed gentleman his polite attention, he had no wish to become involved in any intrigue concerning the government. His eyes darted to the place where she had disappeared into the trees, searching for any sign of her return.

"It could be very profitable for your company, sir. I can give you half now and the other half upon delivery."

"I do not deal in arms, Mr. Wilcox, and I certainly have no wish to be caught between the Hawaiian and *haole* regimes. Your first king was smart enough to realize that weapons were not the way to settle differences. Diplomacy, I think, is what he used to unite the islands." Ryan was aggravated at best. Wilcox had contacted him on the premise of shipping a sugar cargo and now wanted to involve him in some subversive attempt to restore power to a wasteful monarch.

"I should have known better than to expect a *haole* to understand!" the man across from him sneered in contempt. "And if you stay in Hawaii, Captain, then be advised there is no in-between. You will have to become involved on one side or the other . . . and I can well guess where your support will fall."

The man was a fanatic. Ryan shrugged as he reached for the gourd of rum punch and helped himself. "Think what you wish, Wilcox, but bother me no more with your subversive aims. I'm done with business for the night."

At the lazy dismissal, Wilcox spun about stiffly and walked away. Ryan watched him, knowing full well that he had made an enemy. He had seen men like Wilcox before. No doubt there was reason for the fevered dedication that burned in his eyes. Colonization, annexation . . . they were often the price paid for the progress business brought to a primitive land.

"Damnation," he cursed, slinging the remainder of his drink on the ground. His mood had been dampened by all this political rubbish.

"I'm thinkin' much the same thing, sir. Them wenches ain't comin' back. No doubt their givin' that young buck the time of his life, but there's more to be had," Amos observed with hungry eyes. "And them with more flesh on 'em's more to my likin' anyways. That little 'un made me feel downright guilty for some o' the things I was thinkin'," he added with a snort. "But that 'un, now, is another story."

Ryan followed his first mate's lusty gaze to one of the dancers, just in time to see the woman smile at them, her ample hips never losing the beat of the music. She was a comely wench in her thirties, the captain guessed, although it was difficult to judge with some females. And she was definitely a warm one by the way she continued to stare at them. Perhaps another time, Ryan might have been interested himself, even though he preferred the more willowy types . . . like Meilani. Leaning over the mate's shoulder, he raised his voice above the music. "I'm going back to the ship. See that the men are there in time to sail with the tide tomorrow."

"Aye, sir, but I'd not be too hasty," the mate answered, pointing past the dancers to where the native girl Meilani burst into the clearing. "Now, if she won't make you forget

26

"That," Ryan answered sardonically, "I shall give to the lady."

A tobacco-stained grin stretched across uneven teeth. "But of course, *mon ami*. I shall speak to her at once."

Out of the corner of her eye, Melanie saw the Frenchman making his way toward her, his weight shifting heavily from side to side with each step. But instead of the apprehension she had felt earlier, she lifted her chin and glared, as if challenging him to recognize her. Beyond reason, she wanted anything that would upset 'Io. He had followed her when she did not go home, demanding she leave the *luau* before she was recognized and her reputation ruined. He was nearly shaking with frustrated anger for he dared not make a scene, giving her the weapon to exact her revenge.

"Mademoiselle, the captain wishes to see you dance with the others," the Frenchman informed her, his small eyes shifting from Melanie to 'Io in speculation. If the native caused trouble, he'd have him locked away until the girl was gone.

"She is not going to dance," 'Io spoke up, stepping in front of Melanie. "I am taking her home."

With a strength that surprised the Hawaiian, Melanie shoved him aside. "I would love to join the others."

Her eyes glowed triumphantly at 'Io as she allowed the host of the *luau* to escort her to the line of dancers. She would make him pay for what he had done to her. He wanted to stop her and he couldn't. It showed in his eyes as they followed her. Damn you, 'Io. Her lips formed the words as she fell into the rhythm of the strumming guitars and beating drums.

How ironic that the song was a love song written about a beautiful flower that grows on the island of Kauai, the flower actually being a lovely young girl. Ever so delicately with her hands Melanie described the enchanted place where the flower grew to maturity and blossomed, kissed by the dew and nourished by the sun. As she turned, gracefully swirling her arms above her head to imitate the tradewinds that brought her lover home, she noticed the golden stranger leaning against a sloping palm tree. Knowing that 'Io watched her every move, she blew the kiss the heavenly flower sent out to meet her love to the captain and dipped her lashes provocatively as he met it with a smile.

My God, she knew what she was doing and he was acting like a moonstruck boy, Ryan Caldwell scolded himself. He fought to control the desire that flooded through his body at the sight of Meilani's lithesome form swaying to the rhythm of the guitars and drums. No, she moved to the rhythm of the island, he corrected himself, lifting his eyes to the palm fronds that moved to the same cadence overhead, in an effort to distract his mind from the direction it was taking. He wanted her now, and it was all he could do to keep from obeying the primitive instincts she aroused in him to carry her off to the nearest private tree and make love to her.

But he would wait. His features hardened, reflecting his anger at himself for his impatience as he stared at the stars above the trees. It had already cost him good money for what he could have had for nothing. But he didn't know what hold the Frenchman might have on the girl, what kind of arrangement they had between them, he reasoned in his defense. And there was little time between now and the morning tide to play any game but that of the islanders.

With the change of the tempo to an ancient chant to Pele, goddess of the volcano, Melanie became lost in the wild and untamed enchantment of all that was Hawaii. Now she was a part of it, one with the land upon which she had been born. She moved like the leafy branches in the breeze. She stomped like the angry voice of Pele bellowing from the mountain top. She lifted her face to smile at the sun and laugh at the tickling raindrops. Her arms flailed in wild grace at the winds of the hurricane, only to be calmed by the rising of a gentle moon over placid waters. The magic of the islands flowed from her being — exotic, mysterious, fragrant, embracing. . . .

Thunderous. Melanie's eyes widened at the reverberating explosion that interrupted the chant of the islands. The skies were brilliantly clear, she noted, bewildered at the sound of the thunder that was not part of the chant. A woman's shriek called her attention to the main road leading into the plantation yard, where a group of uniformed men were assembled, men whose dress she recognized as that of the law enforcement officers of Lahaina.

"Wilcox!"

Another shot rang out and the clearing became a mad scramble of confusion. Melanie remained glued to the spot, uncertain of where to run or why she should. The constabulary knew of the Frenchman's *luaus.* It was no secret that many of its members attended regularly, although names were not revealed. So why were they here?

"There he goes!" one of them shouted.

"Meilani, go home! Quickly!"

'Io's words broke through the dull thought processes that stumbled through her mind. She looked about frantically. Where was he? " 'Io!" she cried out, the surrounding panic beginning to infect her. People were everywhere, running and shouting, shooting and cursing.

"Meilani!"

Melanie turned and ran into the strong arms that offered her refuge and sanity in the chaos. She clung to 'Io's waist and buried her face in his chest. He afforded her only a brief squeeze of reassurance before he ushered her into the safety of some nearby trees.

"Men of the *Liberty Belle,* to me!"

Melanie gasped at the imperious command that erupted from the man she held on to, noting for the first time the unlaced shirt that no more belonged to 'Io than did the voice that roared above the din of confusion. She made an effort to pull away from him, but he caught her firmly by the shoulders.

"It's all right, Meilani. I won't let anything happen to you," Ryan promised gently. "Just stay by me."

Melanie stiffened, her eyes widening warily at the golden stranger who offered his protection. Dared she trust him?

Ryan Caldwell cursed in frustration at the language barrier between them and glanced around in relief to see Amos

31

leading a group of men, whom he recognized as part of his crew, toward him. The first mate had hardly reached them when Ryan shoved Meilani at him.

"Take her with you to the *Belle* and explain that we'll take care of her. I'm going after the others. Hell, they're just primed for a fight. Jack, Mason, come with me."

"Whoa there, Meilani," Amos exclaimed as Melanie tried to pry apart the locked fingers that held her prisoner. He began again in broken Hawaiian. "You no hurt. Safe with captain. Umm . . . You go sleep, he take home when sun is in sky. Big trouble here. He try to fix. You want home, you come us. Oh, shit!" he added, lapsing into English. "I ain't makin' a damned bit of sense to 'er."

Melanie would have laughed at Amos under any other circumstances. It was obvious that he was trying to hold her without hurting her, and she could not help but believe that he told her the truth. Her mind reeled as she tried to make sense of what was happening, making her regret the rum she had forced down to spite 'Io. She managed to turn in the circle of Amos's rough arms to search his face for any hint of deceit, but all she saw was friendly grey eyes that tried to assure her where words had failed.

"But I must go," she explained slowly in Hawaiian, wondering at the sudden shift in her hazy surroundings. "Thank your captain . . ."

Melanie broke off at the sound of a familiar voice, roaring across the plantation yard as if it came from the pulpit in her father's church, condemning the sinful acts that had transpired. It couldn't be!

"You, sir, are an abomination to this island! It was God's own doing that led these good men here this night! I demand, Constable, that this French cur and his whores be brought before justice, and every man here fined for his sinful pursuits!"

Melanie felt the blood drain from her face as she looked blindly at the changing face of Amos Cobb. She blinked her eyes in disbelief. Instead of the first mate's image, she saw her father's condemning countenance glaring down at her, his holy voice thundering in her ears. "Bring the whore to justice!"

"No, Papa!" she cried out in a voice that was little more than a whimper as she sought refuge in the swirling vortex of blackness that enveloped her.

In the haze of her semiconsciousness, she was aware that she was being carried by the golden captain's men, which served to prevent her discovery by her father. God, she couldn't bear that! Then she was on a ship, judging from the gentle sway of the hard bunk she'd been deposited on. It was so hard to tell, for her mind was so clouded, making clear thought impossible. But the man called Amos had promised she was going to be safe . . . from whom? Her father? The police? It really didn't matter, for Melanie found herself so sleepy, lulled by the rhythmic rocking of her bed.

And then she had dreamed . . . or was it reality? She'd heard 'Io's voice calling out to her and then he was at her side, distraught over the way he'd treated her. He smothered her face and neck with tiny, urgent kisses, which drew her from the warm reaches of her slumber into the torrid throes of a passion she'd never dreamt of.

The things he did to her made her body dance, like a puppet dangling in a fiery limbo of desire. Never had Melanie known such wicked sensations as spread through her, robbing her of breath and sanity. The searing invasion that joined them in love's most intimate union could not stop the wild tide he stirred in her, until the discomfort was of little consequence and she was tearing at his back, crying out . . . for what she didn't know. It wasn't to stop the sweet madness sweeping through her shuddering body, yet she wondered that she could survive.

Then, when at last she'd drifted back down to a more earthly realm, she'd smiled up at him, calling him her mighty hawk, and crooked her finger under his chin. But to her astonishment, it was not 'Io who gazed back at her, the embers of passion still glowing in his eyes, but the golden stranger—the man still in possession of her desire-ravaged body.

While her body still gloried in that ultimate embrace, her mind rebelled violently. This wasn't the way it was to be! Closing her eyes, she willed the golden image away and replaced it with that of her raven-haired hawk. Thus satisfied, she sank into slumber, contentedly cradled in the arms of her lover.

Chapter Three

The first light of day was blossoming on the eastern horizon when Melanie awakened, roused by a soft grinding noise beside her. Gradually, her eyes became accustomed to the room and grew rounder in amazement, coming to rest on the man sleeping next to her. The golden stranger was sprawled naked on the edge of the mattress, one leg carelessly thrown across her and an arm encircling her waist, making any movement impossible without waking him.

No! That was the last thing she wanted to do . . . to face him. Not until she knew what had happened. But that didn't take a lot of deduction. She was in his bed, as naked as he, and the secret ache within her of muscles unaccustomed to a man's possession were evidence of the fact that she had permitted this man to make love to her. What confused her was why. She hardly knew him.

Her smooth brow furrowed with her struggle to put the elusive memories of the night in order. Her head ached abominably, making it difficult to concentrate. In her dream, 'Io, her childhood sweetheart, had come to make up for the harsh way he had treated her. His molten kisses had made her swoon with pleasure, his lovemaking more than she'd imagined in her wildest fantasies. But then he had had the face of the golden stranger called Ryan and she'd willed him away . . . or thought she had.

Color flooded her face at the memory, her cheeks burning in spite of her conscious condemnation of her behavior. Dear God, how could she face him after the way she had behaved? What must he think of her? Her stomach churned uncertainly at the thought. Perhaps she would die before Ryan woke up, she thought miserably, her eyes welling with tears.

A thin film of moisture clung to her skin. It was suffocatingly hot in the confines of the bed. Swallowing hard, she fought to control the nausea that washed over her with a wave of dizziness. If only he would go away and give her time to get herself composed, to think. It was so hot, she thought, moistening her dry lips with her tongue. If she could just get some air.

She tried inhaling deeply, but the heavy leg across her abdomen seemed leaden, adding to the illusion of the room closing in on her. A rise of panic began to set in. She had to get away from him, to get some air, or she was going to be ill. Desperation taking over, she shoved the sleeping figure away from her, sending the precariously perched captain tumbling off the bunk. But she did not care. Melanie was only intent on reaching the open portal above. Oblivious to her nakedness and the startled curse of her sleeping partner as he hit the floor with a thud, she struggled to her knees and breathed deeply of the fresh morning breeze that ventured through the opening. Her fingers were clenched white about its brass frame, as if she feared being dragged away by the man she heard moving behind her.

Gradually, the dampness on her skin began to evaporate, but still Melanie felt weak and queasy. From somewhere in the room she heard pouring water, but she could not bring herself to satisfy her vague curiosity and look. The air was the only thing that kept her from falling into that dark void that had claimed her frequently during the night.

She seized her lower lip with her teeth, shivering from the aftermath of the hot flash. What on earth was wrong with her? It was like the time she had had the fever, but not quite. Her mind felt as though it were filled with clouds that blocked logical thought, allowing only bits of it to slip through like revealing rays of sunshine shedding light on the past night.

"Meilani?" The mattress sagged with Ryan's weight behind her. A sun-bronzed arm slipped gently around her abdomen as a cool wet cloth was folded against her forehead.

Dear heaven, she couldn't face him—not now, not like this. She tried to be brave, but her skin felt like thousands of minute icicles pricked it, giving rise to gooseflesh. With a whimper of defeat, she leaned into the curve of his warm body for comfort, silent tears spilling down her cheeks.

"Shush, blue eyes. You'll be all right. Try to lie back down and I'll cover you."

To illustrate his intentions, the captain gently drew her down on the mattress and began to tug a corner of the sheet up from the mass of tangled bedclothes they had slept on. He fluffed up a pillow and tucked it under her head, his fingers lingering in the silken tresses of her hair. But when he leaned over to brush her lips with his own, Melanie stiffened, drawing the sheet tightly to her neck and shaking her head vehemently. The action made her pay with a throbbing increase of blood rushing to her temples.

"Don't worry, blue eyes," the captain assured her. "Although you are undeniably tempting, I'd rather not frolic with someone who looks like they are about to heave their insides out." His voice was sympathetic, but his green eyes twinkled, reflecting his good humor. Unlike Melanie, her lover seemed to have weathered the night quite to his satisfaction.

Melanie did not move. Instead, she watched the man stroll over to a chair where he had abandoned his clothing the night before. Her face regained its color as she studied Ryan for the first time. He was a magnificent specimen of a man. Broad shoulders tapered down to a narrow waist, his flat and muscular stomach sun-darkened to his naval and white below. The wiry mat of burnished gold hair on his chest followed a similar pattern but formed a narrow line leading down past his naval to a thicker growth, where the weapon that had taken her maidenhood stood proudly, indifferent to her shocked gaze.

"I did say I was tempted," Ryan remarked dryly upon

catching her scarlet appraisal. He pulled up his trousers and proceeded to button them. That she had seen him nude didn't seem to bother him at all. In fact, it seemed to amuse him.

Melanie said nothing. Instead, she turned her face away, ever alert to the man's movements as he continued dressing. She now recognized the category to which he belonged—that of the womanizers. He was not much better than the Frenchman, simply more polished. He had seduced her, she concluded defensively, and she, thinking that he was 'Io, had allowed him to dissolve every shred of self-discipline she possessed until she was beyond stopping him.

Surely it was the rum punch that had weakened her will. Hadn't her father condemned alcohol for that very reason? And she had gulped it down to defy 'Io. 'Io. Her throat constricted. Would he want her now that she had been spoiled by another man? Oh, Melanie, you fool! She gasped in an attempt to swallow the sob that rose from her chest, then rolled over, facing the wall. But his name tore from her aching throat. " 'Io . . ."

"Meilani?" Ryan's voice was full of concern as he reached for her, placing his hand on her shoulder.

It was his fault, she thought madly. Like an irritated cat, Melanie swatted his hand away and withdrew to the corner of the bunk, her eyes brittle through her tears. His sudden concern for her welfare was a bit belated.

Ryan's face took on a bemused expression. He stared at the change in the native girl, wishing he knew what was going on behind those swirling pools of sapphire. She was certainly an enigma to him. Nothing about her seemed to make sense. Were it not for the language barrier between them, he'd demand to know just what he had done to earn the open hostility blazing in her eyes. Or perhaps this was a sample of what the Frenchman had warned him about. If it was, he would straighten her out, communication problem or not.

But for now she was ill, no doubt hung over. Her angry outburst had cost her, for even now he could see her slight body trembling beneath the sheets he had tucked about her. Besides, he had a ship to get under way, he reminded himself, fighting the urge to try to comfort her. She'd be all right after she slept it off. In the meantime, he'd leave Meilani to Amos Cobb.

Melanie collapsed on the pillows with the slam of the door, relieved that the captain was gone. Perhaps he was done with her now. From the clouded look on his face, his good humor had deserted him. Her mother had said men like him use women and then abandon them. Hadn't Amos said she would go home this morning? She put her fingers to her temples in an effort to clear her swirling thoughts. Thinking to momentarily give in, to rest long enough to regain some strength, Melanie closed her eyelids and became lost to the world around her once more.

The dream world she entered was more frightening than the one of the previous night, for instead of a passionate lover, it was her father who came to shake her from her sleep. His face was a stern mix of anger and disappointment, but his tone was unforgiving, his accusing names tearing at her with blades of shame, condemning her as the whore she had become.

She'd tried to tell him what had happened, how it hadn't been entirely her fault. She'd begged his forgiveness, and to her surprise, he took her in his arms and comforted her, cushioning her sobs of remorse against his chest.

But when Melanie awoke again, Abner Hammond was gone. A quick look around told her that she was still in the ship's cabin. This time she really had been dreaming. As she tossed back the sheets and swung her legs over the side of the bunk, she realized that she was no longer naked, but was instead engulfed in linen. A closer examination of her makeshift nightdress revealed it to be a man's shirt. It was clean and had the fresh scent of clothes recently dried by the sun and island breezes. The same scent as the bed linens, she thought, noting that the bunk was neatly made except for the small indentation she had created in the tightly tucked sheets.

Why, her hair had even been braided, she discovered, fingering the long, uneven braid with a leather thong tied about the end in wonder. On a chair beside the berth was a washbowl containing soap and a wadded-up towel. Her cheeks flushing at her suspicion, she picked up the soap and sniffed it first, then her skin. Someone had bathed and dressed her . . . either the captain or Amos or both! Melanie grew hot with embarrassment.

Well, she would no longer stand for such advantage to be taken of her weakened state. Although her stomach growled, it was for food, not because she was nauseous. Her head was relatively clear, the clouds of drowsiness rapidly disintegrating under the rush of growing indignation.

She would find her shift and march off this boat without so much as a second glance at the men who had deceived her. But a quick search of the cabin failed to produce her own clothing and her ire flared higher. What did they intend to do? Keep her imprisoned for their amusement? Melanie froze in panic and then burst rapidly into action, dropping to her knees and throwing open a chest jammed against the stern wall of the cabin.

It was only then that she noticed the vibration of the deck beneath her. My God, they were moving! She shuffled through the neatly folded garments, inadvertently noting that the owner must have acquired some measure of wealth to possess such finely made clothes. Under what appeared to be a gentleman's topcoat and coordinated vest was a pair of fawn trousers. She yanked them out without care for the disorder she created.

Hastily, she pulled them on, despairing at the loose fit and length of material extending from her feet. With resolve, she rolled up the pant legs and tied the overlapping material of the waist into a cumbersome knot. By the time she reached the cabin door, she was forced to pull them up again. After readjusting the ill-fitting garb, she found the door unlocked and opened it.

There was no one on the lower deck, she saw with relief. Determinedly, she marched past a dining table with long benches on either side and an armchair at its head, and on to the steep steps leading topside. She was going to demand this vessel be turned around. She would tell this presumptuous and opportunistic captain exactly what she thought of his underhanded abduction of her and make him see the error of his ways. 'Io would kill him for what he had done, but if he gave her no trouble, she would protect his identity from her fiancé.

The sun was blindingly bright on the decks of the cargo ship as Melanie emerged from below, one hand holding up the trousers that kept sliding down on her hips. The wind caught her braid, whipping it about her face and molding her loose clothing to her body. A commotion in the towering square-rigged masts above her head distracted her temporarily. She had often admired the large ships in the harbor, but this was the first she had traveled on. Sailors were scurrying up the rope ladders among the network of lines and cables, apparently intent on unfurling the great white rolls of canvas lashed to the riggings.

At that moment, the great ship seemed to shudder under her feet and the vibration died. The steady hum that she had become accustomed to gave way to silence, disturbed only by the flapping sheets of unfurling canvas and the shouts of the men intent on their tasks. The momentary still diminished the plowing momentum of the vessel so that it became more subservient to the rolling swells of the sea. With a lazy groan, it listed to the starboard, causing Melanie to tack sideways toward the rail. Her arms flailed out ahead of her to cushion the impact, but her feet tangled in one of the cuffs of the trousers that had come unrolled, sending her sprawling facedown on the deck with an undignified grunt.

She lay still for a moment, trying to retrieve the wind that had been knocked from her by the fall. If not for the material of the trousers, she would surely have bloodied her knees, for even so, they burned as she awkwardly struggled to her feet. She grasped the rail firmly, her bare feet seeking footing in the drain that carried water in rough weather from the decks back to the sea. Her eyes grew wide, rivaling the color of the ocean that stretched to the distant horizons on either side of her. Nowhere was there the tiniest speck of land. Good heavens, how long had she slept? she wondered in dismay.

"Well, now, it seems our sleeping beauty has decided to join the living again."

Melanie started at the sound of the captain's deep voice and whirled to face him, nearly tripping over the pant legs again. She steadied herself on the rail and straightened with as much dignity as she could muster.

"I demand that you turn this thing around and take me back to Maui this instant!"

Ryan folded sinewy arms across a broad chest bared to the elements that had colored it, his feet spread to accommodate the movement of the vessel. Slowly a smile, white and devoid of humor, spread across his face, his green eyes glittering as they assessed the indignant figure swimming pitifully in his clothes. He was so enraged over the tearful and staggered confession she'd given in his arms the previous night that he wanted to shake the fire out of her. But loss of temper would not bring him the answers he desired.

She had duped him into thinking she was an illiterate native incapable of speaking English. She had flirted outrageously in some sort of game with her boyfriend to make him jealous, arousing him to the point of recklessness — a recklessness that had cost her her virginity according to the stains on the sheets he had taken from the berth. And she'd made him the ignorant patsy of a man he was coming to despise by the moment. Now it appeared the crafty Frenchman had cheated him of his warm nights as well as of his guarantee of an uninterrupted good time for him and his men.

"And just who are you to demand such a thing, Meilani . . . if that is indeed your name?" In view of her anger, he might taunt her to find out what he needed to know from her. "And by all means, continue in my language since you have suddenly developed a talent for it."

Melanie blanched at her slip. She did not want him to know who she was. She could see him laughing at her now if she told him she was a missionary's daughter.

"I am a young lady who was taken to this ship under the pretense of concern for my safety," she retorted haughtily. "And then you—"

"Odd," Ryan interrupted, scratching his chin thoughtfully. "I don't recall spending the evening with a *lady.*"

Melanie gasped at the insult. Indifferent to the group gathering about them in interest, she stepped forward and raised her hand to slap the insolent smirk off Ryan's face, when her trouser leg caught onto a rough edge of decking and tripped her. To her horror she lunged against him, knocking him partially off balance. Ryan stepped back to steady them and he caught her as she fell.

"Don't you touch me, you contemptible animal!" Melanie shrieked, pummeling him about the face and shoulders with her fists. "Let me go!"

"Behave yourself, Meilani, or suffer the consequences." To illustrate his threat, the arms tightened further, until she thought her ribs would collapse.

Melanie dug her nails into his flesh in a struggle of wills, gaining small satisfaction from his wince of pain. Still, the vise that threatened to break her in half would not let up. Incensed by his use of brawn to force her into submission, she glared up at him and bit into the hard flesh of his shoulder.

A curse exploded from the captain. He hurled her across the deck and touched the bleeding wound in disbelief. Melanie gasped for air and, ignoring the pain of her scraped elbows and knees, unsteadily pushed herself into a crawling position. Gathering her courage, she raised her defiant gaze to the man who had tried to master her. She could feel the singe of the hellish green fire leaping from his eyes as they glared past his bloodied fingers at her. The loud silence chilled her, making her aware that in addition to herself, his men waited as well to see what their captain was going to do to her.

A thousand damning sentences passed across his face—a face flushed purple with a rage that shook the muscles of his body as he struggled to control it. His jaw was clenched, white teeth grinding to hold back a building torrent of curses she was certain were not meant for delicate ears. Without twitching a muscle, Melanie futilely searched the deck for a refuge, a place she might escape to until he could be reasoned with, for certainly his rein on his emotions was short at best. If she could make it back to the cabin, she could use the bolt she had noticed on the inside of the door.

Breaking the foreboding stillness of the scene, she sprang into action with a mad scramble toward the main hatch. But only a few yards short of her goal, her trousers caught again, causing her to turn in frustration and see Ryan's foot firmly planted on the oversized pant leg. Modesty prevailing, Melanie hesitated at abandoning the cursed garment altogether—a move that was her downfall, for in a flash, the enraged captain seized her by the excess material of his shirt and trousers and hoisted her into the air to the cheers of his men.

"No!" she screamed, arms and legs flailing helplessly as he carried her toward their destination.

He paid no need to the way her body bumped against the rails as he made his way down the steps. Upon reaching the cabin door, he stopped and let go of her shirt to open the latch. Melanie stretched her hands out to catch herself on the floor, but her fingers fell short of the wide wooden planking.

"Amos!" Ryan roared, his voice filling the closed-in deck and echoing from starboard to stern.

"Aye, sir!" Amos answered, scampering down the steps behind them.

"She'll be needing clothes."

"Amos! . . ." Melanie cried out, using the doorjamb to swing herself around and face the retreating mate. "Help me!"

But Amos acted as if he had not heard her, and Melanie gave a shriek of despair. As the captain attempted to take her through the doorway, she grabbed the jamb again and held on stubbornly. She had wanted to get to the cabin to get *away* from the captain, not to be caught in it alone with him. Her fingers ached as a superior strength pulled at them. Her waist was cut by the taut pinch of the trousers wound in his hand. A muffled curse, followed by a swift jab in the ribs by a hard knee, collapsed her resistance, and she was hauled inside and dumped unceremoniously on the floor.

Stunned, Melanie used the desk in the center of the room to pull herself to her feet as Ryan closed the door behind them with a loud slam. She involuntarily stepped back as his angry countenance was focused on her again. "H—how dare you!" she croaked, her mouth suddenly dry. Yet her show of indignation was just that, for Melanie had never been more frightened in her life. There was no place to run, no one to help her . . . and no sign of mercy in the scathing gaze that raked over her.

"Since you are intent on being the ruination of my clothes as well as myself," Ryan said in a dangerously quiet voice, focusing on the tears in the knees of the trousers, "I'll have them back now."

Melanie's eyes grew rounder yet. "But I haven't any—"

"Now, Meilani," he insisted. A caustic smile tugged at the corner of his mouth. "It isn't as if I haven't witnessed your more charming attributes before."

"You bastard!" Melanie swore. She seized a spy glass that was conveniently nestled in an oak cradle near the edge of the desk and hurled it at him.

Instinctively, Ryan ducked as the glass sailed past his head and crashed against the wall, shattering the lens. He looked down at the broken glass that had been his father's, and the fury that had sorely tested his will earlier surged with renewed vigor through his veins. "You little savage . . ."

He was across the room before Melanie could react, crushing her squirming body in his grip as he dragged her over to the berth. Melanie shrieked as she was turned upside down and shaken out of her trousers. Almost before she reached the floor, she was hauled across his lap and pinned there by a leaden arm. At the first heavy slap across her buttocks, she stiffened in disbelief. The second one stung her into a frenzied protest.

"By God, I'll kill you for this," she screamed, her volume increasing as he struck her again and again.

"By God, woman, consider yourself lucky that I haven't done the same to you!"

Melanie shrieked again as his hand resumed its stinging assault, then she collapsed helplessly, tears spilling down her cheeks. She blinked them away, spying the exposed calf of her assailant's leg. Unable to reach it with her teeth, she sunk her nails into the lean flesh. "Let me go!" she growled.

Ryan cursed profusely at the piercing pain the savage native girl had inflicted, and he increased the strength of his blows. "Madame, I assure you, I can stand this as long as you," he grimaced.

The truth of his words, the sheer hopelessness of her situation, was more than she could bear. "D . . . damn . . . you . . ." Melanie sobbed, her own offense wavering at his renewed onslaught, until her fingers gave up their bloody hold and her entire body trembled, too weak to resist any further. "Stop . . . ple . . . ease."

The spanking halted. "What did you say?"

Melanie gritted her teeth. "Please stop."

"Then apologize."

Her fist clenched. Damn him! If he hadn't provoked her, taunted her, she wouldn't have lost her temper. If anyone should apologize, it should be him for taking advantage of her. But now was not the time to argue the point. She wanted to get away from him.

"I . . . I'm sorry," she whispered shakily.

"I didn't hear you, Meilani." He rested his hand persuasively on her bared buttocks. She wanted to tear him apart for his impudence, his insolence. He was pushing her beyond reason.

"I'm sorry, damn you!" she screamed hoarsely. And she

sobbed, not with remorse but with frustration. She would get even for this. She would make him regret the way he had treated her, somehow, someway. Every man had a weakness and she would find his.

His laughter, rich as it rang out in the room, was nearly her undoing. "Well, I'm glad to hear it, and so are the men topside," he teased, lifting his arm so that she could get up.

Melanie lost no time putting the distance of the cabin between them, her hands inadvertently going to her burning backside. Her chin trembled as she silently blamed him for her discomfort, but she held her tongue. Anger was gone from his face as he studied her and his handsome features were now thoughtful, as if he were determining his next move. She shrank away from the penetrating green eyes, unconsciously noting the way the sunlight that filtered through the portal picked up golden flecks in them that matched his coloring. She sulked in silence, waiting.

A tentative knock granted her a brief reprieve. At the captain's bidding, Amos Cobb entered, carrying her shift and a set of unfamiliar clothes—a smaller pair of trousers and a shirt. He glanced uneasily from Melanie's tearstained face to the captain's pensive one and crossed to the berth of deposit the clothing. To the side, he whispered to the captain in a voice accustomed to being heard over the drone of the powerful steam engines that ran the ship.

"I couldn't find no drawers fittin' to give her, sir."

Melanie inhaled sharply and looked away, her face crimson with humiliation. Surely the whole crew knew of her situation and thought of her exactly as their captain did.

"I think we can come up with something, Amos. You've done fine," Ryan reassured him.

"How 'bout some ointment for that bite?" He gave Melanie an awkward look and followed her guilty gaze back to the captain's bloodied leg. "Sweet Jesus! I'll see to ye right away, sir," he exclaimed, his mouth thinning in disapproval with the look he shot at the girl cowering in the corner as he left the room.

Ryan rose to his feet and picked up the shift from the

bunk. Aware that Meilani was paling with each step that brought him closer, he stopped a few feet from her and held it out. "Put this on."

Without watching to see if she took it, he let go of the garment and went over to his trunk. "Your behavior from now on will determine your treatment, Meilani. If you wish to be treated like a lady, then you must act the part," he informed her, opening the lid of his trunk. He concentrated on sorting through the disorder the girl had made.

Good God, did she disrupt everything she came into contact with? he wondered, alert to her hurried movements behind him. His mind was a quandary of emotions. One minute he had had to fight to keep from strangling her, and the next to keep from pulling her to him and comforting her tears. And what was worse was that through it all, she had stirred him until he ached more with desire than from the wounds she had inflicted on him.

Guilt. That was what was wrong with him, he rationalized. Although she had deserved every blow he had dealt her for such heathenish behavior, he decided in self-defense. But he had taken her innocence. Damn it, what was he going to do with her now? He'd had more than a few women, but he'd never taken a virgin to bed. He was more accustomed to a bedmate who knew what to expect between the sheets and woke up beside him as satisfied as he was . . . someone like Arabella.

He found the box in the bottom of the trunk, containing the silk drawers and camisole he had purchased for Arabella Harrington. She loved fancy lace and silk underclothing, to drive a man wild by parading about in it. Ryan was always pleased to give it to her, and even more so to take it back.

It was made of the finest Oriental silk, a floral design woven in its white-on-white pattern. As he removed it from the box, he likened the feel of the delicate material in his fingers to the satiny skin of his lover. But, disconcertingly, it was not the beautiful and gracious Arabella that came to his mind, but rather the dark-skinned native girl . . . her blue eyes . . . the contrast the pure white would make against

48

her dark skin. . . .

He inhaled deeply and let out his breath. Damn her and her innocence, he cursed, aiming his anger at himself. He ignored the way she jumped as he swung around to face her and handed her the underwear. "You can have these. The lovely lady they were intended for won't even miss them," he added with a half smile.

Embarrassed beyond words, Melanie took the delicate garments from the captain. She couldn't help but wonder what sort of woman this captain would be buying such things for. His sister, perhaps. But one look at the way they were made to fit made her dismiss that idea. She stole a curious glance at the golden stranger, but he was busy picking up the shards of glass from the broken telescope, affording her some degree of privacy.

Grateful, she hurriedly slipped on the drawers under her shift and tied the satin drawstring in a bow at her waist. The camisole unlaced in the front, so she was able to slide it up under her shift as well. In a matter of moments, she had pulled her arms inside the outer garment and donned the silken camisole. She'd just finished rearranging her shift when Amos Cobb reappeared with a bottle of ointment and some clean rags.

"Well, I kin see neither of ye look much the worse for wear since I left and I ain't heard no bloodcurdlin' screams," he commented dryly.

"That will be all, I think. Just leave the iodine there, Amos. I've cleaned up one of her messes. It's time she learned to be responsible for her actions," Ryan explained. He turned to Melanie expectantly. "Well?"

The nerve of the man, Melanie fumed. But she mastered her irritation with a brittle smile and as Amos Cobb reluctantly left the two of them, set about filling the washbowl with water to cleanse the wounds. Ryan dropped into his chair, watching her as she set the bowl of water on the desk and soaked one of the cloths Amos had brought in. Ignoring his disturbing scrutiny, she stood at arm's length and gently dabbed the circular mark that was now inflamed with a bluish edge.

"You can come closer. Unlike some people in this room, I do not bite," Ryan remarked sarcastically.

"It is unseemly, sir, for a lady to be alone in a room with a man." She deliberately left out the term *gentleman*, for this man was anything but.

"It's a bit late to consider such trivial proprieties, wouldn't you think?"

Melanie leveled a hostile gaze at Ryan but checked her heated retort. Instead, she liberally doused a swab with iodine and applied it to the wound. The tightening of his jaw muscles was the only show of pain the captain gave, but it was sufficient to bring a satisfied smile to her lips.

"And what of the future, Captain?" she asked sweetly. "Surely now that you have seen the error of your ways, you'll find another room for me . . . or for yourself."

Ryan tensed, annoyed at the sudden turn of the conversation. He hadn't considered any alternative other than continuing to share the same quarters. "That's impossible, Meilani."

Melanie's smile faltered, but only briefly. "But I don't understand, sir. Surely a vessel this big can afford you some sleeping facility. If you are true to your word that I shall be treated like a lady, then you will find it."

The burn of the iodine on his open flesh was hellish but by no means matched his increasingly ill humor. He had made another mistake. He had underestimated her resourcefulness. Again he wondered who she was. Perhaps the bastard of one of the planters, one her father had seen educated. But educated or not, he was not going to let her evict him from his own cabin on his own ship.

"If you are concerned that you might have to share my bed, Meilani, believe me, your worries are for nothing. As you can see, this is my office as well as my sleeping quarters. It's hardly practical that I should move my belongings elsewhere," he pointed out matter-of-factly. "However, I shall give you every consideration possible, including the sole occupancy of the berth."

"But where will you sleep?" she asked suspiciously.

"Anywhere but with you, dear lady. I am no glutton for punishment, speaking of which," he added, twisting as she was about to cork the iodine, "I've a few other afflictions dealt when you were in a more affectionate humor that you might see to. I don't think the skin is broken, but just the same, a dab of prevention . . ." He broke off and raised his eyebrows, her scarlet blush improving his disposition.

Melanie was horrified. Although she was using every good manner and act of propriety her mother had taught her, he was not going to let her forget what had happened between them. He was going to hold that over her head, humiliate her with the shameful memory of her behavior. How could she have let him of all people take her?

"I was not myself, sir. As you can see, I have had some gentle upbringing. . . ." Ryan's sudden burst of ridiculing laughter cut her off, and Melanie realized her behavior to date had been anything but what her parents had instilled in her. Abandoning her sweet facade, she threw the swab into the water bowl, spraying the desk with a splash, and glowered. "By God, if I were a man, sir, you would not make such fun with me!"

The chair scraped as Ryan rose above her and took her shoulders firmly. "Ah, Meilani," he said with a wicked wink, "no truer words could be spoken." Before his meaning sunk in, he brushed her lips and retreated hastily. The door slammed behind him in time to catch the tin basin of water she slung across the room.

"Clean it up!" came the fading order from the other side of the door.

Melanie considered the mess and groaned in despair— not over the water that ran down the door and puddled on the floor, but over the mess she had made of her life in the past forty-eight hours.

Chapter Four

Supper that evening was served to Melanie in the captain's cabin. The ship's cook had prepared roast chicken, boiled rice, and fresh sauteed carrots from his recently resupplied stores. Starved, she finished every last morsel, including the bits of pineapple and shredded coconut that brought the meal to a perfect conclusion.

As she placed all the utensils on the tray the cabin boy called Sven had brought her earlier, she listened to the banter of the men assembled at the table outside. They apparently did not like the signs Mother Nature was giving them concerning the weather, and if what they read into them was true, there would be a dramatic change by morning. Ryan's authoritative voice occasionally rose above the others as he sought the opinions of his staff and gave precautionary orders accordingly. It was evident by the enthusiastic reception of his commands that the men, some more than a few years his senior, respected his judgement.

Well, she had been given very little reason to respect him, she mused peevishly. The only thing that kept her contained in the cabin was the threat of physical abuse. Even now she found it too uncomfortable to sit on the hard seat of the desk chair and suffered the indignity of having to use a pillow.

But her afternoon had not been a total waste, for the books that lined the high shelf crowning the room contained not only those one would expect to find about ships and navigation, but also a grand assortment of great literary works. What her mother would give to have such a collection! Well, most of them, she conceded, recalling some of the more risqué works she had briefly perused, particularly the one with the handwritten inscription.

It was dedicated to Ryan with all the love of a decidedly wicked woman called Arabella—decidedly wicked considering the nature of the works. Of course, it was only out of curiosity that Melanie had opened it, and she sat on the edge of the berth ready, at the first sign of someone's approach, to shove it back into its proper place. She had wondered, with cheeks afire, that such torrid reading could be found in print.

There was so much of the world that existed outside of Lahaina that she did not know. Her mother had seen to her education well enough. She could read and write and had a particular affinity for working with numbers. In fact, her mother admitted that she as the pupil had surpassed the teacher in that respect. Melanie had been very proud of that achievement, for her mother's praise was scarce.

"You have a sharp, inquisitive mind and a curiosity I have yet to see the match for, Melanie. I pray it will not lead you astray."

Astray, she thought, her misery returning. Her mother would swoon to see her now. With a sigh, Melanie got up from the chair and began to prepare for bed. The sun had long deserted the sky. In the dim light of an oil lamp, she bathed and washed her teeth at the built-in washstand made of the same rich mahogany as the cabin's paneling. The only soap she could find was that in the shaving mug, and although she felt somewhat refreshed, she would have preferred the perfume of the bars her mother made to the masculine-scented concoction she had used.

To settle her dilemma over the lack of a nightdress, Melanie opted to use the captain's shirt. Then, helping herself to the use of the comb and brush set she had found alongside the shaving utensils, she perched cross-legged on the bunk and set about brushing out her hair.

She had no idea how fetching a picture she presented, nor could she guess the reason for the way the captain stared at her when he entered the cabin. Her hair was spread about her shoulders like a black satin cloak, dark and shiny against the crisp white of his shirt. She held the brush poised in midair as she met the heated gaze of the intruder, unaware of the way her upturned breasts were outlined. Although she had done nothing to antagonize him any further, his face was a picture of irritation aimed directly at her.

"Now what have I done, sir?" she exclaimed, folding her arms crossly in front of her.

"I believe you said you would be in bed by eight and, madame, it is half past."

"Well, if I am not in bed, sir, do tell me, where am I?"

She meant it, Ryan thought, his irritation giving way to wonder. She really didn't know what she was doing to him. If it were any other female but this one, he wouldn't fall for that innocent fluster of exasperation. He turned away from her scornful reproach and started to put up one of the hammocks the men sometimes used up on deck.

"From now on, I would appreciate it if you had your hair fixed and whatever else you women find to do that prolongs the ritual of readying for bed, and be neatly tucked in when I enter the cabin."

Melanie made an incredulous exclamation. Nothing pleased this man! Not that she was in any way inclined to do so. She merely wanted to avoid rocking the very delicate balance of temper between them. Yet she could not let this ridiculous notion of his go unchallenged.

"Don't you think that you are being a bit unreasonable?"

But he didn't answer her. Instead, the captain hooked a sling of some sort to a small ring that she had not noticed before on the wall. He secured the other end on a heavy support beam in the center of the room, wrapping the cord around a lantern peg. That accomplished, he turned and strolled gingerly over to where she sat. Melanie hastily drew the sheets up to her neck, a modest blush inflaming her cheeks.

"What do you want?" she demanded, her heart fluttering as he leveled the hypnotic gaze that had first drawn her into its emerald depths.

"A pillow," he answered simply, snatching one from under her head. "And a sheet." But instead of taking one of hers, he leaned over and opened a drawer built under the berth.

Melanie could not help but admire the rippling torso that stretched down and withdrew one of the folded linens. It was the muscular back of a man hardened to work, with skin healthily weathered by the sun . . . and currently marred by the faint scratches of their lovemaking. Guilt washed over her face as Ryan turned and walked away.

She drew up her knees under the covers and rested her head in her folded arms. She could not, would not, be able to lie down and rest until she was certain he was in his hammock. Tension seemed to build inside her like a coiled spring as she listened to his stealthy movements about the cabin.

"You know, Meilani, you would do well to accept my requests without question. It's far safer."

Melanie started at the nearness of his voice, for he had once again moved to her side undetected. She thrust out her chin stubbornly. "And why, Captain, should I do that? To permit you to have me cater to your silly whims? I think not!"

Ryan leaned on the bunk, the mattress giving with his weight. His face seemed only a breath from her own, as if he intended to bully her by his sheer presence. And it was working more than she cared to admit, for her fingers were clenched white about covers that nearly choked her as she pressed them against her throat.

"So you are the impetuous young woman who must have a reason," he mused aloud, as though he played a game with her, one she sensed was undoubtedly dangerous. "In the field of battle, a soldier who fails to obey his superior's command without question often suffers the worse for it." He sniffed the edge of her shoulder and a flicker of amusement danced in his eyes. "I vow, but the sweetness of your lovely body does wonders for shaving soap."

Melanie swallowed dryly. His voice—no, his breath—was right at her ear, warm and infuriatingly disconcerting. "I am neither a soldier nor are you my superior. And if you are bent on seduction, sir, you'd best go back to your hammock, for I vow that you shall have no willing partner."

The length of his arm pressed against her back, causing her to sit erect, her eyes fixed on the portal to escape the persuasive effects of his gaze. While she wanted no part of him, her body was coming alive with the anticipation of his masculine touch.

"But it's *you,* dear Meilani, who seems bent on seduction," he objected softly. "It's you that taunts me with the vision of your naked form pressed against the material of my shirt, so boldly highlighted in the lamplight." His free hand slid to her waist, and her abdomen shrunk way from the warm touch with the sharp intake of her breath.

"Don't . . ." she started, suddenly robbed of air. Her hand closed over his, but it refused to draw the offensive one away. It only checked further boldness.

"And it's *you* who used the bewitching ploy of the most accomplished seductress—brushing your glorious tresses . . . tresses that beg to be combed by a lover's fingers," Ryan whispered as he wound the silken strands about his hands until his fingers stroked the nape of Melanie's neck.

Gooseflesh spread like wildfire from the sensuous contact. It was inevitable that his lips would close upon her own. She knew they were coming, but something kept her from moving away . . . perhaps the hand that held her head captive by the bonds of her hair. Yet they claimed her ever so gently, coaxing her breath away as they bore her down against her pillow. While reason struggled to survive in the heat wave of riotous sensations that engulfed her brain, another tide rose from the swelling peaks of her breasts, tantalized by torturous fingers that had escaped the weak restraint of her hand.

"So you see, Meilani," he cooed softly above her agonized

56

moan of protest, "were I not privy to the knowledge of women such as yourself, I could not help but fall victim to such calculated enticement." Without warning, he drew away from her and tweaked her nose mischievously. "Think well about it, blue eyes."

Melanie, shocked at the sudden chill left by the absence of Ryan's touch, stared at him blankly at first, until his words and actions registered. "Ohhh!" she ground out in a mad mixture of fury and despair at her reaction to the man. Unable to face his smug countenance, she snatched up the covers and twisted her back to him. Her body cringed as he reached over her to turn out the light, her face hidden in the pillow from his scrutiny. But his retreating chuckle was more than she could stand. Without looking at him, she condemned him through clenched teeth. "You are, by far, the most despicable human being I have ever met!"

"And I fear, Meilani, that I have at last met my match."

Her answering shriek resulted in outright laughter. Tears of frustration choked her. "I hope you hang yourself in that contraption! So help me, I do!"

"I'd save your energies for tomorrow, blue eyes. No one rides for free on the *Liberty Belle*, and since you do not seem to fit into the original position I had in mind for you, you'll earn your keep by helping Sven and the cook starting at first light."

"I hate you, Ryan . . . whoever you are!" she blurted out. "And I'll be damned if I'll—"

"Oh, but you will, Meilani," the captain answered coolly, his tone implying the dread consequence if she did not.

"I swear you will pay for this!" she blurted out. "So help me, you will!" She choked on her indignation.

But, other than the laughter that died slowly as he dismissed her and climbed into the hammock, there was no retort. The only sound she heard was the straining of the cords under the captain's weight. She prayed that if it would not hang him, the lines might at least break and dump his insolent and damnably handsome body on the hard deck. But as his breathing became slower and more regular, it appeared that he was not to suffer any of the mishaps she wished on him. Instead, he was going to sleep like a baby, leaving her to deal with the unwanted devil of desire he had awakened in her, until she too at last succumbed to a slumber of a more restless nature.

It seemed as though she had just shut her eyes, when she was roughly shaken and Ryan's disgustingly cheerful voice ordered her out of bed. Melanie sat up, swaying sleepily, and mumbled an incoherent objection as the captain, fully refreshed and dressed for the day, tossed her the shirt and trousers Amos had scrounged up for her.

"Now pull that bottom lip in or you'll never get that shirt over your head," he teased. "I'll go tell Cook you'll be along shortly."

Too tired to object, Melanie nodded mutely and clutched the clothes to her chest as her cheerful cabin mate left her to her own devices. Her wits gradually coming to her, she realized the cabin was still lit by lamplight. One glance at the portal revealed the reason: It was not only early, but also quite cloudy. A steady drizzle of rain beat against the portal that Ryan had apparently closed during the night. This was the bad weather the men had spoken of the night before, she hazily recollected, forcing her relaxed body into motion.

In less than a half hour, she ventured to the top deck. The sails had been trimmed and the *Liberty Belle* barreled under steam through the choppy water surrounding them, in weather that had worsened considerably since she had first noticed it. The wind, not the tropical trades that cooled the islands, beat the rain into the material of her shirt and wreaked havoc in the hair she had tied at her neck with a handkerchief procured from Ryan's trunk.

Upon seeing a group of men gathered foreward around a structure emitting smoke from a short metal chimney, Melanie shielded her eyes with her arm and made her way toward them. A few looked up from their conversations as her small figure awkwardly made its way across the rolling deck. When she reached them, they parted and indicated with a nod that she take cover in the ship's kitchen.

Just as Melanie stepped over the threshold, the ship listed hard to starboard and she stumbled headlong toward the iron cook stove. Her fearful cry was cut off by a huge arm that seized her and yanked her back against a cushion of flesh, only inches short of the hot iron surface.

"You best keep to the for'd wall till you git your sea legs, scrapper." The sweat-covered arm released her, and a round giant of a Swede wedged himself between her and the cook stove. Pale blue eyes that were neither friendly nor hostile looked her over in speculation. "One of you fetch her a slicker 'fore she takes a chill!" he shouted over his shoulder. "And you stay put till you dry out."

Melanie nodded, sensing there was no nonsense about this man whatsoever. The men jumped to attention for him, just as they did for the captain, for one scurried off at his barked command. "I—I'm supposed to help you," she ventured in a small voice. "I often helped Mama in the kitchen." Somehow, she felt compelled to state her qualifications.

The cook snorted as he wiped his hands on a greasy apron, covering a girth that evidenced his liking of his own food. "Well, I'm not your mama and no one cooks in this kitchen but Karl."

Melanie rubbed her cold arms briskly and shrugged. "Well, that suits me fine, since I hate to cook anyway." She started at his loud laugh and was more startled to be hauled up by her shoulders. Her feet practically dangled as she was speechlessly displayed to the few men drinking coffee about the hatchway.

"By golly, didn't I say this was a scrapper?" the burly cook bellowed, the others joining in his amusement at her expense. When they had had their fun, Karl put her down gently as a kitten and patted her head. "Now, scrapper, have yourself some coffee and some of these hot biscuits," he said, pointing to a tempting pan of fresh baked bread. "And then I'll put you to work, ya?"

Although her pride had been ruffled, Melanie decided it was best to go along with the heavy-handed cook. With an impish grin, she answered "Ya!" and proceeded to pour a mug of the strong steaming brew from the tin pot on the stove.

To her delight, the biscuits were filled with dried fruit and sprinkled, not with flour, but with powdered sugar. The sumptuous meal last night had been no fluke of fate. Karl had a reason for being proud of his cooking, she admitted to herself as she timidly asked for another.

"Ya, well, I suppose all that temper needs feedin'," he remarked, his lips pursed to keep from smiling. When she had finished, he handed her the slicker the crewman had tossed in to him and put his hands on his hips. "Now, do you think you could rob the henhouse and make it back here without breakin' my eggs?" His tenor voice always turned up pleasantly at the end of his sentences, especially at the end of a question.

"Henhouse?" Melanie echoed in confusion.

"Aye, the *Belle* has a real poop deck, only it's forward by the henhouse," one of the men snickered.

"I don't hear you complainin' when you have fresh eggs for your breakfast, Mason," Karl retorted in mock indignation.

"Yep, the *Belle*'s becomin' more of a hen's frigate by the day," another piper up.

The reference to a ship housing the captain's woman passed over Melanie's head. She was too intrigued by the idea of having animals aboard to pay it any heed. "You really do have chickens! Where?"

"Eric'll be glad to show you," Karl answered, nodding to a young man who stepped up, his face beaming from under the hood of his oilskin.

Although from what she could see of the body that filled out the waterproof garment, Eric was the opposite of Karl in girth and closer to her age, there was still a resemblance between them that made Melanie suspect they were brothers, or at least cousins. Recalling the cherubic face of the cabin boy, Sven, she wondered if he too were related. They all had strong Nordic noses, the same pale blue eyes, and thick curly blond hair, although Sven's had more red in it than the others. Perhaps when she knew them better she would ask, she decided.

Melanie pulled on the slicker, its hem nearly dragging on the deck, and eagerly took the basket Karl handed her. Eric stood back to permit her to exit the kitchen, his strong fingers offering her support as she regained her footing on the slippery deck. Melanie followed him forward to where a small shedlike structure had been erected. It had a low doorway that even she had to stoop under to get through, and inside were the nesting chickens the cook had told her about.

"These are my Uncle Karl's babies," Eric informed her, answering her unspoken question of relationship as he crouched under the low roof of the henhouse. It was very close quarters, and each time Melanie moved, she inadvertently bumped against the young man. "He and Sven have a name for each one of them, but—" he laughed, his voice strongly resembling his uncle's, "I cannot tell them apart. Some are destined for the pot and others for the heart, according to Karl," he quoted with a crooked grin. "In the long days at sea, Sven and Karl spoil them while I pass my spare time with my guitar."

"Really?" Melanie commented, enjoying the pleasantly attentive company as she disturbed one of the fat hens to relieve her of her produce. "I should like to hear you play sometime."

That she had pleased Eric showed, for, if possible, his face brightened even more. "I would like that very much."

Melanie had just about filled the basket when she reached into the last of the little box nests. "Ow!" she exclaimed, drawing her hand back as one of the hens pecked at her in objection.

"Now that one I know," Eric told her. "Her name is Irmgard."

Resolutely, Melanie let the sleeve of the slicker protect the back of her hand as she invaded Irmgard's nest again, this time triumphantly coming away with two eggs. "Sorry,

Irmgard, but you have to earn your keep," she quipped, a vexed expression clouding her face as she recalled having heard the same words earlier. Heaven forbid she pick up any of the captain's habits!

Eric backed against the wall of the shack to let Melanie out first. "Sven and Karl vow each of the hens has a personality, but Irmgard is the only one I recognize. She was named after our great aunt Irmgard, who used to cuff us boys, even Karl, for no good reason other than to strike terror into our hearts. Mother said she hated men because she was never asked to marry."

Melanie laughed with Eric as they emerged from the henhouse, her cheeks rosy as the rain beat down upon her face. She could picture the shy Sven and, possibly, Eric being terrorized by a giant Viking spinster, but the older Karl was another story. More likely, the cook would have picked *her* up and swung *her* around to further antagonize the woman.

"And you had done nothing to provoke the old dear?" Melanie asked, her eyes dancing merrily. "Not a thing?"

The ship started to lean heavily to one side and Eric slipped an arm about her waist to steady her. Melanie clenched the handle of the egg basket, her free hand covering the top to keep any of her booty from falling out as they swayed the other way. Upon reaching the kitchen hatchway, Eric lifted her over the threshold, holding her momentarily and winking.

"I swear, not a thing," he vowed with a crooked grin, setting her down. "She met Irmgard, Kar . . ."

"The men are double-checking the cargo holds to make sure eveything is battened down for the storm, Eric. I'd suggest you join them," the captain cut in sharply.

Melanie turned away from the door and tossed her hood back, her cheeks flushed. She ignored the irate captain, who leaned against the corner sipping hot coffee, and handed her basket of eggs to Karl. "It's true," she told the cook brightly. "Irmgard pecked at my hand, but I got the eggs anyway." If the captain had expected to dampen her spirits, he was going to be sadly disappointed.

"Somehow that doesn't come as a surprise, does it, Karl?"

"No, sir," Karl quietly agreed to the sardonic comment. He hung the basket on a hook. "I'm goin' to put some meat on some bread for the midday meal, plain and simple, if it's to your likin', sir. I'm tinkin' the men might need something they can eat on their feet."

"You read my mind, Karl," Ryan smiled, handing the empty mug to Melanie. His whole facial expression changed, making his devilish good looks even more appealing in their sincerity. Somewhere from within, a voice that Melanie could not recognize wished the change were for her instead of for the robust cook. "And as for you, blue eyes, you better take some food back to the cabin and stay put. We're in for a pretty rough ride and I'd hate to see you washed overboard. Not even the sharks deserve that," he added with a twist of his lips, before stepping back out into the weather.

Although the captain had told her to return to the cabin, Melanie hated the thought, procrastinating as long as the busy cook permitted her, so as to keep from spending the day alone. However, as the gathering storm grew worse, quite another motive kept her securely nestled in the cozy kitchen. She'd never been on a ship, 'Io's outrigger being the extent of her sea travel, and they'd always gone out in fair weather. Remaining in the kitchen, she helped the cook make the sandwiches and kept the coffeepot full for the seamen who straggled in from time to time.

When the noonday meal was ready, Melanie accompanied Karl to the crew's dining area, just below deck. The force of the wind that gusted and sprayed a drenching mist over the decks nearly knocked her over and the driving rain managed to soak her in spite of her rain gear.

Karl hurried down the hatch ahead of her and was there to take the hamper from her so that she could use both hands to grasp the rail on her way down the steep steps. A few men sat on benches that were bolted to the floor on either side of a plank table. It was much the same dining setup as the officers had at the stern of the vessel, other than the design and finish of the wood table, which was much simpler for the crew.

"I guess you better do like the cap'n told you now, scrapper," Karl told her over the din of the storm. "You should put on somethin' dry, I tink." His heavy hand clamped on her shoulder in approval. "You did good this mornin' for somebody who hates cookin'."

"Thanks," Melanie grinned. She glanced reluctantly in the direction of the cabin. She really hated to go there alone. Suddenly, her face lit up with an idea. "Suppose I take some sandwiches up to the men steering the boat?"

"Sven'll be down for them soon," Karl assured her, a knowing and sympathetic gleam in his pale blue eyes.

"But if I took them, I could ask the captain if I could stay." The thought of having to ask Ryan for anything galled her, but not as much as riding out the storm alone in his cabin.

"Well, now, there's merit to that thought, I tink," the cook relented. He handed Melanie the hamper. "Now be careful, scrapper. I'll follow you up and see that you make it."

The ship leapt forward as it crashed into a wide open gap in the angry waves. Melanie pitched headlong but regained her balance before needing Karl's supporting hand on her arm. She held the food basket tightly against her chest under the cover of the slicker as they passed the kitchen near midships and moved ahead to the charting house.

The door swung open for her, and a gust of ocean spray literally carried her into the smoke-filled room and slung Sven against the wall. As the cabin boy strained to close the door against the relentless gale, Melanie added her weight to the cause, and between the two of them, they managed to latch it securely once more. When she threw back her hood, Sven's eyes widened in surprise. With a weak smile, for the crashing waves on the deck had unnerved her more than she cared to admit, she presented the basket to the cabin boy.

The captain and Amos Cobb hovered over a chart spread on a large table in the center of the room. Ryan was taking

64

some sort of measurements with a compass and Amos was jotting them down in a bold hand. If they had noticed her, they gave no sign. They were so absorbed that Amos's pipe lay on the table, the fire all but out.

"The barometer's still droppin', sir. By God, we're crossin' a horse market to be sure this time," the helmsman called out from the bow section of the enclosure that was separated by a bulkhead, its door open and lashed against the wall.

"What's your heading, Jack?" Ryan asked sharply.

"One-eight-zero, south by southwest!"

Ryan's shoulders sagged. He raised his eyes to his first mate as he pushed himself up from the table. "We've got to put some sail up," he told the mate reluctantly. "It's getting too dangerous to go on scudding. The storm'll suck us right into her center."

"Aye, sir!"

Amos left the cabin abruptly to relay the captain's decision to the men in the forecastle, and Sven followed on his heels. Melanie drew back from the invading spray and huddled unobtrusively on a cushioned bench that ran the perimeter of the back half of the cabin. Instinct told her that this was no time to interrupt the shipmaster. Instead, she watched silently as Ryan gave the chart one last look and went forward to talk to the helmsman.

She could catch bits and pieces of their conversation over the howling weather outside. The captain was taking the ship off course to keep to the outside of the storm. They discussed the coordinates, and Ryan pinned the list of numbers Amos had written down for him on a board for the helmsman and his mate. He was concerned about his foremast hands and was going out with them.

Ryan never so much as glanced at Melanie as he slipped out of the cabin and into the gale. When he was gone she sighed in relief, afraid he'd have made her go below. Then she anxiously got to her knees to peer out of the rain-battered glass overlooking the deck. Her eyes followed the progress of the captain's oil-skinned figure as he joined one of his men and looked skyward. When she raised her eyes she gasped in trepidation, for men were hanging in the riggings, unfurling the sails.

They never seemed to lose their footing, climbing like monkeys among the flailing lines of the ship's nervous system. Melanie's heart was in her throat as the vessel plunged into a wall of white-crested water that crashed down on men and ship alike, knocking many to the deck. Some were washed perilously toward the rail, but ropes tied about their waists and secured to the deck brought them up short and she sighed in relief.

The moments seemed to stretch into an eternity before the white square rigging stretched skyward, although the sails were reefed short of where they had been the day before. Ryan worked among his men, stopping here and there as if to encourage them. His hood had blown back and his golden hair was plastered against his head, but he gave it no heed as he shouted his commands.

And no one stopped to question him, Melanie noted, recalling his earlier words. A wrong move could cost a person his life or the men their ship. No matter what her personal feelings were toward the golden-haired captain, she was forced to admire his courage and dedication to his crew. She settled back down on the cushion and drew the cold slicker about her shoulders, unaccountably reassured.

When the mate to the helmsman noticed the hamper Sven had placed on the bench beside her, he motioned for her to bring it forward. Glad to be able to do something, Melanie carried it and held it while the mate helped himself to one of the delicacies she and Karl had prepared.

"What takes you here?" the mate asked in surprise. "The captain told us you were in his cabin." He bit into his sandwich hungrily and waited for her reply.

"I brought the food up and everyone was too busy to eat, so I waited," Melanie explained. The sandwiches were too tempting for her to resist any longer, so she took one out and joined the man. "I was going to ask if I could stay in the kitchen with Karl." She hesitated, glancing at the man struggling with the wheel to keep to the course Ryan had set. "It's really a bad one, isn't it?"

"I'd say so, though the *Belle*'s weathered as bad and maybe worse. It's still going to be hell till it's over."

Melanie slid down the wall and sat cross-legged on the deck as the mate turned back to his duties. She felt foolish, but the company of the two strangers, each absorbed in his own task, was comforting. She observed them with interest, wishing she could watch the large encased compass they were intent upon and guess at the computations Ryan and Amos had worked on earlier. She had just finished her sandwich when the door burst open on the other side of the bulkhead and Ryan's voice roared throughout the enclosure.

"Meilani!"

"She's right here, Cap'n," the mate called out to him as the captain filled the narrow entrance with his rain-drenched form.

Melanie was helped to her feet, lifted by the scruff of her slicker clenched firmly in Ryan's hand. She could see that he was upset with her and did not resist when he shoved her into the chart room and spun her about to face him.

"I told you to go to the cabin and stay put!" he snapped, green eyes glowering from his fear-whitened face. "I thought you had gone overboard, you stupid little savage."

"I didn't want to. I thought I might stay in the kitchen, but—"

"I know, Karl told me," Ryan cut her off. He ran his fingers through his hair, stripping it of water that ran down his neck, and took a deep breath. Then, forcing it out slowly, he spoke again, his voice much calmer. "But I did not know that when I went to the cabin to check on you."

"I'm sorry . . . I didn't want to bother you when you were busy."

Her apology was a small concession for the distinct satisfaction she felt. He was concerned about her; he really cared for her safety. It showed in the frantic look in his eyes when they had discovered her. It showed in the way he was looking at her even now. Under that anger was genuine concern. Encouraged, she braved his anger and placed a hand against Ryan's cheek.

"Why don't you just eat something and calm down? We need your cool head to get us where we're going," she pointed out with an impish twist of her lips.

Ryan was speechless at the change in her. He watched her fetch the hamper and hand him a sandwich, with a smile that robbed him of his anger. But he was not finished with her. The thought that she might have been washed over the side had sent his heart leaping to his throat, and even now he wasn't sure he could swallow the food being so charmingly served to him.

She deserved to be punished for what she had done to him. He would not tolerate disobedience in his crew and she was no exception. Yet the knowledge that she had been too frightened to stay alone, combined with the disarming smile that was like a burst of sunlight in the cloud-darkened room, merited some consideration.

"You can stay here where I can keep an eye on you until we've weathered the worst, I suppose. Provided you keep out of the way," he stipulated. "Right now, we've a ship to keep afloat."

"Is it that bad?" Melanie asked, eyes widening in alarm.

But his leonine features relaxed into a smile, one just for her. "Just a manner of speaking, blue eyes. Now, out of the way. I need no distraction." To emphasize his point, he gave Melanie a swat on the derriere to speed her along, resulting in a startled outcry.

"Why you — you —" Melanie sputtered, breaking off as he raised a reproachful finger to her.

"Be glad that that is all you received for not listening to me, blue eyes."

He didn't hear the smothered giggle that gurgled in her throat as he rejoined his men at the helm. He had forgotten her already and was now intent on the readings of the instruments. After a while, Melanie removed the slicker that prevented her soaked clothing from drying and rolled it up to use as a pillow on the hard bench. Her eyelids drooped as she kept a watchful eye on the activity in the forward compartment.

Ryan was not still for a moment. He was back and forth from the charting table to the helm and in and out of the gale constantly. The smell of pipe tobacco from time to time announced Amos's comings and goings. Even the raised voices of the team that fought to navigate the heaving and groaning ship through the storm became part of the normal background noise as Melanie catnapped.

Once she awoke with a cry of alarm as the entire vessel seemed to vibrate viciously. She saw Ryan and Amos grab for the instruments and cling to the table as the *Liberty Belle* took a severe roll. In a panic, she started to get up, but Ryan shouted for her to remain where she was and hold on. Surely enough, the ship righted itself, only to continue to list to the opposite side. Melanie choked back a scream of terror as she caught sight of a hideous frothing tide that opened its gaping mouth as if to swallow them. She began to pray, her fingers in a deathlike grip on the edge of the bench.

When they were not awash in the churning sea, she ventured a peep through her clenched eyes and saw Ryan scanning the foredeck, his face pressed against the glass, drawn and anxious. Melanie scrambled to her knees in time to see one of the oil-skinned men lashed to the mast give a signal that all was well. The captain exhaled in relief beside her.

"Keep her to the wind, Mike! The devil with our destination!"

"Aye, sir!" the mate who had relieved the helmsman shouted back.

"You all right?"

Melanie nodded solemnly, grateful for the reassuring hand on her shoulder. "I thought the ship was falling apart and we were capsizing," she croaked hoarsely.

Ryan shook his head. "We got caught in a trough. For a few seconds, the propeller was out of the water."

If his words were intended to assuage her, they did not. That a ship the size of the *Liberty Belle* had been lifted out of the water made her shiver, more from fear than from the chilling dampness of the shirt and trousers that clung to her in a most distracting manner. She wrapped her arms about her shoulders, withdrawing quietly into a corner.

Ryan damned himself for almost forcing her to face the squall alone in his cabin, although in the beginning he had not expected a full-blown typhoon. Right now he wanted to take her into his arms and warm the chill that shook her bedraggled form, to somehow banish the terror that widened her enchantingly blue eyes.

But he could not. Although he was certain this was the worst of it, the fight with the raging squall was far from over. He needed every wit dedicated to the *Belle* and her crew. He could not even allow his own fear—fear of one mistake, one error in judgment that could cost a life or his entire ship and crew—hinder his concentration. The shipmaster was the brain of the mighty network of lines and riggings, controlling the functions through the seasoned sailors and engineers who carried out the orders that kept the *Belle* from foundering in total helplessness.

"The way I see it, we are somewhere near these islets," he told Amos, pointing to the chart. "Which means we had best stay clear of the reefs." He didn't add "If we can," for Melanie's benefit, but the first mate understood the rest

"Then I'd best be out," Amos grimaced, pulling up his hood to brave the decks once more.

"Aye. We need every eye available," Ryan agreed. They had kept on the edge of the storm and been forced into unfamiliar waters near some small, uninhabited islands, according to his calculations. Now the chance of coming up on the coral reefs presented more danger. The *Belle* was an iron ship, but coral was a deadly enemy to the strongest-built vessel. One error in his calculation . . . He banished the thought and, with an encouraging wink at the pallid girl drawn into a ball in the corner, rejoined the men at the helm.

Chapter Five

It was after midnight before Karl was able to feed the crew the hearty stew he had prepared when the storm had dwindled to the point that it was safe to cook. The winds had diminished and the crew was able to pull the ship out of the spiraling course Ryan had been forced to take to avoid the deadly gales surrounding the calm center of the typhoon. At that point, Melanie was allowed to leave the charting house and return to her chores in the kitchen.

After having shared the long, grim hours of the typhoon with the tired men who sat at the crew's dining table, Melanie felt a part of the quiet camaraderie. With relish, she ate the piping hot meat and vegetables she had scrubbed and cut up for the cook. The conversation was not lively as it had been the night before, for most of the men were too drained to talk and looked forward to falling into their bunks. Those that could not were forcing down strong coffee to help them stay awake for night duty, although Ryan had seen to it that they stole a few hours rest as soon as the imminent danger had passed.

But he had not rested himself. He sat at the head of the table and moved his food about his plate in a halfhearted effort to eat. The strain of the last eighteen hours showed on his unshaven face. From time to time he blinked red eyes and mumbled a response to conversation directed at him, but his weary shoulders and the slow sinking progress he made in his chair evidenced his fatigue. Melanie's sympathy

71

went out to him and to all of the men who had fought so valiantly against the thrashing tides of the typhoon. When he finally heaved his body up from the table and excused himself, she was relieved that he was going to get some sleep.

After the men had gone their separate ways, she and Sven cleared the table and washed the tin plates and mugs. With the meticulous care her mother had taught her, Melanie scoured the dishes thoroughly in the water Karl had warmed on the stove, while Sven dried them and put them away for the morning meal. Perhaps it was her nerves that made her so talkative, for she could not help chattering away to her silent partner, who gave abbreviated answers to any questions she directed at him.

When their chores were done, Melanie made a slow exit, reluctant to return to the cabin. She wasn't the least bit tired, although she should have been. It was still raining topside, but it was more like the first drizzle of the previous day. Had it been just hours ago? she wondered incredulously. It seemed like a week.

Lanterns swung lazily along the deck, lighting her path to the main hatch. There were no stars above, for the tail of the typhoon was a long and clouded one. But unlike before, the air held the promise of calmer seas and a brighter tomorrow.

The cabin was quiet when she entered, lit dimly by a lamp that hung on the support post near the desk. Ryan had not put up the hammock he had used the night before. Instead, he lay sprawled facedown, cater-cornered across his bunk. His wet shirt was discarded on the floor, and he still wore his boots and trousers.

Melanie tiptoed over to the sleeping man, loath to wake him up. He had probably decided to lie down for just a moment and had given into the exhaustion she had witnessed on his face at supper. With a resigned sigh, she grasped his boots, their leather still damp, and pulled them off his feet carefully so as not to disturb him. As she leaned over to put them at the foot of the bunk, he turned on his back with an

72

incoherent mumble, immediately resuming the steady breathing of his slumber.

He appeared so harmless, peacefully stretched out with his arms and legs askew. His face was almost boyish in spite of the growth of golden stubble outlining the shadow of his beard. Eyelashes of a darker shade, which would be the envy of many women, were spread on weather-burned cheeks, creating a tender temptation to touch her lips to the eyelids above them. But Melanie was not so foolish as to underestimate his appearance and she exercised restraint. There was no way she wanted to mislead him into thinking that her concern for him was founded on anything more than sympathy and gratitude.

A barely visible white crust, that of the salt left from the ocean spray that had soaked his body, lingered on his chest. Perhaps, if she were gentle, she might at least sponge it away. After all, it was through his efforts and wit that they had outlasted the storm.

She filled the basin with water and lifted it from its holder to carry to his bedside. Quietly, she wrung out the wet towel and gently dabbed his face. For a second, his eyelids fluttered, but upon recognition, they rested once more and he relaxed. She made slow circular motions on his chest, taking particular pains about the red and irritated wound she had inflicted on his shoulder. What on earth had possessed her to act so . . . savagely? she finished thoughtfully, a smile touching her lips at her use of his own description of her.

As she mopped away the salt residue, Melanie's bold fingers strayed from the washcloth to shyly explore his lean and muscular physique. He was much like 'Io in that respect, except that the captain had a burnished growth of crisp body hair that her Hawaiian sweetheart did not. But both were so virile, so very male . . . and so unlike the men her parents introduced her to.

When she had finished with the sponge bath, she gently blotted him dry with a fresh towel and put away the bathing utensils. There was enough water left for her to perform her own toilette before considering the dilemma of where she was going to sleep. As she brushed out the salt-ridden tangles in her hair and plaited it to keep it in order, she found herself longing for a real bath. It would be heaven to wash her hair in fresh water with the scented soap her mother made from the island's hibiscus. And a nightgown and a dress, a pretty one with lace and ruffles, would be a dream come true.

But since that was not to be, she donned the shirt Ryan had loaned her and made up a bed on the floor. The wearied man on the bunk deserved the more comfortable spot and she really didn't mind.

As she snuggled, her back to the trunk and her head on one of the pillows she had stolen from under the captain's head, Melanie wondered what this Arabella of the book's inscription looked like. Not that it really mattered, she sniffed indifferently. She was just curious. When the *Liberty Belle* arrived in Honolulu, she and the captain would go their separate ways. What exactly it was that she was going to do at that point she wasn't sure. And it was with that dominating thought that sleep eventually caught up with her.

Once during the night she stirred with the sensation that she was floating on air, and when she awoke at daybreak, alone in the bunk, neatly tucked in, Melanie realized that Ryan had put her there. His consideration warmed her so that her mood was bordering on exuberance as she made her way to the kitchen, where Karl gave her a hot breakfast of eggs and hash before she was instructed to clean up the meal from the crew's dining quarters.

Sven was among the hands who worked on deck to clean up the debris from the storm, so Melanie worked alone, humming a cheerful, if nondescript, tune that brought smiles to the faces of those close enough to overhear. It seemed that there had been damage to some of the sails and riggings, and she had heard a few of the men talking about engine trouble as well. That was probably so, for when she finished her chores and meandered topside, Amos informed her that Ryan was below with the engineers.

The light misting rain that had started off the day dwindled by noon and a welcome sun peeked through the clouds, absorbing the remaining chill of the storm in its basking rays. She spied Eric, who waved at her from the riggings, and watched as he and his fellow mates took down one of the shredded canvases for the ship's sailmaker, who was already busy on deck mending another. In fact, the breeze in the aft mast and foremast was the only propulsion the *Belle* had at the moment, for the engines were quiet and the mainmast's sails had either been stripped or reefed. There was a general festive air about the ship, which Melanie attributed to gratitude for their deliverance from the wrathful hands of the typhoon.

The midday meal was served topside in the same manner as it had been the day before. It suited Melanie perfectly to sit on one of the hatch covers in the brilliant sunshine and picnic with the crew on deck, although the busy men only stopped long enough to wolf down the hastily prepared victuals before going back to their assigned tasks. The ship was disabled and the primary objective in everyone's mind was to get her under way as soon as possible.

"I heard the captain is going to anchor off that island in the distance until we're shipshape again," Eric informed her, his blue eyes sweeping over her in appreciation. "We'll probably lay over there for a few days."

The news that they were close to land surprised Melanie. After the typhoon, she had thought that it would be weeks before she set foot on dry and still soil again. "Will we go ashore?" Melanie asked, straining to make out the growing rise of land in the distance that Eric pointed out. She envied the men in the network of riggings above, for they surely had the most extraordinary view of their surroundings. And they would also be able to see what sort of port lay ahead.

"I imagine the captain'll send a boat ashore, although Amos says it's most likely uninhabited," the young man added, dashing her hopes of finding passage to Honolulu after disembarking from the *Liberty Belle*. That was where she would start to look for 'Io. Honolulu was where he had been living since her father had run him off. "Still, it'll give us time to recover, and if the main mast is badly damaged, the carpenter will need to finish the spare." Eric pointed to a gigantic log that had been roughly hewn in the shape of a mast, which lay fastened to the deck. "Niles'll have it ready in no time. He's the best ship's carpenter on the seven seas."

"It must be a wonderful feeling to be able to see for miles around up there," Melanie said, her eyes lifted dreamily to the round crow's nest, where a lookout kept a keen eye out for the dark shadows of coral lurking beneath the shimmering surface.

"That it is," Eric agreed. He stood up and bowed shortly to her. "And as much as I would like to spend the afternoon in your company, I had best get back up there."

Melanie finished her sandwich and stretched out on the hatch cover, studying the clearing sky above that served as an azure backdrop for the sails and riggings. Her hands folded behind her head, she followed Eric's progress up the square ladders of heavy jute that led to the boom. From there another rose to the next level of gaffs, and then another to the last and highest, where the lookout was perched.

No one paid any heed to her when she started up the ropes. Each man was intent on his own task. It wasn't until she was on the second level that a startled foremast hand delivered an oath and pointed her out to his fellow crewmen. By the time she was on the third rope ladder that took her to the lookout's perch, several wary eyes were on her lithe and agile figure with sure bare feet curling about the lines and dark hair flowing behind her in the breeze.

Among them was Amos Cobb. At first his heart had stilled at the sight of the native girl nimbly scooting up the ropes, but when he saw the way she laughed as the ship swayed, not missing her step, he checked his shout of alarm. He'd seen a lot in his day, but this had been the damndest voyage he had ever witnessed. He never thought he'd see the day Ryan Caldwell shared a cabin and not a bed with a wench.

But then, Amos had never run into a hellcat like the one in the riggings, and he was certain his captain had not, either. If the barometer in the pilothouse could register the tension between her and the captain, it would be haywire, the mate thought with a rueful grin. She was trouble and had been since he'd laid eyes on her. Hell-bent, that's what he'd call her, he mused, shielding his eyes from the sun to catch sight of her. He put his pipe in his mouth and chuckled at the irony. Just like Ryan Caldwell.

The island loomed ahead of them, a fertile green knoll in the midst of a turquoise sea. Through the spy glass the amazed lookout had loaned her, Melanie scanned the land with delight. None of the banyan trees she had scaled with 'Io and Nani as children had ever afforded such a view as this. There was no sign of a village or any sort of habitation. A thin U-shaped beach strewn with palm fronds and other debris from the storm formed the cradle of a harbor where the ship could anchor, safe from the dark coral that had formed in spots closer to the island's edge. She wasn't certain, but a slash of white farther up the slope of the hill that rose through the dense trees might be just the place she was looking for to get that bath she'd dreamed about. Gratefully, she returned the glass to the uneasy lookout. Excitement built inside of her as the men brought the big ship into the cove.

When Melanie recognized Ryan emerging from the main hatchway, she borrowed the lookout's spy glass again and focused it on the captain. His face and clothing were smudged with soot, she noted as he walked over to where Amos Cobb was giving orders. They spoke briefly and Amos pointed toward her with a shake of his head. As Ryan raised his eyes to the top of the mast, Melanie dropped the glass and waved at him merrily. But instead of returning the gesture, he kicked off his boots and made a determined path toward the foremast.

"Ye'd best be goin' down, missy, if'n I was you," the lookout advised her, peeping nervously over the rail at the man climbing toward them. "Like I told ye, this ain't no place fer a lady."

"But I'm not afraid," Melanie objected, the mate's advice making her as uncomfortable as the ominous progress of the man climbing toward them.

She would simply explain to Ryan that she was accustomed to climbing high places . . . that she loved the thrill of being able to see for miles in any direction. But when she saw his stormy face appear over the rail, followed by a body that almost vaulted into the crow's nest as the lookout bailed out, the strength of her argument waned.

"What in the hell do you think you are doing?"

"I wanted to see the island." Her voice was much calmer than the nerves that screamed warily not to provoke him further.

"At the risk of breaking your lovely little neck?"

Melanie brushed back the wild strands of hair that played about her face in the warm breeze. "I can climb quite well, thank you. I was in no more danger than any of your men. I've climbed trees since I was a wee thing."

"Well, since you have reverted to your childhood again, perhaps I should revert to that sort of discipline."

Melanie bristled at the threat and raised to her full height. "I did not disobey you, Captain. You did not tell me not to come up here!"

Her tactic temporarily diffused the situation, for she was correct and he knew it.

"Damn it, Meilani, anyone with half a wit could see the danger of a female pulling a stunt like this. If for no other reason, consider the distraction of the men!"

"Oh, you are incorrigible, Ryan!" Melanie denounced hotly. "The fact is, there has been no harm done and you well know it." She grasped the captain's arms and stared up at him, her eyes as brilliant as the sky behind her. "For heaven's sake, just look around you! Everything's special from up here. Just experience it and enjoy it! Don't waste it on anger!"

Melanie watched the storm of emotions pass over his clean-shaven face as he struggled to sort through his feelings. When he smiled down at her, she felt a sense of victory that she had made him see reason. Her own lips responded in kind.

"Perhaps there's merit to your words, Meilani."

Melanie's confidence, however, faltered when he stepped forward and clamped an iron arm about her waist, which forced her against him. His misleading smile twisted sardonically as it lowered and claimed her lips, providing the outlet of the rage she had sought to disarm. She opened her mouth to protest, but his tongue savagely invaded it, seeking and probing while his free hand held her head captive, his fingers clenched painfully in her hair.

Fearing this discipline more than the first he had threatened her with, she tried desperately to back away. His hand slipped down and pressed her hips against his, massaging her buttocks painfully with his fingers and thwarting her escape. From below a cheer of encouragement rose as the men sided with the captain and fired her resistance.

"Stop it!" she gasped as his mouth relented its attack and began a wet trail of kisses down her neck, exposed by her futile attempt to escape his embrace.

"I am merely enjoying a challenging experience, blue eyes," he breathed huskily against the swell of her breasts.

That the linen of her shirt covered them did not dissuade his ravishment of the crests that leapt to attention under the damp warmth of his lips, as well as the insane nibbling of his teeth. The supportive shouts below made her want to slink away in humiliation at this blatant display of the captain's dominance over her. Her back felt as though it would break as he leaned her over the rail, demanding his pound of flesh for displeasing him. Unable to bear her weight in the awkward angle in which he forced her, Melanie's knees buckled. Ryan caught her and lowered her to the planks beneath them, his punitive debauchery changing to a gentler nature but not relenting.

The balustered rail protected her from the leering participation of the men below them, but her shame mounted regardless, for her treacherous body responded eagerly to its

79

teacher's bidding. Tears of frustration streamed down her cheeks as Ryan's hands found their way into her clothing, touching, exciting, until her body quivered in hot confusion between will and want. And then his weight was on her and his mouth reclaimed hers hungrily, his breath coming in ragged spurts.

"Cap'n, will ye be wantin' a boat put over?"

Amos Cobb's voice seemed to infiltrate the passion-consumed body that held her captive, shocking it into immobility. Ryan shook himself, throwing off the fiery demon of desire that had possessed him. He looked down at her with a bemused expression, which hardened with accusation as he wrestled with his conflicting emotions. Swallowing hard, he pulled himself to his feet and gave a terse affirmative to the first mate's question, his condemnation never ceasing.

Melanie drew away and rearranged the clothing the man standing over her had undone. She felt defiled by the shameful way he had used her own volatile feelings to his benefit. Amidst the lewd cheers of his men, he had shown his male mastery over her, robbing Melanie of her pride and degrading her to them and worse, to herself, for a part of her reveled in the way he had taken her.

"Come on, blue eyes. You're going down."

She did not protest when he heaved her over his shoulder. The thought that he might drop her as she hung precariously, bobbing with each step he took down the ladder, never crossed her mind. Nothing could escape the arm that clasped her legs to his chest. Instead, she closed her eyes to the speculative faces turned up at them and allowed the animosity eating at her sanity to grow with each rung Ryan took closer to the deck. She would not give him the chance to do this again. She would die first.

Ryan set her on her feet once they reached the deck of the ship, then he curtly ordered her to his cabin. Melanie straightened defiantly and the look she gave him was gravely disconcerting. Her tears had dried and blue eyes pierced him with venomous daggers. Wordlessly, she spun on her heels and started away. But instead of walking to the main hatchway, she went straight to the rail of the ship. Disbelief slowed Ryan's response as she nimbly hoisted herself up on it. With a scathing backward glance, she spat and dove over the side.

"Sweet Jesus," Amos swore, springing toward the side of the ship at the same time as his captain.

"Lower the boat!" Ryan shouted hoarsely, searching the clear water for Meilani. He perched on the rail and, when he saw her dark head surface, dove in after her.

The longboat hit the water simultaneously. Behind him, Ryan could hear the excited voices of the crew manning the oars as he came to the surface of the cresting water and shook his head to clear his eyes. She had to be somewhere ahead of him, yet all he could see was the swells that rolled toward the island. If he could reach Amos, keep her afloat until the men caught up with them . . .

Dear God, what had he done? he admonished himself, sick with fear and remorse. He had only intended to kiss her. Twice she had stricken him with fear for her safety, and he had wanted to exact revenge, for never before had he known such a sickness. But revenge had been far from his mind when Amos had interrupted them. The warmth of her lips, the contours of her soft body trembling against his, had robbed him of reason. That it had taken Amos's voice to restore it repulsed him. Desire's demon had driven him and he had driven her to this.

"Meilani!" he shouted, ceasing his long, even strokes to search for her again.

"She's up ahead, Cap'n, and swimmin' like she was born to it!" Amos reassured him, his voice only yards away. "Stay put and we'll bring ye aboard."

Damn her reckless hide, Ryan thought, his panic thawing at the realization that once more he had underestimated her. So help him, he would tame that savage if it took his last breath. That his lungs were about to burst as he treaded water and waited for his crew to catch up to him gave him cause to think it might. When the boat pulled alongside, he hauled himself aboard and followed Amos's pointed finger to the girl several yards ahead of them.

"Just keep behind her till she wears herself out," he commanded in a breathless calm that brought his first mate's gaze sharply to him.

"Now don't do nothin' else ye'll be regrettin', lad," Amos cautioned warily.

The last thing the captain wanted was to be reminded that he had brought this on, and he glared at the greying member of his crew, silencing him without a word.

"Cap'n there's a reef ahead and she's swimming right over it!"

Ryan seized his bottom lip with his teeth as he watched Meilani straighten her body, allowing the frothing shallows to carry her effortlessly across the coral toward the sandy beach beyond. "Swing around it, Mason," he ordered, praying silently for her deliverance while at the same time cursing her for the sickness he felt in the pit of his stomach . . . sickness born of worry.

Melanie's knees stung, jamming into the sandy bottom of the beach. Unsteadily, she struggled to her feet and gasped to regain her breath. The force of an incoming wave struck her and sent her staggering forward, the churning waters dragging her feet so that she sprawled onto the beach. Every muscle burned from exertion and collapsed, refusing to respond to her exhausted command to go on. The waves washed up around her, so that she had to strain to keep her head out of the water until she regained the use of her limbs.

It had been sheer instinct for survival that had kept her going. No matter how she had wished that the warm ocean would take her under, part of her had refused to accept it. With the skill she had developed swimming at the beaches near Lahaina, she had used the current to carry her in, swimming with it. 'Io had taught her the secrets of the ocean, how to make it the servant by keeping one's head.

But it had taken its toll nonetheless. Her lungs ached, the air she breathed scorching them. Gradually, life came back to her, and she crawled beyond the lapping froth of the surf and rolled onto her back. A groan of dismay escaped her lips when she saw the longboat circling toward the island farther down the beach. Would he never let her be? Her desire to avoid the golden captain and his crew tapped a hidden reserve of energy, and she climbed to her feet unsteadily.

Wildly, she searched the thick tropical growth that edged the beach and lunged blindly into it. A fallen branch caught her foot and she fell against a coconut palm, its rough bark scratching her cheek as she landed. Numbly, she dragged herself up on it, embracing the tree with her arms to support the legs that shook weakly under her weight.

"Meilani, stop!"

Ryan's voice sounded above a thunder of footfalls closing in behind her, yet she could go no farther. If he took her this time, he would not take her willingly, she vowed. Wincing at the effort, she picked up a palm frond that had blown off in the storm. With her back against the tree, she lifted her blurred vision to face him, her weapon brandished before her.

The captain stopped a few feet from her, his face oddly white and contorted as his eyes swept over her. As if sensing for the first time that something was wrong, Melanie glanced down to see the red splashes of color seeping through the clinging shirt and trousers. Vaguely, she recalled the ripping pain of the sharp coral that had shredded her clothing. The palm frond dropped to her feet as she turned over her hands and saw their bleeding palms. With one last look at the man who rushed forward to catch her, she shook her head in a final rebellious attempt and slipped into a blackness where the sting of her wounds did not exist.

The whole way back to the ship, Ryan was tight-lipped as he cradled the unconscious girl in his arms. The night before, he thought he had reached her. Through the thin slits of his eyelids, he had watched the tenderness on her face as she bathed him. Her fascination with his body intrigued him. It had taken every ounce of control to remain relaxed under the tantalizing exploration of her delicate fingers, for he knew if she suspected he was awake, she would have erected that barrier she kept between them—a barrier he was certain was without substance, considering her warm submission to his touch.

But to do this, to nearly kill herself to get away from him . . . He closed his eyes and inhaled deeply. Maybe he had been wrong. Maybe he had read something into the way she had treated him that was not there. He clamped his lips together until they were bloodless. He had to get a hold on himself. No woman had ever tied him into so many knots—knots from which there seemed no escape.

A small moan from the girl in his arms captured his attention. She was regaining consciousness but not one muscle moved. Her body remained limp, drained of fight, as her dark eyelashes fluttered against her cheeks in her attempt to come back to the present. When they finally lifted, blue eyes met his dully. Then with a shuddering sigh, she closed them again and pressed her face against him wearily.

Although she was alert, she could neither protest nor help the men who lifted her like a rag doll over the rail. Ryan carried her straight to his cabin and laid her gently on his bed while Amos Cobb fetched the medical kit. Her skin was like ice and her breathing shallow as he removed her damp clothing to examine the injuries she had sustained skimming over the sharp and dangerous coral reef.

Yet, to his infinite relief, he saw that her hands and her clothing had taken the brunt of the beating. The scratches marring her smooth skin had already stopped bleeding, and in a few days all that would remain would be the yellowed ghosts of her bruises. The cuts on her hands would take longer, but they too were minor in comparison to what he had first thought when he saw the blood seeping through her clothing.

"How bad is she?" Amos asked, entering the cabin with an armful of bandages and ointments. He paused and kicked the door closed behind him with his foot.

Ryan covered the girl protectively, responding to an instinct even he did not notice. "Not as bad as we thought.

There's nothing broken. More bruises and scratches than anything else. I can take care of her, Amos. You see to the men."

Amos glanced at Melanie, who lay acquiescent on the bunk, and he shrugged. "If ye need me, I'll be within shoutin' distance."

As soon as the first mate left, Ryan filled the washbasin and placed it within reach on the edge of the desk. When he began to cleanse the injuries, Meilani opened her eyes. Her nakedness bared before him did not seem to affect her. She merely watched him in silence, her face devoid of emotion, her body obedient to his quiet ministrations. Even the sting of the iodine elicited little more than a sharp intake of breath and a pained wince. By the time he had finished and cleaned up the mess, she had fallen asleep, curled around a pillow with a sheet pulled tightly over her bruised shoulder.

Deigning to skip the meal he heard Sven setting up at the table outside, Ryan withdrew a bottle of brandy from the cabinet and uncorked it with a pop that failed to disturb his sleeping companion. The drink he took was a healthy one, which he swirled around in his mouth, thoroughly savoring the rich burning nectar before swallowing. For now she was complacent, he mused. She seemed to work like that — sweet and agreeable one moment, and hell's fire the next.

Why he even bothered with her was beyond him. Perhaps it was the guilt he felt at having taken her innocence when in retrospect, she very obviously had thought him someone else. He scowled and determined to drown the festering resentment that the sweet, wild passion she had shared with him had been for another man . . . that someone else controlled the flame that burned behind those enchanting blue eyes.

Chapter Six

Melanie ached as if she had been beaten in her sleep, but she stubbornly left the comfort of her bed as soon as she heard Ryan leave the cabin. Since Sven's clothing was ruined, she painfully donned her shift. An empty bottle, lying on its side on the desk, explained the distinct odor that filled the room, but she took no time to puzzle over it. It took all her effort to function as she tormented her matted hair with the brush until the sand from the beach had been shaken free of it.

When her hair was neatly brushed, it hung loosely about her shoulders, its luster dulled by the salt water that had dried in it. Once more she longed for a hot bath and the chance to wash her hair with scented soap. Melanie banished the thought and the homesick tears that threatened, and she made her way topside to the kitchen, defeated in body and spirit.

"You can check to see if there are any eggs, though my ladies may still be a tad distressed from the storm," Karl instructed as she stood mutely in the doorway. He handed her the egg basket and turned back to the hotcakes he was cooking on the large iron griddle. "I'll have some for you when you get back."

The lack of warmth in the cook's voice did little to boost her low morale. Melanie left without comment and trudged to the makeshift henhouse. Of all the hens, only Irmgard had come through. It took two tries before she emerged from the shack with three eggs and a bleeding hand, where the vicious hen had opened one of her cuts. But she hardly noticed such a small hurt compared to the misery she was experiencing.

When she declined the hotcakes Karl offered her, the big cook tossed them on top of the large tray she was to carry down to the hungry crew. Melanie was loath to do it . . . to face the men who had cheered at the way their captain had treated her. But she was saved having to put up a good front for them, because other than a few grunts of thanks for serving them their portions, Melanie was not spoken to. The camaraderie she had felt a part of the day before was now gone. The men acted as if she weren't even there, pointedly excluding her.

It was only Sven who had the nerve enough to say what the men were thinking. Everyone had gone about their assigned chores, and Melanie and the cabin boy were doing the dishes.

"You are really stupid," he told her with a grimace of disgust. He pushed her aside from the wash pan and handed her the towel. "You shouldn't be wettin' them cuts till they heal. I'll wash."

Tears welled in her eyes, not from the hot water that set fire to her palms, but from her private anguish. With lowered eyes to keep the cabin boy from noticing, she let the comment go. She had no one to talk to, to confide the terrible humiliation she suffered at the captain's hand.

"You're doin' things to hurt yourself," Sven observed, dragging her from her wallow of self-pity. "I had a cousin who was like that, but he was crazy. My aunt had to watch him all the time, 'cause even though he was grown, his brain was a baby's. They kept him locked in his room most of the time."

"Is that what you think should happen to me?"

Sven turned a guilty face away from her misty challenge. "No, it's just that you push the captain by doin' stupid things. Nobody blames him for the way he treated you.

Some say he shoulda left you on the island where wild things belong."

Melanie refused to cry. If that's what they thought, to hell with them all. She really didn't care. They were a bunch of inconsiderate brutes who thought of women as nothing more than playthings to amuse themselves with.

"Has the captain ever allowed you in the crow's nest, Sven?" Melanie asked suddenly. She had made a mistake in patronizing Sven, only reinforcing his opinion of her inferiority, and she was not about to let that happen again.

"Ya, when I have no more chores to do," the boy stipulated.

"Do you like it up there?"

"Ya! You can see for miles," he beamed. "Sometimes the watch and me play games, betting pennies on who spots the first sail. One for the sighting, one for the first to identify her colors and another for recognizing what sort of vessel she is."

Melanie managed a wistful smile. "I like to see for miles, too. And yesterday, after I finished my chores, I climbed up there to spend a few spare moments enjoying the view."

Her point was not well received. Sven snorted in consternation. "But you're a girl! And you not only got yourself into trouble, but all of us as well. The captain upbraided us all for not stopping you."

So now the real reason for her social banishment was out. Her impulsive action had caused the crew to suffer. She felt a brief pang of regret but rose to make her point. "And I am more likely to hurt myself because I am a girl?" At Sven's hesitant nod, for she had given him food for thought, she dried the last plate and placed it on the stack to put away. He might be a boy, but he already thought like the captain and his men, she realized with an annoying sense of futility. "Then I'll be finished when I put these in the cupboard, and you can carry out the wash water. I might hurt my back straining with such a heavy burden." With an angry toss of the wet towel across the disgruntled boy's face, she picked up the plates and walked away.

The deck was covered with sail and the sailmaker worked diligently with his hooked needle, his bald head shining in the sunlight. Like the others, he did not raise his head to speak to Melanie, but was intent on his stitches. It would be no pleasure to remain topside under the circumstances and in truth she was poor company, so she started toward the stern hatch, footsteps slowing as she saw the captain engrossed in conversation with Amos Cobb and two blacksmeared men.

Ryan, his gold hair color enhanced by the sun, stood feet apart, arms folded across his broad chest. His legs, exposed by the white trousers he had rolled up, were bronzed and as firm as the sturdy mast beside him. He nodded, a gleam of satisfaction in his eyes at the content of the engineer's words. But Melanie knew she had caught his attention, for his green eyes darted to her as they captured her reluctant gaze, making her unconsciously hesitate.

Feigning ignorance of his presence, she dropped her eyes to the deck and continued past them. Every fiber of her body cringed in alarm when he reached past the engineer and caught her arm, halting her in her tracks. It was a gentle but nonetheless unrelenting grasp that drew her to his side as he finished his business.

"That's the best news I've had, Andy. If that's the case and it was just a result of the vibration . . ."

"That it were, sir. We took a tolerable beatin' down there. Lucky the whole damned thing didn't break loose."

"You're the man who would know," Ryan acknowledged with a hearty slap on the man's back. "Thanks." As the two engineers started below, he raised his eyes to the riggings in speculation. "We'll be out of here day after tomorrow at this rate, although we could go on under steam without the sails readied," he considered aloud, to no one in particular. "Amos, go see what Tom has to say on his progress."

Amos left them with a tip of his cap and an "Aye, sir."

"I hadn't expected to see you on deck." The crisp businesslike manner of his voice had changed to a soothing tone as he reached out and touched the scratch on her cheek with the same tenderness he had used to care for her wounds the night before.

His concern affected her so profusely that she needed to remind herself it was his brash action that had caused them. "You are the one who said no one rides your ship for free," she reminded him flatly.

His fingers slipped under her chin and raised her face to his. "Are you sure you feel up to it?"

Averting her eyes from the green ones searching them, Melanie shrugged indifferently. "It doesn't matter what I feel."

Ryan swore under his breath. "Meilani, you are making this very difficult."

It was a strain to keep her voice even, considering he was the one who had made their predicament impossible from the start. "I apologize, Captain. I do not mean to. If I show any sign of pride or attempt to retain some shred of dignity, forgive me. I realize that as your—your *mistress*, I am not entitled to such things." She folded her arms across her chest defensively and looked up at him with an impassive gaze. "May I go now . . . please," she added in a whisper.

Her muscles tensed to disguise the fact that she trembled inside. And when he released her arms, her shoulders drooped heavily with relief. Her eyes remained blindly focused on her feet as she retreated to the cabin, unaware of the expression of dazed frustration she left on Ryan's face. She was frantic to get away from those arms that tempted her to seek the embrace she knew could offer her comfort, for she was not willing to pay the high price the captain demanded for it.

There was much to do that afternoon. After serving pancakes rolled up about a meaty hash at noon, Karl had her scrub-peel potatoes and onions for the fish fry the men were going to have on the island. A few of the hands had spotted a school of fish swimming near the boat after Sven had dumped the morning table scraps over the side. They had hurriedly tossed a net over, insuring a quick change of menu for the evening meal.

When she finished with the vegetables, Melanie joined Sven on the foredeck, where he cleaned the morning's catch. The task was not foreign to Melanie. Without a word, she straddled the board opposite the cabin boy, her dress hiking to her knees, and proceeded to scale her silvery victim with practiced strokes of the sharp knife Karl had given her.

"Next you take off its head and fins. I'll show you."

Sven's patronizing manner annoyed her. She had cleaned fish since she was old enough to use a knife. "Like this?"

Melanie made quick, clean work of the fish, not giving the cabin boy a chance to demonstrate his skill. The head and fins tossed over the rail, she slit its belly and gutted it before tossing the entrails over the side, too. Then, dipping her hands in the bucket of salt water where she deposited the cleaned carcass, she glanced up at her silent partner.

"Well, hand me another and finish that one up before someone thinks this poor ignorant, female knows a thing or two about the most menial of tasks."

Sven slapped a fish on the board in front of her, his pale blue eyes narrowed and his chest puffed up with indignation. "Thor's thunder, I didn't mean to hurt your feelin's this mornin' and I never said you couldn't clean a fish! All you natives eat is fish! Of course, you can clean 'em! Your *kanes* catch 'em and you *wahines* clean and cook 'em!"

"*T'a puhi,*" Melanie responded peevishly. Yet her lips twitched with the first humor she had felt that day. Sven reminded her of a sputtering blowfish and his reference to her Hawaiian background amused her.

"What did you call me?" the cabin boy fumed.

A grin broke free of her restraint and she giggled. "Blowfish." She poked a playful finger at his chest. "One poke and

91

all the hot air escapes, sending you flying overboard."

"Irmgard!" Sven retaliated. His pinched lips twisted as he struggled to contain his own humor. "Even if you're nice to her, she still pinches you."

With mock indignation, Melanie dipped her hand into the fish water and flicked Sven's face, her laughter robbing the offense from the gesture, so that the cabin boy joined her, wiping the water from his face with the back of his hand. "What's it called when you natives fish and cook?" he asked, settling back to the task at hand.

"That is the *hukilau,*" Melanie answered. "All the people of the village haul in the great nets of fish and there is festivity. We eat and dance and give thanks to the gods for the bounty of our land and sea."

She put down her knife and began an impromptu song. It was the song of the *hukilau,* and with it she made the motions imitating the hauling in of the nets, the preparation of the feast, and the dances that followed. After each line, she hurriedly explained to Sven in English what she was saying. When she finished, a clapping behind her gave rise to color in her cheeks.

Eric Johannson, his shirt slung over his shoulder, walked over to them. "So how is it that my brother is privileged to a private audience?"

"Well, I never got to go ashore with the rest of you when we were in port!" Sven declared indignantly. "And Scrapper was showin' me how they catch fish in her village. You sure sing pretty, even if it isn't in English." His face suddenly brightened. "Maybe you can sing and dance tonight, and we can pretend its like a *huki* — " He frowned as he searched for the word she had used.

"*Hukilau,*" Melanie supplied for him. "But I don't think it would be quite the same," she added shyly.

"Just the same, Sven has a good idea. I'm going to take my guitar. You did say you wanted to hear me play," Eric reminded her, agreeing with his brother's idea.

Melanie hesitated. Perhaps going ashore with Eric and

Sven would lighten the burden that seemed to weigh down her spirit. The fact that he had been reprimanded by the captain on her account did not appear to have changed the friendly way Eric had treated her from the first . . . and Sven had even apologized. Perhaps she was not as alone as she had thought, for as she glanced from one fair smiling face to the other, Melanie felt she at least had two friends.

"Now, I would prefer not to dance, but I would love to go with you and hear you play," she agreed.

"With the captain's permission, of course," Eric spoke up.

Melanie's face fell at the dampening reminder. "Of course."

It was foolish of her to have thought for a moment that she might do something of her own volition, without first asking permission of the *Belle*'s all-powerful captain. He controlled everyone and everything on his ship with invisible strings. The master puppeteer, she mused bitterly.

But she could not sustain her ill humor. After Eric went ashore to prepare the fire pit, Sven plied her with questions about life on the island, his eager young face clinging to every word she said in answer. Melanie's own eyes were alight as well, as she became caught up in her passion for the Hawaiian ways. The two comrades snickered at the ignorance of some of the ancient superstitions as they washed down the deck where they had cleaned the fish. Neither of them was aware of Ryan's approach until his shadow fell across them.

"It does my heart good to see such high spirits among my crew. Never have I seen such merrymaking over the carcasses of cleaned fish."

Melanie stopped mopping the wet planking and decided to take advantage of whatever had brought that devastating smile to the captain's face. "I was amusing Sven with some of the silly superstitions of the ancient ones." She stepped toward him, her soaked shift clutching her legs in the process. "The men are having a fish fry. . . ."

"*Hukilau*," Sven interjected exuberantly, caught up in the

light mood that had been set.

"Hukilau." Melanie chewed her lower lip in apprehension. "May I go ashore with Sven and Eric?" she blurted out in a rush. A sidelong glance at the cabin boy revealed him looking at Ryan in somber expectation.

"How do I know I can trust you?" Ryan's words punctured her inflated spirit.

"What do you mean?" Melanie asked, bewildered.

"What's to keep you from plunging headlong into the forest like you tried to do before?"

"I did that because I was upset. I wouldn't—" Melanie broke off abruptly as the brows reached higher for the cocky tumble of golden hair on his forehead. He wouldn't understand, she thought sourly. If he had the capacity to, he would never have treated her the way he did. "Never mind. It wasn't important."

"Good, because I have a task I want you to do," he told her. He took her by the arm and walked her to the rail. "Since most of the men will be ashore, it will be an ideal time to scrub down the crew's deck and fo'c'sle."

"Why, it'll be dark before I'm finished . . . even if I start right now!" Melanie objected, snatching her arm from his grip.

Her eyes strained to hold back the tears welling behind them. It was unfair! She had worked as diligently as the others, and yet she was being made to stay aboard and work while they enjoyed an evening ashore. He was using his authority to drive home the fact that she had no alternative but to obey his commands.

"Then I suggest you leave Sven to his task and carry out my orders immediately."

"Aye, sir," Melanie grated out with a spiteful salute.

How she hated this man! She hated the satisfied gleam in his eyes and the haughty way he stood over her. Picking up the dripping hem of her shift, she whirled away from him, her foot stomping in protest as it hit the deck.

"Hop to it, wench!"

Melanie gasped as Ryan's hand swatted her backside with a resounding clap against the wet material. She froze and clenched her fists, a hundred means of revenge coming to her mind. The silence around her made her realize that they had an audience, and with a monumental effort, she willed her coiled body to relax. She understood his game — provoke her and then humiliate her. It was too fresh for her to fall victim to it again. Lifting her head high, she continued on, her back straight and her teeth clenched so tightly they hurt.

Ryan watched her retreating figure, unconsciously holding his breath until she disappeared below deck. He had been perfectly miserable since their encounter that morning. Her dejection had infected him with guilt and a myriad of emotions he'd yet to identify. He couldn't seem to concentrate on anything but her words and the dead expression in her eyes.

He had wanted to tame her spirit, not to kill it. It was that part of her that intrigued him, captivated him. And just when he was about to capitulate, so sick with remorse over the way he had treated her that he would do anything to bring back that sparkle to her eyes, he had found her singing and dancing with his cabin boy and foremast hand. Damnation, but she was resilient . . . and full of surprises. Well, he had a few of his own, thought Ryan. He crooked a finger, motioning Sven over to him.

As Melanie predicted, the sun had set when she turned over the scrub basin and swept the dirty water toward the scuppers to drain out the side of the ship. From the portal, she could see the blazing campfire and hear the men's raucous laughter across the water. No doubt Eric and Sven were among them, she thought wistfully as she put away the basin and mop.

But it was just as well she hadn't gone. Her only garment smelled of fish and was sorely in need of a wash. And although her scratches and cuts were white from their constant soaking in the harsh, soapy water she used to clean the crew's quarters, she was extremely conscious of them.

Thank heaven 'Io could not see her now, she thought, gaining some consolation from that. She wasn't fit to be seen by anyone. Tonight she would wash out her shift and do the best she could with her hair. Even the captain's shaving soap was better than this.

Only a few members of the crew remained on deck as she walked toward the captain's cabin, but they were too intent on watching the distant scene on the beach to notice her. Ryan must have gone ashore, she thought, for the cabin was dark when she entered it. She felt her way to the corner washstand and searched for the matches kept in a tin on a shelf by the lamp.

"Heavenly Father!" she swore under her breath as she tried to pry the lid off the tin. It would not give and her nails threatened to break under the strain.

Suddenly, from the other side of the room, there was a scrape of a match against wood, followed by its bursting flash. Melanie cried out in alarm, dropping the can. It crashed to the floor, its lid still firmly on, and rolled away from her feet.

"My, such harsh profanity, Meilani. My ears are singed," the captain of the *Liberty Belle* admonished wryly. He lit the lamp hanging over the bunk and, with a shake of his wrist, extinguished the match.

Melanie's hand rested on her chest, trying to assuage the frantic heart beating within. "You frightened me to death, hiding in here like that!" she accused. Exhaling deeply, she leaned against the paneled wall behind her and closed her eyes. Then, as it registered that something about the room was different they flew open again.

This time her sharp intake of breath was a combination of surprise and delight, for between her and her observant companion, in the place where the desk had been, was a bathtub. It was a simple design, constructed of metal and raised at one end to support the back—just big enough to sit in with one's knees drawn in slightly. But it was filled with hot water and looked like heaven to her. "Oh!" she exhaled in disbelief, rushing over to touch it to reassure herself she was not dreaming. "Where did you get it?"

The captain assumed a mysterious air and, in a conspiratorial tone, whispered, "Many things are hidden in the spare compartments of this ship."

Melanie frowned. "I thought you said there were no spare rooms on the *Liberty Belle.*"

Damn, she was quick. "There aren't," Ryan answered quickly, cursing himself for his inadvertent slip. "They are filled with items such as this . . . for storage purposes," he explained. He moved forward and dipped a towel in the water. "What do you think?" he asked, holding the wet towel up to her nose.

Melanie's eyes widened in amazement. "It's scented! But this is a ship full of men. Where—?"

Ryan was beside himself with satisfaction, inspired by Meilani's excitement. "So some of my lady friends will find themselves short a gift or two when I return home," he shrugged indifferently. "I thought that this one needs them more. I believe it's jasmine," he informed her. He let the towel slip back into the water and wiped his hands on his trousers. "Aren't you going to try it?"

Melanie looked uneasily from the inviting water to Ryan's quizzical green eyes. "Are you going to stay?" she asked, her voice suddenly shy at the thought of a man's presence, even one who had, as he had once put it, witnessed her charms.

"Do I have a choice?" His velvet-edged question was oddly disconcerting. He moved behind her and put his hands on her arms, awaiting her answer.

Melanie stiffened warily. "Do I?" she countered. She would have little alternative if he told her no. He certainly could strip her and force her into the water, and she had no desire to fight him. She just wanted to relax and enjoy her unexpected treat—although she would do so much better without his presence than with it.

97

His chest shook with private amusement, but there was no sign of it in his voice as he granted her reprieve. "The soap's in the bottom somewhere. I'm off to fetch some rinse water for your hair. Aside from that, you'll have your privacy, blue eyes." At her audible sigh of relief, he added mischievously, "Although you do tempt me."

Melanie swung her face to him in time to catch his devilish wink and realized that he had baited her. Impulsively, she dipped her hand in the water and shook it in his face.

Instinctively, he leapt back. His green eyes darkened with mischief as he wiped the droplets away with the back of his hand. "I vow, is that an invitation to join you?"

"No!" Melanie declared, moving back as he appeared to be having a change of heart.

After some thought, he heaved a regretful sigh. "Alas, I thought not." He paused at the door and pivoted with second thought. "Oh, when you've undressed, put your shift outside the door. I'll see that it's washed for you."

Melanie was speechless. The bath, the scented soap . . . and now this. But she shook her head and offered a grateful smile. "It's very considerate of you, sir. All of this is," she added, "but I would prefer to wash it myself with the soap . . . if you don't mind."

"Meilani, surely you don't think I would make off with your only clothing," he tormented her with mock reproach.

"In truth, sir, I do not know exactly what you will do," she admitted with beguiling candor. "But my reasons for keeping the shift are as I said. Besides, you've a trunk full of clothing I might borrow should you make off with it," she added with a sly grin.

And he did not doubt that, Ryan thought. Even in the shapeless blue shift with the grime of her hard labor, she was quite enchanting. She was half-woman, half-child, a diverting combination if there ever were one. "Well said, blue eyes," he credited her, his mouth quirking with humor. "Well said."

Melanie had to shake herself from her dumbfounded

state as she gazed at the closed door he left behind him. She could not guess the purpose of the captain's lighthearted humor, but whatever it was, she intended to make the best of it. It was a refreshing change. Delightful, in fact, she decided, testing the water once more before removing her clothing and stepping into the tub.

Her body reveled in the caressing warmth of the hot water, each muscle seeming to say "Ahh" in euphoria. For a while, Melanie rested against the back of the tub and let her salt-dried skin soak in the scented oils. Jasmine, she mused dreamily. Such an exotic fragrance compared to the pure and sweet hibiscus her mother used. Hadn't some of the Orientals brought over the sweet shrub for the beautiful gardens they planted around their homes?

She searched her mind for an appropriate word to describe the scent and chose *sophisticated*. Sophisticated, she mouthed silently. Was his Arabella sophisticated? she wondered. Unconsciously, her lips pursed, forming a peevish pout. Or perhaps the scented oil was for another adoring admirer of her golden captain, it occurred to her. *"Some* of my lady friends," he had said.

But of course a man with his decidedly good looks would have more than one feminine admirer. As much as he annoyed her, even she was not immune to those good looks. She recalled the sensuous undertone of his voice when he had first said her name. Why, he might as well have run his skillful fingers up her spine, for the infinitely disturbing effect it had had on her. And when he had nibbled at the food in her fingers, boldly licking them with his tongue, she had had to draw back to keep from falling victim to those hypnotic eyes that kept her from straying too far.

"Oh, damn!" she mumbled, seizing the washcloth with one hand and seeking out the soap in the bottom of the tub with the other. If she continued to think in that direction, she would end up in more trouble than she already was. Melanie chastised herself severely. As if to eradicate the recollections her body had begun to respond to, she punished

99

her skin with a thorough scrubbing.

She had just rinsed the soap from her hair with the scented bath water, when Ryan knocked to announce his return. "Stay put! I promise not to look," he assured her, entering the cabin with a bucket of freshly warmed water and a long-handled dipper.

Closing her eyes in embarrassment, Melanie curled up in a ball, her knees clasped to her chest as he set the bucket beside the tub.

"Dear Meilani, *I'm* the one who said I wouldn't look!" His quiet chuckle so close to her ear brought her astonished and irritated gaze to his in an instant.

"You liar!" she fumed helplessly, tightening her grip about her knees.

Nonplussed, Ryan shrugged and drew up a chair. The material of his fawn trousers stretched across his muscular thighs as he straddled the chair. "I'm only human, Meilani. Besides, if I hadn't said that, you would be running about the cabin frantically searching for cover and dripping all over the floor." He picked up the ladle of the rinse water and, with a wicked smirk she would have loved to slap, questioned, "Do you need any help?" When her only response was a low growl of denial, he clicked his tongue in disappointment. "Well, in that case, you rinse off and wrap this around you," he instructed, reaching for one of the folded towels lying on the desk, "and I will get the ointment to treat your injuries before you dress."

Melanie puffed with indignation as he got up and walked to the cabinet over the washstand, where the medical supplies had been stored. "You are incorrigible!"

"You use some pretty big words for a simple native girl, blue eyes," he observed thoughtfully, his broad back to her.

"You are beyond salvation, sir! I think that Lucifer trembles at the thought of your impending occupancy in his domain!"

"Meilani," he tutted, his voice damnably patronizing, "I am only going to be preoccupied for so long with my back to you. Try to make the best of it." He kept his face turned as he placed the bottle and swabs on the desk and opened his trunk.

Choking back her retaliatory remark, Melanie seized the handle of the ladle and dipped it into the rinse water. For a moment she held it poised and considered the target of her ire, but then thought better of it and turned the contents over her head instead. She paid little heed to the water that spilled on the floor, for she was determined to rid her hair of soap before the captain found whatever it was he searched for in the bottom of his trunk.

She stood in the tub and, after a cautious glance toward Ryan's back, emptied the remaining contents of the bucket over her body, bringing an end to the heavenly respite of her bath. Hastily, she snatched up the towel Ryan had left within her reach and wrapped it about her snugly, tucking the end in the valley of her breasts to secure it.

She attained decency just in time, for the captain made a satisfied exclamation and withdrew a paper-wrapped package from among the garments he had disturbed. He gave it a sling toward the bunk and motioned Melanie over to where he stood. At her hesitation, he reached for the bottle of ointment and held it up.

"Be a good little girl, Meilani, and we shall have no problem. And wrap your hair in that before we're forced to swab the deck," he added, pointing to a second towel.

Although he smiled, Melanie recognized the threat and complied grudgingly. She fashioned a turban about her dripping black tresses, piling them high on her head, and stood stiffly as Ryan soaked a swab of cotton with the stinging ointment. He became strictly business as he applied the ointment to those cuts still raw enough to require it. Her skin was red from a combination of the hot water soak and her mortification, but she meekly submitted to his methodical ministrations, moving the towel to permit him access to those hidden wounds he recalled from her previous treatment.

"There we are," he announced when he had finished. He disposed of the swab and recorked the bottle. "You are disinfected and fresh as a daisy . . . or some such flower," he added, bending down to sniff her bare shoulder. "Is Meilani some sort of tropical flower?"

"No, it is not!" she denounced curtly, an unwelcome flush coming to her cheeks. She now knew how the mouse felt when the cat played with it. The captain was deliberately manipulating her, and the knowledge was strangely alarming and somewhat heady at the same time.

"Now, hurry and dress. I have dinner waiting for us at the table."

"Dinner?" Melanie repeated blankly.

"As I recall, you have not eaten today, blue eyes. You've wounded Karl's feelings, you know," he chided gently.

The distance between them was so nil that Melanie moved against the bunk in an effort to retreat from the heat of his body. "And what do you expect me to wear? This towel?" she questioned, assuming a most proper tone of indignation.

"It is an intriguing idea, blue eyes," Ryan told her, injecting a huskiness into his voice that told of its effect. His hands slid to her waist. "But I could not guarantee that the fish Karl has prepared would not be replaced by another delicacy far more tempting."

He moved closer, as if to illustrate the subtle threat. Melanie had nowhere to go as she arced her back over the edge of the bunk, one hand righting the turban that toppled sideways while the other clutched the front of her wrap to keep it from falling down. "You have the unfair advantage over me, sir," she objected breathlessly. "You mustn't—"

"You injure me, blue eyes," Ryan pronounced, his lean body just brushing hers, his lips almost touching her own with each syllable he spoke. But instead of kissing her as she fully expected, he reached beyond and grabbed the package he had taken from the trunk. "Actually, I thought you might prefer something a little more substantial than that most becoming towel," he informed her, holding it over her head as he looked down at her with eyes that thoroughly enjoyed her discomfiture. "And I, wounded gentleman that I am, will wait for you outside," he told her, sealing the promise with a light peck on the tip of her nose before leaving her in dumbfounded silence.

Chapter Seven

When Melanie first opened the package and removed the scarlet swathe of silk brocade, she was confounded. It bore no resemblance to anything she had ever worn. She shook it out and laid it on the bed, only then recognizing the Oriental design of the garment.

She put on the sarong with the thrill of a child at Christmas, trying to capture her full image in the captain's shaving mirror from across the room. She secured the silk ties, which drew the luxurious fabric that clung lovingly to her freshly bathed skin about the curves of her youthful body almost shamefully, Melanie thought, as she turned to see the back of the garment. Why, if she were to roll up her hair and decorate it with tiny red bows, she would look just like the wealthy Oriental ladies who kept a sharp eye on their servant shopping at the fish market.

But without pins, that was impossible. Undaunted, she towel-dried her long black tresses and brushed them to a sheen rivaling that of her garment. She tied up her hair with a matching scarf she discovered in the bottom of the package, so that it swung in a shimmering cascade down her back. With one last critical glance at the mirror, she started for the door, anxious to see if the captain was as pleased with her appearance as she was.

When she opened it, Ryan was seated in the armchair at the head of the table. It was set for two, with china and silver-covered dishes containing their meal. Presiding over them, a tiered candelabra was aglow, its flames dancing on the low ceiling. The captain turned at the sound of her entrance and his wine glass stopped just short of his lips, his eyes drinking in every inch of her silk-swathed figure.

Melanie was just as still, for suddenly she was intimidated by the beautiful and gracious women he must have known, and one particular Arabella. She was like a child who had been caught playing dress-up, pretending to be something she was far from. That thought was probably going through those green eyes right now, she fretted, her stomach knotting beneath the wide cummerbund that accented the smallness of her waist and the ripe fullness of her breasts . . . those eyes that seemed to see past the silk to the real Melanie, simple, unsophisticated, and unaccountably frightened.

She flinched as Ryan rose, shoving the chair back with his knees, and put his untouched glass on the table. It required all her courage to stand her ground as he approached her with long, fluid strides that closed the distance between them with each heartbeat. His hand engulfed her own and raised it to his lips, a gallantry that halted her in mid-breath.

"Meilani, you never cease to amaze me," he said, a kindling warmth in his voice that affected her profoundly. "You must keep this dress, for no other could do it equal justice."

The tentative smile that twitched at the corners of her mouth was the only response she could manage. Yet her spirit soared at his words of approval. The heat of his hand through the thin silk at her back made her intensely aware of the virile man escorting her to her seat. He held her chair and bent over her shoulder as she slid it under the table, his voice resonant at her side.

"Will you have wine with your meal?" At Melanie's nod, he filled the crystal goblet at the head of her place setting and handed it to her. Then taking his, he lifted it in toast.

"To my breathtakingly lovely dinner companion. May all the misunderstandings of our past be banished by pleasant memories we've yet to make."

Puzzlement reflected in the sapphire gaze Melanie directed over the rim of her glass as she sipped the sweet, clear nectar. She ran her tongue over her lips, tasting the fruity essence that lingered. It was stronger than the communion wine her father used in church and, aside from the rum punch she had so recklessly swilled to spite 'Io and some medicinal sips of brandy, her first truly alcoholic beverage. Yet her nerves were such that she needed its calming effects.

"It's very good," she commented, breaking the uncomfortable silence and meeting the gaze that still observed her every movement. "Thank you." She folded her hands primly in her lap. "And thank you again for the bath and—and this dress. You can not know how wretched I felt smelling like fish."

"It was worth every ounce of effort just to see you now, blue eyes," Ryan assured her. "And there is plenty of wine, so you needn't ration it. It will go perfectly with this supreme culinary delight Karl has prepared for us."

He uncovered the largest of the dishes to reveal a bigger fish than the ones she and Sven had cleaned. It had been baked with vegetables and topped with a rich white sauce. The captain served her a healthy portion and insisted she take one of the fresh yeast rolls that were nested in another dish. Melanie waited politely until his own plate was prepared and followed his suit when he began to eat.

"I didn't know such finery existed on a ship," she marveled, lavishly buttering one of the warm rolls.

The dishes were far prettier than the broken set of china her mother's sister had sent them to use as their Sunday best, and the silver was so ornate compared to her family's meager service for four. Whenever they entertained, the guests used her mother's silver and her family used the everyday bone-handled cutlery.

"Well, there really hasn't been time to entertain you properly, blue eyes. These sort of things," he said with a sweep

106

across the table, "are best left packed and secured under the type of weather we've had. And besides, I only use them when we carry passengers."

"Do all the passengers occupy your cabin?"

"Only the prettiest ones," countered the captain with a crooked grin. At her thin grimace of doubt, he pulled a straight face. "Actually, all of these doors you see are passenger compartments." He motioned around them. "The fancy dinnerware is only used when I have guests. Otherwise, I eat with the men. But this particular voyage was one of business speculation. I intend to set up regular shipping routes between here and the States. There is a never-ending demand for coal, and your plantations seem to have a need for transport of their sugar and other exports. At any rate, I needed no passengers worrying me about schedules."

Melanie chewed thoughtfully, mulling over his words. "Then why did you bring me along?"

"That is one of those past misunderstandings I would just as soon forget, blue eyes." He handed her her glass and touched his to it. "My concern is, what am I going to do with you now?"

"Take me to Honolulu." Melanie chased the roll with the wine, finishing the contents of her glass.

"And what will you do there?" Ryan contained his annoyance at her glib reply. Although that was his full intention, to hear her speak so eagerly of leaving the *Liberty Belle* disturbed him more than he cared to admit.

Melanie watched him fill her glass. Feminine instinct told her not to reveal her reason for wanting to go there. Even now she sensed her companion's suppressed disapproval. His strong fingers jammed the cork in the wine bottle a little too forcefully and the lightness of his mood had dampened. Something inside her balked at having let this happen. She was so enjoying him in his present humor. He was positively enchanting company.

"I'm not really sure."

"Have you relatives there?"

Melanie shook her head. She couldn't be specific about her plans if she was intending to share them with Ryan. She only knew she wanted to find 'Io. How and where remained to be worked out.

"You'll need money," he pointed out. "What did you do to earn a living before you left Maui?"

"I lived with my parents and helped them."

"Let me guess. Your father was a fisherman."

Melanie laughed, releasing her relief at not having to come up with a plausible background for herself. "How did you know?"

"Madame, few women I have known can slay a fish with such practiced hands . . . and I have seen no one swim like you. I can say that you gave us the scare of our lives when we saw you shooting over the coral. I thought we'd have to piece you together and—" he paused, a devilish glint brightening the somberness that had momentarily clouded his face, "we would have been hard pressed to do as good a job as Mother Nature has."

Melanie felt her face warm with color. She modestly brushed away the compliment. "It was body surfing. Mostly we use boards from old buildings in the village. It's fun to ride them in on the waves. I would be glad to show you." Her eyes gleamed as she went on. "There is something about the ocean, an energy perhaps, that is all-healing and . . . invigorating." She placed her hand over his arm eagerly. "Even in the terrible storm—not that I wasn't frightened, mind you, but even so—I was excited . . . or . . ." She gave a shrug of frustration at her loss for words.

"In other words, you thrive on the sea. It runs in your blood, feeding you, giving you life as no other source can. It can soothe your wearied mind or torment you, but it is your mistress, always drawing you to her with your insatiable need for her."

Wonder filled her eyes at the poetic words that flowed so effortlessly from the man who covered her hand with his own. The intensity of his emotions as he spoke of his first

108

love surged from him into her, meeting its match. "Exactly," she murmured in agreement.

Candlelight played in the captain's eyes. He chuckled softly, not with amusement but with continuing amazement at the fascinating brown-skinned girl, who took another dainty sip of wine and licked her lips in unsuspecting provocation. They shared a kindred spirit he had not guessed, drawing them closer in a tangled web that he was completely ignorant of.

"You would have made a good captain had you been a man, blue eyes," he teased, unaccountably uncomfortable and wishing to break the spell they had been caught up in. "But for obvious reasons," he said, raking his eyes over her boldly, "I am glad that you are not."

Melanie struggled with his double-edged compliment, her affront at his reference to the inferiority of her sex outdistanced by the leap of her heart as she gazed upon him. The breasts his green eyes lingered on strained against the thin silk, forcing her to hide her reaction by concentrating on her wine.

"But my femininity should not be the only reason for your gratitude to fate, Captain," she demurred, mastering the thrill of his attention, "for I would surely have your ship as well and leave you to swab the decks of the crew's quarters."

"Then by all means, blue eyes," he said, his voice fraught with amusement, "let us drink to fate!" Their glasses touched, each one miles apart in their thinking as they drank to the unpredictable lady who had brought them together.

Dessert was a coconut creme concoction containing just a touch of almond liqueur. When she had scraped the last of it from the cut glass custard dish and Ryan rose to help her up from the table, Melanie was full and dreamily contented. She had enjoyed the captain's company, falling in with his teasing good-naturedly and returning it with her own spontaneous wit. She was inclined to agree with his toast to bury the past, for they had given each other little chance to get to know one another.

"Will you have more wine? I can carry it topside and we can toast the stars," he suggested, lifting the second bottle from the white linen cloth.

Melanie laughed, a velvet gurgling sound emerging from her throat as she swung her head from side to side and then stopped suddenly to keep from losing her balance. "No, thank you!" she declined. Her fingers grasped the back of her chair to restore her balance. "I've had far too much, I fear."

"Then a walk on the deck is my prescription."

Melanie preceded Ryan up the steps of the hatch, grateful for the hands that steadied her. Above the network of lines and riggings, the stars glittered against the velvet sky, like the smoldering embers of a freshly stirred fire. She leaned her head back to study them, touching it to the chest of the man behind her, his hands about her waist. The warmth of his lean body invited her against it and she heaved a melancholy sigh as she accepted its unspoken invitation.

"Maybe we should have," she said almost to herself.

"Should have what, blue eyes?" His question was whispered into her hair as he savored the exotic scent of her.

"Toasted them," she quipped.

His chest shook with amusement as he pulled her even closer. "Judging from the delightful sway of your step, my dear, I believe the stars will not hold it against you. In truth," he told her, "I had fully intended to take you ashore after our meal, but you seem a bit too at ease. Are you tired?"

Melanie was moved by his thoughtfulness and felt a hint of remorse for the terrible fates she had wished on him earlier as she had scrubbed the forecastle. She knew now that he had only made her do this so that he might prepare her bath and the other considerate surprises he had in store for her.

"A little," she admitted. The day had been long and the weariness of her hard work was beginning to take its toll. She stifled a yawn, not wanting the moment to end. "Ryan . . ." She hesitated and then went on at his grunt of acknowledgment. "The lady that you bought this dress for . . . what is she like?"

Ryan smiled to himself, recognizing the feminine curiosity about a possible rival, which had survived the centuries. The image of Arabella Harrington came to his mind, her polished grace and beauty, a pretty veneer over unbridled passion. Polished, he mused. That was the only advantage his Boston beauty had over Meilani—polish and experience. Arabella was the cultivated rose, Meilani the wild orchid.

"She is tall and slender, with auburn hair and startling brown eyes flecked with gold that dance when she laughs and burn when she is angry."

Melanie scowled at the picture the captain painted with his words. "And her skin is white, like fine porcelain, and her lips the deepest red of the rose," she added, her voice betraying her irritation.

"Do you know her?"

"Of course not!" Melanie huffed, disengaging herself from Ryan's arms. "I only know that she reads filthy novels and must be decidedly wicked. But no doubt that would appeal to the likes of you."

"So, the native girl can read and is prone to pry among another's private belongings." The captain crossed his arms, his manner infuriatingly superior . . . and all the more so because of the reproachful way he looked down at her. "Did you enjoy the book?"

"I did not lower myself to read it," Melanie lied with mustered indignation.

"Then how, my flashing blue eyes, do you know the nature of its contents?"

That smirk, Melanie fumed. How she hated it! She held her tongue, for she had blindly fallen into his trap and

111

would not further her embarrassment. Why did she have to ask? she chastised herself angrily. It had been so lovely between them, and now the cordial mood was over due to her stupidity.

Her eyes glazed with misery, she stiffened against the rail and tilted a proud chin upward. "Thank you again, sir, for the pleasant evening. As you noted earlier, I am tired and think I shall go to bed. Karl will be needing me early."

"Meilani . . ." Ryan objected. He stepped into her path.

"Good night, sir," she insisted, sidestepping to pass him. But in her stubborn haste, she forgot the wide scupper in which she stood and her toe caught painfully on its edge. While she would have raised her foot to minister to the throbbing member, her balance, impaired by the wine, was lost. Before she realized what had happened, she was gathered up in Ryan's arms.

"Madame, you are a study of bullheaded impulse," he swore in exasperation, shifting her weight to better his hold. "And were you not so damnably beguiling, I would be sorely tempted to pitch you over the side."

But instead, he carried her toward the main hatch. Melanie, bemused by the circumstance that had delivered her back into his warm, if annoyed, embrace, hardly noticed the discomfort of her toe. She rested her head against his shoulder complacently, glad that she had toasted the lady fate.

"And I suppose I was a bit churlish in not telling the truth about Arabella," Ryan admitted, dropping to a sitting position on the top step so that he caught her in his lap. He lifted her chin so that he could see her face in the moonlight. "She is actually a shriveled hag with a wart on the end of her nose."

He cringed inwardly, imagining Arabella's livid reaction to such a blatant lie, but the snicker of delight that bubbled from the wild and unpredictable beauty in his arms banished all thought of Arabella Harrington. "Although, methinks thou art the wicked one for taking such pleasure in

112

another's misfortune," he quoted facetiously.

His mouth curled sensuously above hers and Melanie was certain that he was right. Not for the reason he stated, but because she wondered what those lips might feel like on her own without the instigation of anger. Her eyes shimmered with anticipation as she bashfully voiced her thought.

"Can you kiss without hurting me?"

Ryan could not believe his ears. He had hesitated to taste her lips, longing to do so all evening. She had such a volatile temperament and he had not wanted to set her off in one of those tirades that drove him beyond the limits of his control. And now it was another control he was forced to exercise, for her buttocks wriggling maddeningly in his lap already flushed his loins with a desire that made him want to ravish her right there on the hatchway steps.

"I can, blue eyes and," he promised huskily, "I will . . . inside our cabin."

The delay was sheer torment. By the time he crossed the threshold of his cabin with her, his heart was beating furiously and his manhood fought the restraint of his trousers. He went straight to the bunk and placed her on it, as gently as a baby. She was a vision in scarlet, her breasts thrusting against the silk as she took a deep breath and exhaled it shakily in anticipation. And her eyes. He could get lost in the fluid gaze that blinked at him with the curiosity of one inexperienced but eager to learn.

That he would be her teacher aroused him further. But he would have to exercise patience . . . if that was possible, he thought heatedly, his hand going out to touch the beating pulse in her throat. Deliberately, he moved it down over the smooth swell of her breasts, his palm passing lightly over their tips, causing their rising and falling pattern to falter.

"Ryan . . ."

"Shush, blue eyes," he whispered hoarsely, silencing her momentary panic with soldering persuasion.

Her lips were as sweet as the wine that lingered there, her breath locked within her still chest. He coaxed them apart,

113

his tongue playfully tracing and probing until the barrier vanished. His hand moved down her abdomen in slow circular motions, which evoked a shudder of desire throughout her deliciously soft and yielding body. God, he wanted her. He wanted to feel the satin of her flesh beneath his own, to seek out the moist cache of her womanhood in intimate possession.

"Ryan!" Melanie gasped as he drew away to rid himself of his clothing. "Please hold me!"

"Let's take off your dress, Meilani," he urged her softly, drawing her to a sitting position to assist her.

His fingers shook as they fumbled with the ties of the garment. She did not offer to help but clung to him instead, her legs spread so that she could press her body against his, the contact flaming the fire in his blood to unbearable heights.

"Let go, blue eyes," he cajoled, breaking the urgent grip of her arms about his waist in order to remove the silk that covered her warm, intoxicating flesh. "Come on."

"I'm falling!" she whimpered, her arms reaching for him as he lowered her back to the mattress and exposed her exquisite body to his lust-crazed eyes.

"No, sweet," he assuaged her, giving her the reassurance of his body against her.

"Don't leave . . ."

"I won't," he murmured, inhaling her breath and claiming her lips once more in reassurance, until he felt her go limp in surrender, the arms that kept him from removing his own clothes falling away from his neck to the pillows beneath her. "Meilani?" he whispered hoarsely, a dreaded suspicion taking root in the passion-infected labyrinths of his mind. "Meilani?" He raised up and shook the still girl beneath him gently, his face flushed with incredulity.

"Mmmm . . ." she breathed quietly, cuddling his supporting arm to her and nuzzling it gently.

He remained frozen in shock, anger flaring at the innocent figure that curled peacefully about a pillow, totally oblivious to his unrequited passion. It was the wine. The damned wine had unexpectedly presented this golden opportunity and had just as quickly snatched it away. Damnation, he should have known better! He should never have coaxed her into sharing the second bottle with him. He had known then by the pink flush of her cheeks and her overbright eyes that she had had too much.

His nostrils flared with the heavy breaths he forced through them in an effort to control the desire that was to have no outlet, for he would not stoop to taking Meilani in her sleep. That would only cheat him of the immense pleasure of her participation, and this time he wanted her to know it was he who made love to her and not this 'Io she had talked about during her nightmare.

He sighed heavily. He did not blame her. How could he? he mused, redirecting his angry exasperation inwardly. He looked at her face, angelic in quiet repose. It was justice, he supposed guiltily, for he would have taken advantage of her wine-sweetened warmth toward him. After all, seduction had been his primary intent when he'd brought her into the cabin.

Damn! He unclasped her loose fingers from his arm and stood up. The sound of pulled stitches echoed in the room as he yanked his clothing off, venting his frustration with each jerk until the pieces lay, balled at the other end of the room where he had pitched them. He looked back at Meilani again and somehow tenderness managed to surface from the boiling pit of exasperation.

Hold her, she had said. So help him, that was exactly what he intended to do, he decided. Gently, he nudged her over so that he could cradle her in his arms. In reward, she turned with a low murmur of contentment and snuggled up to him, abandoning her pillow for his shoulder. And it was to the rhythmic fan of her breath against his skin that he eventually managed to sleep.

Perhaps it was the flash of lightning in the distance or the faint roll of thunder from a storm on the other side of the island that stirred Melanie from her slumber. She blinked her eyes to adjust them to the black stillness of the room and was about to stretch in a lazy arch, when she became aware that she was wrapped most intimately about the warm and naked body of the captain. Heat rippled under her skin, not from embarrassment but from the recollection of what had transpired between them.

He had kissed her and undressed her with a sense of urgency, which infected her entire being with sweet, burning anticipation. He had wanted her, desired her. Even now the memory bestirred a raw, unsatisfied need. Her mind had whirled in a vortex of pleasurable sensations that seemed to engulf her body and soul and, then, her consciousness.

She sighed dreamily and moved her hand over the muscled ridges of Ryan's chest, picturing the coarse golden hair she idly ran her fingers through. He was perfect, she mused, her fingers feather light as they inched up to trace the sharp line of his jaw. Careful not to awaken him, she drew herself up on an elbow and, in the darkness, found his chin and then his lips with her own. Her hair fell forward, the scarf having fallen out of it during her slumber, and veiled her shy kiss.

At first she experimentally brushed them. Then, gaining courage, she tasted them, her tongue following the outline of his mouth in imitation of his own masterful seduction. But when it was met by another, she gave an astonished cry and tried to push away, only to be captured by invisible arms dragging her on top of him. His voice rumbled low in his chest.

"Welcome back, blue eyes."

"Th—there's a storm coming," she stammered, glad for the pitch darkness that covered her disconcerted features. She had thought him deep in sleep or she would have never been so bold.

"Aye, there is," he agreed, his hands sliding down along the hollow of her back to cup her buttocks. "But it's nothing to worry about. I heard it make up and it's moving away," he explained, squeezing the rounded flesh until she wiggled uncomfortably. " 'Tis the rising storm in this bunk that interests me. Can you feel what you do to me, blue eyes?"

He raised his hips and Melanie felt the hardening of his passion against her flat stomach. She contracted her abdomen in retreat from the shockwave of desire that spread from that electrifying contact to the far-most reaches of her body. Conflicting arguments sprang to her mind, undermining her already-weak resistance. Shameless, she condemned herself, while her lips demanded more from the lover who so readily obliged her.

Her fingers locked in his golden hair as she smothered his neck and ears in the tiny kisses that had driven her wild, hoping to return some of the delight his roaming hands evoked. At his bidding, she raised up, her hands pressed against his shoulders, exposing her breasts to him. An ecstatic moan tore from her throat as his lips found each throbbing rosette with unerring direction, alternating from one to the other without prejudice before he buried his face between them with a hungry growl. As the intensity of his ardor grew, so did her own, until she clutched his head to her chest and tremulously called out his name.

"Now, Meilani," Ryan rasped, tearing away from her clamant embrace. He firmly grasped her hips and shoved her down against the eager shaft of desire that awaited her.

"Nooo . . ." Her arms sought his neck in panic, checking the downward movement that grated hot flesh against hot flesh. The memory of the tearing pain of his possession was still fresh.

"Don't be afraid, love. It won't be so bad this time." His patient words were strained as he wrapped reassuring arms about her and kissed her longingly, until her body shook with molten fire and molded to his in surrender.

In one fluid movement, Ryan rolled her over so that he could more readily control the delicate situation. The coarse hair of his legs brushed her inner thighs with an insane caress. In a mindless attempt to check the sensation before she swooned in ecstasy, Melanie clasped her legs against them, unwittingly inviting the manhood pressed against her to take her. But instead he remained poised and ready, as if awaiting her total consent, and began a sensual exploration of her body, his expert fingers everywhere at once until her mind was overrun with frantic messages demanding relief and she ached from the very core with the compulsion to feel him around her, within her, as one with her.

"Ryan," she pleaded, arching her body to receive him. All memories of what had been were gone, replaced by what was now, desperate and demanding.

"What, blue eyes?" His voice betrayed his barely controlled restraint.

"Ple . . . ease." Her nails dug into his taut buttocks, imploring him to put her out of her misery.

"Please what, Meilani?" he whispered urgently, beginning to press against her yielding flesh.

"Love me."

She had not gotten the words out when he drove her against the firm mattress of the bed with a thrust that took her breath away. Her body embraced him totally, shuddering violently in response to his lovemaking. She called out his name, her voice catching with rapturous breaths that seemed to heighten the force of his possession. They moved together, need for need, their passion rising in a mindless crescendo. Building and building, it carried them both to its explosive peak and then plummeted back to a languorous reality, where they lay exhausted and content in one another's arms.

Chapter Eight

After two glorious days on the deserted island, two days in which they frolicked in the water, Melanie teaching Ryan to surf of a flat wide board like the natives of Lahaina, and made love on the beach, the captain assuming the role as teacher, the *Liberty Belle* was fit to travel again. As she cut through the water, her decks hummed with the rhythm of the steam engines.

Melanie, having said her good-byes to the island as the sun rose over its lush blue-green peaks, straightened from her task of scouring the deck of Ryan's cabin and wiped the perspiration from her forehead. A smile tugged at her lips as she recalled the way Ryan had slipped up behind her, catching her misty-eyed farewell. She still couldn't believe what he'd said when she'd told him how she hated to say good-bye.

"Then don't, blue eyes," he said softly. "What we had here could be just the beginning if you don't get off the ship at Honolulu. You could go to San Francisco with me." With a grin that had a melting effect on her heart, he bussed her on the forehead. "I can't think of anyone I'd rather share the voyage with or show the city to."

She shook herself, banishing the warm recollection that had slowed her progress all morning, and surveyed the work she had accomplished in spite of it. The brass portals looked like new, the freshly laundered curtains for the empty rods over them hanging topside, along with the airing mattress

119

and pillows. The glass had been washed in vinegar and water until every trace of the salt film was removed. Each book had been taken from the shelf, dusted, and put back. The paneling gleamed, its thirst for oil satisfied. Each item in Ryan's trunk had been taken out, refolded, and put back neatly.

All that remained to be done was to hang the curtains, make up the bed, and tackle the organization of his desk. Since the curtains were likely still damp and she wanted to leave the mattress till last, Melanie decided the captain's desk was her next chore. She took the bucket out and emptied the dirty water before putting it away with her mop and scrub rags. Then, wiping her hands, shriveled from a full morning of scouring, she returned to finish her work.

When she'd told Karl of her intentions, he had assured her that Sven could relieve her of her duties in the kitchen. She wanted to surprise Ryan, for by the look of the dust and mold she found in the compartment, his compulsive neatness did not necessarily mean cleanliness. Men, she supposed with an indulgent smile, saw only the cover dirt. More than likely, his desk was a mess as well.

A contented sigh slipped from her lips. Then, dropping purposefully into his chair, she opened one of the drawers. To her surprise, everything was meticulously categorized in files for business contracts, alphabetized by customer name, for receipts, and for prospective clients. She idly scanned the names written in his bold hand, recognizing some of them as having been mentioned over the dinner table at her home.

It was only when she started to close the drawer that she noticed the company heading on the printed stationery. Melanie jerked the drawer back open, her breath frozen in her throat. Caldwell Lines! She shook her head in disbelief. It couldn't be. As if in a daze, she withdrew the receipt file and examined the first few. *Paid to Captain Ryan Caldwell, the full sum of* . . .

A sick wave of nausea swept over her and she closed her

eyes. Ryan Caldwell of the Caldwell Lines! He could be no other, she realized miserably. That would be too much to charge to coincidence. He had to be related to Gilbert Caldwell, husband to her mother's sister, Petula. Aunt Pet's brother-in-law, she groaned. Ryan was family!

But she had to know for certain. Methodically, she began to search the desk, coming up with a box containing letters—letters that confirmed her fear. She recognized the similar hand of Gilbert Caldwell on some. They mostly referred to business and always fondly expressed his wish that Ryan grace his home with his presence on a return voyage. There was little or no mention of Aunt Pet and Cousin Priscilla in any of them other than, "My family and I, as always, pray for your safety and your swift return to our home."

As she put them back, she saw another bundle, neatly tied with a lacy green ribbon. The hand was delicate, yet elegant, and a quick sniff confirmed the faint scent of jasmine. Before she looked, Melanie knew these letters were from Arabella Harrington. She only read one, for that was all she could bear. The fine Boston lady and the captain of the *Liberty Belle* shared a deeply intimate relationship, one Melanie realized had endured for a long period of time.

A blade, sharp and cutting, lodged in her throat as she retied the packet with the ribbon, no doubt once belonging to the beautiful Arabella, and placed it back in the box. Was she foolish to think, to hope, that it could be over between them? After all, Ryan had told her he had never met anyone like her and that he didn't want to end what they had shared on the island. Wasn't that reason enough to believe he had forgotten Arabella?

How she would love to have seen his reply to Arabella's letter. Or would she? reason questioned doubtfully. What had Ryan said about love to her? Melanie tried to recall his exact words on the deck as the *Belle* had left their private island. Nothing of love, she realized with a sinking feeling. He had been so vague. He wanted to *share* the voyage to San

Francisco with her. At least he preferred her over Arabella for that, although the thought brought little consolation. She was here; Arabella was not.

What a reckless, stupid fool she had been, Melanie condemned herself, a sob catching in her throat as she buried her face in her folded arms on the desk. She was reckless, for she had become involved in an illicit affair with a member of her family . . . her mother's family! A stranger would have been bad enough, but family! The shame of such a thing, the heartache she would bring to her mother, was too awful to think about. Lydia Hammond spoke of Aunt Pet and her daughter as if they were demigods of Boston society. What would this do to them . . . to the Caldwell family?

And she was stupid because she had mistaken the captain's lust for love. She had believed his endearing words, gloried in his love, nay, lust-making. She had dared to think that he had meant to take their relationship seriously.

Thank heaven she had not betrayed her true identity to Ryan Caldwell. She shuddered at the thought. If she could get away from him in Honolulu, Meilani would disappear forever from his life. He need never know what had become of the foolish native girl he had corrupted without conscience. A pain, so intense it twisted her insides until her body was racked with sobs, tore at her heart.

But she loved him. She didn't know how or when it had happened, but surely that was why it hurt so badly just to think about parting. He had made her a woman. He had taught her things about herself she had never dreamed existed. Not even 'Io had managed to reach her as Ryan Caldwell had. She took a deep, ragged breath and exhaled it slowly. Why, he had all but erased 'Io from her mind, she thought in wonder.

Ryan mustn't know that, she decided resolutely, her resilience beginning to bring her back from the pits of despair. A plan began to come together, a plan that would tell her exactly how much she did mean to Ryan Caldwell. She washed her face and soaked her swollen eyes in cool water until she regained her composure. Tonight she would see, for tomorrow they would be in Honolulu. Tonight the captain of the *Liberty Belle* would declare his love for her or lose her forever.

Melanie took great care in setting the table for the two of them. She bathed in the scented soap, swallowing her pride that it might possibly remind him of the woman for whom it was intended. She wore the satin dress he had given her and filled their wine glasses, draining one as she waited for him to change for the special meal she had planned. The violent war of nerves waging inside of her was well concealed by a calm veneer.

During the meal, she made an effort to keep up small talk about the ship. Although he frequently topped off her glass, Melanie was not so foolhardy as to overindulge, for she had come to know her limit and needed every ounce of wit to carry out her plan. Over dessert she planted the seed, her eyes devastatingly blue with an emotion Ryan mistook for eagerness and curiosity.

"Have you ever been to Honolulu before?"

Ryan nodded, extremely content with the meal and prospect of the evening at hand, although he had noticed that Meilani was unusually talkative, as though something bothered her. To wait until she was ready to discuss it seemed the most practical way, for few women would reveal their temperamental irks until they were ready.

"A few times," he answered. "Mostly for refurbishing supplies. Why?"

Melanie shrugged. "I was just wondering what it was like."

"Well, it's more modern than Lahaina. They've trolleys and a grand hotel, mercantile shops lining the streets, a shipyard—" Ryan paused over his wine glass. "I'm planning on taking you ashore. You're going to need more clothing than that . . . nothing for nights, mind you," he teased, his hand slipping familiarly under the table to her leg. "Just few dresses and accessories for San Francisco."

Melanie bit her lip and mustered her courage. "I—I'm not certain I want to go to San Francisco," she said softly. She watched Ryan closely, praying that he would try to make her change her mind. But her words made him sit up with an irritated start, the placid green of his eyes coming to life.

"What do you mean, Meilani?" he asked. The forced calm in his voice was like that before a storm.

"I mean, I am not certain that I want to go with you. I think it might be best if I were to remain in Honolulu." Her explanation was not enough. She could see it in the eyes that stared right through her, demanding more. She swallowed dryly. "I need some time to think about your proposal to go with you. . . ."

"How long, for God's sake? We're only going to be there two days . . . just long enough for me to make a few business contacts and resupply the *Belle*."

"What I meant was . . . if . . ." she faltered, fearing the confrontation that was building, fearing its outcome, "if you still want me when you come back and I still . . ."

"If I leave you in Honolulu, Meilani, I will not come back," Ryan stated flatly. He shoved the china out of his way so that nothing came between them. The shatter of one of the delicately shaped cups made Melanie grimace. "Now," he began with a low rumble of discontent, "you tell me what this is really all about, because I am rapidly losing my patience."

Melanie met his gaze through an azure mist. She tried to recover from the hurt of his adamant disclosure, which was so void of the emotion she had hoped for. "I do not think I know you, Ryan Caldwell . . . not well enough to leave my home and go halfway around the world." If she could only see what was going on behind his suddenly inscrutable face. There had been anger at first. She had expected that. But now there was no sign of any emotion other than a clenched jaw that held his stony mask in place.

"Do you mean you do not wish to leave your home . . . or your 'Io?'"

Incriminating shock registered on her face, for she could not imagine what Ryan Caldwell knew of the young Hawaiian. "What do you know of 'Io?" she whispered, only to be ignored.

"It didn't seem to bother you about running away with him, Meilani. A young buck who fled at the first gunshot and left you to fend for yourself at the Frenchman's *luau*. Does cowardice appeal to you?"

The glaze of hurt in her eyes iced over as she came to the defense of her friend. " 'Io is no coward! He would die for me as I would for him!" she averred dramatically.

She had no idea how effective her words were. Only the cruel flicker of Ryan's eyes in the candlelight betrayed his jealous outrage. He casually leaned against the back of his chair and lifted his wine glass to his lips, pausing just long enough to taunt, "Then, blue eyes, he very plainly didn't give a damn what happened to you. If you recall, it was I who got you out of that hornet's nest."

The ring of truth to his words staggered her. 'Io had left her. He had warned her and then left. Like an animal cornered, she rebounded in bitter retaliation. "For your own pleasure, sir!"

"Indeed it was," he reflected, his eyes taking on the vindictive glow of smoldering embers. "Seven days and nights' worth of pleasure, to be exact, blue eyes. Seven days and nights, bought and paid for," he reiterated harshly. "Seven days and nights of which I have only enjoyed five. You owe me two more, blue eyes."

Melanie blanched, her face foundering in bewilderment. "Bought and paid for?"

Ryan jumped to his feet and slung aside his empty glass. "Bought and paid for, by damn," he swore. "And I'll not be cheated by you or that French bastard who pawned off an

125

untried virgin on me."

Melanie recoiled in shock. What had the Frenchman to do with this? Her expression raced from confusion to discovery, as the relevance of his words became clearer. The Frenchman had sold her services to Ryan Caldwell. She had been bought and paid for like common goods. She had only been spirited off to the ship to insure the captain his money's worth. She could not even claim the hope that Ryan had wanted her for herself, but rather because he had expected the wicked and experienced services of a whore.

How well he had hidden his disappointment, she reflected bitterly . . . until now. She had never known such boiling rage as that welling inside her. "How . . . dare . . . you," Melanie grated out, her hand reaching for the empty wine bottle at the same time.

With a furious cry, she swung it at him, but the side of his hand came down like a knife across her wrist, effectively knocking it from her grip. Her wrist throbbed, but her frenzy was such that she availed herself of a table knife with her free hand, slashing out at him wildly. Its blade sliced across the white silk of his shirt.

Melanie was stunned as his blood seeped through to underscore her strike. She had only meant to fend him off.

"You bloodthirsty little bitch!" Ryan sprang at her, the palm of his hand exploding against the side of her face.

Her vision blurred as she fell to the deck. She shook her head in an attempt to clear it, to focus on the giant figure standing over her, reaching for her. He hauled her to her feet by her collar, the silk of her dress cutting into the flesh of her throat. Her voice and breath were strangled as she was bodily forced through the door of the captain's cabin. Just as she thought she was going to pass out from lack of air, she was slung against the bunk.

"By God, you'll pay for this!" she heard Ryan swear, but she could not make out his features in the darkness of the cabin. "Seven nights I paid for and seven nights I'll have, Meilani!"

The silken ties that held her dress in place were no match for the violent jerks Ryan used to remove it. Through the reverberating ache in her head, his intentions became clear to her. Blindly, she began to fight, digging at his face with her nails until he seized her wrists, cursing profusely. For what seemed an eternity, he pinned her against the freshly laundered sheets of the bed with his full weight, then she felt the cut of the satin ties he used to bind her wrists.

"Nooo!" she shrieked, her voice little more than a gasp.

But the cords only drew tighter, lifting her arms above her head and holding them there as he secured them to the lamp hook bolted to the bulkhead. When he relieved her of his weight, she lay stunned for a moment, trying to regain the breath he had crushed from her. She had to get free of the bonds that encumbered her arms, she thought in drunken desperation. She drew up her knees to inch her body along the bulkhead, only to have her arms nearly dislocated by a vicious jerk of her feet, which forced her to stretch out again.

Suddenly, a heavy weight fell upon her, naked hot flesh against her own fear-chilled body, forcing a strangled cry from her aching throat. Hands, oddly slippery, squeezed her breasts until she cried out, but her pleas to stop were brutally silenced by punishing lips. Melanie thrashed her head from side to side, inadvertently breaking the delicate flesh of her mouth against his angry teeth. She tasted her blood and kicked in a helpless frenzy, for his knees bruisingly forced her thighs apart in preparation for her ultimate degradation.

He hurt her when he thrust the sword of his violent passion into her tender and unprepared body. Yet he might as well have run a shaft of steel through her heart, for his brutal invasion rendered her as still as death beneath him. As he had his vengeful way with her, her skin grew icy cold, while her mind and body became mercifully numb. Her breaths were shallow under his weight, and her eyes watched him blankly.

It wasn't until he had finished his shuddering climax that he noticed her wide, unseeing eyes and the heat of his desire for revenge turned to a fear-stricken chill, which doused the white fire of lust from his head. "Meilani!" he shouted, his voice cracking dryly as he straddled her small body and grasped her cool, immobile form. "Meilani!" He lifted her from the bed and shook her roughly, her head lolling back like a broken doll's.

His pale face came into focus slowly above her, his strained voice penetrating the senseless world she had retreated to. Her feeling came back and, with it, the returning aches of her victimized body. A slow burning hatred for his defilement of her, and for the sweet memories of what they had shared, obsessed her. She summoned all her reserve, every ounce of her emotion, to force out her words with a lethal impact.

"Go to hell, Ryan Caldwell!"

The captain froze, his face contorting in an odd mixture of relief and contempt. He should have known she'd rally for the last word, the last blow. He ignored the stinging wet pain of the cut she inflicted and leaned over her, his voice cursing. "I've just been there, blue eyes." Then, sickened by what he had done and the seeming hopelessness of it all, he pushed himself away from her and staggered toward the door.

Melanie followed him with her eyes, for she could not move. Her body was paralyzed with shock—a shock that gradually gave way to weakness and despair. She began to tremble at first, and then shake violently. Small rasping sobs rose to choke her as she curled up like a shattered child and cried herself to sleep.

It was well before daybreak when the ship's engines were cut and the resounding splash of the anchor announced their arrival in the Honolulu harbor. Melanie woke with a start at the stillness. Her battered body was stiff, but she managed to unhook the red cords that had all but cut off the circulation to her numb hands. Like a frantic and frightened animal, she tore at the knots with her teeth, the wounds on her swollen lips cracking under the strain and bleeding once more.

Once free of the constricting cords, blood rushed to her fingers like thousands of prickling needles. She had to flex them several times before she could use them effectively. There was little time, and if she were to escape, she would not have the luxury of allowing for her discomfort.

She fumbled for her shift in the darkness and donned it. Using the cord the captain had bound her with, Melanie tied her hair securely at her neck for the long swim to shore. With luck, he was either sleeping or occupied with the mooring of the *Belle*. In the semidarkness, she stood a good chance of slipping over the side of the ship undetected. But when she tried the latch on the door, she discovered it locked, as if he had anticipated her plan.

Melanie struggled with the icy blade of fear in her chest. She had to keep a cool head, she told herself sternly. She could not fly off, not now. It had cost her dearly on more than one occasion, and she did not ever want to give Ryan Caldwell the chance to dole out his cruel retribution again.

Her eyes traveled around the room, furtively seeking, in the pale dawn light filtering in through the portals, anything with which to force the lock, when they came to rest upon the portal itself. An idea began to take root. While its size would preclude a man from climbing through it, a child . . . or a petite female just might be able to squeeze through. Melanie climbed up on the bunk and studied the size of the opening, judging it to be close, if not impossible.

It was a long fall, several decks in fact, to the water. If she were to hit the water wrong, she could injure herself and the chances were great that no one would notice her splash with all the commotion topside. She thought for a moment, weighing the risk, when she noticed the dark stains on the sheets she had so lovingly laundered for Ryan earlier. Her face paled as she realized it was blood, his blood. The slippery substance on his hands when he had accosted her, the lubrication between their bodies, had been his blood, she realized, her stomach contracting uncertainly.

Dear God, what had she done? How badly had she injured him? She could not remember any more than slashing out at him in blind fury. He had staggered to the door, she recalled vividly, and he had not been drunk. He had had not more than a few glasses of wine with a good meal. What if he were lying on the other side of the door? . . .

No! She would not finish the dreaded thought. But still, even if he were not injured badly, she could be accused of attempted murder. Would he turn her in to the authorities? He had raped her, but who would believe *her?* Everyone on the ship knew she had given herself to the captain. She was his mistress. That's how she had acted.

Perhaps ordinarily she could not have made it through the round opening of the portal, but fear born of panic is a strong motivation. The backs of her arms scraped against the cold metal edge as she worked her upper torso through. Then, half out, Melanie shoved against the side of the gently rocking *Belle,* wincing as her hips cleared the opening, one of the brass bolts catching in her shift and raking her mercilessly down one side.

She gasped as she fell awkwardly toward the dark water, her impact knocking the air from her body. Her momentum carried her downward until she thought her lungs would burst, but she remembered 'Io's council and forced herself to remain calm. As she began to buoy up, she sped her progress until she broke the water's surface and hungrily took in the precious breath her body craved.

Her muscles relaxed at her willful command. She treaded water until her breathing became regular, assembling her strength for her long swim to the building-studded docks ahead of her. As she started out, she was momentarily taken by the sudden appearance of the sun peeking over a dark rise of rock in the distance. Was it an omen, she wondered, one promising hope and strength? Whether it was or not, it somehow offered her a primitive sense of reassurance and the courage to face the future as she reached out in quiet, steady strokes to leave the troubled past behind.

Part Two
Boston, Massachusetts 1893 . . .

Chapter Nine

Silver-grey clouds hung over the ragged skyline of Boston, highlighted by a setting sun that had struggled against them the entire day. An occasional ray of it managed to glance off the partially frozen offshoot of the river, where children walking home from the elite school for girls gazed at it with longing, hoping that it would soon freeze so that skating parties could again take place there.

Inside the two-story brick structure that blackened the sky with smoke from the coal stoves located in each classroom, Melanie Hammond lifted her head from her study of her student's math assignments with a start, at the mournful sound of an incoming steam trawler somewhere in the nearby harbor.

Nearly six years, and it still managed to unsettle her and rob her face of color. Against her will, the memories came flooding back. Ryan's brutal parting, her desperate escape . . . the long and painful road back to recovery.

Weak and tired from her swim to shore, Melanie had wandered the streets and alleys of Honolulu in a daze, until she'd heard the bells of Kuwaiahao Church ringing and had followed the sound that reminded her of home and security. But the trauma of what had happened caught up with her, and she got only as far as the gardens in the back before collapsing in a weak faint.

It was there that Amanda Cummings, the elderly wife of the Reverend William Cummings, had found her and taken her in after the rainstorm that had chilled Melanie to the bone. The dear woman and her servant, Kela, had nursed her through the days of fever—days in which Melanie wanted to die.

From her incoherent ramblings, they were able to gather much of what had happened to her and her identity, which led them to notify Abner and Lydia Hammond. But Melanie's parents did not come for her; 'Io did.

It was only then that Melanie began to recover. Going against her gentle upbringing, Amanda Cummings permitted the young man to stay at the sick girl's bedside, for it was only to the strange young Hawaiian who offered Melanie the tenderest of care and devotion that the patient began to respond.

A spark of life entered the dull and emotionless eyes that had been burned out by fever and whatever had happened to her, and gradually she began to regain her strength and will to live. Her parents hadn't cared enough to come, but 'Io had. 'Io, who would not let her down. 'Io, who loved her.

He'd told her how distraught her parents were, but Melanie could read between the lines. She had disgraced them and they would never forgive her for that. But she had 'Io. Or at least she'd thought she did, until the somber Hawaiian youth revealed what had happened that night at the *luau* and why.

He was beside himself with remorse because he had not revealed the secret that, while it would have broken Melanie's heart, would have saved her this . . . the secret that Abner Hammond had finally come out with when 'Io, having been knocked senseless by a bullet that had grazed his forehead during the police raid and had left him unconscious in the tropical forest surrounding the plantation, had come to him in a panic to see if Melanie had made it safely home . . . the secret that Abner Hammond was not only Melanie's father, but 'Io's as well.

And so it was with desolation and a terrible trepidation that she left the loving sanctuary of the Cummings home and returned to Lahaina to face her parents. She had lost not only 'Io, but all chances of returning to a normal life with her parents. Aside from the secret that had spurred her mother to seek a cold and silent revenge against the husband who had fallen from grace in her eyes and broken their lifelong ties with 'Io's mother and all the Kuakinis, Melanie was with child.

It was simpleminded Kela who had first suggested to Melanie the reason her monthly curse had not come . . . Kela, who had come to the Cummings house under similar circumstances years before. Except that the native Hawaiian, unlike Melanie, had not recovered from the terrible abuse that had brought her, battered and beaten witless, to the steps of the Kuwaiahao Church. In many ways she was like a child. Yet she was sharp enough to commiserate with Melanie and know her condition before Melanie did herself.

Lydia Hammond knew also, the moment she saw Melanie. Melanie did not have to say a word, for her mother confronted her the evening of her arrival, throwing in her face that the child was God's punishment for her sinful behavior, and as such, she would neither have Melanie nor her fatherless child in her house.

Instead, her mother had already worked out a plan to rid herself of the painful reminders of her husband's past surrender to the sins of the flesh. Melanie was to go to Boston to live with Lydia's sister, Petula Caldwell, as the grieving widow of a captain lost at sea shortly after their wedding.

That had nearly been Melanie's undoing, for she couldn't imagine living with Ryan's family. Once more, it was 'Io who helped her come to her senses and prevented her from running away again. Not knowing the real reason she didn't want to go to Boston, he convinced her that she had to think of her child now and stop thinking of herself alone. In Boston, Melanie could rebuild her life as a widow with a child, using her mathematics skills to acquire a teaching position. And if she found living with her mother's family so terrible, she could certainly find quarters of her own once the baby came and she was settled.

So, taking the greatest risk of her life for the sake of the one growing inside her, Melanie went to Boston as Mrs. Jeb Lyons, grieving widow and expectant mother. And she prayed. She prayed fervently that Ryan Caldwell would stay at sea as his brother's unanswered invitations indicated, until she had time to start an independent life for herself and their unborn child. A child she already loved. A child she vowed would never know the rejection she'd felt when her own mother had turned away from the dock before the gangway of Melanie's Boston-bound ship had even been lifted.

Only her father had remained until the ship turned and made its way out of the harbor. He and Melanie were the seed of seed, so her mother had declared, each paying for his sin of the flesh in his own way. No longer the pillar of piety, Abner Hammond had a thousand words of regret on his face but had not spoken one. Yet, after the weeks of silence when Melanie had been home, weeks in which he suffered in a hell of his own, his singular wave managed to convey what Melanie so desperately needed to know . . . that at least one of her parents still loved her.

"Mrs. Lyons. I vow, sometimes I think you are as absent-minded as some of your students!"

Melanie looked up from her desk at the familiar voice of Gilbert Caldwell and gasped in distress at her forgetfulness. "I was supposed to meet you out front! Oh, Gilbert, I am so very sorry. I am not a fit mother to let my daughter's birthday party slip my mind so easily. Do you think she suspects?"

"She is moping dreadfully and is convinced that everyone has completely forgotten her," the distinguished dark-haired gentleman replied ruefully. "She's made me feel so wretched at my part in this deceit that I left for my office early for fear of giving it away."

Melanie smiled with affection and turned so that Gilbert could drape her woolen cape about her shoulders. "You do spoil her, Gilbert Caldwell. Kristen is only five, and she thinks she should be able to attend balls and parties with Boston's debutantes."

"An uncle's prerogative, dear girl. Pet and I were not blessed with a baby of our own, and while Priscilla is as good a daughter as a man could ask for, surely you would not deny us the joy your Kristen brings us."

"You and your family have been so kind to me, how could I deny you anything, sir?" Melanie asked, the fondness in her voice as genuine as that in her heart.

She had had full intentions of leaving the Caldwell home as soon as Kristen had been born. But after she had recovered from the difficult breech birth and mentioned the possibility of renting a cottage, none of them would hear of it. So, to satisfy her pride and to keep her and the baby in their spacious three-story manor, they agreed to accept a token fee for room and board once she took the position at the private girl's school—a sum Gilbert Caldwell promptly invested in Kristen's name with a stubbornness equal to Melanie's.

Melanie enjoyed her own apartment of rooms in the Caldwell home. Her bedroom and parlor were strictly her own, but Kristen's nursery was public property, where she could find any of the Caldwells playing with her daughter at any time during the child's waking hours. Gilbert was always bringing her toys, and Aunt Pet and Priscilla fawned over her constantly, seeing the young miss clad in the most adorable clothes a little girl could wish for.

As usual when Melanie and Gilbert were together, they shared their gay camaraderie as they hopped the Little Green Car to take them to Beacon Street. Gilbert went on about some young swain on the car who could not take his eyes off Melanie, declaring he was the envy of every dapper young man who saw them together. But when the young man asked if Melanie needed assistance to get her father home, it had been all she could do to decline with a straight face, considering her uncle's stricken expression.

She was still giggling as they made their way up the brick-paved street to the mansion at Number Eight Beacon, where the door burst open and a small child charged into them, squealing in delight.

"Oh, Mama, Uncle Gilbert, please hurry! It's my birthday and I can't wait a moment longer!"

"Kristen Elizebeth Lyons!" Melanie chastised sternly, her tone belied by her twinkling eyes. "What on earth are you babbling about?"

She held her beautiful daughter away from her, drinking in the joy that bubbled from the golden-haired angel before her. Kristen had been born with Ryan's fair coloring and Melanie's eyes. Clad in a new smocked dress of white eyelet over pink ruffled petticoats, she was irresistible. Her rosy lips formed a perfect O as she tried to smother a giggle over her slip of the tongue. Melanie looked expectantly to the stout nurse standing in the doorway with both hands clasped to her pink cheeks in dismay.

"To be sure, I'm sorry, mum," Megan Leary apologized. "I would not have spoiled the surprise for the world, mind ye, but the wee thing was so sad . . . I just couldn't help meself."

"Such weakness in your position could lose it for you, Megan Leary," Priscilla's sharp voice rang out from inside the hall. "And for heaven's sake, close the door!"

Megan Leary turned on her heel and put her hands to her ample hips. "And who gave the lass a small gift to tide her over till the party as soon as the words were out of me mouth?" she challenged.

Priscilla Caldwell stopped on the stairwell and looked down at the group assembled in the foyer. Her gangly shadow was half again as tall as she in the glow of the gaslit chandelier that rattled in the draft of the door Gilbert closed behind them. Her face was thin and smug, as though it had been groomed to look haughtily prim. But her pinched lips twitched as she broke the brittle features with a sheepish grin and retreated guiltily up the stairs.

"Is there going to be a party, Mama? Did you get me a present, Uncle Gilbert? Oh," Kristen exclaimed with a cross stomp of her kid-slippered foot, "will *someone* talk to me?"

Melanie folded her hands, her eyes cracking a gentle whip. "When everyone is calm and can remember their manners."

Kristen filled her chest with air and let it out slowly in a great show of gaining control. Her blue eyes sparkled as she curtsied first to her mother, and then to Gilbert Caldwell, who held his hand over his mouth suspiciously.

"Good day, Mother. Good day, Uncle. Have either of you any idea what day it is?"

Melanie might have maintained her composure but for the grand snort from Megan Leary and Gilbert's outright peal of laughter. She dropped to her knees and opened her arms to the accomplished little actress who had managed to put them all in stitches.

"Happy birthday, darling!" She clung to the child who had been her salvation from total despair in that first desperate year of adjustment. "And, yes, there is to be a party. Can you tell us when, Megan?" she teased the flustered nurse.

"As soon as everyone is freshened up and ready for supper," Megan replied with a polite dip of her head. "Will ye be comin' with me or your mama?" she said to the excited little girl who had given her away.

"Mama," Kristen answered, slipping her small hand in Melanie's in such a way that her mother's heart melted.

Melanie climbed the steps, having to rush to keep up with Kristen's bounding pace. Once in her room, she removed her bonnet and let Kristen, after trying it on, put it away. She washed her face, smiling indulgently as her daughter imitated her, and then set about rearranging the short fringe of curls about her face. The balance of her hair was parted and swept into a dignified chignon. Through the mirror she could see Kristen puffing her own ringlets of gold with pink fingers.

"I wish I could wear my hair like yours," her daughter remarked, blue eyes admiring the raven locks that shone in the light overhead. "Megan spits on my curls to make them stay in place, and you tell me ladies aren't supposed to spit."

Melanie thought for a moment, trying to come up with an answer that would not incriminate the Irish nanny Petula Caldwell insisted Kristen have. "Well, darling," she began hesitantly, "in some cases it is acceptable . . . such as grooming. But I shall speak to Megan and request that she try water first." She rose from the vanity stool and held out her hand. "Are we ready to eat a good supper so that we might enjoy cake and ice cream afterward?" Melanie received an enthusiastic affirmation that was most unladylike and was fairly dragged from her room by the anxious youngster.

Supper was a simple fare in order to leave room for the special dessert to follow. The cook, like everyone else at Number Eight Beacon Street, sought to please the birthday girl by serving her favorite meat pasties and beef stew. Kristen was beside herself as she tried to finish the portion Melanie had put on her plate and listened to the adults converse as though there were no rush to get to the dessert.

"Melanie dear, Gilbert tells me young Walter Otis introduced himself to you on the Green Car today. May we expect him to call?" Aunt Pet asked, holding her silver fork and knife poised at her plate.

"I think not, Aunt Pet. He is quite young."

"And a damned poor judge of one's age," Gilbert interjected in mock indignation. "Father indeed!"

Aunt Pet ignored her husband and reasoned with Melanie. "Dear, you are not over the hill at twenty-four. I believe young Otis is about that. He is doing graduate work in law to follow in his father's footsteps. A very good and wealthy family," her aunt informed her, looking meaningfully at Kristen.

"Pet, isn't it enough that you run my life, without meddling in Melanie's?" Gilbert piped up in her defense. "I believe she's doing quite well for herself."

Petula Caldwell swelled and shot a stinging look at her husband. "You need someone to run your life for you, Gilbert Caldwell. I was preoccupied with the cook this morning and what do you do? Go out without your hat in this cold damp weather! It would be dreadful for you to spend the holidays abed and I forced to attend the parties without

142

you."

"Gad, how thoughtless of me! I had forgotten our social schedule," Gilbert countered with a surreptitious wink at his niece.

Melanie lowered her head to keep from smiling and cut a piece of meat on Kristen's plate that was too large for her. Her aunt and her mother had much in common besides their dark, greying hair and blue eyes. Both were strong-willed individuals accustomed to running the household with an iron hand. Abner Hammond's salvation was the fact that he looked at things in the same light as his wife. But Gilbert Caldwell did not. It was only due to his easygoing nature that Aunt Petula had her way. However, when he really objected, everyone in the house tiptoed about to avoid becoming involved in the clash of stubborn wills.

"Speaking of which, have you written your acceptances, Melanie? I should think you and Priscilla will be beset with gentlemen callers and dance partners this season."

And like Lydia Hammond, Petula Caldwell did not think a woman could live without the financial security and protection of a proper husband. Melanie nodded. "I have some of the finished."

Were it not for the constant line of men being forced upon her by hostesses who felt sorry for the young widowed niece of Petula Caldwell, Melanie would enjoy the glamour of Boston's social circuit so much more. She certainly did not lack for invitations, for as soon as sufficient time had passed after Kristen's birth, she was inundated with them. The beautiful gowns, the lavish table settings, the lively theatre, and the graceful dances were part of a wonderful life she had never experienced. She supposed she should be grateful, for if anyone were eligible to introduce her to it, Aunt Pet was.

There the two sisters differed. Lydia Hammond would frown at the blatant display of wealth and frivolity. Her idea of entertainment was a simple meal where discussion centered around charity and her school. Her dedication was to the mission and to the children. Yet Aunt Pet was no less charitable. She simply found a merrier way to help the needy, by raising moneys through social affairs. Their intentions were the same, their methods different.

"Well, if you do not reply, dear, your name will eventually be dropped from circulation and that would break my heart. Priscilla and I have done our utmost to see you included."

"And then you'll *never* find me a daddy!"

There was an astonished silence around the table as Kristen stared at Melanie, her little hands at her waist in a show of exasperation. Melanie found her voice, certain that the child had picked this notion up from something she had overheard, no doubt in their very house. "I wasn't aware that you felt so slighted, Kristen."

The child shrugged. "Everybody has a daddy but me. I want one with yellow hair, so nobody at the Garden can say that he isn't really mine, even though mine is dead."

Melanie clutched her hands under the table at a loss for words. But Kristen, with the fleeting attention of a child, had already dismissed the subject. She finished the last of her food and announced that it was time for her party. If Aunt Petula was stubborn, she was also sensitive enough to recognize the blow Kristen had inadvertently dealt her mother. She brightly instructed everyone to bring in their gifts and rang the hostess bell for the table to be cleared.

"Children can be so cruel, but she doesn't really mean anything by it," Priscilla consoled her as Melanie retrieved the box containing the white velvet dress with a scarlet satin sash, which she had made for Kristen with the upcoming holidays in mind. "And that goes for Mother, too, bless her."

Melanie had to smile at her cousin's last remark. Theirs was an odd relationship. While she and Priscilla were not the best of friends, they both had Aunt Pet hovering over them with a watchful eye, attempting to model them in her image. It was a common bond that sometimes led to mutual sympathy and understanding between the cousins.

Priscilla was one of those girls who never seemed to outgrow her awkward stage. She went through the motions of

144

acting the proper Bostonian lady under her mother's tutelage, knowing that she was neither as beautiful nor as graceful as Aunt Pet would have her be. It was heartbreaking for Melanie when she received more calling cards in one day from the eligible bachelors of the town than Priscilla had in a week. Unlike her, Priscilla's one aim in life was marriage and a family. And although at first Priscilla was jealous of Melanie's popularity, she eventually came to recognize the advantage it offered—the chance as Melanie's cousin to meet young men who would never have introduced themselves to her otherwise.

The cake was a masterpiece of pink and white confection. The cook brought it in as the family sang "Happy Birthday" to the thrilled five-year-old. Kristen stood on her knees in her chair and blew out the candles after making a wish—one that she was cautioned to keep a secret in order to have it come true. Then the presents were opened with great fanfare.

Aunt Pet and Gilbert gave her a sled. It was an apple-red affair with long metal runners. A curled front offered protection from an accidental run-in with a tree and a braided cord provided a means of pulling it back up the hill. It was long enough for Kristen to lie completely prone. "So there's less chance of her falling off," Aunt Pet explained.

"Oh, I want to use it now! Please, Mama! Uncle Gilbert could take me to the park and—"

"Tomorrow, I promise," Gilbert intervened for Melanie. His eyes twinkled at the thought. "I haven't been sledding in years."

"Well, do take your hat this time and wrap warmly. I should hate to—"

"—attend all those Christmas parties alone," Gilbert finished wryly. "I know, dear." He gave Aunt Pet an indulgent peck on the cheek.

The doll her Aunt Priscilla gave her made Kristen's eyes light with joy. Its round face was made of china, with pink painted cheeks and large blue eyes. Its stuffed body was dressed in a white gown embroidered with pastel flowers, and a matching bonnet covered its painted tuft of brown hair.

"And I made this to go with it," Priscilla announced proudly, handing the little girl a smaller box containing a change of clothing.

"You are the bestest sewinger in the whole word, Auntie Pris!" Kristen told her with a big hug that made Priscilla's normally miserable face shine in delight.

"Seamstress, dear," Aunt Pet corrected primly.

When she opened Melanie's present, Kristen assumed a smug little sniff, "I'll bet this is clothes."

"How keen you are, Kristen!" Melanie remarked, knowing that there was more of a surprise in store for her daughter than just another dress.

Each time they had gone shopping during the past few weeks, Kristen had always halted her in front of the store window to point to the dress on display. Melanie had explained, to the child's dismay, that it was for bigger girls and would not fit. Then she had slipped back and commissioned the seamstress to make one like it several sizes smaller, for a special five-year-old.

"Mama!" Kristen gasped, folding back the tissue. "It's the one! The very one I saw at the shop on Charles Street! Why, it's almost like your good dress, and it's velvet, too! And it's red for Christmas and white for angels. And . . . how I love you, Mama!" she exclaimed, crawling over the box into Melanie's arms.

"Young lady, we do not crawl over the table, we use the floor!" Petula Caldwell scolded gently.

Kristen tore herself away from Melanie and, in a similar tone, answered, "But, Aunt Pet, this *is* my birthday!"

"Kristen!" Melanie chided at her daughter's impudence. "That is no way to speak to your elders."

But the general amusement that resulted took the edge off the reprimand, and with a hurried "I'm sorry, Aunt Pet," the little girl wriggled out of Melanie's lap and declared that it was time for cake. Although her daughter's retort was charming, it only served to point out how spoiled she was becoming. Melanie made a mental note to speak to her later in private about manners, then got up to help with the dessert.

Kristen soon finished her portion and, when Melanie was firm about there being no seconds, played quietly in the corner with her new doll while the adults relaxed over hot tea. Aunt Pet and Priscilla were busily discussing the dinner party they were giving only two weeks before Christmas and making up the order for Quincy Market. There was only one thing the Caldwell women liked more than attending parties and that was giving them.

"What about Master Meyers, Melanie? Should we include him on the invitation list?" Aunt Pet asked, referring to the professor of science at the boy's academy across the street from Miss Gravenor's School for Girls.

Melanie blushed at Gilbert's raised brow. "I should think it would be proper, considering he has asked me to accompany him to the theatre."

"My word! So we are coming out of our shell, are we?"

"And afterward," Melanie went on, ignoring Gilbert's teasing remark, "we are going to Otis Place at the Apthorps' invitation. Some of the actors are going to be there."

"Oh! I am just green!" Priscilla moaned. "I should be the envy of the Footlight Club if I could attend." The Footlight Club was an amateur theatre group to which her cousin belonged. The fact that professional actors and actresses were to attend the Apthorps', William Apthorp being an eminent musical critic, certainly would lend a degree of superiority to an amateur who could claim to have discussed the art with them.

"This is the sixth call Master Meyers has made at Beacon Street," Gilbert observed, reaching into his pocket for his pipe. "You don't suppose he's smitten with a certain eligible widow, do you?"

"Sam is a friend and colleague whose company I enjoy," Melanie replied smoothly.

"So it's Sam, is it?" Gilbert went on, frowning as he withdrew a letter at the same time as his pipe.

"I think Sam smells funny," Kristen observed from the chair where she rocked her doll.

"Master Meyers to you, Kristen," Melanie reminded her daughter in exasperation. "And the smell is from the chemicals he works with in the laboratory."

"Oh gad, Pet," Gilbert exclaimed as he opened the missive. "I forgot to tell you that I received a letter from my brother today. He will be in Boston for the holidays, so you might keep that in mind when making up your invitation lists."

Petula Caldwell groaned and rolled her eyes to the ceiling. "God forbid that I have that scoundrel in this house, Gilbert. You know how he behaved the last time he was here. Why, I could not show my face afterward."

"For heaven's sake, Pet. It was hardly Ryan's fault that old man Vaughn could not hold his liquor and fell into the punch bowl!" Gilbert snorted in amusement. "It was the most refreshing entertainment of the evening! And he has not been here since he sailed to the Pacific Islands. I can not refuse him his own family home."

"But, Father," Priscilla whined, "he's liable to bring that *woman* here again. Although she claims to be an actress, we all know fully well what she is."

Gilbert smiled and winked at Melanie. "Ah, the lovely Miss Harrington. What a pair they make! You, my dear, are in for a treat," he told her wryly. "My brother Ryan is the black sheep of the family, if you listen to Pet. What she fails to admit is the fact that the family business has tripled under his far-reaching efforts. But this should come as a shock to you, Pet," Gilbert announced, squinting to make out the boldly written lines without his glasses. He read aloud. "I have purchased a plantation on the outskirts of Honolulu. It not only seems a worthy investment, but I am entertaining the idea of settling there."

"Good heavens, Melanie. Are you all right?" Priscilla questioned suddenly. "You look positively ill!"

"Too much ice cream too fast," Melanie explained with a weak laugh. She put her hand to her aching forehead. "I think I'll take Kristen upstairs and retire myself after I put her to bed."

"Nonsense. I'll send for Megan," Petula Caldwell insisted.

"No, please. It is her special day and I would like a few moments alone with my daughter."

Melanie rose from the table, fighting the urge to run up the stairs in panic. She had known this day would eventually come. But the prolonged absence of the wayward sea captain from his home had lulled her into a false sense of security. She looked at Kristen who, upon hearing it was her bedtime, climbed out of the rocker and came to stand at her side, her doll clutched under her arm.

"Can I sleep with her, Mama? I promise I won't let her keep me awake," the child averred seriously.

"Of course you can, darling! Now say good night to everyone."

"Shall I send you up some hot cocoa, dear? It might counter the effect of the ice cream," Petula suggested as she bent over to receive her good night hug from Kristen.

"No, thank you, Aunt Pet. I'm sure I'll be fine in a little bit." She extended her hand to the little girl at her feet. "Good night everyone."

Her mind raced as she prepared Kristen for bed and tucked her in. It was with half an ear that she listened to the child's prayers, for all she could imagine was Ryan's reaction to finding her there—and worse still, to finding his beautiful daughter. She *had* to think of a reason to go away for the holidays. Once the captain left Boston, she could return home.

She remained at Kristen's bedside until the little girl closed her eyes, exhausted from her big day. Five years seemed to melt away the mental wall she had built to contain the memories of Ryan Caldwell. As she sat before her vanity table and took down her hair, her initial panic subsided, and she began to view her quandary with reason. Her fingers went to the creamy white skin of her face, so stark a contrast to her ebony hair.

Ryan Caldwell knew Meilani as a brown-skinned native.

Dare she count on his not recognizing her based on that chance? She had changed a great deal since she had come to live in Boston. Dressed in the tailored dresses with her hair pinned up demurely, she did not look at all like the foolish girl he had carried off. She lifted her waist-length tresses with her fingers in quiet contemplation.

Making her decision, she withdrew a pair of scissors from her sewing basket and began to cut her hair. With each slice of the silver blades through the raven tresses that were her pride, Melanie winced. They were not fashionable, anyway, she consoled herself when the floor lay covered with the hair he had worshipped with his fingers.

She left just enough to reach her shoulders, just enough to sweep up off her neck. Relieved of its weight, the silken locks curled in untamed disarray. With the help of a powder to lighten her skin even more, Ryan Caldwell might never guess the mild-mannered schoolteacher from Lahaina was the fisherman's daughter, Meilani.

But if he did, was she prepared to do battle with him? The steely gaze of her eyes, mature and determined, told her the answer. She had not only changed in appearance, but inside as well. He would find her a more worthy adversary than the young girl-child he had corrupted. She was older now, more sure of herself. Hurt and betrayal had calloused her heart against anything he could do to her. And if that were not enough to give her the strength she needed, there was one other thing that had changed that would. She was a mother now . . . and no more formidable opponent existed where the happiness of her child was concerned.

Chapter Ten

Otis Place was noted for its late dinner parties for visiting divas and stage professionals. Cabs made straight from the theatre to the Apthorps', where a buffet had been spread that was as beautiful as it was delicious. A grand piano was the center of attention, where one of the many talented guests played familiar tunes while his comrades, now well in their cups, strained to hit the notes of selections not especially in their range.

Across the grand salon that had been constructed specifically with entertainment in mind, a three-piece ensemble competed, their music certainly more organized for the couples that tried to dance in the Bohemian chaos. Above it all rang the dramatic addresses of "Dahlings" and "Luvs" as the guests greeted one another, often from opposite sides of the room.

Ryan Caldwell adjusted the starched collar of his shirt and cursed the frock coat that restrained his wide shoulders. The wide knotted tie at his throat threatened to choke him each time he took a sip of the champagne the maids were passing out freely from silver trays. To add to his ill humor, Arabella was fashionably late. His green eyes darted around the room, catching a flirtatious smile from a tall, willowy blonde near the piano, but he refused to rise to the lure.

All he intended to do was to put in the appearance he had promised the lovely actress, then take her back to her apartment. He had arrived early in Boston, and not wanting to suffer the insistent invitation of his brother to share the family home on Beacon Street right away, had gone straight to Arabella's. After an appropriate show of displeasure that he had avoided Boston for six long years, displeasure softened by the exotic gifts he presented to her, his auburn beauty welcomed him as warmly as she always had.

He did not stop to ponder her fickle change of nature. That was Arabella. She was ever-changing like the wind, as refreshing as a summer breeze one moment and as blustery as the worst of gales in a temper the next. She neither made possessive demands of him nor would have them made of her. And that was the factor responsible for the endurance of their relationship. But this small request to attend the Apthorps' so that she might make a dramatic appearance was becoming tedious.

To think that at one time he had actually enjoyed this facade of glitter was laughable. He'd had the best tailors on Charles Street outfit him in the dandiest and most uncomfortable wear to see him through his Harvard years. The suit he wore now fit him no less perfect, but he had changed. Perhaps he was getting set in his ways, he mused wryly, recalling Amos's favorite expression. Too many years at sea in comfortable clothing and a casual atmosphere had spoiled him.

A maid paused in front of him, her smile offering more than the champagne she served. His polite "Thank you" as he exchanged his empty glass for a full one was met with a provocative "Anytime, monsieur." Ryan's smile was cynical as she walked away, the white voile bow of her apron swinging with her hips. She was no more French than he, but like everything there, she exemplified the falseness he had come to disdain.

Damn Arabella, he thought, glancing at his pocket watch irritably. He would give her until midnight, and if she did not show up by then, she could find her own way home. He was no stage door johnny who would wait around forever for a favor, no matter how appealing her many charms were to him. Bored with the liquor-distorted renditions of Gilbert and Sullivan, he meandered toward the opposite end of the room where the musical ensemble provided dance music.

His trousers, narrow cut with a black braid stitched at the side seams, moved with his muscular legs with a virile grace that drew more than one feminine eye to his impatient progress. Even if his skin were not so healthily bronzed in comparison to the garish made-up faces of some of the actors who strutted about like proud peacocks for their admiring flock, his self-assured manner set him apart.

He found an inconspicuous spot near one of the florentine columns that supported the beautiful arched ceiling, when a velvet laugh drifted his way. His glass froze at his lips as he looked in its direction to seek out the owner, knowing that she could not be the one he was reminded of. The couples whirled to the waltz in a kaleidoscope of colors, consuming the one who had disrupted his thoughts.

Ryan tossed down the rest of the champagne as if to drown the memory that unexpectedly reared to the forefront of his mind. It had taken a long time to put it to rest once he was convinced that that was all it would ever be . . . a memory. But laughing blue eyes haunted him, making him weak with guilt and self-inflicted rage.

To hell with this place and to hell with Arabella, he fumed in a defensive effort to redirect his anger. He put his glass on an empty tray and started to search the room for the host and hostess, to pay his respects, when he heard it again. He pivoted to see a young woman waltzing on the arm of her beau, responding in delight to some witticism.

She was a lovely creature with raven hair, upswept and adorned with royal-blue plumes that matched the satin of her gown. Tiny curls fringed a delicate face as though kissing her skin. Alabaster came to Ryan's mind to describe it, although her cheeks were flushed with the effects of the champagne and the lively step of the waltz. But it was her eyes that made him grateful for the support of the pillar behind him, for they were like sapphires outshining the real gem on the broach of the black velvet ribbon tied about her neck.

153

"Meilani . . ." slipped from his lips against all reason.

"So there you are, Ryan darling. I realize I'm late, but I promise I'll be even naughtier later!"

Ryan hardly heard Arabella's husky whisper against his ear or felt the brush of her lips on his cheek. He watched the woman on the dance floor curtsy prettily at the end of the dance and accompany her dour-looking escort toward the punch bowl.

"Darling, are you feeling ill? You look as if you've seen a ghost."

The shake of Arabella's hand on his arm momentarily broke his fascination with the woman in royal-blue. His short laugh was humorless as he replied, "I thought I had."

But Meilani was dead. For months he had refused to accept it. He believed against all hope that she had somehow managed to reach the island. He would not face the implications presented by the fact that his men had searched the city, asking everyone along the docks if they had seen the blue-eyed native girl, and had come up with nothing. He had gone ashore himself, his stomach wrapped in gauze from the wound she had frantically dealt him.

It was superficial, however, when compared to the blow of her death. He had killed her as surely as if he had tossed her over the side and held her under. He had lost his own control and, in so doing, had driven her to her end. Like the wild bird he had captured as a boy and caged, she had killed herself trying to escape.

Every night for months afterward, he had dreamed of her, waking up in a cold sweat as he saw her lifeless blue eyes staring up at him from a watery grave in his nightmare. No amount of alcohol would banish his guilt or his anguish at her loss. He had not realized how much he had come to care for her until it was too late.

"Who is she?" Ryan asked, nodding toward the subject of his attention.

Arabella's emerald eyes slanted as she observed the girl who had captured his interest. "Someone *not* in our social circuit, darling," she mused, the corner of her sensuous

154

mouth tilting slightly. "And hardly your type, I might add. Why, she hasn't a touch of make-up. She does look a ghost compared to the other ladies here."

"She doesn't need it, cat." Ryan chuckled at Arabella's snort of indignation and hugged her to him. In the shadows of the column, he nibbled at her neck playfully. "Don't tell me you're jealous."

"Me?" the actress protested, snapping a practiced fan open and peering over it at the couple partaking of the sumptuous buffet. "Of course not. But I do wonder why Sam Meyers would bring such a prim little mouse to this sort of thing."

Sam Meyers. Ryan tucked the name away, for he was going to find out who the woman was that now looked around her in wonder at the gay festivities—the same sort of innocent wonder that had once secretly ensnared his heart. "And who is Mr. Meyers?"

"Ryan, you are becoming a bore," Arabella complained, turning in his arms to face him. But upon seeing that her escort was not to be dismissed as easily as the men she was accustomed to, she relented. "He is a professor of science at the Bayside Boy's School and a member of the Omega Club. Why even he bothers to come is a mystery to me."

"You are, as ever, as informative as you are beautiful, my sweet," Ryan complimented. Ignoring the people standing nearby, he tasted the lips so provocatively turned up to him. "And if you are willing to leave here, I can think of a place where I will not be nearly so boring to you."

"Only *you* could drag me away and you know it, you degenerate sea dog," Arabella teased, her long fingers sliding down the stiff pleated front of Ryan's shirt.

"Then I'll get our coats and hail a cab."

"Oh!" the actress gasped, startled by the hand that managed to evade her resilient bustle to pinch her encased bottom. Her cheeks flamed deeper than the rouge they wore as she smiled at the guests who looked at her quizzically for the cause of her outburst. But the cause was already yards away, making a straight path for the foyer, leaving her to follow in his wake.

"Good night darlings. Do carry on without me," she said with a graceful sweep of her gloved arm. "My prince awaits."

Melanie stared after the strikingly attractive woman who seemed, not merely to walk, but to glide across the marbled floor through an adoring crowd. The crystal light from the chandeliers sparkled in the sequined bows that adorned her generous auburn curls—curls that cascaded to one side of her emerald-bedecked neckline.

"Why, she must be royalty!" Melanie remarked in utter awe of the woman's stately beauty.

"Hardly, my dear Mrs. Lyons," Sam Meyers responded dryly. "But she is a vision worthy of such a title. She is Arabella Harrington of theatre fame. She has a voice like a bird and a foul temperament, so I've heard."

Melanie cut her eyes at her companion's humorous attempt and laughed. "Mr. Meyers, your wit leaves me breathless."

But what had actually left her breathless was the flawless beauty of Ryan Caldwell's Arabella. Not even in her wildest imagination had Melanie done justice to the actress for whom the captain had purchased so many gifts. There was no doubt at all now that Meilani had only been an amusement for him . . . a substitution in the queen of his heart's absence. Well, she was welcome to him!

Melanie guiltily checked her green and spiteful train of thought. Wounded ego, she diagnosed grudgingly. That was why her spirits had suddenly deflated like a punctured balloon. She had been floating on air in Sam's arms. The fact that he fawned over her in a very proper adoration fed the sudden need she had for male attention. Since the news of Ryan Caldwell's impending arrival, she had had too much time to dwell on her inadequacies, particularly since she had impulsively cut her hair.

Although Sam helped to buoy her faltering self-assurance, Melanie found herself wishing the evening she'd been enjoying so much was over. And when the coach came to a halt in front of Number Eight, bringing the evening to its conclusion, and Sam walked Melanie up to the steps, she fell into his polite embrace so desperately that he was encouraged enough to kiss her, a kiss she returned warmly, as if suddenly starved for something that once had been.

It was then that Gilbert Caldwell opened the door and discovered another means of bringing color to Melanie's cheeks, with his mischievous and well-intentioned teasing during the days leading to the Caldwell Christmas party.

Aunt Pet was a bundle of nerves the day of the event. She sent the servants on first one errand and then another, changing her mind so many times that Melanie had seen the frustrated staff cross themselves as they shifted in midstream of their assigned tasks. Yet somehow, in spite of all the confusion, the house was spotlessly clean and decorated, and by evening the meal was coming along nicely in the basement kitchen.

With school closed until after the holidays, Melanie enjoyed the weekdays off with her daughter, enlisting little helping hands with the decorations that had been her assignment. Kristen ate more popcorn and cranberries than she strung on the garland, and by the time the pine boughs and mistletoe had been tied together with scarlet ribbons to hang over the doorways and windows, she was sticky with resin, but her effervescence made the day go by so quickly and pleasantly.

All through her bath she protested that it was unfair for her to help like the adults and then not be allowed to join the party with the rest of the family. As Melanie scrubbed off the pine resin, to which unsightly dirt had now adhered, from her daughter's pink skin, she explained once more that the party was for adults and would last well past Kristen's bedtime. Over a meal in the nursery which she supervised, Melanie finally compromised, promising her daughter she could come downstairs before going to bed to bid everyone good night.

So Kristen picked out her best negligee of pink and ruffled flannel to wear for the occasion, as carefully as Melanie chose her gown of ice-blue taffeta. They dressed together, each one helping the other, like two schoolgirls laughing at each other's antics. Kristen eagerly furnished ribbons for Melanie's hair, which she wore swept off her neck with the exception of two short ringlets that hung to one side.

"Oh, Mama, you are the most beautiful woman in the whole world!" her daughter exclaimed in awe as Melanie stood before the floor-length mirror and studied her image critically. "I hope I'll be as pretty."

Melanie was pleased with the ice-blue satin creation trimmed in royal-blue velvet bows that was one of her favorites. "I do feel pretty," she admitted, drawing her daughter to her. "But, darling, you are already lovely and growing more so everyday. I shall have to hide you to protect you from the young men," she teased.

Kristen gave an indignant snort. "No you won't, Mama. I can pinch them and send them squalling to their nannies."

"Kristen Elizabeth!" Melanie gasped in astonishment. "Where did you pick up that unladylike habit?"

"The Garden. It's only fair, Mama," her daughter spoke up in her own defense. "They pull our curls!"

Melanie smiled, but that was as far as she allowed her amusement to go. "Then perhaps if you acted like ladies, they might act like gentlemen."

"The wee divils do not know how, Mama!" Kristen remarked abhorrently with such a brogue that Melanie could not help but guess whom her daughter had learned it from.

"Well, I had best go down and help Aunt Pet with the last-minute details, darling. You run along, and if you're good, perhaps Megan will read you a book before bedtime."

"I'll sneak into the kitchen," Kristen announced with a sparkle of glee, "and sample the dessert. I'll bet that's where Megan is."

Melanie started to object but stopped herself. She knew that the cook would run Kristen out if she got in the way, as surely as the stern woman had run Melanie herself out on occasion.

The guests began to arrive promptly at the appointed hour. Gilbert was grandly attired in a deep russet evening coat, which set off the touch of red in his brown hair. The perfect host, he saw everyone accommodated with a drink of their choice until all the guests were accounted for. When dinner was announced, the group moved across the foyer to the dining room to find their seats marked on the place cards Aunt Pet had had printed.

The banquet table was beautifully set with the Caldwells' best linen, silver, china, and crystal. All of the extensions had been used to seat the twenty head that gathered about it, making complimentary remarks about the tiered centerpiece of fresh cut greenery interlaced with ripe red apples and festively decorated cookies and tarts.

Melanie was seated between her host and Professor Sam Meyers, and she held her breath at what Gilbert might say to embarrass her. Her uncle, however, was on his best behavior. He conversed with Sam about his position at the boy's academy in a most civil manner, but his teasing eyes kept Melanie on edge. She demurely sipped the sauterne from her delicately stemmed goblet, leaving most of the talk to the men.

She listened with half an ear to Gilbert and Sam, for Priscilla and her gentleman dinner partner, a young man from her theatre group, were involved in an animated conversation concerning the backstage antics at their most recent performance. Melanie nearly choked on her wine in amusement, for she could hardly picture the prim and proper Priscilla chasing a stray dog, who had wandered into the theatre through a back door, across the stage during the production.

"I say, I met your brother at the Omega Club the other day. Dashedly cordial fellow," Sam told Gilbert cheerily.

"Ryan at the Omega Club?" Gilbert echoed in surprise. "Gad, I had thought they'd bar him after nearly burning it down."

Sam laughed. "That was a good one . . . what? Barney Minot told us about it. Odd," he said suddenly, "I had thought he might be here."

Gilbert sighed wistfully. "Ryan made the same impression here as he did on the Omega Club Board," he said with a meaningful glance at the opposite end of the table, where Aunt Pet chattered away without thought to the food getting cold on her plate. "He promised me he'd spend the holidays, though, with or without the consent of my dear wife."

Christmas Day, Melanie thought, her total attention ensnared by Sam's mention of Ryan Caldwell. If she could get through that one day, then he would go back to sea and she could breathe easier again. The tiny ring of the silver hostess bell drew her back from her mood-dampening thoughts as Aunt Pet rose to lead everyone back to the parlor for a game of charades.

There was much confusion as teams were selected. Melanie sat on the arm of the loveseat with Sam at her side and watched Gilbert go through his frantic mime. He was entirely too funny as he narrowed his eyes in reprimand at her wrong guesses and with a wave of his hand erased his previous actions to start over.

"My, but you two are thick!" he exploded in good-natured frustration when his time was up. "I was Scrooge and I wasn't picking lice, I was penny-pinching! And you are the teachers of our children?" he teased. Suddenly, a wicked gleam came to him eye. "Look!" he said, pointing to Sam.

Melanie looked up at her partner in bewilderment.

With an audible groan of exasperation, Gilbert took her hand and bade her rise from her precarious perch on the divan. Calling her attention to the green boughs over Sam's head, he said, "Mistletoe, you adorable dimwit."

Blood rushed to Melanie's face at his meaning. "Oh, no, I couldn't . . ."

"Gilbert Caldwell, will you please behave!" Aunt Pet declared huffily from the opposite side of the room.

Gilbert frowned, fully aware that he had an audience, and shook his head. "You're quite right, dearest. This won't do." With that, he pulled Sam out from under the mistletoe and shoved Melanie beneath it. "That's better!" he declared proudly. "Well, go on, Sam."

There was a general applause as Sam awkwardly pecked Melanie's scarlet cheek. Then, at the clicking of Aunt Pet's tongue, Gilbert deviously pinched a piece of mistletoe and, holding it over her head, bussed her on the tip of her nose, deflating her indignation to an embarrassed giggle.

"What am I to do with you, you rascal!" the older woman scoffed fondly. "Now, who's next?"

At the appearance of the servant at her side, Melanie rose, certain that Kristen, who had apparently talked Megan into more than one story, was ready to say good night.

But the uniformed gentleman leaned over and said, in a low voice, "There is a Captain Jeb Lyons waiting in the foyer to see you, madame."

"What?" Melanie gasped in disbelief, drawing the attention of those nearby.

The servant nodded apologetically. "He says he is Captain Jeb Lyons, madame, and he is asking to see you."

She stared numbly at the man, her face draining of its color. "It can't be," she whispered almost to herself as Aunt Pet rushed to her side.

"But it is, darling Melanie," a familiar voice came to her from the foyer.

The servant stepped aside as Ryan Caldwell entered the room and took her hands. Melanie could neither move nor speak. She looked up into hypnotic green eyes, her blood frozen within her veins.

"What is the meaning of this outrage!" Aunt Pet fumed beside her.

Ryan's lips curled into a humorless smile as he answered, but his gaze never left Melanie's. "I am here to rectify an outrage, dear sister-in-law, not commit one."

"Ryan, I do hope you have an explanation," Melanie heard Gilbert say sternly.

"In living up to the opinion you good people have formed of me, I took this innocent young lady as my wife under the name of Jeb Lyons some five years ago. We were separated before I could set things right, and until this last week, I had thought her dead and my guilt irreconcilable. This time when we marry, I shall give her and my child my real name."

Gasps of astonishment echoed around the room, but Melanie did not hear them. All that rang in her mind as she slumped to the floor were the words *my child*.

Ryan lunged forward to break Melanie's fall as her head lolled back in a faint. She weighed not an ounce more than the last time he had held her in his arms, but the slippery material of her gown made it difficult to secure a good hold on her. If he had had any doubt that she was Meilani, the look in her eyes when he mentioned the child affirmed it.

He'd met Sam Meyers at the Omega Club and, after an afternoon of poker with the stiff-mannered professor, had found out the lovely woman he'd seen at Otis Place was none other than the niece Gilbert Caldwell kept referring to in his letters. The following morning, Ryan went straight to the Caldwell offices to find out more about the intriguing widow from Honolulu with the five-year-old child.

"Someone get the salts," Petula Caldwell called out in near hysteria. "Gilbert, do something!"

But everyone, including Ryan who rose with Melanie in his grasp, froze at the bloodcurdling shriek from the stairwell in the foyer. He looked up to see a little girl scampering down the steps in a flurry of pink ruffles, her nurse at her heels. Her blond curls bounced with each frantic step as she raced toward him.

"Mama!" the child screamed, tearing at his trouser leg. "What have you done to my mama?"

"Kristen . . ."

Gilbert tried to pull the sobbing child back, but she jerked away and seized Ryan's hand, nearly costing him his hold on Melanie's inert form. Ryan grimaced as the child sank her teeth into the back of his wrist and yanked away awkwardly.

"He's taking my mama!" she shrieked, her blue eyes spilling frightened tears down her face. Gilbert caught her and drew her up into his arms.

"Hush, Kristen. He's not taking your mama anywhere but to her room." Gilbert Caldwell assured the child in a soothing voice, clutching her small, trembling body against him.

"Where?" Ryan asked, his own face pale beneath sun-bronzed skin at the unexpected appearance of his daughter—a daughter who, until a few days ago, he had not even known existed.

"Follow me," Petula Caldwell said hastily, having regained a degree of composure "Priscilla, please see to our guests."

Ryan did not feel the least bit smug about the way things had turned out. He had known there would be guests. It was something he had counted on. For once, his rakish past had served him well. By admitting having led her false, he publicly vindicated Melanie's reputation and yet locked her into marriage before she could run away again. She hadn't been able to deny him. He had hoped that her shock at his use of her own lie would be so great that she would go along with him. It had been a gamble that had worked precisely as he had anticipated . . . until she fainted and the child appeared.

He followed Petula Caldwell into a feminine room with floral printed wallpaper, a room he barely recognized as once having been his own, and deposited Melanie on the white eyelet bedspread. As he withdrew his arms from under her, she began to stir with a soft moan. He started to lean over her when a bare foot walked over his booted one, and the crying child wedged herself between him and her mother.

"Mama?" she sniffed, taking Melanie's hand and holding it to her face. "Mama, please wake up."

Melanie opened her eyes, focusing on the tear-streaked face of her daughter. "Kristen?" she murmured in confusion, wondering if it had all been a horrible dream. But as her vision cleared, she saw Ryan Caldwell behind the child and knew that it had not.

"Maa . . . ma," Kristen pleaded brokenly, crawling up on the bed with the help of the stranger. "Mama, are you sick?"

"Dear, your mother is all right, but she needs air," Petula Caldwell suggested from the foot of the bed.

Melanie did not need air. She needed exactly what her daughter offered—strength to face this totally unexpected turn of events. "I'm fine, Kristen," she whispered shakily, adding in an attempt to console the child, "Your silly mother just fainted."

Kristen hugged her tighter. "I—I thought that man was going to take you away," she mumbled against Melanie's chest. "I thought you were dead like my daddy." With that, the little girl became hysterical again.

"Are you satisfied, sir?" Petula Caldwell condemned Ryan viciously. "Do you see what your crude sense of humor has caused? Well, do you?"

Melanie managed to inch her way up on the pillows so that she could cradle her small daughter against her. She looked at Gilbert Caldwell plaintively. As if reading her mind, Gilbert took his wife in one hand and his grimly mute brother in the other.

"I suggest we leave until Melanie can get the child calmed down." But it was not a suggestion at all by the way he ushered them both out into the hall.

After a while, Kristen's sobs became less ragged. Melanie cooed softly to her, promising her over and over that she would never leave her, that no man would take her away. She stroked her daughter's blond curls away from her face, kissing her forehead gently as her eyelids fluttered in exhaustion. When they at last lay fanned against her tear-reddened cheeks, Melanie pulled back the covers and tucked the sleeping child snugly beneath them.

Without thought to her appearance, she tiptoed into the hall to find Megan waiting outside the door. The nurse was distraught over having lost control of the child and, more so, from Kristen's hysteria.

"Is the wee thing all right now, mum?"

"She's sleeping in my bed," Melanie answered quietly.

164

"Please sit with her until I return."

Megan's head dipped in acknowledgment. "Master Gilbert said to tell you the family waits in the library, mum."

"Thank you, Megan."

As Melanie walked down the dimly lit corridor to the library that adjoined the master suite, she calmly steeled herself. Ryan had caught her completely off guard. Never would she have suspected him of this! How had he found out about her and Kristen? How could he know that Melanie Hammond Lyons was Meilani? The questions continued to surface as she neared the library door, raised voices meeting her.

"Had I known, sir, that you intended to shock that poor gentlewoman like that, I would not have been so eager to tell you about her!" Gilbert Caldwell denounced hotly. "What do you hope to attain by such tasteless airing of your despicable deceit?"

"Gentlewoman!" Ryan echoed incredulously. "You do not know what she is capable of! This is what your *gentlewoman* did to me when we last saw each other."

Melanie stepped into the room, her chin tilted defiantly as Ryan yanked his shirt up to show the thin white line slashed across his flat abdomen. "It's a pity I did not know how to use a knife. Then I would not be forced to suffer this embarrassment." Her eyes glittered coldly as she went on, "Unlike you, I cannot show the scars our last encounter left me with. Instead, I bore a child and," her voice softened slightly, "I'll not refer to Kristen in any way but with love." Gilbert was dumbstruck by her bold admission as she turned to him calmly. "Where is Aunt Pet?"

"I convinced her to rejoin the guests. I believe she's seeing them off," he answered, his eyes showing that he still did not believe his ears. "Kristen?"

"Asleep in my bed," she assured him. "Megan is with her."

"Then," Gilbert paused, disconcerted, "my brother is really Kristen's father?"

Green eyes challenged her from across the room, but their challenge was needless. Melanie was tired of lying,

165

tired of running. "He . . . is," she admitted brokenly.

She ignored Ryan and turned to his brother. Her eyes were glazed with remorse as she began her confession, for the shame of the past five years had caught up with her. The admission of her deceit came hard. This sweet gentleman had opened his home and his heart to her, and this was a sinful repayment for such kindness.

"I—I did not want to lie to you and Aunt Pet. There was never any Jeb Lyons. I ran away from home and crossed paths with your brother. When I discovered who he was and realized how . . . that our relationship was meaningless, then I left him, praying he'd never find me." Melanie inhaled deeply and went on. "When I finally did get home, I was with child. Here was the last place I wanted to come because you were Ryan's family, but my mother had no idea of the child's father's identity and insisted it was the only way—not for me, but for my baby—that I could build a new life," she added with a sad and ironic smile.

She took Gilbert's hand between her own. "I wasn't going to stay. I was foolish to have done so, but . . . you and Aunt Pet made me feel so welcome and . . ." her voice broke, "my own mother wouldn't have me . . . Please forgive me, Gilbert. I would not hurt you or any of your family for the world! I owe you so much."

Her guilt bore her to her knees like a crushing steel weight upon her shoulders. The anguish at the shame she had caused the family that had taken her in twisted inside her. She held her arms across her abdomen and swallowed the wretched sob that hung in her throat. "I cannot face Aunt Pet or Priscilla," she managed as she felt the gentle stroke of her uncle's hand on her hair. "Kristen and I will be gone by morning."

"You'll do no such thing!"

"The hell you will!"

Ryan's and Aunt Pet's voices chimed in together, Aunt Pet having slipped in unnoticed in time to hear Melanie's tearful confession. In a rush of taffeta, the older woman hurried over to where Gilbert gathered Melanie up in his arms and

166

held her tightly.

"You adorable little dimwit," he cajoled with his usual affection, "you do not owe us a thing. It is we who owe you, for sharing your daughter and yourself with us. And if that is not enough," he said, lifting her trembling chin so that she looked him in the eye, "you have caused my brother and wife to agree for the first time in family history."

"Oh, Gilbert," Melanie sniffed through quiet tears. "You always make me laugh."

"Another debt I owe you, dimwit. You are the only one who shares my sense of humor," he mumbled gruffly against the top of her head. "Pet, shall we leave these two youngsters to work out their problems in private?"

Petula Caldwell, however, was not as easily assuaged as her husband. She tucked Melanie in her generous embrace and glared over the girl's shoulder at the golden-haired gentleman casually perched on the edge of her husband's desk. "That is entirely up to Melanie," she stated brusquely. "She may not wish to be left alone with the scoundrel. Are your intentions honorable, sir?"

"Absolutely," Ryan remarked cynically, meeting Petula's gaze with mutual dislike.

"Humph!" her aunt snorted. "I'd just as soon take the word of Satan himself."

"Petula!"

At Gilbert's warning tone, Petula Caldwell turned to Melanie. "Now don't you worry about us, dear," she cautioned. "It's obviously all his fault and no one expects any better of him. You take care of yourself and my little niece." Although Aunt Petula was not a large woman, she puffed up her chest in a foreboding manner and directed a scathing look at Ryan while questioning Melanie. "Are you sure you don't need me to stay with you?"

Melanie shook her head. She didn't need Aunt Petula or Gilbert to face Ryan now. Their forgiveness and support gave her the fortitude she required to deal with him. She was no longer alone but was reinforced with a family now . . . a real family. When they left the room, she walked over to one of the large leather chairs by the potbellied stove and sat down, all too aware of the green eyes that followed her curiously.

"Very well, sir. What have you to say for yourself?"

She primly arranged the flouncing on her skirt as she awaited his reply. When it did not come, she raised her eyes to him with the demanding look she often gave her students for an answer. The fact that her hair had come undone and hung in loose curls about her face, giving her an unkempt appearance, was appealingly contradictory to her demeanor of propriety.

"Damned if I know," Ryan replied candidly, shaking himself to keep from staring.

Nothing had gone right and everything had. He had found Meilani, a schoolmistress and mother of his child, in one fascinating creature that now snapped her eyes at him as if rapping him with a map stick. She acted like a schoolmarm and looked like a combination of the native girl and another more refined, yet equally passionate woman he had yet to meet.

"What happened to your hand?" Melanie asked, noticing for the first time the handkerchief wrapped around his wrist. She loathed the green-eyed scrutiny that seemed to see everything there was to see about her . . . that looked right into her soul and read its secrets.

Ryan's lips curled at the irony. "Your . . . *our* daughter bit me."

"She what?" Melanie exclaimed with the indignation of a horrified mother. His correction of *your* to *our* struck her suddenly, the common bond oddly appealing in spite of her reservations concerning the captain and her daughter.

"She . . . well, you heard what she thought," Ryan reminded her. "She came running down the stairs like a screaming pink banshee and attacked me," he finished with a chuckle at the similarity between the child and its mother. "Like mother, like daughter."

The reference brought to the forefront the enmity that existed between them, and Melanie raised her guard again.

It was difficult, for Ryan could be so devilishly appealing when he laughed like that. He looked so much more himself with his evening jacket discarded and his waistcoat unbuttoned to reveal a pleated front shirt. The tie hung loosely about his neck and he had unfastened the turned-down collar.

"What exactly is it that you want, Ryan?" she asked sharply, irritated at herself for her inadvertent admiration.

Ryan started to answer "you," but he checked himself, reverting to his original strategy. It annoyed him that his thinking became so muddled when face-to-face with this woman. And there was no doubt she was all that now. "I want my daughter."

Melanie recoiled as though his verbal blow had been physical. Her worst fears became realized, her eyes reflecting the terror they invoked. They mirrored those of her daughter's earlier that evening, and the same stabbing guilt at his actions made Ryan want to reach out and comfort her. He didn't want to hurt her anymore. He wanted her.

"You don't have to lose her, Meilani . . . Melanie," he corrected in frustration as he slid off the desk and strode over to her. "I think marriage will solve both our dilemmas." When he dropped his tone like that, it seemed to stroke the back of her neck with its velvet touch, raising the silken hairs of her flesh.

"How can that be when I cannot stand the thought of your touch, sir?" She slapped away the hand that caressed her neck and glared hatefully. It was the same hand, she reminded herself, that had tied her to his bed and painfully assaulted her. She shuddered involuntarily, reliving the nightmarish memory.

Ryan stiffened, his ego battered by her evident repudiation of him. And along with its sting came the bitterness that had risen when he discovered Meilani had resiliently bounced back from their affair, circulating in Boston's elite society, while he had wallowed in guilt and remorse, thinking her dead.

"It's simple, blue eyes. I have confessed in public that I

married you under false pretenses and have come to make it right. I get my daughter, you do not lose her . . . and you can save the family further disgrace, for surely the tongues will wag if the whole truth be known about the wild savage girl who was not always forced against her will to enjoy the intimacy normally set aside for the marriage bed."

Melanie's face grew hot with horrified disbelief. "You wouldn't!"

The cynical twist of his lips threatened her, but he answered simply, "I don't have to. I can take Kristen from you, Melanie. There is nowhere on this earth where you can hide that I would not find you," he told her matter-of-factly. "And I do not think you would submit her to that kind of life."

Melanie wanted to slap him. Fire fairly leapt from her eyes as she rose abruptly and stood toe to toe with him. He used reason to do her injustice. But life was not always fair. Wasn't that what she tried to teach her daughter? He could provide Kristen with financial security and, as he said, protect their reputations. And she could give her daughter the selfless love a little girl needed—love she knew him to be incapable of.

It galled her, but Ryan Caldwell had had her in the palm of his hand the moment he'd discovered Kristen was his. She had underestimated him, for he had taken the one reserve she had counted heavily upon and used it against her. She looked him squarely in the eye and averred brittlely, "You leave me little choice, sir." She picked up the hem of her gown primly and, with a contemptuous rake of her eyes, bade him a stilted "Good night."

Chapter Eleven

A wet kiss planted loudly on her cheek woke Melanie from the sleep she had finally won after a long night of clock watching. She opened her eyes to find two like her own staring down at her mischievously. With a giggle of delight that only a child could feel first thing in the morning, Kristen scurried back under the covers to hide from her. Although she had watched the milk wagon pass at four when the morning light had not yet begun to peek over the eastern horizon, Melanie wiped the sleep from her eyes and dove under the flannel sheets after her impish charge.

"Mama!" the child protested as Melanie tickled her until she came out for air. When her cackling laughter had exhausted itself and she lay with her head on Melanie's shoulder, Kristen sighed dreamily, "I love to sleep with you, Mama. You're so soft and warm."

"And you're like having my own living doll to sleep with," Melanie told her, snuggling closer as she fell in with her daughter's mood.

It was a special treat to be able to lie in bed on a weekday and share this closeness with Kristen. From outside she could hear the distant tootings of factory whistles calling the workers to their jobs across the river and the clinking hammer of the blacksmith shop a few blocks away at the stables. Twisting her fingers idly in the fine hair that shone like spun gold in the morning light, Melanie wondered if her mother had ever felt like this toward her, for she could only recall dutiful attention from Lydia Hammond. Any real warmth she remembered had come from her father. She kissed the top of Kristen's head, suddenly feeling very sorry for her mother over the joy the woman never knew she had missed.

"Who was that man, Mama?" Kristen asked, wriggling until she was propped on her elbows. "The one who carried you in here?"

Melanie's heart stopped at her daughter's question. For a moment she had forgotten the disturbing events of the preceding night, events that had made sleep impossible. She had practiced a number of ways to explain Ryan to Kristen, and now not one would come to her mind. No amount of embellishment would alter the plain and simple truth.

With great reluctance, she answered her daughter. "His name is Ryan Caldwell, Kristen."

"Uncle Gilbert's captain brother?"

Melanie nodded, working up the nerve to complete the identification. "And he is also your father, Kristen."

Kristen's face screwed into protest. "But my daddy is Captain Jeb Lyons and he is dead."

Oh, what a tangled web, Melanie thought as she wove a more detailed story to explain the name so that Kristen would accept the truth. "It was a game, darling. We used different names, like when you and Charity Lowe play dress-up . . . and then we were separated and couldn't find each other. . . ."

"Because he thought we were dead, too?"

"Yes," Melanie agreed lamely.

There was no point in explaining that Ryan had not known of Kristen's existence. That would only lead to more uncomfortable questions, for her daughter had inherited her inquisitive nature. She watched Kristen digest the news. Her golden brows knitted and her pink lips pursed in a rosette that would shame spring's most prize rosebud.

"Is he why you fainted, Mama? Did you think he was a ghost?"

Melanie laughed nervously and dragged her precocious

offspring to her. "Something like that, darling."

"Is he here now?"

"I—I would imagine," she decided. It would be too much to hope that Ryan had disappeared as quickly as he had shown up. He was enjoying her discomfort too much to give it up so easily. That he wanted Kristen was an excuse to punish her. Melanie had reasoned that out in the darkness of the long night. He had found her and the way to pay her back for what she had done to him. His money's worth, she recalled him saying that last horrible night.

Kristen's shriek made her start. "Mama, why are we in bed when we need to see him before he goes to work?" In a mad scramble, Kristen slid off the bed onto the carpeted floor and ran to the door that led through Melanie's parlor to the nursery. "I'm going to wear my new dress so he'll think I'm pretty!" she called back in breathless excitement.

"Not your velvet!" Melanie objected, tossing back the warm covers to face the chill of the December morning.

After considerable persuasion, Melanie convinced Kristen that her smocked birthday dress of white eyelet over pink petticoats would make a satisfactory impression. When Megan showed up to take over her daughter's preparations for breakfast, having heard the young lady's exuberant squeals from the hall, she was bombarded with the news that Kristen now had a real father with gold hair just like hers and he wasn't really dead.

Melanie left her bubbling daughter to her nurse and set about getting dressed herself. Her first instinct was to reach for one of her newer dresses, but she mastered it with a firm resolve to remain coolly indifferent to the fact that the captain of the *Liberty Belle* was back in her life. She would not allow the fact that Ryan Caldwell would now be raking those all-seeing eyes of his over her affect her normal mode of dress. Besides, she thought, recalling her chance view of Arabella Harrington, there was little point anyway.

So she chose one of the day dresses she wore when she taught school. Its jacket and overskirt were a gold alpaca, the underskirt and the frogging black in contrast. She pinned up her hair in a singular twist under which she fastened a yellow and black Alsatian bow.

In spite of her late start, she still had to wait for Kristen. The little girl stood more quietly than Melanie had ever thought possible, watching every move Megan made in the mirror as the nurse fashioned each golden ringlet that hung from the cascade of locks and tied it up with pink and white ribbons. When the last shining coil was carefully put into place, Kristen leaned forward and pinched her cheeks unmercifully.

"Oh, Mama, I need some color," she whined, casting a forlorn look at Melanie.

"That is exactly what you'll get if you keep that up, young lady. One black cheek and one blue one," Melanie chided. "Now come along."

"Is it true, mum? Is Master Ryan truly your lost husband?" Megan asked, almost biting her tongue for her impudence and yet too anxious to care.

Melanie took a breath and held it, along with her answer, before carefully rearranging her words. "Yes, Megan. Ryan is Kristen's father."

"Oh, ye must be beside yerself, mum!" Megan squeezed Melanie enthusiastically. "To be sure, I'm so happy for ye and the wee lass."

Melanie forced a smile. "Thank you, Megan."

The tantalizing smell of fresh coffee and bacon that rose to meet them as Melanie walked down the steps with Kristen in hand failed to tempt her appetite. She tried, for her daughter's sake, to act normal as they neared the dining room and heard Gilbert and Ryan discussing the plantation Ryan had purchased in Honolulu. Although Kristen had practically dislocated Melanie's fingers, pulling eagerly to meet her father, when faced with the man in person, her vivacious daughter suddenly turned shy.

"Good morning, ladies," Gilbert beamed, breaking the sudden silence at their arrival and rising from his chair as Melanie hesitated in the entrance with Kristen clutching her skirts.

174

Ryan rose as well, but he remained mute. Melanie could have sworn she saw panic in the eyes that moved from Kristen to hers, but he contained it quickly. It was the disgusted sniff from Aunt Pet, who held her spoon poised over her hot cereal, that spurred him into leaving his place and meeting them. He took Melanie's free hand and brushed her cheek with cold lips.

"Good morning, Melanie." He paused again, his eyes searching hers, as if looking for a clue to what to say to the child who was all but hiding her face from him in her mother's skirts. When no help came, he stubbornly rose to the occasion with his most charming smile and dropped to a squatting position so that he was at eye level with his daughter. "And you must be Kristen."

"Don't you know me, Daddy?" the child asked, the idea striking her as preposterous.

The room was so silent that the ticking of the mantel clock seemed thunderous. "Well, Kristen, you've grown into a pretty young lady," Ryan remarked with an awkward glance at Melanie.

Cautiously, Kristen let go of Melanie's skirt and held out her hand. "It's all right, Daddy. I don't remember you, either," she admitted sheepishly. "But I am most pleased to make your acquaintance again."

Picking up on his daughter's initiative, he took the small hand, so white and tiny in his own, and kissed it, causing Kristen to cast an impressed look at her mother before returning her wide blue eyes to the gentleman at her disposal. "You're not mad?" she asked in astonishment.

Ryan frowned, somewhat taken aback. "Why should I be mad?"

"Because I bit you," came the timid and apologetic reply.

The golden-haired captain laughed out loud, more from relief than from amusement, and snatched up the penitent child into his arms. "Not in the least, sunshine," he reassured her. This time he kissed her cheek and received a hearty one in return.

"Why did you call me that?" Kristen asked as he carried

her to the table.

"Because that is what you remind me of . . . sunshine."

"I like that," Kristen approved with a bouncing shake of her curls. "Are you going to stay here with us now?" She ruffled his hair with her fingers and tried to compare one of her long ringlets to it. "Can you come to the Garden with me after breakfast? Can I sit in your lap and eat?"

Melanie listened to the barrage of questions directed at the newfound father. Kristen did not give him time to answer one before another came out. She settled in Ryan's lap and spread her dress over her petticoats, making him guess how many she had on to make it stand away so prettily. When he reached for a spoon so that she could eat the hot oatmeal placed before them, she spied the small wound where she had bitten him and kissed it.

"Mama can really make it feel better. She kisses all my hurts," she told him authoritatively. Then, as if just remembering Melanie, the child turned to her. "Mama, please sit next to us so we can be a family."

"Well, brother, you can see who really runs the house now," Gilbert Caldwell remarked wryly. He walked around to where Melanie stood frozen to the spot and seated her next to Ryan. With the natural knack her uncle had for putting things at ease, his remark caused a general round of quiet amusement, after which the conversation seemed to become more normal.

"Where's Priscilla?" Melanie asked her aunt as she took one of the delicious baked apples from the platter in front of her.

"She's not feeling particularly well, dear," the woman answered evasively. She darted a quick glance at her husband. Then catching sight of Kristen picking up the cream pitcher to lavish her cereal with it, she hastily warned, "Do watch her with the milk, Ryan!" It was apparent from the disapproval on her face that she did not think the sea captain capable of handling the child.

Ryan's tanned hand covered Kristen's, steadying her as she poured a puddle of white over the oatmeal. Melanie

176

thought that he deliberately teased her aunt as they dribbled honey from the dish to the cereal, twisting the honey dipper just as the amber thread threatened to drop on the linen tablecloth. They were a perfectly impish pair, she mused grudgingly as her daughter giggled in delight over Aunt Pet's needless gasp and exchanged a conspiratorial look with Ryan.

Melanie picked at the baked apple the maid had placed before her without interest and listened to the day Kristen planned with her new father. Ryan had agreed to go to the Garden with her and afterward promised Kristen lunch at a restaurant. It became more and more evident that he intended to woo their daughter, Melanie was certain, to make sure of his hold on her. With Kristen firmly attached to him, how could she fight him?

"Kristen must be home in time for her nap," Aunt Pet reminded Ryan, quite ruffled at the idea of her grandniece spending the day with him and, more so, at her helplessness in preventing it.

"I am sure Melanie will have me do whatever is proper. You will come with us, won't you, Mother?" Ryan asked, his mocking gaze fixed pointedly at Melanie.

The thought of watching Ryan capture her daughter's heart so effortlessly for the entire morning repulsed her. "I had made other plans for the morning, sir. But I am sure even you can follow such simple instructions as having Kristen home by one-thirty."

"I'll have Megan go along," Aunt Pet decided aloud, not at all warm to the idea.

Ryan ignored his sister-in-law's intervention and, with a calculating look, smiled at Melanie. "Whatever it is, it cannot be so important as our marriage. After Kristen returns for her nap, I had hoped to go to the church to speak to the minister about our wedding this Christmas Eve."

Melanie dropped the spoon with a clatter against the china cup of coffee she was stirring, but she spoke with a placid grace that surprised him. "I was not aware there was such need for haste, sir."

177

"Indeed!" Aunt Pet denounced emphatically. "Why, I could not possibly make the arrangements on such short notice. The extra staff alone would be an impossibility to acquire on that particular day, and the printer needs at least two weeks advance notice for invitations."

"Melanie and I prefer a quiet ceremony, Petula." Ryan interrupted, placing his hand over Melanie's. "Just the family . . . right, darling?"

"Yes," Melanie replied icily.

"Can I be in the wedding?" Kristen asked excitedly. "I can wear my velvet then, can't I, Mama?"

"Your mother and I wouldn't think of having a wedding without you, sunshine," Ryan answered with a hug. "Right, darling?"

"Of course not."

Her helplessness was almost as infuriating as the way he watched her every reaction. How he was exalting in all this, she fumed inwardly. "But I cannot join you this morning. I have some errands at the school that must be taken care of while the girls are on vacation."

It was a lie. She didn't have to change the decorations in her room that very day. Mrs. Gravenor would have the school open the day before the young ladies returned, but it was the one act of defiance she could fling at him.

"Very well, then," Ryan conceded, but Melanie's victory was brief. "Since you are going to the school, you might as well tender your resignation. It's only fair to give the board as much notice as possible, since you'll not be returning after the holidays. The *Belle* will be leaving for Honolulu after the New Year."

"Oh dear God, I can't take any more!"

Aunt Pet's distressed cry distracted Melanie from her own reaction. With an accusing look at Ryan, she left the table and ran after the older woman, who had retreated in tears to the parlor. Melanie found her aunt collapsed in her favorite chair, her face buried in her hands. Her shoulders that were always straight and proud were now rounded in shaking anguish.

"I cannot bear it," she sobbed, clinging to the embrace Melanie offered. "It is bad enough that he"—the word *he* spoken as a curse—"comes to claim you and Kristen, but to take you away . . ." Her aunt's voice became hysterical, "Whatever will Gilbert and I do without you both?"

"You will go on as you did before," Melanie soothed her.

"But you and Kristen have brightened this house . . . those precious squeals of delight . . . I . . . she is as much my granddaughter as you are my daughter." Aunt Pet managed to stop crying long enough to blow her nose and then started again.

It was with mutual affection that the two women held each other. Melanie's own tears trickled down her cheeks as she patted her aunt's back and tried to find words of solace, but they eluded her. She could not imagine living apart from the family that had come to be her own, and she hated Ryan Caldwell even more for what he was doing to her.

This was a dismal day for her, Melanie thought later as she looked out the window, following Ryan and Kristen's progress down the street in the booby the family used when the streets were covered with snow. Although she could not see them, she could imagine the ecstatic joy on her daughter's face at showing her daddy off to the friends who had teased her. Part of her accepted that gratefully and part of her resented it.

With a frown, she let go of the drape and put on her wrap to go to the academy. Just to escape all the volatile emotion of the morning was enough to hurry her along. Priscilla came down the steps as she emerged from the parlor but did not reply to Melanie's greeting. With a resentful sniff, her cousin walked past her and into the dining room beyond. Allowing for the malady that had kept the young woman in bed through breakfast, Melanie thought little of it as she bade her aunt good-bye at the door and rushed out to catch the Little Green Car at the next block.

It was a chilly ride to the Back Bay area where Miss Gravenor's School for Girls was established. It was Melanie's fortune to see the light on in the upper floor office window, indicating that the school madame herself was working and that the building was open. She walked up the cobbled drive that circled in front of the school. The sun disappeared overhead, thick grey clouds having drifted in from the west, and a light dusting of snow began as Melanie closed the heavy oak door behind her and stomped her booted feet in the hallway.

Her room was cold, for no fire had been lit in the stove since last Friday. Melanie kept her coat on until the fire could catch up and the little stove began to afford some warmth to the classroom. The morning's events had been so disturbing that although she had gotten away to ponder them, she set them aside and buried herself in the task of taking down the holiday decorations that she and the children had made.

Hers was a melancholy mood when the boards were empty and the classroom was as barren as it had been on her first day there. She had so enjoyed the time she spent there, for she had felt a profound sense of accomplishment with each class she sent on its way to the upper grades. Her independence was going to be difficult to give up, she mused. Piqued, she sat down and wrote out her letter of resignation.

After packing the books her mother had given her and the items she had purchased and made over the course of her tenure, she set the box by the door, to be picked up later, and delivered her letter to Miss Gravenor. When she told the schoolmistress the content of the missive she handed over to her and the reasons behind it, the older woman was graciously understanding but was distressed that she had not had more notice, for not only would there be the difficulty of replacing Melanie, but she was certain the other staff members would regret not having had the chance to say good-bye.

The bell in the schoolhouse tower rang twice, announcing the hour of two, when Melanie caught the horse-drawn bus near the school. Her eyes widened in alarm, for she had taken much longer than anticipated at the academy and

Ryan would be waiting for her. With an obstinate purse of her lips, she thought, let him wait. He had waltzed in and disrupted her life and the lives of those she cared for, so a little inconvenience on his part would be well deserved. She might even stop at Charles Street and listen to the street corner carolers, she decided with stubborn defiance.

The cold air felt good on her face as she walked along, window-shopping. The scattered snowflakes that fell sporadically melted against her cheeks, turning them a decidedly Christmas red. Delivery pungs glided along the white snow-packed street, pulled by one- and two-horse teams. Young boys ran after them to hitch a free ride on the runners. Their shouts of "Cut, cut behind!" echoed above the din, but no driver begrudged them the play enough to wrap his whip about them.

The enticing smells coming from Chater's Bakery on the east side of Charles reminded Melanie that she'd had only had a half-eaten apple for breakfast, and she gave in to the urge to warm herself with a bowl of hot soup. Their lunch counter was not crowded as she took a seat and ordered the clam chowder featured on the chalkboard menu. The soup was served with a crackerlike biscuit, and Melanie ate every bit of it ravenously. For dessert she guiltily bought a sweet confection stuffed with cream and ate it as she walked toward the stop to catch the next car toward Beacon.

To her dismay, the wintry weather had intensified during her warm respite at the bakery and the bus was so full she could not find standing room. The sky was darkening prematurely and the temperature dropped accordingly, decreasing even more with the wind that picked up off the riverside. To avoid its chilling lashes, she backed under an awning against the front of the variety store and pondered her situation.

Home was several blocks away, but she supposed she could walk it. If she did not, she was likely to have to wait another hour for the next car. This was a fine fix, she chastised herself severely. She should have gone on home as she had started to. Deciding she'd as soon spend the hour walking as standing, she stepped away from the building and raised her arm to protect her face from the wind. In doing so, she blocked her vision of the gentleman emerging from the store and soundly knocked into him.

"Madame, forgive me!" the astonished patron apologized, reaching to steady her as she tried to regain her footing on the slippery surface.

Melanie raised her face to the victim of her recklessness and saw Professor Meyers. "Sam!"

"Melanie! What takes you out in this horrible weather?"

Melanie explained how she had been at the school and had stopped off at Charles Street to window-shop. "I really shouldn't have. I've missed the recent bus now and am forced to walk."

"I'll not have it," Sam objected indignantly. "I was running an errand for a friend and am certain he will not object if I use his cutter to deliver a lady in distress."

"I would be most indebted, sir."

The one-horse rig was parked on a side street. Sam helped Melanie in and tucked the heavy rug about her before climbing in the vehicle himself and taking up the reins. As they rode along, a dapper young man with a scarlet scarf wrapped about his neck pulled along beside them, challenging Sam to a race. The conservative professor declined the top-hatted sport with a shake of his head.

"I am always asked to race when I borrow Derby's vehicle. I believe the only reason these young bucks purchase them is for sport," he remarked with a wry chuckle.

"They do race a lot on Beacon Street, I've noticed," Melanie commented. She thought for a moment, torn between discretion and the urge to confide in a dear friend, then told him, "I've handed in my resignation, Sam."

"Then it's a sad loss for the academy, not to mention myself. I take it you are going off with your husband." Sam clicked his tongue at the horse and turned onto Beacon Street. He spoke to her over his shoulder, so she could not see his expression. But there was a pang of regret in his tone that saddened Melanie.

"I shall miss you, Sam. You have been a wonderful friend."

"And I shall miss you as well. I wish you—"

"Don't!" Melanie objected, unable to bear one more wish for happiness, especially when she knew the well-meaning wishes were for the impossible. Miss Gravenor's had been enough for one day. Her eyes misted and she looked away as Sam turned at the distress in her voice. "If one more person tells me how happy I am going to be, I shall scream."

Sam directed the horse to Number Eight and brought it to a halt. His face mirrored his sympathetic concern as he hopped down from the cutter and removed the blanket from Melanie's lap. He found her hands, squeezing them in brief consolation. "I was only being polite," he admitted. "Actually, I am gravely disturbed at this wretched turn of events. But I do not fault you. You did not know of your husband's existence." He lifted her hands to his lips. "And when I am sufficiently recovered from my disappointment, I promise, I shall pray for the happiness you do not seem to think possible. You see, Melanie, if you loved him once, you may come to love him again. One can only hope for the child's sake . . . as well as for your own."

Touched by his candor and sensitivity to her feelings, Melanie threw her arms about her friend and held him a moment before backing away. "I am richer for having met you, Sam," she confessed with a wistful smile. "Your kindness and understanding are an inspiration to me. Good day, dear friend, and thank you for everything."

Not wishing to prolong the punishment of the farewell, she turned away from the somber young man and ran up the steps to the house. The door swung open as she reached for the latch and Gilbert Caldwell stepped back to let her in. He took her snow-covered wrap and bonnet from her, handing them over to the doorman as she stomped heavily to shake off the ice that clung to her wet boots.

"Where on earth have you been, Melanie?"

Melanie glanced up from unlacing her boots. "I stopped off at Charles Street from the academy and missed the last transport. Sam was good enough to give me a ride home."

"Hmm," Gilbert acknowledged in a troubled tone. "Ryan is out looking for you. He's quite concerned."

Her eyes flashed. "Is he? Good!" She walked to the edge of the stairwell and sat unceremoniously on the steps to remove her wet footwear.

Gilbert followed her. "Melanie, I know you and Ryan are not on the best of terms. That is your affair, I realize. But my brother is used to—"

"—having things his way?" she finished, arching a challenging brow at the man standing before her. At his nod, she shrugged. "Then he might as well get used to the change, because I will not be dictated to like some slave. I am no longer the impressionable young girl he bullied about. I am a woman who is used to her independence, and that will come hard for me to give up. I won't give it up," she declared fiercely.

Gilbert stared at her in amazement. "I don't believe I've ever seen you quite so obstinate."

Melanie tossed her boots aside and got up. "Dear Gilbert," she smiled affectionately, "I don't believe you have ever vexed me as your brother has."

There was a gleam of humor in his green eyes as he pondered her words and his brother's reaction. "I wonder if my brother realizes—"

A cold rush of air filled the entrance as the front door burst open and the subject of their conversation stomped through, slamming it shut behind him. Like an angry bull, he charged straight for Melanie. His golden hair was flecked with rapidly melting snow, his overcoat nearly white with it. He stopped before her and seized her arms with wet gloved hands.

"Where in the hell have you been?"

Melanie leveled a cool gaze at him, refusing to be intimidated by his aggressive manner. "At the school and—"

"I went to the school and it was closed," he interrupted hotly.

"If you will stop ranting, I will give you the answer you

184

are so desperate to hear," she admonished sharply. She glanced down at the hands that held her arms disdainfully, then back to him, demanding release without saying a word.

Gilbert watched the scene, totally bemused as his brother dropped his hands. Theirs was a relationship he did not understand but hoped would work out. He could think of no woman he would rather see as his sister-in-law than Melanie, no better mate for his younger brother. But he wondered if the two independent spirits would ever reach the compromise necessary to make their marriage work.

"You're dripping on the carpet," Melanie reminded Ryan sternly.

Ryan's eyes glared as he began to rip off his overcoat.

"I'll take that, Ryan," Gilbert offered genially. "Then I think I'll see what Pet has in store for supper. The parlor may afford you two more privacy."

Taking his brother's tactful hint, Ryan ushered Melanie into the empty room and closed the doors behind them. His hair dripped melted snow onto his wind-reddened forehead as he stood with feet apart and demanded, "Well?"

Melanie turned her back to him to study the muss her bonnet had made of her hair in the gilded oval mirror on the wall. She spoke, nonplussed, as she rearranged the dark curls, securing them with pins.

"As I said, I went to the school and lost track of time. It was two when I left and—" she cut her eyes sideways to his reflection behind hers, "thinking it too late for your purpose, I went window-shopping." Her heart skipped a beat when he stepped up behind her, the front of his broad chest brushing the material at the back of her dress.

"So while I was waiting to go to the church, you thought you would go window-shopping!"

"You had done such a wonderful job of arranging my life thus far without my input, I hardly see what difference it made whether I went along or not," she shrugged indifferently.

"And that is where you met Sam Meyers?"

Her fingers froze in her hair. "Yes, it was," Melanie admitted stiltedly. For if Ryan knew she was with Sam, it had to be because he had seen her with him. Besides, in spite of the guilty flush of her cheeks, she had nothing to hide. "He kindly offered to bring me home when there was no room on the Green Car."

"How very convenient."

Melanie rose to the acetic slur. "Indeed it was. I was overjoyed at the chance to see my dear friend once more and say good-bye." With Ryan to her back and the pedestal table between her and the wall, she had little choice but to shove against him in order to gain freedom from his overwhelming presence.

But Ryan had no intention of letting her off so easily. He caught her waist and maneuvered her against the wall, his hands pressed on either side of her. "A dear *friend,*" he mocked, looking down into her eyes in cynical disbelief. "It was a rather touching parting."

"Professor Meyers did nothing out of the way, sir, if that is what you are insinuating!" Melanie declared heatedly in Sam's defense. "Unlike you, he is a man of honor and propriety."

"I doubt it not!" Ryan chuckled menacingly. "He is so uncommonly proper, he no doubt asked your permission to kiss you the night of the Apthorps' party."

"He did not, sir!" Melanie caught her breath at her blunder. How on earth could Ryan have known about Sam's boldness, unless . . . No! She would not entertain the idea that Sam had discussed her with Ryan at the Omega Club. Men!

Ryan bent over until his face was level with her own. "*Very* dear, this friend of yours." He tired of his game, for she could feel the heat of his gaze penetrating her eyes and spreading rapidly throughout her body. "But who could blame him for his thirst to drink the nectar of champagne from your lips, my sweet." His mouth moved even closer to her own, but Melanie could not bring herself to move. "The temptation has been on my mind ever since I saw you danc-

186

ing in his arms, a vision in royal, a ghost come to life," he murmured against her lips as he claimed them gently.

A breathless "No!" was all the protest she could utter, for the arms that had barricaded her escape now fully imprisoned her, his kiss sealing all verbal resistance. He drew her hips against him as he bent over her, forcing her back to the wall. Her mind screamed in panic, for although he did not hurt her, she recalled the terror of his last embrace.

In the background the grating sound of the pocket sliding door being shoved open, followed by her daughter's astonished "Daddy!" brought an abrupt end to her sweet torture. With a muffled curse, Ryan straightened, one arm still firmly about her waist as he faced Kristen and, with a rueful grin, moaned, "Caught by the light of my life in the act of kissing another woman! Can you ever forgive me, sunshine?"

"Daddy . . ." Kristen cackled at her father's outrageous admission. "It's all right to kiss *Mama* . . . but only if you kiss me, too!" The five-year-old barreled into them both, enveloping as much of them as her outstretched arms could hold.

Melanie managed to quell the dizziness that threatened to overcome her, clinging desperately to Ryan for support. As their daughter hugged them, he stole a look at her face, her pallor wiping away the quick smiling cover he had put on for the precious intruder.

"Why don't we sit on the sofa and I can have both my girls at my side while you tell your mama about our morning in the park," he suggested brightly to the little girl who jumped up and down to be picked up.

His arm never left Melanie's waist until she was seated against the high-tufted back of the brocade settee, then it cradled her shoulders firmly but gently. Melanie managed to smile as Kristen told her how her daddy had pushed her in the swings higher than all the other girls and how he had given them all piggyback rides, with Kristen, of course, getting the most. And then they had walked down by the river that was freezing over, and her daddy had said if it continued to freeze, he would take her ice-skating at the same place he had skated with Uncle Gilbert when they were little boys. Melanie nodded when the little girl asked if she would go, too, so that daddy could teach them both. And then they had had lunch at a cafe where they had hot chocolate covered with whipped cream and a cherry on top with their meal. And tomorrow daddy was going to take her to see the *Liberty Belle* and . . .

The way Kristen's eyes sparkled as she talked about Ryan and the way he himself listened as if mesmerized by the bigger-than-life character his daughter portrayed him to be eventually brought a real warmth to the shallow smile Melanie had mustered. She had been so caught up in her own world of the working mother that she had not given much thought to the void that no father had left in her daughter's life.

It was the only bright point concerning their impending marriage, but it was a very vital one. Melanie hardly realized it when she rested her head against his broad shoulder, her panic subsiding to something subtly deeper, and looked down lovingly at the little girl babbling away about the wonderful life ahead of them. For a little while, her mother, too, dreamed with her.

Chapter Twelve

Social calls nearly doubled that weekend. Aunt Pet was certain that the guests had come more out of curiosity than social protocol, to find out the whole shocking story about Mrs. Jeb Lyons and Capt. Ryan Caldwell. The kitchen staff was hard pressed to provide sufficient pastries and confections for the afternoon callers, and several pots of tea were served graciously by the hostess, who managed to parry their questions tactfully with the unexpected support of Ryan Caldwell.

Melanie did not recognize the charismatic cohost who fed the gossip-starved visitors with the tragic tale of his and Melanie's separation during the typhoon that had actually drawn them closer. His suffering at the presumed loss of the girl he had admittedly taken aboard his ship under false pretenses won him forgiveness for his deceit and more than one misty-eyed expression of sympathy. But everyone loves a tale with a happy ending, and there was no end to the heartfelt good wishes bestowed upon their reunited family.

There was little else to do except accept Ryan's devoted attention and return the warm smiles he often directed at her during his stirring account. In the midst of it all, if there was one who had not been favorably impressed with the Caldwell family's unusual predicament and was inclined to spread malicious rumor, Kristen won them over. The bright-eyed child never missed a chance to make the family that would be truly united on Christmas Eve a threesome.

Nor did Melanie have much opportunity in the week that followed to fret about the wedding that would dissolve all barriers between her and Ryan. The long sea journey ahead to the warm climate of her native Hawaii had to be prepared for. There were dresses to be ordered for Kristen, for she had outgrown last summer's wear, and the packing of Melanie's own gowns. The lone trunk that had held all her earthly belongings on her arrival in Boston would not begin to accommodate her wardrobe, so new trunks needed to be purchased as well.

Aunt Petula was able to help her immensely by turning the plans for the holiday meals over to Priscilla. Although Priscilla's mood had not changed overmuch since the morning after Ryan's arrival, she dutifully accepted the responsibility. Melanie could not fathom what she had done to alienate her cousin and tried to smooth over the difference between them to little avail. Aunt Pet insisted she pay it no heed, and if her aunt had any idea as to the cause of Priscilla's alienation, she gave no hint.

Aside from calling hours, Melanie was spared Ryan's company. Privacy in the big house was impossible, much to her relief, for she deliberately avoided being alone in a room with her intended husband. During the day, Ryan was either at the shipyard or at the offices of Caldwell Ltd. At night, he and Gilbert were often closeted in the library, settling business that would carry them through the next long period of his absence, Melanie assumed.

She could not complain about his treatment of her. When he was around her, he gave her every consideration, his ire over her day shopping apparently forgotten. He even took to heart her acid suggestion that he see to the marriage arrangements without her consultation and, accordingly, the nuptials were to take place at Trinity Church the afternoon of Christmas Eve. Afterward, a small dinner reception was being given for them at Number Eight Beacon Street by Gilbert and Aunt Pet, with only a few close family friends and associates invited.

Christmas Eve morning Kristen awakened Melanie before dawn, already dressed in the white velvet dress she was to wear in the wedding. Melanie coaxed her excited daughter into changing into one of her other dresses, lest she soil the beautiful velvet before the appointed hour, and sent her down to the kitchen to order a surprise breakfast for just the two of them to share in her room.

She felt as if a heavy chilling weight burdened her chest as she donned the robe Amanda Cummings and her friends had made her. It was quite light for the cold temperature of her room, but its sentimental value somehow managed to offset its inadequacy. She stoked the fire in the coal stove in her private parlor and sat next to its open door for warmth, staring blankly as it began to catch.

In a few hours she would be Ryan's wife. Her reactions were so varied and contrasting that she could make sense of none of them, except that she was uneasy and frightened at the prospect. To hear him speak of her to others, to bask in the glow of his green eyes as he did so, almost made her believe he had desperately sought to find her. And the more she saw him with Kristen, the more certain she was that she was doing the right thing for her daughter. She had seen the near worship in his eyes as he watched the little girl, unaware that he, too, was being observed.

But she could not bring herself to face the thought of him touching her, possessing her as husband. She had dreamed—no, had had nightmares about it. Her body had neither forgotten the ecstasy he had given it nor the humiliating agony he had inflicted upon it.

"Melanie? Melanie, dear?" Aunt Pet's voice outside the parlor door interrupted her troubled thoughts.

"Come in, Aunt Pet," Melanie called out, closing the door to the ornate little stove and moving the stool she had been sitting on away from it.

Aunt Pet's face was worried as she entered the room, her buxom figure clad in a heavy wool dressing gown and her head covered with her ruffled nightcap. "I saw Kristen in the hall, dear, and she said you were taking breakfast in your room. Are you ill?"

"No," Melanie denied with a shake of her head. She looked at her folded hands. "I suppose I am a bit nervous, but that's to be expected."

"Of course it is, dear," her aunt sympathized. The corners of her mouth twitched humorously. "I apologize, Melanie, but Kristen was so cute. She had dragged Ryan out of bed and was taking his breakfast order when I came across them." At Melanie's alarmed look, her aunt reassured her. "I straightened them both out by explaining to the little miss that it was bad luck for the groom to see the bride before the ceremony on the wedding day."

Although it was hardly appropriate in Melanie's particular case, that particular tidbit of information kept Kristen preoccupied the remaining hours until the wedding. Melanie could not step outside her room without her daughter first checking the halls to make sure Ryan was nowhere in sight. At one point, Aunt Pet insisted the little girl leave her mother in peace to bathe and dress, but Melanie assured her aunt that Kristen was no trouble. In fact, she drew strength from her daughter's constant presence.

As the hour of departure neared, Priscilla sent the upstairs maid, a young French girl named Lisette, to help Melanie dress. Not wishing to offend her cousin for the first civil act she had demonstrated toward her recently, Melanie invited the girl in and submitted to her heavily accented fluster. Most of the wealthier homes boasted a French maid on the second-floor staff in order that the ladies of the house might practice their French and improve their fluency. In Melanie's case, she was certain the well-meaning Lisette was practicing her English on her, and the help was tedious at best.

When Melanie emerged from her room, it was almost a relief to be going to the church. She rushed down the hall in the tea gown she had chosen to wear, in spite of Aunt Pet's reservation that it would be too informal, its delicate train slung over her arm. The lighter gauze material, a rose floral

MORE PASSION AND ADVENTURE AWAIT... YOUR TRIP TO A BIG ADVENTUROUS WORLD BEGINS WHEN YOU ACCEPT YOUR FIRST 4 NOVELS ABSOLUTELY *FREE*
(AN $18.00 VALUE)

Accept your Free gift and start to experience more of the passion and adventure you like in a historical romance novel. Each Zebra novel is filled with proud men, spirited women and tempestuous love that you'll remember long after you turn the last page.

Zebra Historical Romances are the finest novels of their kind. They are written by authors who really know how to weave tales of romance and adventure in the historical settings you love. You'll feel like you've actually gone back in time with the thrilling stories that each Zebra novel offers.

GET YOUR FREE GIFT WITH THE START OF YOUR HOME SUBSCRIPTION

Our readers tell us that these books sell out very fast in book stores and often they miss the newest titles. So Zebra has made arrangements for you to receive the four newest novels published each month.

You'll be guaranteed that you'll never miss a title, and home delivery is so convenient. And to show you just how easy it is to get Zebra Historical Romances, we'll send you your first 4 books absolutely FREE! Our gift to you just for trying our home subscription service.

BIG SAVINGS AND FREE HOME DELIVERY

Each month, you'll receive the four newest titles as soon as they are published. You'll probably receive them even before the bookstores do. What's more, you may preview these exciting novels free for 10 days. If you like them as much as we think you will, just pay the low preferred subscriber's price of just $3.75 each. *You'll save $3.00 each month off the publisher's price.* AND, your savings are even greater because there are never any shipping, handling or other hidden charges—FREE Home Delivery. Of course you can return any shipment within 10 days for full credit, no questions asked. There is no minimum number of books you must buy.

4 FREE BOOKS

TO GET YOUR 4 FREE BOOKS WORTH $18.00 — MAIL IN THE FREE BOOK CERTIFICATE T O D A Y

Fill in the Free Book Certificate below, and we'll send your FREE BOOKS to you as soon as we receive it.

If the certificate is missing below, write to: Zebra Home Subscription Service, Inc., P.O. Box 5214, 120 Brighton Road, Clifton, New Jersey 07015-5214.

FREE BOOK CERTIFICATE

4 FREE BOOKS

ZEBRA HOME SUBSCRIPTION SERVICE, INC.

YES! Please start my subscription to Zebra Historical Romances and send me my first 4 books absolutely FREE. I understand that each month I may preview four new Zebra Historical Romances free for 10 days. If I'm not satisfied with them, I may return the four books within 10 days and owe nothing. Otherwise, I will pay the low preferred subscriber's price of just $3.75 each; a total of $15.00, *a savings off the publisher's price of $3.00.* I may return any shipment and I may cancel this subscription at any time. There is no obligation to buy any shipment and there are no shipping, handling or other hidden charges. Regardless of what I decide, the four free books are mine to keep.

NAME

ADDRESS _____ APT _____

CITY _____ STATE ____ ZIP _____

( )
TELEPHONE

SIGNATURE _____ (if under 18, parent or guardian must sign)

Terms, offer and prices subject to change without notice. Subscription subject to acceptance by Zebra Books. Zebra Books reserves the right to reject any order or cancel any subscription.

109002

print, floated in the air over the white silk liner. Velvet ribbons of deeper rose were woven through the lace that ruffled the low décolletage and high back. The princess waist and flounced hem were adorned with the same ruffle and larger velvet bows at each drape of the hemline.

Suddenly the door to Kristen's nursery burst open and her daughter ran out to block her way. "Mama!" Kristen protested loudly. "Daddy is downstairs. He'll see you!"

"No he isn't, sweetheart," Gilbert Caldwell called from the foyer on the first floor. "It's not only safe to come down, but prudent. I fear we are going to hold up the ceremony." Gilbert's face lit up as he watched Melanie and her daughter descend the steps hand in hand. "My dears, you are breathtaking!" He took Melanie's hand as she reached the bottom step and kissed it. "My brother is a lucky man indeed."

"What about me?" Kristen demanded imperiously. Dressed in her white velvet dress with the wide contrasting red cummerbund, she was adorable. Matching red slippers and white longstockings completed the ensemble.

Gilbert feigned horror. "Forgive me, miss. I quite forgot myself."

As he attended to her small gloved hand, Kristen giggled. "Oh, Uncle Gilbert!"

The ride to the church in the plush upholstered booby did not take long, which was just as well, for with Melanie, Kristen, and the three Caldwells, it was quite crowded. Aunt Pet cross-examined Priscilla on the details of the wedding supper, which was to be a buffet in order to accommodate the growing list that eventually outgrew the dining room capability. The parlor had been cleared of the carpet and the furniture placed along the wall so that a pianist could furnish music for dancing afterward.

When Gilbert walked her down the long center aisle of the church, Melanie's fingers clutched his arm more firmly than she realized. The pat of his hand on hers and his reassuring smile somehow managed to restore reason to the mind that was nearly frozen in panic. She could see no one but Ryan, tall and virilely elegant in a cutaway coat and narrow tapered trousers, not even the gruff Amos Cobb who stood at his side in his best store-bought suit.

It was only Amos's muffled "Sweet Jee . . . hosophat," which changed in midstream with an apologetic glance at the frowning minister, that temporarily distracted her enough to nod to the bearded first mate in equally startled recognition.

Kristen took her place proudly at her side, her normal bubbling demeanor as somber as the occasion dictated. During the ceremony, which Melanie went through mechanically, the child occasionally peeked around her mother's skirts at her father and Amos Cobb, but only the first mate noticed, for Ryan did not take his eyes off Melanie's pale face. At the minister's blessing to kiss the bride, Ryan took Melanie in his arms and softly touched his lips to hers.

As they turned to face the small assembly that cheered at the announcement of Mr. and Mrs. Ryan Caldwell, Melanie caught sight of a movement in the back of the church. A woman, clad in a hooded dark green cape, slipped through the doors in a hasty retreat. Melanie did not need to see her face to know that the woman was Arabella Harrington, but she had little time to digest the knowledge before she and Ryan were bombarded with congratulations.

Ryan's rented coach delivered the new family back to Beacon Street, where the drive was lined with the vehicles of the guests Aunt Pet had invited to the reception. In the dense afternoon fog, every window of the house was ablaze with lights of welcome celebration. On the front steps, to Kristen's squeals of glee, Ryan swept Melanie off her feet and carried her through the door and into his family home. Caught unawares, Melanie was flushed with embarrassment when he set her on her feet in the foyer and kissed her once more for the benefit of those who did not attend the wedding.

The bride and groom were soon separated. The men gravitated toward the refreshment table, where a uniformed servant served champagne, liebfraumilch, burgundy, and assorted cordials, as well as French brandy and cognac. The women all gathered about Melanie to see the expensive ring Ryan had slipped on her finger during the ceremony, a large diamond set in a circle of glittering sapphires on a band of ornately engraved gold.

"It belonged to Ryan's mother," Aunt Pet informed them, her pale blue eyes twinkling with affection. "His father gave it to her on their Christmas Eve wedding at the same church."

"How positively romantic!" one of the admirers sighed.

"I do suppose he has some redeeming qualities," Petula Caldwell reluctantly admitted, draping an arm over Melanie's shoulders. "After all, he had the good sense to marry my niece."

Even Melanie had to chuckle at her aunt's words, from surprise if nothing else. Aunt Petula and Ryan waged war daily, in which Gilbert served as the mediator. The wedding itself was a compromise of wills, Ryan insisting the ceremony be kept to family and Aunt Pet holding firmly to the belief that Melanie should not be denied the presence of those who had come to know and love her in her past six years in Boston.

Priscilla outdid herself with the delicious buffet. Pâtés of every description, stuffed chicken breasts in sauce, rolled marinated filets of beef on skewers with vegetables, served over a bed of curried rice, roast duckling basted in an orange sauce, and sautéed shad roe set a royal table. Throughout the downstairs rooms, platters of cheeses, pickles, olives, and other hors d'oeuvres were set out to temper the effects of the bountiful wines and liquors.

Although Melanie was the bride, Priscilla herself won her own share of the attention at the piano, playing sprightly music for the dancers. Besieged by willing partners, Melanie eventually managed to plead exhaustion and found an inconspicuous spot in the parlor. She tapped her toe to the music as she relaxed with her second glass of wine and watched her daughter skip to Gilbert's shortened steps of a polka. It was Kristen's special day as well. Her golden curls bounced down her back as she tossed back her head with gay laughter. When the dance was done, Gilbert was promptly replaced by another beau.

"She's absolutely tireless, our daughter," Ryan observed wryly at Melanie's side, startling her with his unexpected appearance.

"Wait until we try to put her to bed," Melanie responded with a rueful grin. "I fear we'll have our hands full. She has a frightful temper at times, especially when she's overtired."

A mocking golden brow arched in feigned horror. "Like her mother?"

"Like her father," Melanie countered with a smug twist of her lips.

Ryan gathered her to him suddenly with a low growl. "For that, madame, you shall pay." He smiled down at her, adding with rakish charm, "With a waltz for now."

The remark had been made in fun, Melanie realized, but that fact did nothing to inhibit the spark of apprehension fanned by it. Tonight he intended to take her as his wife in every sense of the word. It was in his eyes, the way they hungrily devoured her as he swept her about the dance floor that had cleared for the bride and groom. She was totally in his grasp now. He controlled her life as he controlled her in the dance, expertly guiding her through the graceful steps with practiced ease. His closeness, the strong male scent of him, and the powerful body that moved with hers all served to reinforce his superiority. She foundered in it and, when the dance was gratefully ended, needed the arms about her until she could assemble her panic-stricken wits.

Mistaking the way she leaned against him, her breath shallow and rapid, her husband bent over and promised against her lips, "Later, my sweet."

The guests began to politely make their excuses at a reasonable hour. Melanie managed to slip away under the pretext of getting Kristen ready for bed, leaving Ryan to see them off. As she predicted, Kristen was in no way ready to go to sleep. Her eyes were overbright as she bounced on the bed, but she was not cross. Instead, she was hyperactive from the excitement of the day and the confections she had been popping into her mouth with unsupervised license.

Melanie sent for some warm milk and, with her daughter in her lap, settled in the parlor to read from a book of Kristen's favorite stories. She hoped the combination would eventually have a sedating effect on the child. But Kristen was too enthralled by the party to listen and kept interrupting Melanie to tell her about this particular dance or that particularly funny thing one of the guests did.

"And everybody said you and Daddy were the handsomestest couple . . ."

"Handsomest," Melanie corrected, interrupting with the ultimate threat to settle a child on Christmas Eve. "Kristen, you are going to have to calm down. You realize tonight Santa Claus comes and what would he think to find you babbling on like this?"

"But, Mama," Kristen replied, wrapping her arms about Melanie's neck, "I got my birthday wish for Christmas!" She hugged Melanie tightly. "I got my daddy, and I don't care about candy or toys or anything else."

Melanie returned the hug, clinging to Kristen for the nourishment of her troubled mind. For Kristen, she told herself firmly. For Kristen, if for nothing else, she must try to make their marriage work. "I love you, darling," she whispered against her daughter's cheek, her eyes misty with affection.

"Can we wait for Daddy to tuck me in?"

Ryan's voice sounded from the door behind them, causing both of them to start. "No need to wait, sunshine."

"Daddy!" Kristen admonished, holding her hand to her heart dramatically. "You scared us!"

"Did I now?" Ryan mused, his gaze moving past Kristen, as he picked the child up, to meet Melanie's. "Well, I was rendered speechless at the door when I came upon two such lovely creatures as this and just had to stand there a while." He carried his light bundle of ruffles and flannel over to the bed and dropped her onto the mattress with a bounce. "Tucking in is a new experience for me, Mother. Is this how we do it?"

Kristen cackled as Ryan threw the covers over her head and tucked them around her tightly. "Daddy! I can't move or breathe!" She wriggled the covers off her and looked up at him with large blue eyes framed in a mass of golden curls. "Just up to my neck and not so tight," she instructed him through giggles. When he had obeyed, she held out her hand to Melanie. "Now, Mama must sit here," she said, patting the other side of the mattress, "and you must sit on this side to tell me a bedtime story."

Ryan looked at Melanie quizzically. "Do we do this every night?"

Melanie smiled. "Megan usually does the story and I do the tucking."

"But this is Christmas," Kristen pointed out, "and a special night."

Ryan looked at Melanie again, his green eyes kindling meaningfully with warmth. "So it is, sunshine," he answered his daughter. "Now let me see . . . a story . . ."

Melanie rested her back against the white iron headboard, cushioned with the spare pillow, as the fair-haired man began to spin a tale that captivated not only Kristen but Melanie, too, as she recognized her part in it.

"There was a pirate called Lion, because of his thick mane of golden hair, and one day he saw a beautiful native girl named Meilani while he was in port with his men. Now, his being a scoundrel, he tricked the lovely Meilani into coming aboard his ship and he sailed away with her."

"I would have kicked his chins!" Kristen snorted indignantly.

"She did worse than that," Ryan told his daughter, eyes twinkling with mischief. "And the pirate didn't know what to do with her. He tried telling her what to do and that didn't work. It only made her angry and made her cry. And he didn't want that. You see, he really wasn't as bad as she thought he was."

"Why didn't he just say he was sorry and take her home?"

Ryan inhaled deeply and slowly let out his breath. "He tried in his own way, and he was going to let her go when

198

they got back to land. But something happened that even he didn't realize until it was too late."

"What, Daddy?" The little girl's eyes were no closer to sleep than Melanie's.

"They got to know each other and the pirate could have sworn Meilani liked him as much as he liked her."

"They fell in love," Kristen sighed.

Ryan gave Melanie a wistful smile. "Something like that. But when they got back to shore and it was time for the pirate to let her go, he didn't want to. They had a terrible argument. . . ."

"Because she wanted to go?" Kristen injected.

"Yes. And the pirate was so hurt because of that, that he wanted to hurt her. So he locked her up until he could change her mind." Ryan's face was deadly serious as he went on. "He thought and thought about what he had done and discovered the reason he didn't want her to go was because he more than liked her. He loved her and wanted her to stay with him. But when he went down to tell her, she was gone."

"Where?"

"He didn't know. But he thought she had drowned trying to swim to shore."

"Like Mommy thought you did," Kristen commented. Temporarily distracted, she raised up on her elbows. "I can swim," she told him proudly. "Mommy takes me to the shore every summer and I can ride on the waves, if she's with me."

"Then you'll like our plantation, for it has a beach on its south side."

Kristen dropped back against her pillow with an ecstatic sigh. "I just can't wait to live there." Her smile faded suddenly. "Did the pirate ever find her?" At Ryan's hesitation, she added, "I don't like unhappy endings, Daddy."

Melanie's heart melted as Ryan leaned over and hugged the little girl. "Then why don't we let you make up the ending," he suggested, "and then it's to sleep with you."

Kristen put her finger to her chin and screwed up her face in thought. "We . . . ell," she drawled, "He went ashore with all his men and looked in every house in the town. And when he still couldn't find her, he went to church to pray for God's help." Her face brightened. "And guess who was there?"

"She wasn't!" Ryan denied with a teasing look of doubt.

"She was," Melanie nodded as Ryan questioned her comment silently.

"Mama, *I'm* telling this story!" Kristen objected with a frustrated heave of her chest. She tugged on Ryan's arm, dragging his attention from Melanie. "Anyway, Mama was right. The girl was there and so was the preacher, and they got married and lived happily ever after."

"Sounds good to me." Ryan winked at Melanie before bussing his daughter on the forehead. "Good night, sunshine."

"Night, Daddy. Mama?" Upon receiving Melanie's kiss, she sighed, "I'm so glad you and Daddy stopped playing games and found each other."

"I'm glad for you, darling," Melanie told her, avoiding the green gaze cast her way from the other side of the bed. "Now you go right to sleep, because Santa might even be in the neighborhood right now."

"How long will it take her to close her sweet little eyes?" Ryan asked, having followed Melanie through the parlor to her room.

"Well, Megan's room is just on the other side of the nursery, so she'll keep her in her room if she decides to get up for something," Melanie answered quietly, closing the door behind her husband. "I think it's safe to go on downstairs and get her things. . . ."

She halted as she saw the covers turned back and a man's dressing robe beside her gown on the bed. A familiar trunk lay butted to the foot of the bed and next to it a pair of boots. On the lamp table near the window sat a bottle of champagne and two glasses. At the touch of Ryan's hands at her waist she spun away from him, backing toward the door. Her face had gone white and panic widened her eyes.

"I . . . it's Christmas Eve," she stammered, coming to a halt against the wood paneled door. "We have to play Santa."

Ryan closed the distance between them in two easy strides. "I won't pretend to understand this. Did you expect to continue sleeping in separate beds, Melanie?" His expression was neither hostile nor friendly, but inscrutable.

Melanie shook her head. "No, but we must—"

"Gilbert and your aunt have already taken care of the stocking," Ryan interrupted impatiently. "They know where you hid her things."

"Oh." Her remark was lame, but she could not think further than that. The moment she had most dreaded was upon her, for she could see that Ryan was near his patience's end. He had given her and her child his name, righting in his mind the injustice he had dealt her. Now he expected what was his right as her husband. Kristen's words about playing games echoed in her mind and she drew herself upright, determined to try. "Then I suppose we should be getting ready for bed."

She ducked under Ryan's arm and walked over to the dresser, her hands attempting to unfasten the hook at the high neck of her gown. Silently cursing Lisette for managing to tangle it in the threads that formed the eye, she struggled with it until fingers warmer than her own took over. The cool rush of air chilled her skin as her gown parted at the back and caught on her underskirt.

"I can manage now, thank you," she told him, meeting his diverted gaze in the mirror with an innocent plea.

When Ryan obliged her by leaving her to her own ministrations, Melanie snatched up the lace peignoir set Aunt Pet had given her and hastily retreated behind the Oriental dressing screen. It had to be her nerves, for her fingers would not work on the ties of her bustle and laces of her bodice. By the time she had divested herself of her undergarments and donned the ivory lace gown, her skin was covered with a thin film of perspiration, despite the cooler bedroom temperature.

Its princess lines skimmed her body, silhouetting it in the translucent lace. The bodice was scooped low in the front and back in a Juliet fashion, and gathered with a satin ribbon under her breasts. As Melanie tied it, she noticed the darker circles of her bosom, visible through the thin material, and she blushed profusely, shocked at her aunt's selection. She pulled on the dressing gown in a rush and tied the ribbons at the front.

The uncorking of the champagne bottle heralded her emergence from the screen. Ryan stood clad in a dark loden robe that fell open at his chest, revealing the thick curling mat of hair she recalled shining golden against a bronzed chest in the tropical sun. Her heart fluttering like that of a wild bird, she walked over to her dressing table and sat down. She watched in the mirror as he filled two glasses with champagne, her fingers picking nervously at the silk rosettes Lisette had pinned in her hair.

She stiffened as the satin lapel of his robe grazed her back when he placed her glass of champagne on the table in front of her. His eyes rested heatedly on the thin bodice that Melanie could have sworn revealed more to him than the mirror showed, but instead of taunting her, he smiled crookedly at her scarlet color and meandered over to the bed. It creaked under his weight as he sat back against the headboard and contented himself with watching her.

"You know, for the first time I am beginning to rejoice that you cut your hair," he remarked when she had finished the last of the champagne he had poured and had run the brush once more through her shoulder-length tresses. "Were it still waist-length, the dawn would see us exactly as we are now."

Realizing that she had exhausted his patience, Melanie put the brush down and closed her eyes. She heard the creak of the bed and his footsteps light upon the carpet as he came up behind her. His hands came to rest on her shoulders, his fingers working the tight muscles that would not relax, even under the influence of the champagne.

"I believe my beautiful wife is suffering the same malady that befalls many brides on their wedding night, although I had not anticipated this," he admitted, his lips in a grimace of a smile.

He reached over her shoulder and turned out the lamp, flooding the room in darkness aside from the tiniest bit of light cast through the shuttered windows. Melanie rose quietly at the mute coax of his hand upon her own and allowed him to lead her to the bed. She made no effort to stop him as he sought the pretty satin bow she had tied at the bodice of her robe, but it took all her concentration to keep from bolting away.

The tension between them seemed to grow with the silence as he slid the robe off her shoulders and let it fall to the floor. She heard him inhale the scent of the soap she had used to shampoo her hair, the same concoction her mother continued to make and send to her along with her biannual letters. His breath was hot as he spoke against her neck.

"You are wearing the same perfume you wore your first night on the *Belle*."

She was taken aback that he recalled such a minute detail. "It—it's made from the same flowers I wore . . . the hibiscus."

"I thought you were the most exquisite creature I had ever seen that night, but as I watched you earlier with Kristen, I find you've grown even more captivating. Motherhood becomes you, Melanie." His hand glided over the curves of her hips as the other spread against her back. The brush of his cheek against her own as he sought her lips was slightly abrasive, his smooth morning shave having begun to grow once more.

"Ryan, please!" Melanie turned her head away from the lips that found her mouth in the darkness. She placed her hands against his chest and rested her cheek on his shoulder as he stiffened. "Please talk to me."

Although she could not see his face, she could feel his eyes upon her. It was terribly confusing the way her body leaned against his, seeking the warmth of his flesh where the robe had parted, and yet she could not bear the thought of him touching her in any other way. She wanted his arms about her, she needed their comfort and understanding, yet she feared anything more intimate.

"What do you want me to say, Melanie?" His voice reflected the strain that tightened the coiling muscles of his chest and arms. At her silence, he suggested, "Perhaps you'd best do the talking . . . but in bed under the covers would be best. I feel a distinct chill coming on."

The abrupt absence of his warmth shocked her as he left her, and climbed into the bed. She stood at the side of the bed, staring blankly at his shadow, barely perceptible against the white flannel sheets. "I . . . are you on your side?" She bent over to feel her way cautiously.

"Oh, for God's sake, get in here!"

Melanie gasped as her wrist was seized and yanked, pulling her headlong into the soft feather bed. With one arm under her and her body partially covered with his own, Ryan snatched up the heavy quilts and embraced her in a human cocoon. The overwhelming closeness, the muscled entrapment, smothered out the last flicker of reason and Melanie began to fight him desperately.

"Melanie!" Ryan growled, pinning her under his weight and shaking her. "Damnation, what is wrong with you?"

Melanie thrashed her head from side to side, her pulse beating erratically in her temples. She was no longer in her own bed but on the hard mattress of the bunk, with Ryan forcing his weight upon her, her arms held fast with his hands. Her eyes grew large with terror at the heavy shadow hovering over her.

"Don't . . ." she whimpered, her body trembling beneath him. "Dear God, please don't."

"Don't what?" Ryan's voice exploded in her ears. "I was only trying to cover you up! It's December, woman, and whether you realize it or not, your skin is like ice."

His words managed to penetrate her frenzy. Feeling miserably foolish, Melanie inhaled shakily and tried to will her body still. But for that very brief moment, she had panicked. She no longer fought him, but her muscles continued to quiver with each ragged breath she took.

"I . . . I'm sorry, Ryan," she said when she could finally speak. "I promise, I shall try to be a good wife to you . . .

for Kristen's sake. But I need more time to get to know you."

His body jerked with a laugh devoid of humor. "Melanie, I can think of no better place than this to get to know someone!"

"But when you touch me like that," she said, her voice bordering on hysteria at the cup of his hand under her breast, "all I can feel is the terror of the last time you did so . . . and I am so frightened of you I cannot bear it!"

A sob wrenched from her chest at the agonized admission that made the body next to her grow rigid. Ryan rolled away from her, as if he had been burned by her words, and lay still at the far side of the bed. Aside from the rapid breaths he forced through his nostrils, Melanie might have thought him vanished. When the silence of room grew to unbearable proportions, he spoke, his voice low and even.

"In that case, madame, I think it best that I find other accommodations for the evenings until such time as you find yourself . . . *comfortable* as my wife."

He tossed back the covers on his side of the bed to rise, when Melanie stayed his hand. "Ryan, I didn't mean—"

"Your request is not unreasonable under the circumstances, Melanie. I assure you, I am not angry." He removed her hand from his taut arm and kissed it before rising abruptly.

"Ryan, I didn't mean you to leave me!" she called out, confused by what she really did mean. She scrambled out of the bed and padded across the chilly carpet to where he pulled on his clothing. "Ryan, I—I need you."

He looked hard at her as he fastened his trousers and then sat on the edge of the trunk to don his boots. "For what purpose, madame?" he grunted sharply as he pulled them up and stepped into them.

"To hold me?" she sniffed in uncertainty, tentatively snaking her arms about him.

Her skin was covered with gooseflesh as she lay her head against his starched shirt, seeking his reassurance. And when he scooped her up in his arms and carried her back to

205

the bed, she cuddled against him in relief. But as he deposited her on the bed and tucked the heavy quilts around her, she realized it had been premature.

"Ryan . . ." she broke off, silenced with as brief kiss.

"Now you *are* being unreasonable," he told her sternly. Then, softening his voice, he bade her "Good night, blue eyes" and left the room.

Chapter Thirteen

Melanie was awake and dressed when Kristen charged into her room Christmas morning. The fact that she had hardly slept showed in the circles under her eyes. Although she was on the second floor, she had sensed the opening of the front door. Hurrying to the window, Melanie had seen Ryan's lone figure walking down the lamp-lit street, until he had disappeared into the darkness. Throughout the remainder of the night, she had tossed and turned between fits of cursing herself for her foolishness and despairing over the fact that her husband had spent his wedding night in Arabella Harrington's arms.

"Where's Daddy?"

And now another type of despair ensued, one that made the other small in comparison as she hugged her daughter. "Darling, he's—"

"—right here in the parlor, having been completely ignored by his own daughter as she barreled past. Where's the fire, sunshine?"

"Daddy," Kristen chided, pulling free from Melanie's embrace and running to the man in the doorway. "It's Christmas morning! And Megan said she heard the door open last night and thinks it might have been Santa Claus! Why don't we go see?" the little girl suggested excitedly.

"Why not?" Ryan agreed amicably. He hoisted his daughter up in one arm and held out the other to Melanie. "Mother?"

Melanie had to check the tears of relief that misted her eyes and govern the urge that made her want to charge across the room to him like her daughter. Last night she had feared that she had driven him away forever. The reason for his return was evident as he bounced Kristen on his hip and teased her about finding coal in her stocking. Melanie's earlier reservations that he used Kristen merely to exact revenge upon herself completely dissolved as she basked in the newfound love so obvious between the father and his offspring.

"I have never in all my life had coal left in my stocking!" Kristen denied indignantly upon reaching the bottom of the steps. Her rosy lips puckered peevishly. "You are a divil of a tease!" she accused Ryan, repeating Megan's constant reprimand of herself.

Ryan's belly laugh filled the hallway, bringing Gilbert Caldwell and his wife out of the dining room with greetings of "Merry Christmas!" Gilbert gave Melanie two kisses— one, he said, for his niece, and one for his new sister-in-law. Aunt Pet surprised even Ryan with a loud buss on his cheek, after which she primly informed him that he needed to shave.

"Has anybody been in the parlor?" Kristen demanded pitifully, unable to stand the wait any longer.

"Why, I do believe Auntie Pris is doing some cross-stitch by the hearth," Aunt Pet answered, drawing her cheeks in to smother her amusement. "Why do you ask, dear?"

"I am starved," Gilbert announced cruelly. "How about a nice hot breakfast?"

Kristen put her hands to her temples with the most pitiful wail. "Oh, I hope I never get so old I forget Santa Claus!"

"Oh!" Gilbert groaned, slapping his hand to his forehead. "So that's the old coot I showed to the door last night." At Kristen's look of absolute horror, he added mischievously, "With all the cookies his fat belly could hold and a bottle of milk."

This was too much for the little girl to bear. Kristen grabbed Ryan's shirt with a squeal, "He was here!" Unable

208

to hold his squirming daughter any further, Ryan let her slide down his leg to the ground and followed with the group as she scampered across the foyer and slung aside the paneled doors to the parlor. "Auntie Pris, are you blind? Didn't you see my stocking?"

Kristen stood transfixed before the hearth when they entered the room, staring with sparkling eyes at the mantel where she had hung her stocking the day she'd helped Melanie decorate. "In case Santa should come early," she'd explained to her mother. The stocking, a larger one that Priscilla had knitted for her, bulged at the sides, but the little girl was enchanted with the one item that would not fit in it and sat just above on the mantel.

"A gingerbread house!" the child exclaimed in awe. "A real gingerbread house!" She turned to face the adults, her arms folded across her chest to contain her delight. "I'm going to eat it just a little at a time to make it last forever!"

There was no coaxing Kristen into any breakfast. She was too enthralled with the treats she discovered in her stocking. Besides the delicious candy and fruits, she discovered a silk embroidered purse just like her mother's best, only smaller and a small brass telescope. It was all Melanie and Megan could both do to get her dressed for church, for each time they'd leave her unattended, she was at a window peering out at the neighborhood.

Ryan could have acted no more devoted a husband when, after the services, they were once more inundated with congratulations. His arm about Melanie as the family traveled back home for the afternoon of exchanging gifts and the traditional Christmas dinner they shared with the household staff only served to make her more miserable for the way she had denied him.

The parlor was closed off from the rest of the hubbub of activity so that the family could exchange their gifts in private while the staff made the final dinner preparations. Everyone agreed to start with the youngest, much to Kristen's satisfaction. She received mostly summer clothing for the trip ahead from Gilbert and Aunt Pet, and matching outfits made by her Auntie Pris for her doll. Raised under Aunt Pet's heavy influence concerning fashion, she was quite tickled with the pretty dresses, particularly the yachting attire that amused Ryan to no end.

"She's traveling on a coal freighter, Pet," Ryan snorted, his eyes twinkling as he gave his brother a conspiratorial wink and teased, "not a blooming yacht!"

"Nevertheless, she shall be properly attired!" Aunt Pet responded good-naturedly.

"I wonder what your aunt would have said had she seen you as I first did," Ryan whispered wickedly into Melanie's ear.

She could not resist taking part in the merriment. "Behave!" Melanie chided, enjoying the retaliatory squeeze of her shoulders for her harmless slap on his cheek.

But it was the small pair of ice skates Ryan had insisted he and Melanie give Kristen that brought the loudest shriek of glee. It was inevitable that the skates came with a promise to take her ice-skating the next day, since the river had frozen and Ryan had seen several young folks out the day before. Kristen put them on under the pretense of having to practice and wobbled about on the carpet much to Aunt Pet's dismay.

"Kristen, you are going to break your neck! I must insist you take them off," Aunt Pet declared in exasperation after the child had grabbed one of the tables to keep from falling, toppling an Oriental vase. Thankfully it did not break, but the fright was enough.

"You can skate all you want tomorrow," Ryan reminded the little girl whose lips began to pout in defiance, "provided you can act like a polite young lady today."

Melanie recognized the stubborn jut of Kristen's chin as the child leveled a steady blue-eyed gaze at her father. There was no doubt in her mind that her daughter was measuring Ryan to see if he would indeed hold true to his words, for he had not yet crossed her. Apparently, Ryan also recognized it for what it was and narrowed his eyes.

"Your mother looked at me exactly the same way when

210

she considered disobeying me, and I had to soundly spank her to make her listen."

Kristen's gasp was echoed by Melanie's, but Aunt Pet's indignant "Indeed!" drowned them both out. "Putting such nonsense in that child's head, sir. You should be ashamed of yourself! Come sit over here by me, dear, and we'll finish opening our presents."

Kristen went to Aunt Pet eagerly, for she wasn't as certain that Ryan had been pulling her leg as Petula Caldwell was. It was Priscilla's snicker at the child's stolen glances at Ryan that touched off the laughter needed to diffuse the situation. Aunt Pet fussed as she untied the skates, saying that it was foolish to have bought them when the child would be leaving the next week anyway. Melanie forgot her irritation over Ryan's explicit threat when she saw her aunt sniff and dab her eyes with a handkerchief.

"Actually, Petula, Melanie and I aren't going quite as early as we'd planned." Ryan grinned, looking like the cat who'd swallowed the goldfish as all eyes came to rest upon him. He nodded to his brother and leaned back against the sofa, drawing Melanie with him. "Go on, Gilbert. I'm not taking all the fire."

Gilbert Caldwell cleared his throat awkwardly. "Well, as you know, Ryan and I have been talking a good deal lately about land on Oahu. And it seems Ryan has not only purchased a plantation, but a large home in Honolulu. It's quite an investment, actually. I think we could easily gain—"

"My brother the accountant," Ryan interrupted wryly. "In simple terms, New England winters are hard on Gilbert's health, you women are sniveling because you're going to miss each other, and I have two homes. What Gilbert is trying to say is that he has agreed to bring the whole family to Honolulu to see if you like it. I'm going to hold the *Belle* over another month and we'll all go."

Aunt Pet's hands flew to her cheeks in shock. "Leave Boston?" she murmured, looking at Gilbert for affirmation.

"Oh!" Kristen gasped, throwing her little arms about

Aunt Pet's shoulders. "Isn't it the most wonderful idea in the whole world? You can get a dress just like mine to wear on Daddy's boat!"

"Oh, dear," Aunt Pet fretted, "I never thought of leaving Beacon Street." She followed Kristen with her eyes as the child danced around the room, drumming up support for the idea.

"Father, how could you make such a decision without consulting us?" Priscilla demanded, rising sharply from her chair. "Why, the place is crawling with heathens! There's no theatre, no—"

"Priscilla, that's not true! You're speaking of the Hawaii of the past," Melanie objected, sitting on the edge of her seat in earnest. "Why, Honolulu has everything Boston has, except on a much smaller scale. There's a rather cultured society, with balls at the Iolani Palace and the band concerts. And the homes are every bit as grand. It is truly one of the most beautiful places you'll ever hope to see." She smiled at the recollections of her home. "Some call it paradise."

Ryan interjected, "If you are looking for culture, it might interest you to know that Hawaii is becoming the Mecca for great writers and people of the arts. While I was looking for a plantation house, I met Robert Louis Stevenson at a *luau* given by King David."

"And Ryan is not suggesting we abandon Boston forever," Gilbert went on. "He thinks we should stay the year to help Melanie and Kristen adjust and go back home after next winter. It sounds quite tempting to my aching joints to summer in Boston and winter in Hawaii."

"The food would do you wonders, Gilbert," Melanie assured him. "As much as I stuff myself with the rich fare served here, I know the fresh fruits and vegetables of the tropics are so much better for me."

"How on earth can I pack what I will need in only a month?" Petula Caldwell mused, oblivious to all that was being said around her.

To Melanie's astonishment, Priscilla grabbed her hand,

pulling her to the distracted woman, then dropped to her knees, urging Melanie beside her. "We'll help, Mother. We must think of this as an adventure, right, cousin?"

"You mean you're considering going?" Melanie asked blankly.

Priscilla shrugged her angled shoulders and snickered. "If the literary greats can vacation in the South Pacific, it's the very least I can do. But I must take Lisette," she stipulated.

"And I must have Megan," Kristen announced, picking up her aunt's tone.

"Then I'd recommend you ask them," Gilbert said practically. "Ryan and I had thought you'd want to take some staff with you. Well, Pet?" he asked, coming up behind his wife and hugging her shoulders.

"Have you arranged things at the office so that you can just take off?" Pet asked, turning to question him authoritatively with her eyes. "And, of course, I'll have to decide which of the staff should remain to keep the household going until we return," she added before he could answer. "I'll have to check on your lighter-weight suits. There is some mode of heating on this ship of yours, is there not, Ryan? You know how easily Gilbert takes a chill, not to mention the fact that you should be concerned about Kristen."

"We have heat, Petula, and—"

"What about menus? I haven't the faintest idea how you manage at sea without a market nearby, so I shall need—"

Melanie exchanged an amused glance with her cousin and turned to see Ryan's scowl. She placed a discreet hand over her mouth and moved aside as her husband rose from his seat and crossed the room in determined strides to halt in front of her aunt.

"Pet," he interrupted, using Petula Caldwell's nickname in uncharacteristic familiarity. Once he had her attention, he crooked his finger at the woman, beckoning her to lean forward to hear what he had to say. "Just so there are no misunderstandings from the very beginning." He pointed to himself. "*I* am the captain of the *Liberty Belle*. I run the ship like you do your house. *You*," he said, pointing to her, "are the passenger, and as such, your only function is to ride and look at the passing scenery. Are we clear on that?"

Melanie held her breath as Aunt Pet parried Ryan's finger with her own and smiled. "Of course, dear brother-in-law. I haven't the faintest idea how to run your ship, and Kristen shall afford me all the entertainment I need," she said, reaching for the little girl who was carefully putting her skates back in their box.

"Why is it that I get the feeling I have just put my head in a noose and tightened it," Ryan remarked under his breath after the grand meal featuring turkey and goose, which had to be served on tables running out of the dining room and into the hall in order to seat the household. Aunt Pet had not stopped talking about the trip since she had been told about it.

From behind him, Melanie locked her arms about his trim waist as they watched Kristen and Megan dance to the jig Priscilla played on the piano. "I think you've done a wonderful thing for all of us. I know how she gets on your nerves, but she does mean well."

"Well, if she invites one more servant to go along, the bathtub will have to go in the hold," he chuckled, dragging her over to a chair and pulling her down on top of him as he dropped into it.

It seemed so natural to curl up in Ryan's lap, her legs hanging carelessly over the arm of the chair. His shoulder was invitingly comfortable as she rested her head against it. Aunt Pet replaced Priscilla at the piano, to give her a break, and the tall young woman took a seat next to Melanie and Ryan.

"You look positively exhausted, Melanie. Do you want me to tuck Kristen in tonight?"

Gilbert tutted loudly, "That is not exhaustion, Priscilla. That expression is bliss."

"Go on, Gilbert!" Melanie laughed softly, her face a becoming pink. "I really didn't get much sleep last night."

"You're not supposed to on your wedding night, silly!" Priscilla twittered, her face sobering with a mortified "Oh!"

as she realized her terrible breach of etiquette.

Startled by her cousin's risqué twist of her words, Melanie opened her mouth to object, only to have Ryan clamp his hand over it. "Say no more, blue eyes. This particular shade of crimson suits you well."

Gilbert cleared his throat. "I, for one, am genuinely shocked at the turn of this discussion." He winked at Ryan. "Which do you think is a deeper red, your wife or my daughter?"

"Oh, Father!" Priscilla leapt from her seat and fairly ran from the room.

"With one having fled, it's difficult to tell," Ryan reflected, his own voice edged with fatigue.

"You two are horrible," Melanie accused. She punched at Ryan playfully before calling to Megan Leary. "Megan, I think it's time we put the little one down for the night."

Ryan promised Kristen he'd be upstairs when she was ready for bed, then left Melanie and Megan to settle her down. The little girl plagued Megan, who had been overcome with tears at the prospect of remaining as Kristen's nurse, with questions about which toys she thought best to take on the trip to their new home. As they bathed and dressed Kristen, Melanie told them as much about Honolulu as she knew herself.

"But your Uncle 'Io lives there," Melanie pointed out when Kristen expressed disappointment that the grandma and grandpa she had never seen were on another island. She did not have the heart to tell Kristen that in six years her mother had not once mentioned the little girl in her letters. And her father never wrote at all except to say hello through her mother.

"Oh, mum!" Megan exclaimed suddenly. "The present the young man sent this November last for Kristen's Christmas!"

In all the holiday confusion and with Ryan adding to it, Melanie had completely forgotten the package 'Io had sent to give to her daughter on Christmas Day. He had written regularly during the Kalakaua's and Liliuokalani's reign, but since the overthrow of Hawaii's queen, his letters had been few, with months passing between them. When they did arrive, their postmarks were often different, so that Melanie could only hope the one address he had given her would serve for the return correspondence she sent him.

Melanie went to her room and found the brown wrapped package where she had hidden it on the top shelf of her closet. The familiar printing on the address made her smile as she thought of her brother and wondered what he would think when he discovered she had married the fair-haired captain he had suspected of carrying her off. Her smile faded upon the recollection of his anger, and she made a mental note to write him immediately to diffuse any trouble that might result. The last thing she wanted was 'Io attacking her husband.

"I wonder what it is?" She shook the package over Kristen's head curiously before dropping it into her outstretched arms.

Kristen tore into the package, her face twisting in confusion as she withdrew what appeared to be a bundle of rags. "Uncle 'Io sends me the strangest things."

Melanie took the small bundle and shook it out, somewhat puzzled herself until all the green shreds of cloth hung down from the narrow circle formed by a tied band. The note that fell from it to the floor confirmed her suspicion.

"Darling, it's a hula skirt," she informed Kristen over the edge of the paper before reading on. Mrs. Cummings and Kela had sewn the garment together out of the cloth 'Io had purchased, since a real grass skirt would not last long. Two more bundles, smaller than the skirt, turned out to be *leis* made of cloth hibiscus. The thoughtfulness of the friends she had left behind brought a smile to Melanie's lips.

"Can I try it on?" Kristen asked eagerly.

Melanie tied the grass skirt over Kristen's flannel gown and draped the *leis* around her neck. "Do you remember the dance Mama taught you?"

Kristen wrinkled her nose. "I think so. How about if you do it with me?"

"Oh do, mum!" Megan encouraged her.

Melanie obligingly stepped up beside her daughter. "Now remember to start with a friendly smile and move your hands just so."

As if it were only yesterday, Melanie sang the words of the song in the melodic Hawaiian language, her feet keeping time as she began to move through the motions that told her story. Her eyes were on the little girl mimicking her as she dipped and swayed, moving her arms over her head in a swirling motion. Although Kristen's syllables were not exactly coherent Hawaiian, her words resembled the ones Melanie sang. At the end, the little girl lowered her head and crossed her arms gracefully, a tumble of golden curls falling over her shoulders.

"Wonderful!" Megan applauded enthusiastically. "I feel like I'm in the islands already."

"Malio," Kristen thanked her.

"Mahalo, sunshine," Ryan Caldwell corrected from the parlor door. He clapped his hands together in belated applause.

"Daddy! I didn't know you spoke Hawaiian!" Kristen ran across the room to her father as Megan excused herself quietly. "Look what Uncle 'Io gave me for Christmas. It's a grass skirt, just like the hula dancers wear!"

The smile on Ryan face faltered as he looked past Kristen to Melanie. *"Uncle* 'Io?" he questioned skeptically.

"He's my uncle in Honolulu," Kristen answered. "He always sends me the funniest things. I have *pu'ilis* in the closet. They're bamboo sticks that are cracked—"

"Well, he's made a regular little Hawaiian out of you then," Ryan told her, his sarcasm not lost on Melanie as he tossed his daughter on the bed. "You should feel quite at home on the island."

"Can we have a *luau?"* Kristen asked as her father unfastened the tie of the skirt and tossed it aside.

Ryan gave Melanie a cutting look. "Why not? *Uncle* 'Io can dance for us."

Melanie's lips thinned at the way he kept slurring 'Io's

name, but she said nothing. She would explain 'Io when they were alone.

"Mama can dance too . . . and me. Did you know that Uncle 'Io and Mama used to dance together when they were little just like me? Uncle 'Io's mama and daddy taught them first and then they learned in a *halau* hula," Kristen said carefully. "That's a hula school. Can I go to one when we get to Hawaii?"

"Why don't we wait till you get there, sunshine." Ryan tucked the child in and kissed her on the forehead. "Good night."

As her daughter stretched out her hand to her, Melanie rounded the bed and did the same. "Good night, darling. Sleep well."

"Daddy," Kristen called out as they started out of the room, "do you think the river will still be icy in the morning?"

"I imagine so. Just listen to that wind blowing across it and let it whistle you to sleep," he advised her with gentle indulgence.

But there was an abrupt change in his manner when the door was closed between the parlor and the nursery. Ryan outdistanced Melanie, stalking into the bedroom and over to the window. At the click of the door sealing them from the parlor, he pivoted, his face dark and brooding.

"*Uncle* 'Io?" His lips twisted in mockery. He jabbed a thumb toward Kristen's room. "If that little girl in there had had black hair, I wouldn't be here."

Melanie returned his heated gaze as his meaning sunk in. "She could have taken after me," she countered quickly. She didn't know whether to be insulted or to laugh. He was jealous, she realized with incredulity.

"What did he do, kick you out when you returned to him carrying my child?"

Blue eyes flashed at the jeer, reminding Ryan more of Meilani than the woman he had married only yesterday. "No. He came after me and nursed me back to health from the pneumonia I had caught lying unconscious in the

218

churchyard overnight. He held me and gave me comfort and a reason to go on after you had stripped me of my pride."

"But he didn't offer to marry you," Ryan sneered, reaching for her. "And did he tell you why he didn't try to help you the night of the *luau?*" His fingers caught the sleeve of her gown as she attempted to sidestep his advance.

"He was shot, you pompous self-centered fool!" Melanie cursed, wrenching away from him. "And he would have married me and been a good father to your child, but he couldn't very well do that when he was my brother."

Ryan laughed, replying sourly, "I'm not an innocent five-year-old, Melanie."

"No," Melanie agreed, "you're just a jealous, hotheaded fool!"

Incensed by the words she flung at him with a defiant toss of her head, Ryan reached for her again, this time catching her arms in his hands and pulling her to him roughly. He practically lifted her off the floor, his face only inches from her own. "Unless you are, in addition to a deceitful little temptress, prone to incest, blue eyes, *you* are the fool. The first time I made love to you, you called me 'Io and welcomed my touch most eagerly."

From the midst of her angry shock rose the memory of that confused limbo in which she had drifted between dream and reality. She had given herself to Ryan, as he had accused, most eagerly. And she had thought him 'Io. Her face darkened guiltily in spite of her innocence. "But I didn't know!" she protested. 'Io had refused to tell her the reason for his rejection at that point, she remembered.

"Because you were drunk out of your mind after your little quarrel with *Uncle* 'Io," Ryan reminded her bitterly.

At his misinterpretation, Melanie cried out in frustration and grabbed at the front of Ryan's shirt, pulling his face down to her own. "We quarreled because I wanted to run off with him and get married, and he turned me down. He wouldn't tell me why because he promised my father!" she said in an angry rush. "I didn't know he was my brother until after you had finished with me, you stupid, arrogant—" She yanked at his shirt and pushed him back in a repeated effort to shake some sense into him.

"—fool?" Doubt played heavily on his leonine features, giving way to incredulity. He released her and turned away so abruptly that Melanie lost her grip on his shirt. Running his hands through his hair, he muttered under his breath in disbelief, "Your brother!"

Sensing his outrage exhausted, replaced by another less tangible and intimidating emotion, Melanie ventured her arms about his waist and hugged him. Her heart felt ridiculously light when she realized it was because of her that he had been so furious. "I forgive you, Ryan," she whispered sweetly, her cheek pressed against his back. "I kind of like the idea of your being jealous."

He reacted to her words as if she had slapped him. To her dismay, he threw her arms away from him and whirled around to face her. "Well *I* don't, Melanie," he snapped, his voice as razor-sharp as the look he gave her. "I'll see you in the morning."

Melanie flinched at the slamming of the door behind him and stared at it dumbfounded. As the stupor wore off, her temper reached its boiling point. He had to be the most unpredictable, bullheaded, hot-tempered individual she had ever come across in her life! If it weren't for Kristen, she'd have broken a lamp over his hard egotistical head. Well, good riddance, she fumed, taking out her animosity on her clothing as she undressed.

She stomped on her petticoat in answer to the slam of the front door. But when the finality of it registered, she ran to the window. Hurriedly, she wiped away the condensation in time to see her husband walking in the same direction he had taken the night before, and her building wrath gave way to absolute wretchedness.

Chapter Fourteen

The week between Christmas and the New Year was filled with parties and social calls. Aunt Pet became the queen of the circuit with her announcement that the Caldwells were going to Honolulu. Although included in the invitations, Melanie and Ryan did not attend many, nor were they expected to as newlyweds. But that was not the reason they did not go.

Each night after Kristen was put to bed, Ryan left. As on Christmas Day, he could have acted no more sweetly to Melanie. He even apologized for his reaction to 'Io's gift. They went skating as he had promised Kristen, although Melanie declined to participate, happy to watch father and daughter from the shore. The other days he spent at the shipyard, coming home with Gilbert precisely at six to spend the early evening at Kristen's disposal.

Melanie longed to confront him as to where he went. One evening, just after they had said good night to Kristen, she summoned her nerve. Gilbert and Aunt Pet had gone to the Vaughns' home for a dinner party in honor of their impending departure at the month's end, and Priscilla was at a rehearsal for the Footlight Club. Things had not gone particularly well for Ryan that day . . . something to do with the engines on the *Liberty Belle*. He had even been short-tempered with Kristen. Melanie watched, chewing her bottom lip apprehensively as he drew on his jacket and buttoned it with jerky motions.

221

"You're going out again?" she asked, feeling somewhat ridiculous for her simple statement. It was apparent that he was.

His fingers stopped on the last button. "I am." His eyes took in her soft blue gown that seemed molded to her womanly figure and the wispy childlike curls that could not be made to fit in the chignon at her neck. "Have I reason to stay other than to watch you sleep?" His lips curled wryly at her wide-eyed hesitation. "I thought not." He lifted a stray silken coil off her forehead and smoothed it in with the rest of her coiffure, only to have it spring back contrarily.

"You're going to her, aren't you?" Melanie challenged, brushing his hand away irritably.

"Her?"

"I saw her at the church, Ryan. I am not an innocent fool. I know what she is to you."

The bemusement on his face gradually changed to mockery. "You mean Arabella! The hag with the wart on her nose."

Melanie rolled her eyes in annoyance and turned away from him. "The very one . . . and I've seen her, so don't speak nonsense."

"Tut, tut, blue eyes. Green does not become you." She snatched her shoulders away from him as his hands clamped down on them, only to have them captured again. "Arabella and I are old friends, Melanie. That she came to the wedding did not surprise me, but I hardly think you saw her close enough to note her wart."

"I saw her at the Apthorps' and believe me, Ryan, she had no wart." Melanie crossed her arms, irritated at the course of the conversation. He had managed to put her on the defensive, when it was *he* who was philandering about at all hours of the night.

His hands slid down the back of her arms, the tip of his fingers brushing the rounded swell of her bosom as they passed. Melanie tensed when his arms crossed over her own and his lips moved against her ear, taunting with a sigh, *"I kind of like the idea of your being jealous."*

"Ohh!" Melanie gasped, tearing out of his hold and running to the door. She yanked it open furiously. "Get out!"

His amusement was like fuel to the fire as he bowed cockily and started past her. But at the last moment, an arm hooked about her waist, drawing her against him, and his lips claimed hers, smothering her shocked indignation. Her eyes flashed angrily and she twisted her head, but the hand that cradled it halted her would-be retreat. All that escaped was her hair from the chignon, smitten in the struggle.

The fire that raced through her veins was subservient to two masters that battled in her mind—the incensed pride of her conscious will and the waking desire of her body that had slept fitfully since Ryan's arrival. His fingers entwined in the disarrayed silk of her hair, lending monumental support to desire as they massaged her neck. The clenched muscles of her jaw slackened at the erotic coaxing, parting her lips to a mind-shattering invasion. Her emotions swirled and skidded in confusion so distracting that instead of remaining stiff, her body surrendered against his, soft voluptuous curve against lean hard flesh.

When Ryan lifted his mouth from hers, Melanie waited, her mind oblivious to everything except the delightful sensation of being in his arms. Her head lolled back, cupped in his hand to expose a white stretch of throat pulsing imploringly for more. Gradually, the momentum of the freshly awakened desire slowed without further fuel and cognizance of the situation began to prick her awareness. Blinking to break the spell, she lifted her head and met his flickering green gaze with curiosity at first, and then mortification at what had just happened between them.

"So tell me, blue eyes, am I coming or going?"

It was all she could do to will her body to leave him. Her arms did not want to give up the hold they had found on their own about his neck. Her breasts were loath to abandon the intoxicating crush of his muscular chest against them. Her hips balked at the loss of the hand that pressed her stomach to his, impaling the metal buttons of his coat into her flesh.

Melanie's face mirrored her confusion at the battle going on within her. She turned away, wrapping her arms about her shoulders in the chill of her self-inflicted loneliness, and answered unconvincingly, "Going!"

The telltale click of the door closing brought frustrated tears to her eyes. She began to tremble, but not from fear of him forcing himself upon her. If he had pursued his ardor, she would have given herself to him willingly. That was what she feared — that voracious desire he had the talent to summon, no matter how enraged she was. Despairing of reason, she flung herself on the bed and wrapped the heavy quilt about her shoulders. With such an awesome power over her, she wondered why he had ever resorted to force — unless he was not aware that he possessed it. The question played heavy on her mind until the wee hours of the morning, when sleep eventually erased it without satisfaction.

Saturday was an overcast day. Kristen was up early, dressed in her warmest coat and woolen leggings to go ice-skating. At her daughter's insistent plea, Melanie borrowed Priscilla's skating costume and ice skates so that she, too, could take part in the fun. It was a long walk from their Beacon Street residence to the designated skating area, but there was no wind and they were dressed warmly, so Melanie found it refreshing.

She listened to Ryan tell his daughter how he and her Uncle Gilbert used to play crack the whip with other neighborhood boys. Gilbert was the oldest and had been quite put out at having been sent along by Ryan's mother to keep an eye on the younger lad. Thus perturbed, he took the lead and led the younger boys on a riotous skid across the ice, which sent them sprawling into a snowbank. Ryan, at the end of the whip, did not land as softly as the others and fell on the ice, striking his head with a terrible crack that rendered him bleeding and unconscious.

"I can't imagine Gilbert doing such a terrible thing," Melanie told him incredulously.

"He was in love and preferred Petula's company to mine and my friends," Ryan grinned. "Of course, he was overcome with remorse, not only for my cracked skull, but because Father forbade him to go out, except to the office, for a month. There we go!" he added, pointing to a line of youngsters skating in wide arcs and circles over the scratched icy surface. "Only they're playing it safer. See the rope."

Melanie took a seat on one of the makeshift log benches to watch the boys, protesting that Ryan and Kristen practice and give her time to muster her courage. The boys' ages ranged from ten to fourteen, she guessed from their assorted sizes and builds. They laughed and shouted for the leader to go faster. Each of them clung about six feet apart, with gloved hands, to a long rope, which kept the lot of them together with a tail of jute to spare.

"Mama, look at me!"

Melanie watched as Ryan let go of Kristen's hand. The little girl skated away from him on wobbly legs that reminded her of a newborn foal struggling to walk. Moving a little farther along, Kristen gained more confidence and her gliding steps became more certain. Her father skated after her, his hands clasped casually behind his back.

His astrakhan round hat, black against his golden hair, gave him a distinctively different, yet none-the-less striking look. The straight tunic-type jacket of grey wool, embellished with black braid around the slashed pockets and buttons, reminded her of the Russian cossack hero in one of the books she had read.

Eventually, he passed his daughter and herded her into a turn. His grey breeches buttoned at the knees over woolen stockings, stretched over powerful legs as he crouched on his skates as easily as if he were wearing boots, in case his charge could not make the maneuver. His precaution was needless, for Kristen leaned to her left and turned, her arms spread wide for balance. When she turned and faced her mother, her eyes sparkled with satisfaction.

"See!" she called out, tossing the matching muff to her

coat over her back and starting toward Melanie. "Your turn!"

Ryan skated over to the edge of the bank and reached for Melanie's hand. Wobbling as awkwardly as her daughter, she stood on the metal runners. "Now's my turn to get even for all the ribbing I took over a damned board," he threatened mischievously under his breath.

With an equally impish smile, Melanie started to knock his hat off playfully, but to her surprise the two feet firmly planted under her began to slide apart at her change in balance. With a startled cry, she grabbed Ryan about the waist, nearly taking him with her as she went down in an awkward split. As Priscilla's borrowed felt bowler skittered across the ice, Ryan grasped her under the arms and hauled her upright, an infuriatingly superior look of amusement on his face.

"Mama, you look so silly!" Kristen laughed from a short distance away. "But we all do when we first start," she added with the conciliation of an experienced skater.

"If you concentrate more on balance and less on mischief, madame, you will fare much better," he remarked with mock cynicism.

Melanie made no retaliatory comment, for it was all she could do to stand. Her fingers bit into Ryan's arm as she tentatively ventured forth with one foot. Meeting with success, she shifted her weight to the other.

"Not bad," Ryan consoled her when she had traveled an excruciating few yards.

In spite of the cold weather, Melanie found she was sweating. "It looks so easy when you do it."

"So did the surfing," he reminded her. "Come on, hold on to me. Kristen, stay near the bank!" he called back to his daughter.

Melanie gave a short cry of alarm as he pushed forward, carrying her with her. His arm was hooked around her waist, fingers firmly clenched about the loose material of her coat in case she should fall. His other hand supported her elbow. When they had gone a good distance, he leaned

226

to the left, coaxing her to do the same, and to Melanie's amazement, they made a circle much like the other young couples were doing.

She uttered an "Oh!" of astonished satisfaction when Ryan brought her back around to where Kristen skated in small circles near the bench. They drifted to a halt, Melanie beaming up at her husband. "That was nice. Perhaps we could do it again?"

Ryan gave Kristen a conspiratorial wink. "I think we've got her hooked."

"We knew you'd like it, Mama, if you just tried it."

"Miss Lyons! Miss Lyons!"

At the unexpected call of her name, Melanie turned abruptly to see a young girl skating toward them. In doing so, her feet promptly went out from under her and, her tutor temporarily distracted, she landed with a grunt on the hard ice. In a fluster of frustration, she snatched up the runaway derby and pulled it down over her head.

"At least one didn't break their neck falling into a wave!" she declared in low voice to her chuckling husband, just as Ena Otis skidded up to them. "Hello, Ena. How was your holiday?"

Ena's face was a clashing wind-parched red to the tight carrot-colored braids that hung on either side of it. "Perfectly wonderful," the girl said, looking down at her sprawled teacher somewhat disconcerted.

Ryan bent over and hauled Melanie up again, whispering in her ear merrily, "I don't think your neck is the victim of that fall, blue eyes."

"Is this your dead husband?" Ena asked bluntly, staring at Ryan in utter fascination.

"Yes, Ena. May I present—" Melanie gasped as Ryan brushed the snow from the back of her skirt familiarly, "Capt. Ryan Caldwell."

Ena wrinkled her freckled brow. "I thought his name was Lyons."

"It was, Ena," Ryan told her with a grim look that almost made Melanie laugh. "I was on a secret mission and had to marry the girl under an assumed name."

Ena looked at Melanie in awe. "Wow! So that's where you get our math stories from."

"What's a mission, Daddy?" Kristen asked, glancing sideways at Ena.

"Is this your little girl?" Ena asked, diverting Kristen's answer. "I'd love to skate with her."

Kristen leapt at the chance to have someone to play with. "Oh, can I, Mama? Daddy?"

Melanie smiled. "I suppose so. Daddy can't keep both of us up at the same time. But be careful, Ena," she cautioned.

"And stay away from that roped-off area," Ryan added sternly.

"We will," the two new friends chorused as they skated off slowly, hand in hand.

"What math stories?" Ryan asked, taking Melanie by the waist and elbow to try again.

Smiling, Melanie told him about her imaginative classroom tactic of making up adventures that required mathematical solutions in order to see them to their conclusion. The tanned lines of Ryan's face stretched with his humor at the idea, but his eyes were taking in the rosy cold blush of Melanie's cheeks and the tip of her nose, a cute turned-up nose like Kristen's that just begged to be kissed. Unable to resist, he pecked at it in the midst of Melanie's story, so astounding her that she grabbed at him in preparation for the fall that was sure to come.

He straightened quickly, bearing the bulk of her weight with his arms but, in doing so, overcompensated for the two of them. As a result, he went over backward, pulling Melanie on top of him. Except for the hat that cushioned the crack of his head on the ice, he might have been seriously hurt, but he hardly felt it.

He was too conscious of the soft body sprawled over him in a most unladylike fashion. As Melanie tried to climb to her knees, her leg brushed over him, stirring the desire he had held in check too long. He muttered a curse under his breath when she slipped and fell on him again, her soft breasts burning through her clothing to his very soul.

"I'm sorry!" she laughed helplessly. Her hands clasped his face and she dragged herself up in a maddeningly arousing fashion to meet him eye to eye. "Are you hurt?" At the shake of his head, she lowered her voice, decidedly and innocently seductive, and teased, "If you concentrate more on balance and less on mischief, we'll fare much better."

"I say, folks, might I be of assistance?"

Ryan fought back the irritated urge to say no and accepted the help graciously. The young gentleman paid particular attention to Melanie, holding her, to Ryan's notion, a bit longer than necessary for her to regain her footing. Although he could not blame him, he admitted to himself, noting the way she had pulled Priscilla's hat down over her ears to keep it on. With the bright blue eyes she had given their daughter and her hat almost over her eyes, she was devilishly irresistible.

"Thank you, sir," Ryan said, offering his hand in gratitude. "My wife is unaccustomed to the ice." His annoyance was assuaged by the downfallen look on their rescuer's face as he insisted it was no trouble at all. Ryan felt a selfish sense of pride when he slipped his arm around the woman at his side and led her off.

Melanie had not missed the subtle male challenge and her spirit became even more lighthearted. Ryan's possessive claim on her waist and her arm fed the insecurity of the long nights without him. She found herself wishing the day would last forever.

Kristen, who was having less and less trouble keeping up with Ena, kept skating by them with her partner, for Ryan was slowing his pace intentionally to keep himself and Melanie upright. It delighted the little girl immensely to outdistance her parents. Her red lips pinched in a smug smile each time she passed them.

"Are you getting chilled?" Ryan asked after Melanie had lost count of the number of times they had skated the circumference of the roped-off area.

"Not really." The exercise alone had kept her warm, but

his closeness even more so.

"Then how about trying it backward now that you have forward under hand?"

He moved in front of her and took her hands as if preparing to dance. "Now point the back of the runners out and bend your knees slightly . . . like so." Melanie stared down at his feet as she started forward from his pulling motion. "Now you try," he told her softly, coming to a stop.

His voice seemed to caress her as he gazed into her eyes and his instructions fled her mind. Her eyes became limpid pools of blue, dropping to a sensuous mouth that had robbed her of anger and fired her with desire. They sparkled with the recollection.

"Ryan, please don't leave tonight," she heard herself say, her lips moving toward his of their own accord.

"Mama, Daddy, look!"

Melanie had to drag her gaze away from the man who'd responded with a tightening of his hands about hers and a volatile kindling in his own eyes. When she did, her body tensed with maternal fear. Kristen and Ena had picked up the end of the rope where the boys played crack the whip and were sailing across the ice entirely too fast for either of them.

"Kristen, let go!" she screamed, starting for her daughter without thought to her precarious footing.

"I'll get her," Ryan called back, already shooting past Melanie as she plummeted forward to her hands and knees.

To Melanie's horror, the girls obeyed just as the whip rounded a turn. The backlash sent them skidding out of control toward the roped-off area. Everything seemed to slow down in anguishing slow motion as the last of the boys on the whip noticed what had happened and called for the leaders to turn back. The girls fell, their bodies sliding under the barrier rope onto the dangerous thin ice.

Behind Melanie, some of the adults caught on to what was taking place and several young men started out after Ryan, who was streaking determinedly toward the screaming girls. Her gloves stuck to the ice as she tried to get to her feet, but at the thunderous crack followed by horrified gasps of the onlookers, she froze with unprecedented fear.

She heard Kristen's terrified "Daddy!" as the girls slowed to a halt well beyond the barrier, then Ryan's answering "Don't move!" His skates sent a spray of crystallized ice as he took up at the barrier and commandeered the rope the boys had been playing with. The ice cracked again and Ena, in panic, scrambled to her feet. Suddenly, the surface opened up with a horrible crunching sound and an invisible hand seemed to drag the red-haired child feetfirst into the river. Kristen screamed as she saw Ena digging at the ice to fight the pulling current, which tugged at her legs, and the widening mouth of the monster coming toward her.

"My baby!" Melanie cried helplessly, giving up trying to stand and starting to crawl toward the scene of terror that became blocked by a line of men. Her knees ground painfully on the hard surface as she frantically tried to reach them. Suddenly, she found herself picked up by two men who all but carried her toward the chaos at the edge of the safe area.

When they reached it, all Melanie could see was the young man who had followed Ryan spread belly down near the edge of the gaping hole. There was no sign of the girls or Ryan. Near hysteria, she dropped to the ice, tearing at the runners strapped to her boots.

"Miss . . . Miss! What are you doing?" one of her assistants inquired, bending down to help her up.

Melanie did not answer. Free of the skates, she climbed to her feet and tried to go over the rope, only to be snatched back forcefully. "My baby!" she screamed, tugging at the arms that held her.

"Miss, you can't help. They're doing all they can!"

"Look, he's got one!"

Melanie whipped her head about to see Ryan holding tightly to the rope that was anchored by the skaters on firm ice and shoving Ena's limp form out of the hole. The young man lying at its edge dragged the child out of the water and started inching his way back toward solid ground with her

231

as Ryan disappeared again.

Fear, stark and vivid, stabbed at her chest until Melanie could not breathe. She shook her head from side to side, denying what had happened, her face whiter than the peaceful landscape disrupted by the terrible commotion. Her eyes were riveted to the spot where her husband and daughter had disappeared, and her lips moved in silent, fervent prayer. The seconds were like hours until the answer came and Ryan's head emerged again.

At first he appeared to be alone as he grasped the lifeline, but when his other arm came out of the water, it dragged a small pink-clad figure. The other man, having turned Ena over to the crowd, crawled back toward the captain, who was trying to pull himself and his daughter out of the icy river with one hand. The ice cracked under them, plunging them back in, but Ryan clung to the rope with superhuman strength.

Finally, the men and boys on the lifeline began to work together, hauling the two drenched figures out of the hole and dragging them across the ice to safety. The men who had helped Melanie escorted her over to where Ryan worked furiously on his unconscious daughter. Melanie's legs felt like water but she managed to reach them, only to have Ryan shove her away with a growl of impatience.

Helpless to do anything more than watch, Melanie clutched her arms about herself and rocked back and forth, praying for some sign of life from the little girl being flipped and tossed like a rag doll by her father. She thought Ryan would break the child's back as he pushed on her, the width of his two hands totally spanning the width of her body.

On the third crushing attempt, Kristen issued a gagging sound. Ryan bore down on her again relentlessly. The child choked, eyelids fluttering as she spit up seawater on the ice and went into a spasm of coughing. From somewhere behind them, heavy lap robes from the boobies and sleighs parked along the riverfront appeared. Ryan took the one someone draped over his back and rolled Kristen in it.

"This one's coming around, too," someone shouted a

short distance away.

At the cheers that went up among the crowd, Melanie tore her gaze away from her husband and daughter long enough to see the young man who had helped Ryan, bundling up Ena Otis. As he was helped to his feet with his burden, she saw his face and recognized the dapper young man who had offered to help Gilbert on the Little Green Car as Ena's brother, Walter.

"Let's get her home. Someone send a doctor to Number Eight Beacon," Ryan commanded crisply, the second blanket that had been wrapped about his shoulders falling off as he started for the bank with Kristen in his arms.

"You can use my cutter," one of the gentlemen who had helped Melanie offered, his hand at her elbow as she ran along on the ice to keep up with Ryan.

Ryan waited long enough for Melanie to climb in the sleigh, before handing Kristen over to her and getting in beside her. His face was grim as he leaned over and pulled back the lap blanket, noting his daughter's deathlike pallor and blue lips, which were much like his own. Melanie rocked Kristen and kissed her cold forehead, grateful for the tiny whimpers and shaky breaths she felt against her face as she did so.

"Mama's here, darling," she half sobbed, cradling her child in the curve of her body to afford her some warmth.

"Here," Ryan said in a terse tone, sinking down and drawing a blanket over them all. "Put her between us."

Melanie obeyed without question, enveloping Ryan's wide shoulders, together with her child's, in her arms as the cutter whizzed along the streets. The houses they passed were a blur through her glazed eyes. She patted Ryan's head nervously and cooed to her daughter, her fingers breaking the icy crust that had formed in her husband's wet hair. They appeared to fly, but at the same time, it seemed hours before they pulled up in front of their Beacon Street home.

Ryan lost no time leaping from the cutter and taking Kristen from Melanie. He was kicking the front door open as Melanie hurried up the walk after him, mechanically thanking the good samaritan over her shoulder. Her husband's long legs had carried him halfway up the stairs when Aunt Pet came out of the dining room to see what the ruckus was all about and met Melanie.

"It's Kristen," was all Melanie could say, leaving her aunt to shriek in distress behind her and following Ryan to the nursery.

She set right to helping her husband strip the child and getting Kristen into the warm flannel sheets of the feather bed. When Megan burst into the room, staring wild-eyed at Kristen's still form, Melanie ordered her to have two hot baths drawn immediately. She took off her damp, cold outerwear, discarding it on the floor, then laid down beside her daughter, embracing her tightly.

As she lay there, her warm cheek against Kristen's cold one, she looked up at Ryan. Her husband had dropped to his knees at the side of the bed, heedless of the wet clothes frozen to his body, and stared as if numbed by all that had happened. His breathing was shallow and his body trembled involuntarily. Reaching across the mattress, Melanie put her hand over his and squeezed it. After a moment, she broke through the iced glaze of his eyes, pouring all the love and gratitude she felt into them from the swirling and turbulent depths of her own.

Chapter Fifteen

When the doctor arrived, he checked Kristen over thoroughly. Her lips had lost their blue coloring, although she was still ghostly white. She whined as he lifted her head, complaining that it hurt. The physician felt her skull through her damp golden curls and announced that she had apparently knocked her head on the ice, resulting in a mild concussion.

"Just keep checking her periodically, waking her every four hours to make sure she's all right. And keep her warm . . . some hot broth will do wonders. She's been a very lucky little girl to get away with a mild case of shock and a concussion." He looked up gravely at Ryan, who leaned against the wall, his forehead knitted with concern. "I don't know how you managed to get her out before the current took her away."

"The cord of her muff snagged on the ice," Ryan explained tiredly. His eyelids were half closed and he looked as if he would collapse without the support behind him. "If it hadn't been for that . : ."

Melanie put her arm around him, absorbing his shudder at the possible alternative. But it did not stop, for although it was barely perceptible, her husband was still quivering in spite of the blanket Gilbert had insisted he wrap around his shoulders. He had refused to change his clothes or leave Kristen's bedside until the doctor came, only asking for brandy to take away the chill.

The doctor closed up his black bag, his eyes narrowing as he studied Ryan for the first time. "I think I'd better check you out as well, sir."

Ryan shook his head in protest. "If she's fine, I'm fine."

"I think he should, Ryan," Melanie spoke up in agreement. "You're shaking right now in those wet clothes."

"For God's sake, man, you're courting pneumonia!" the doctor exclaimed incredulously. Dropping his chin with a shake of disgust, he questioned Melanie. "Where can I examine him?"

"In our room," she answered, raising her eyes to Ryan in a plea to cooperate.

His face was inscrutable as he considered her request, but to her relief, he conceded with only a little protest. "But there's nothing wrong with me that a hot bath and a healthy dram of brandy won't remedy. You'd be better off to get down to the other little girl's home and check on her."

The doctor clapped Ryan on the shoulder as they left the room, assuring him, "My colleague is there right now, Captain Caldwell. Are you feeling sleepy?"

"Mama!" Kristen called out to Melanie as she walked to the door to look after Ryan.

"I'm not going anywhere, darling," she reassured the child, going back to the bed. "Would you like me to send for some hot chicken broth? You haven't had lunch."

Kristen declined with a shake of her head, wincing. "I'm just sleepy," she yawned, feeling the lump with her fingers. "It hurts, Mama. Will you kiss it?"

"Of course."

Melanie gently touched her lips to the back of Kristen's raised head, then sat down so that the child could use her lap for a pillow. Aunt Pet came in just after the little girl's eyes had closed. She wrung her hands about her white starched apron and stared down at Kristen, her expression worried. Melanie repeated what the doctor had told her, and Petula hastily left to have the cook prepare some broth for Kristen.

Gilbert appeared shortly after to tell Melanie that Ryan

was fine, aside from extreme exhaustion. According to the physician, that was a normal aftereffect from the icy exposure in the river. He was soaking in a hot bath, sipping brandy, and no doubt would soon be tucked into bed. The gentleman who had given them the ride from the river had stopped by to tell them Ena Otis was doing equally well, thanks to Ryan's quick thinking and action, along with the prompt care she had received from the standers-by.

"So all is well," he announced brightly before fixing his gaze on Melanie. "And what about Mother? How is she faring?"

"Fine now." Melanie managed a weak smile. She had died, stricken with fear and forced to watch the horror of her husband's and child's impending deaths. And now she was torn between staying with Kristen and going to Ryan. There was so much she needed to tell him, things that might never have been said if things had turned out differently.

Gilbert sat on the edge of the bed in front of her, his green eyes dubious. "That was not very convincing. How about some hot tea laced with a healthy shot of bourbon for those nerves?"

"I really don't think I could stand a thing, but thank you." Her eyes watered with emotion at the kind show of sympathy. She sniffed in irritation at her weakness. "I'm sorry, Gilbert. I am joyous that Ryan and Kristen are safe, really."

Gilbert picked up the quilt folded at the foot of Kristen's bed and spread it over Melanie's shoulders. As he did so, he embraced her reassuringly. "It will work out, Melanie. I know Ryan loves you."

Melanie questioned Gilbert with her eyes as he straightened up and gave her a knowing look.

"I am aware that he leaves the house at night. I've let him in early some mornings," he explained somberly. At the wretched look on her face, he averred, "No one else knows." He pretended to flick a piece of lint from his lapel. "I don't know what the problem is between you, but I can tell you this: Whenever you're present, my brother worships you

237

with his eyes. All I can ask is that you remember that Ryan is two things . . . a man and a Caldwell. That makes him aggressive, irascible, thick, and possessive of that which he cares for."

"You're not that way, and you're a male and a Caldwell," Melanie pointed out to the contrary.

Gilbert grinned, his eyes as devilish as she had ever seen Ryan's. "Madame, I am half again as old as my brother and have learned to temper my faults with subtlety. Ask Pet sometime about our courtship."

Melanie remembered Ryan's earlier account of Gilbert's mischief and accused, in an amazed tone, "Why, Gilbert Caldwell! You awful man!" A twinkle came to her eyes as she asked, "Am I to hope that Ryan will become as much of a dear as you?"

Gilbert twisted his lips wryly to one side. "Let us not hope for too much, dear niece. There's a wicked little light in those blue eyes your aunt never possessed, which leads me to think you might not be as angelic an influence as my Pet. In fact, I think my brother has married his match."

"Mama?" Kristen mumbled sleepily, stirring beneath the covers.

"Right here, darling." Melanie gave up her answer to Gilbert and brushed Kristen's forehead gently. "Are you hungry?"

A moan of denial was all that emerged from the little girl as she turned her back to Melanie and snuggled around her pillow. Gilbert Caldwell tiptoed to the door, so as not to awaken the sleeping child, and slipped through it, mouthing the words silently that he would check back with Melanie later. After he had gone, Melanie curled around her daughter's back and, with the blanket tucked around her shoulders, catnapped peacefully.

It was dark outside the windows when Megan came in with chicken broth and crackers for the invalid. Although she was not hungry, Melanie ate a bowl of the hot soup to encourage her daughter to do the same. The few spoons of broth seemed to exhaust the little girl, and as the nurse piled the dishes on the tray to carry them back downstairs, Kristen fell asleep again.

Assured that Ryan was also in bed, Melanie laid back down with her daughter, giving her comforting pats on her shoulders when she whimpered in her dreams. She, too, must have drifted off again, for the next time the nurse came in, three hours had passed.

Megan insisted she go downstairs and have a bite of something that would "stick to her ribs," as the nurse put it. "And then get yourself up to bed. You've had as hard a day as the sick, if not harder." When Melanie objected that Kristen might wake up and need her, Megan informed her promptly that as Kristen's nurse, she was perfectly capable of handling that situation. She added that if Kristen should want her mama, she would not hesitate to call Melanie. "But, like as not, your husband needs ye as well."

Melanie doubted that but was too tired to argue. Ryan had been asleep since his bath, according to Gilbert, and probably would not know whether she was there or not. But she needed Ryan. Not that she intended to disrupt his slumber. She wouldn't think of waking him. All she wanted was to share his warmth and feel his arms about her. Thanks to God's answering her prayers and sparing his life, there would be time to talk later.

She went downstairs to fix some tea, only to have Aunt Pet and Priscilla fawn over her They insisted she sit in the dining room while they brought up some cold leftover meat and cheese. Melanie ate it with an appetite she had not been aware of, listening as her aunt and cousin told her about the number of calls they had had from concerned neighbors and friends inquiring about Ryan and Kristen.

"Everyone was talking about how Ryan hit the water almost the same time as the girls," Aunt Pet recounted.

"He didn't even take time to tie the lifeline to him," Priscilla chimed in. "It was truly a miracle he did not lose his hold and get swept away."

"Priscilla, Melanie does not need to dwell on what might have happened," Petula Caldwell reminded her daughter.

"I'm sorry, Melanie. It's just that he was such a hero . . . him and that Otis girl's brother."

"Well, I certainly wasn't any help," Melanie asserted shamefully. "I was panic-stricken."

"Gina Maxwell said she never felt so sorry for anyone in her life. She told us you were crawling toward them until some men helped you get over to the scene. It must have been horrible," Priscilla shuddered.

"I'm sure it was," Aunt Pet commiserated, refilling Melanie's cup with hot tea. "And I'm certain Melanie would be better off to forget it." The woman swallowed hard, her eyes watering suddenly. "I only thank God you all are safe!" With a loud honk of her nose in her scented handkerchief, she got up. "And I intend to give my thanks right now and leave you in peace."

Taking the hint, Priscilla patted Melanie's hand and got up to follow her mother. "Call us if you need us, cousin."

The house was dark when Melanie finished the last of her tea and went upstairs to check on Kristen before retiring. A crack of the nursery door revealed her daughter sleeping peacefully, Megan's plump figure lying beside her in a gown and nightcap. Her concern appeased, she made her way past the parlor to her bedroom.

Since Ryan had retired before sundown, the shutters were still open and the room was bathed in the gaslight shining through the windows from the street below. She could hear his regular breathing as she undressed near a window to avoid lighting a lamp, stopping more than once to stare at his sleeping figure on the bed.

Her nightgown was not laid out on the foot of the bed as usual, the upstairs maid not wanting to disturb Ryan, so Melanie fumbled in the dim light searching for it. The stubborn catch on the wardrobe refused to give at her gentle pull, and in the end, she reconciled herself to wearing Ryan's dressing robe to keep from making any noise. She washed in front of the nightstand and afforded herself the luxury of dusting scented talc on her body before tying the cumbersome garment about her waist. After a quick run of

240

the brush through her hair, she made her way to the bed, refreshed but tired.

The bed creaked, causing her to wince at the noise, as she climbed into it and slid beneath the covers. Her side was chilled, but as she moved over, she found the warmth generated by her sleeping husband. He looked so peaceful, his finely chiseled features outlined against the white linen pillowcase. She smiled at his sprawled position, which reminded her of the night after the typhoon when he had fallen asleep in her bed.

He looks so vulnerable, she thought, her heart swelling with all the things she wanted to say to him. Very gently, she slipped her arm over his chest and snuggled closely. Against the palm of her hand, she felt his beating heart and closed her eyes in grateful prayer that he was here with her. Her fingers spread out, reveling in the coarse hair that covered his chest. She had almost forgotten how wonderful it felt against her cheek or pressed to her breast.

Slowly, she worked them downward to the lean stretch of abdomen. A groan of remorse hung in her throat as she traced the thin ridge of the scar she had left there. She hadn't meant to hurt him. She had been crazy that night . . . crazy with hurt and anger. As crazy as Ryan had been? she wondered. Did she dare believe his fairy tale . . . that he had loved her?

As if seeking that reassurance, she placed her head on his shoulder, smiling as his arm came down around her and he turned drowsily to take her in his arms. It didn't matter. She loved him. She hadn't realized just how much until she had seen him disappear under the ice. A tear slipped down her cheek, spilling onto his chest. Inadvertently, she sniffed and wiped her eyes, her body shuddering with a long, ragged breath.

"Melanie?" Ryan's voice slurred above her head.

"Hmm?" she responded softly. She held her breath, damning herself for waking him and at the same time hoping she had. Would any reaction she ever had toward this man be sane? she mused.

"Is Kristen all right?" His body tensed in alarm as he came to his senses.

"She's sleeping. Megan's in there with her," she whispered. What would she do if he woke up and left her? That, along with a thousand more doubts, bombarded her mind.

Relaxing at the news, Ryan shifted completely on one side and propped up on his elbow, condemning her head to the feather pillow. "What time is it?"

"A little after eleven."

The quiver of apprehension in her voice made him stiffen again. After a moment's silence, he exhaled irritably. "I have no intention of touching you, Melanie. Here . . ." He took half of the bolster and shoved it between them. "You're safe, and I'm too damned tired to leave or argue." He fell back on his pillow and snatched the covers up to his chin.

Shocked by his misinterpretation of her feelings, Melanie sat up and stared at him. She didn't know whether to laugh for joy or to shake him in exasperation, so she did neither. Instead, she threw herself across the narrow pillow and found his lips, kissing him long and hard until his arms drew her completely on top of him in a tangle of quilts. Her fingers inched up the back of his neck, locked in his thick hair, preventing him from possible escape.

But Ryan did not try. He lay perfectly still, holding her loosely in his embrace. Melanie covered his neck with tiny imploring kisses, receiving no more response than the deep breath that caused his chest to rise and fall, carrying her with it. She nibbled at his earlobe, her tongue tentative as it explored the sensitive area around it. At his lack of cooperation, her trepidation grew even more.

Did Arabelle Harrington keep him so well satisfied? she thought miserably. Having made the first overture, she did not know what else to do. The unwelcome burn of resentment and humiliation rose to her face, and she was grateful for the darkness. In despair at her inability to reach him, she pushed against his chest to roll away, but the loose prison tightened, keeping her in place.

"Sit up and take your clothes off, blue eyes."

His voice reached out to her, low and taut with restraint. His hands anchored her hips as she straightened to obey. The contact of his naked flesh between her thighs made the blood course through her veins in a heated rush. The knot of his robe defied her stubbornly, her fingers fumbling at the distraction of his thumbs trailing silkenly along the curves of her body. By the time it was free, he had separated the front of the robe and her hardening breasts strained toward the outstretched palms that taunted them, close enough to make his presence known, yet not quite touching.

"Now move back just a little," came the terse instruction, his hands guiding her. Beneath the discarded garment that had fallen from her shoulders, the hard evidence of her success met with her. "Get rid of the robe."

Although he was not actually touching her, this close heated distance he maintained knotted her stomach with primeval cravings that threatened her control. The graze of the heavy silk material across her buttocks as she pulled it away made her oversensitive nerves clench involuntarily, and by Ryan's quick intake of breath, she could only guess its effect on him. Her own breath was quick as she awaited his next command, for all she was aware of was the titillating brush of his instrument of passion.

"Touch me, blue eyes."

Melanie held her breath. Knowing what he meant, she could not bring herself to such boldness. Hoping to assuage him, she tripped her fingers lightly over the muscled ridges of his chest, splaying her hands over the tightened circles of his nipples. The brush of her own breasts against his body sent a tremor of anticipation through her, and her hands unconsciously clawed. A flood of warmth flushed her loins, with fire forcing her to grind against him instinctively, seeking relief.

"Touch me, Melanie!" His voice was more demanding this time, as if his patience were giving out.

"I . . ." Melanie swallowed her words of protest, for his abdominal muscles extended and contracted beneath her, promising . . . if she would obey. If he only would love her as he used to . . . drive her wild with those maddening caresses he knew exactly how to administer to make her his victim. Yet strangely, her body was aroused as if he had a thousand hands upon her, all possessed with erotic missions.

Holding her breath, she reached behind her, touching, drawing away sharply . . . and then grasping as need overcame modesty. Desire charged through her body from her hand, as if the steel member exuded an incendiary force that only it could kindle and extinguish. So shocked was she at its effect on her that she was barely able to replace the breath she had anxiously held.

With an inborn intuition, she loosened her hold and slid her hand away, her nails dragging lightly along the hot flesh. At the groan of pleasure that rumbled in his chest, she repeated the newly discovered method of arousal in a fevered wonder, until Ryan's breathing was as uneven as her own. Certain that he would surely take her at any moment and end this terrible torment, Melanie increased her efforts to the sensitive surrounding area, until every tendon in the muscular body beneath her strained for control.

But his instruction came in an even voice, which belied his body's desperate state. "Lie down. I want to feel your breasts against me."

It was more than she could stand to wait any longer. To prolong this agony for them both was cruel, she thought feverishly. "Ry . . . an!" Melanie moaned in protest, leaning forward and hugging his sweat-filmed torso to her. "Plee . . . ez . . ."

She wanted him as never before. Shamelessly, she slithered against him, the friction of naked flesh against naked flesh sending lightning bolts of white fire to her mind, rendering her senseless to all but the man holding her to him. In a torrent frenzy, she worked her way down to the only source of release for the wildfire of desire consuming her, unaware of the gentle hands that slipped over her hips to guide her.

The initial contact made her cry out in breathless pleasure that the sweet fulfillment of this mindless hunger was at hand. Intent only on its satiation, she wriggled downward, taking him viciously. The arching movements under her as Ryan coordinated his ardor with her own shook her until her moans of pleasure vibrated within her chest. His hands locked at her waist to keep her from breaking the volatile junction in the frenzy.

A pure and explosive delight spiraled her spirits higher and higher, her nails digging at his ribs as she tossed her head and trembled violently in release. She could not get close enough to him, could not take in enough of him. She clutched his body with her thighs in depraved starvation, only to be lifted in the explosive climax of Ryan's own passion. Her hair fell forward across her damp brow as she was rocked by its shuddering intensity.

When the fire died down, she collapsed like a rag doll against him, her ear against the thundering pad of his heart. His coarse body hair stuck to her cheek as her own raven locks clung to his damp flesh. Another need, more subtle and deep than the one expired, began to take root, and although she lay upon him, she cuddled as if to move closer, locking her arms around his neck. In answer, Ryan embraced her and, lifting his head, kissed her tenderly upon the forehead.

"Are you always so impatient, blue eyes?" He sounded too tired to affect a teasing tone to his voice.

"It's been six years," she sighed with a secret smile at the delight of the quiet possession he still maintained. She had never felt more of a woman than right now. Ryan's very masculinity seemed to bring it out in her, compelling her to complement it. Ironically, she could not see the same smile on her husband's lips as he closed his eyes and fell victim to the fatigue that claimed her only moments after.

She had not slept so well in a long time. The fiery liberation of her mind and soul left her in a druglike state, cradled in the arms of her lover. Her dreams were the sweetest, often causing her to smile in her slumber and move closer to the warm body in the bed beside her. And such were her thoughts when she awakened in the early glow of dawn to find a pair of deep green eyes staring down upon her.

Meeting them, she smiled drowsily. "Good morning, sir."

Ryan's mouth twitched, but he did not answer her greeting. Instead, he assumed a puzzled expression. "I had the strangest dream last night that you did not stay on your side of the bed." A telltale twinkle came to his eyes. "And imagine my surprise to wake up and find you naked as the day you were born, nestled peacefully in my arms . . . looking nothing at all like a schoolmarm, I might add."

Melanie traced her fingers along the line of his jaw, her nails scratching the stubble of his morning beard. "Then it was not a dream," she murmured. She rolled onto her side to feel the length of him against her, nuzzling the bristle of his chest with her nose, inhaling him. His scent infiltrated her body, with seeking fingers of warmth reaching to the very core of her being. With raised lashes, she prompted coyly, "And what did I look like?"

This time a full smile showed white against his weather-tanned face, forming dimples on either side of it that Melanie had not noticed before. "A raven-haired seductress." A scowl darkened his features momentarily as he added in reproach, "And if you ever lay scissors to your hair again, madame, I shall be forced to deal you a terrible punishment."

Melanie tried to feign horror, her mouth contorting in unconscious provocation as she attempted to smother her grin. "And pray tell, what would that be?"

Ryan's eyes glowed wickedly. "Given your hot-blooded nature, I can think of a dozen delightful sentences."

The hand that rested on her hip turned her on her back, gliding across the taut flesh of her abdomen to seek the haven at the meeting of her thighs. At his masterful strokes, she involuntarily contracted her muscles and inhaled sharply, only to have her breath sealed with his lips. A melting sensation spread from his fingers to the farthest reaches of her body, clashing and growing turbulent with the white water of desire invoked by the sensuous exploration of her mouth by his demanding tongue.

Carried away in the crashing tide, Melanie opened her

arms and body to receive him, closing around him as he gently took possession of her. His movements were painfully slow and deliberate. His mouth retreated from her lips down a hot trail of kisses that tenderly assaulted her breasts, pink and hard in anticipation of surrender. Incensed by her own possession, she arched against him. He was a part of her. He belonged to her. Clenching his firm buttocks with her nails, she dragged him harder against her.

"You impatient little wildcat," Ryan chuckled with broken breath, the tremor of his humor within her driving her mad.

He made as if to draw away but, at her miserable groan of protest, drove her accommodatingly to the mattress. Melanie cried out in mindless rapture, unaware of the knocking on the door until Ryan clamped a hand over her mouth and called out in answer to it. A wide grin stretched across his face as he stared at Melanie, her crimson color deepening by the second as she realized there was someone outside the door. But when she went to move away, he thrust against her and shook his head.

"Beggin' your pardon, sir. Your little girl is awake and askin' for her mama and daddy," Megan informed them from the hall.

"Is she all right?"

"Oh, sure, sir. She's just restless to get out of bed."

"Then dress her and tell her we'll join her for breakfast as soon as we're dressed, Megan," Ryan told the nurse, cupping one breast mischievously and squeezing it. Upon Megan's acknowledgment, he bent over and closed his mouth over it, growling in a low voice, "I'll have my breakfast right here. But I'd best put a pillow over your mouth to keep you from calling the house down upon us."

Melanie was too mortified to answer. The hot waves of passion had been iced down by the interruption and her embarrassment. All that still held the fire was her skin, glowing against the white sheets. "We'd best get dressed," she mumbled disconcertingly.

Ryan made a circular movement with his hips, increasing

the effects of his possession, and lifted his lips from the bud of her breast to speak. "We will, my innocent blue eyes," he promised huskily. "We will." And then he proceeded to make her forget all but him.

Part Three
Honolulu, Oahu 1894 . . .

Chapter Sixteen

The tradewinds ever present off the coast helped cool the shaded gardens at Kuwaiahao Church, where a retirement party was being given for the Reverend William Cummings. Both *haoles* and Native Hawaiians gathered for the tribute to the man and his wife, who had won a place in the hearts of both peoples. Both the influential and those who made a meager living mingled on the lawn in the shade of the giant banyans, enjoying the delicious picnic prepared by the ladies auxiliary of the church, seated at tables and on mats and blankets spread to the edges to keep from being run down by the laughing children playing games around them.

"I say, Captain Caldwell, I can think of no one any more eligible than yourself as a candidate. After all, you have land holdings here in Honolulu. Surely you would think along the same lines as the rest of us."

Melanie cast a sidelong glance at her husband. She knew how Ryan hated to become involved in politics, and yet everywhere they went, that was the main topic of discussion. This was supposed to be a retirement party for the Reverend William Cummings, not a political rally for the Provisional Government. But with the May election date rapidly approaching, supporters were anxiously trying to get prominent and respected men of the community to run as delegates to create the new constitution.

"I do not consider myself qualified, Mr. Samuels. While

251

I own property, I know nothing of the Hawaiian people's wants or needs."

"But as a businessman, sir, you know the needs of your fellow entrepreneurs," Samuels insisted. "We need stability. If the States will not take us under their protection, then we need a strong government with a sound constitution to follow. You know as well as I if the States do not annex us, some other major world power will. The way we are divided, how can we stand? And what will happen to you and your family . . . your lands, this pineapple kingdom of yours and Dole's?"

Melanie knew from the lift of her husband's golden brows that the man had at last captured Ryan's attention, even though his words were nothing her husband had not previously considered since the arrival of the Caldwell clan in Honolulu. She had heard Ryan and Gilbert discussing the delicate situation between the Royalists supporting their queen and the Provisionalists led by Sanford Dole. But Ryan did not like to be pushed. He had admitted to her the time would come when a choice would have to be made, but he wanted to make up his own mind. She began to feel guilty for asking him to give up one of his few days away from the plantation for the affair, but she had wanted to come for William and Amanda. She owed that much to them.

"Ryan, I hate to interrupt, but I would like to say something to the Cummings before we sit down to eat." She gave her prettiest apologetic smile to Lem Samuels. "Might I borrow him just for a second, Mr. Samuels?" She linked her arm in Ryan's, feeling the steel of his tension through the lightweight material of his jacket. "Are you terribly upset that I dragged you away?" she asked impishly, once out of earshot of the political enthusiast.

"Extremely." His eyes darted toward the back of the churchyard, to the secluded screw pines where children dashed in and out in a game of tag, Kristen among them. "And were the place not so crowded, I'd be tempted to lure you into the thicket and show you." His inconspicuous pinch of her hip made her start with a giggled reprimand.

"Ryan, this is a church picnic!" She didn't suppose she'd ever get used to her husband's penchant for doing such things at the most inopportune times, but she wouldn't change him for the world.

How their relationship had changed since that night when she had finally become his wife in body as well as in name. Their voyage had been like a honeymoon . . . almost, she conceded, recalling some rather awkward situations with Kristen sleeping in the adjoining cabin Ryan had remodeled during the long nights before the consummation of their marriage. And there had been a few confrontations with Petula Caldwell, but only a few, for the woman had spent the better part of their time at sea locked in her room suffering from mal de mer.

The rest of them had thrived on the voyage, which, aside from Aunt Pet's seasickness, had been perfect. The weather had held up well, and even the deathly pale Priscilla had a pretty pink flush to her cheeks when they entered Honolulu harbor. It was a metamorphosis that even Ryan noticed, his compliment to his stepniece sending the gangly young woman off in a titter of giggles.

And for Kristen, it was the "most wonderful thing in her entire life, next to getting a daddy," she'd announced one evening as they'd tucked her in. She'd thrilled to climb the heights of the great masts, clinging to Ryan's back like a little monkey. She delighted the crew, particularly Karl, who fixed her special treats just like the staff at Beacon Street. Kristen became her father's shadow, marching about the ship in her adorable sailor suit that had been washed so many times it was worn out by the time they reached their destination.

The only thing that marred their arrival was the news they received at the Caldwell office Ryan had set up in Honolulu. Lydia Hammond had passed away. A rare letter in the bold hand of her father told Melanie of her mother's passing after a fever that had slowly drained away her strength. Her heart had ached as she read the lines that told of his anguish and regret over all the heartache he'd caused Melanie and her mother, heartache that his wife never forgave, even in the end.

At Ryan's insistence, they left immediately for Lahaina. A visit that Melanie dreaded turned into a purging of the soul for her, a return to a place where she buried painful memories of the past so that she could look to the future. Her father was as delighted with Kristen as his granddaughter was with him, spending most of the two days with her instead of with Melanie. Melanie thought her heart would melt when Ryan suggested the retired minister return to Honolulu with them, but Abner Hammond refused, stating firmly that Lahaina was his home.

But before they left, he spoke privately with Melanie, his words leaving her numb with shock and filled with pity for the woman who, even as she breathed her last breath, had sought revenge for the life he'd led her to. Her mother's dying words, brittle with bitterness, had tossed at him the fact that she, too, had kept a secret all those years. The precious daughter he had loved was not his own, but rather that of a dashing young architect who had courted her at the same time as the pious minister.

Melanie had cried. She'd cried for 'Io; she'd cried for herself; and she'd cried for the broken man holding her in his arms, his own eyes glazed with pain. Not that she was sorry for not having married 'Io. She loved Ryan so much that her heart swelled to the point of bursting with it. But her mother had caused so many people so much anguish.

The pity was that the brunt of it fell on her, for of them all, Lydia had been the most miserable. Her mother had never known what it was to truly love and now she would never know.

"It's been two weeks, blue eyes," Ryan whispered with a devious twist of his lips, bringing her back to the present with his reminder.

But he did not need to remind Melanie how long it had been since she'd lain in his arms and soared to passion's height with him. Ryan had been at the plantation working on the main house—a house Melanie was not allowed to see until its completion. The project not only interfered with their nocturnal bliss, but it presented other problems as well.

Although she loved the idea of his surprising her, it was very difficult to furnish a home one had never seen. She spent hours ordering specific pieces based on a room size her husband had given her, and she was still not certain the drapes would fit. "About the same as those," he'd told her when she'd asked him for the measurements, pointing to the windows of the town house in which Gilbert and Aunt Pet had set up residence.

From what he had told her, it was a large wooden structure, three stories in all. The first floor had a veranda wrapped around its entire circumference, with windows and doors opening from every room onto it. The shade of the surrounding palms, bananas, and banyans, in addition to the ever-present trades, kept it cool during the hottest hours of the day. Having belonged to a successful sugar exporting merchant who had given up his Hawaiian residence at the beginning of the political unrest upon Kalakaua's death, no extravagance had been spared. It appeared designed for entertaining. Therefore, it suited Petula Caldwell perfectly.

Gilbert often rode out with Ryan on his weekly sojourns, leaving the women to help Melanie with her blind planning and to become the most favored hostesses in Honolulu. Hardly a week went by that Aunt Pet did not have a sewing circle meeting or an afternoon tea. Even today's affair was a result of her committee work in honor of the reverend and his wife, who had become regular visitors to the Caldwell home on King Street.

"Melanie, how lovely you look!" Amanda Cummings exclaimed upon seeing their approach. Her white hair shone almost silver in the midday sun and her matronly figure was swathed in a lilac shift. "I know you must be proud of her, Captain."

"Indeed so, Mrs. Cummings," Ryan confirmed, his eyes sweeping over Melanie's ice-blue clad figure appreciatively. Even in the heat that sent beads of sweat trickling down the hollow of his back to soak his shirt, his wife looked as fresh and inviting as the sea that matched her eyes. Her dress, quite feminine with short puffed sleeves and a ruffled hem, was tailored to enhance the curves he had committed to his memory. He mastered the direction of his thoughts and focused his attention on pleasantries. "Tell me, what are you and your husband going to do now that your ministry will no longer fill your days?"

Amanda Cummings's eyes warmed in amusement at Ryan's words. "Dear Captain, our work is never done! There is the orphanage that needs us more than the parish."

"An orphanage that needs a teacher," Priscilla Caldwell put in with a surreptitious wink at Melanie. "A math teacher." Melanie thought her cousin looked particularly pretty today. She wore an ecru blouse tucked into a wide belted loden skirt that seemed to lessen the effect of her tallness. The short fringe of hair Melanie had styled framed her heart-shaped face, making it appear more round and diminishing the sharpness of her features.

"Actually, just a volunteer for a few days a week. The pay only enriches the soul," Amanda sighed regretfully.

Ryan cast a suspicious look at Melanie, with the definite feeling that he was being manipulated. Wide blue eyes looked up at him with such beguiling innocence that for a moment he experienced a twinge of guilt for even thinking the angel he beheld would be party to such a plot. But when the corners of her mouth turned up ever so slightly, her rose lips full of silent admission, he not only realized he was being maneuvered, but he actually enjoyed it.

"It's only a few days a week . . . and you are at the plantation so much," Melanie pointed out. She held her breath, for she was not certain Ryan would go along with the idea. He had been quite adamant about her not teaching in Boston, but she hadn't known if it was the idea of her pursuing the career or only the fact that they would be leaving that had made him feel that way.

Ryan pretended to consider the idea, aware of the anxious feminine eyes watching him, and then nodded, with a stipulation. "But only until we move. I would think it will take your full time to make our house livable, as you women put it."

And he wanted time alone with his wife and daughter, apart from his family and all the well-meaning visitors. There had been no real honeymoon for them. While they shared their evening hours in intimacy, their daylight hours crowded them with obligations that forced him to sneak about like an adolescent schoolboy to steal a favor from the woman he had never grown tired of. If anything, his appetite for his enigmatic wife grew with each new facet of her personality he discovered.

"Oh, Ryan!" Melanie showed her appreciation with an impulsive kiss, which made him resent the affair even more for the way his body responded to the soft curves suddenly crushed against it, then unwittingly but cruelly withdrawn.

"That's wonderful, Captain . . ."

"I wish you'd call me Ryan, Mrs. Cummings," Ryan insisted.

His teeth showed white against his tanned face as he smiled at the woman who seemed to him the perfect image of a grandmother. He considered his comparison a compliment but knew better than to pass it on. Women were women, and few liked to be reminded of their age.

"Only if you call me Amanda. That's how it should be among friends, anyway," she declared in agreement. "And I think our Melanie should be proud of her husband as well."

Melanie stepped into the circle of her husband's arm. "That I am, Amanda. There is none sweet—" She lost her thought completely as she stared at the pine thicket, for emerging from it, children hanging on each hand and one perched on his shoulders, was 'Io Kuakini. " 'Io," she breathed in disbelief.

The dark-skinned Hawaiian wore an austere brown short coat with matching trousers and a gold embroidered waistcoat beneath, none of which reminded her of the melancholy young man who had bade her good-bye on the docks of Lahaina over six years ago. But his smile and those sparkling brown eyes that teased the youngsters, who began to crowd around him as if he were the pied piper, were the same. And when they found Melanie, she started for him.

It was only a sixth sense that preserved propriety and held her in check, an intuition reinforced by the stiffening of the man standing beside her. She knew even before she looked that Ryan was not watching 'Io but was watching her. The penetrating green scrutiny spread caution throughout her thoughts, advising patience until such time as she could speak to her friend privately.

The last thing she wanted to do was provoke her husband, she decided, recalling the night he had discovered 'Io's gift to Kristen and, worse yet, his reaction when he'd discovered that 'Io was not her brother. Although he'd accepted her explanation of her tears, that they were not over what might have been with her Hawaiian sweetheart, there had been a difference in the way he'd acted toward her for a while, until he'd come to terms with it.

Not that he'd treated her cruelly; he'd just been more distant for a while. As if a trust had been broken and needed to be reestablished. She'd understood his reaction, even though it was unfounded.

" 'Io, I did not expect you to come!" Amanda Cummings stepped forward and embraced the young man warmly after he shed the last of his charges and sent them scampering off. "And look who has moved to Honolulu since you left us!"

"Did you think I would miss this for anything?" the young man responded in kind. He glanced past Amanda Cummings at Ryan and back to Melanie, suspicion flickering in the dark brown of his eyes. His movement was frozen, as if waiting for Melanie to explain the presence of the golden-haired stranger from the past.

Melanie reached for his hand, the gesture seeming so inadequate to express the joy she really felt. " 'Io, how good to see you! I want you to meet someone very special to me," she told him, emphasizing her description to distract the outright distrust he shot past her at Ryan. "This is my husband, Capt. Ryan Caldwell. Ryan . . . 'Io Kuakini."

Melanie knew immediately from the wash of astonishment on 'Io's face that he had not received the letter she'd posted the week after the holiday wedding. He still clung to her hand, staring at her as if he could not believe what she had just told him.

"Ryan and Melanie bought the Davidson home and plantation. His brother and family live in the city home," Amanda Cummings informed him in an attempt to break the awkward silence and give the young man a chance to recover. She knew from the first day he arrived that he loved Melanie, although the mystery as to why they never married remained unanswered.

'Io cleared his throat and stuck out his hand. "My congratulations, sir. I hope you'll overlook my rude hesitation, but I did not know my . . . that Melanie was married. I am pleased to meet the husband of my childhood friend."

"Mr. Kuakini," Ryan answered politely. "I've heard a lot about you."

Ryan had seen the young man that night at the Frenchman's *luau*, but this was the first time he had gotten a good look at him. Although he appeared polished and reserved, there was a smoldering emotion Ryan could well guess at behind those dark eyes tempered with civility. He imagined there would be more than the disapproval he sensed if 'Io Kuakini knew that Melanie was not his sister.

"Daddy, Daddy! Look what we found!"

Leading two other equally excited children, Kristen

came running up to them, an abandoned bird's nest clutched in her hands. "Can you put it in the tree outside my nursery window so I can watch a bird family live there?"

"Kristen," Melanie interrupted, relieved by her daughter's timely appearance. "I want you to say hello to your Uncle 'Io."

Kristen's mouth formed a perfect "Ohh!" as she turned and studied the somberly clad young man who returned her appraisal with a smile.

There was no need for him to compare the golden locks bedecked in ribbons to those of Captain Caldwell to ascertain her parentage. Nor was there any further question that his original suspicion concerning the identity of Melanie's abductor was untrue. But as he looked at the beautiful child with Meilani's eyes curtsying in front of him, he reserved judgment until later.

"I am honored to meet you at last, *maka polu li'i.*"

"That means little blue eyes, doesn't it?" Kristen asked smugly. "My mama speaks Hawaiian and she's teaching me. That's just what you called her when she was little like me, didn't you?"

'Io squatted in front of the little girl, his eyes narrowed. "And how do you know that?"

"Mama told me. She told me all about you and how you taught her to swim and all kinds of things. You sure are special to Mama and me, too. I really liked those funny things you sent . . . and I can do the hula!" Suddenly, Kristen turned to Ryan and Melanie, backtracking as an idea struck her. "Why can't I have a brother?"

Melanie stood dumbstruck at her daughter's unexpected request, her mind racing for an appropriate reply. Ryan's devilish nudge at the small of her back did not help, for he was apparently dumping the entire responsibility for resolving Kristen's question on her.

It was Priscilla who came to Melanie's rescue. "Oh my goodness, what will that niece of mine come up with next!" She hugged Kristen and held out her hand to 'Io

Kuakini. "I am Priscilla Caldwell, Mr. Kuakini. Melanie is my first cousin by blood and my . . . aunt by marriage?" she finished with a puzzled expression. "Oh, anyway, I am delighted to meet you after all these years of hearing about Uncle 'Io."

"And Auntie Pris made my dress," Kristen informed the young man, holding out her hem and swirling so that it billowed. Her foot snagged on a root, but Ryan quickly caught her up in his arms before she fell.

"It's very pretty," 'Io acknowledged, fully aware of the unspoken claim to Melanie and her daughter. "And I am pleased to meet you, Mrs. . . ."

"Miss," Priscilla corrected, her cheeks pinkening.

"Miss Caldwell," 'Io finished with a smile. "You're quite talented with a needle."

"You should hear her play the piano and sing. The children at the orphanage adore her," Amanda Cummings interjected. "We now have Priscilla and Melanie helping us out." Her mouth formed a regretful pout. "I do wish you could come back. The children miss you."

'Io hugged the minister's wife under one arm. "There's certainly more incentive than ever to come back then . . . not that I need it." His smile faltered with the troubled thought that crossed his mind. "And I promise, someday I will return. You know my reasons."

Before 'Io could elaborate, the Reverend Cummings rang a bell calling everyone's attention to the fact that the meal was about to begin. The families placed their woven mats and picnic blankets in long rows that formed a large circle and helped themselves to the buffet set up on the tables next to the church. After William Cummings asked the blessing, they began to eat.

Kristen asked 'Io to join the Caldwell clan, keeping him busy with questions about his involvement with the orphanage. It seemed that 'Io had managed to secure substantial donations and arrange fund-raisers in conjunction with the functions at the Iolani Palace, due to his connection with the royal family during its last days of rule. In

261

addition, he'd spent his spare time there teaching and arranging activities for the children.

"You're quite a well-rounded individual, Mr. Kuakini," Gilbert Caldwell acknowledged over a plate heaped with fried chicken, roast pork, plantain, sweet potatoes, and other samples of the various dishes supplied by the cooks of the parish, which were buried from eyesight. "To have served in public relations at the palace and teach orphans on the side is commendable."

'Io shrugged modestly. "I earned my living at the palace, and I paid for my room and board by helping at the orphanage. It's the very least I owe Amanda and her husband." He rested his eyes on Melanie.

"By your association with the queen, are we to assume you are a Royalist?" Priscilla asked curiously.

"I am, although I do not think that is the most popular cause among most of these people. What about yourself?"

Priscilla blushed, flustered at the turn of the question. "Well, I'm neither. We Caldwells have tried to remain neutral, since we have not been here long enough to judge what is right and what is wrong for the islands. Besides," she added with an uncomfortable cough, "we women try to stay out of politics and leave that to our menfolk."

Again 'Io's eyes went to Melanie. She smiled to herself, for Melanie knew he did not believe that of her. And he was right. She had her own opinion and believed strongly in maintaining "Hawaii for the Hawaiians," as the motto called for.

"Do you think the monarchy stable enough to stand independent among the major governments of the world?" Ryan challenged quietly.

"Not only to stand independent, sir," 'Io answered, "but to command their respect. King David was the only monarch in history to travel around the world to visit the other countries. He strove to improve Hawaii with the things he learned."

"And in doing so, ruined its economy," Ryan quipped

sourly.

"Ryan, if the *haoles* were not bleeding us, we might have the chance to recover economically," Melanie spoke up. "And even now they seek to create a constitution that will further strip the natives of their voice in their own government. Look at who tries to get you to run as a delegate to the convention, Ryan . . . the very ones who preach that only money and land give us the right to govern ourselves. And who has the land and power . . . the *haole*."

Ryan's face was inscrutable as he leveled his gaze at her. "The last time I looked, you were a *haole*, Melanie. I should be careful of the condemnation of your own kind."

But Melanie was undaunted. "You know the kind I speak of, sir," she countered evenly. "Those of us at this blanket are not the same. I know that."

"Then I'd suggest you try to maintain neutrality like the rest of us."

Melanie bristled at her husband's advice, for there was more demand in his voice than suggestion. Her blue eyes sparked. "I am a born Hawaiian, Ryan. Unlike you and your family, I have seen what the money *haoles* have done."

"Loaned the spendthrift government the money to pay for frivolously incurred debts until it nearly sold itself out?"

Melanie frowned, for Ryan had made a point. The monarchy had borrowed extensively from the wealthy businessmen. The country's debt far exceeded its ability to repay without better management by a stronger government than Kalakaua's had been. But the Hawaiian people had surely learned from past mistakes.

"Do not try to argue, Meilani. His mind is made up," 'Io advised coolly. "It is only a matter of time before he falls in with his friend Dole and the others."

"Your fanatical friend Wilcox said the same thing," Ryan chuckled humorlessly. "Fanaticism will not help your cause either, Mr. Kuakini."

'Io's mouth turned up slightly. "Is that what you think

263

me, Caldwell . . . a fanatic? Your own country is based on rule by the majority. Citizenship is the requirement to vote, not wealth. What is happening here is that a few rich *haoles*, in order to secure their investments and insure future ones, are contriving a government for themselves. The majority of people who work and live here will have no say. The government will be elected by the elite. I am as much against that as your forefathers were. Would you call them fanatics?"

"My forefathers fought against a monarchy. You seek to instill one."

"One favored by the majority," 'Io stipulated.

"Nonetheless a monarchy."

"Oh brother! Is politics all you men can discuss?" Priscilla exclaimed in a huff of irritation designed to diffuse the growing antagonism.

"It is boring," Kristen agreed, putting down a half-eaten chicken drumstick. "Daddy, do you think birds will come to this nest if I put seeds in it for them?"

Between Priscilla and Kristen, they managed to get the topic tactfully dismissed. When the picnic was over, two of the members of the parish brought out fiddles to start the dancing. Amanda and William led the group off in a reel that sent both of them panting to nearby benches at its end. But the ceremony was finished and soon the younger folks took over. Kristen immediately claimed 'Io as a partner and skipped off to join the fun.

Melanie tapped her fingers against her skirt and watched them. 'Io had to bend over and shorten his steps so that the bouncing youngster could keep up with him. When it came their turn to sashay down the two lines, the dancers clapped and cheered for the oddly matched couple. 'Io had not changed, she mused dreamily. He had always been good with children and Kristen was no exception to his charm.

"I hadn't realized I had such an ardent Royalist in my house," Ryan remarked with a degree of cynicism after the others had joined in the dancing and Melanie was alone with him.

"Not ardent, just sympathetic." Melanie leaned into him. "I fear the cause is lost for the reasons you stated . . . but my heart is with the Hawaiians. Justice does not always prevail."

Ryan buried his face in the back of her hair, inhaling its flowery scent. "Then stay out of it until the dust settles. This is not our fight."

"I hope we can, Ryan," Melanie mused aloud. She enjoyed his closeness, knowing full well his mind was not on politics any longer. She missed the intimacy they'd shared on the *Liberty Belle*. Since their arrival in Hawaii, there had been a constant list of things to be done and Ryan had been needed at the plantation. Also, Aunt Pet was now fully recovered and gave him no peace—not that he did not provoke her sharp speeches from time to time. "When will the house be done?"

At the sudden change of the subject, Ryan chuckled. "You're as bad as your daughter. Why?"

"Nothing really . . . I just . . . well, it will be nice when we have our own home," she blurted out awkwardly. "I love Gilbert and all the family, but—"

"I know," Ryan cut her off. "I've been thinking along the same lines of late. And apparently, so has Kristen."

Melanie twisted her head to see a mischievous grin on her husband's face. "How's that?"

"She wants a brother."

Melanie was suddenly snatched toward the dancers before she could reply, but her face was aglow when her husband bowed to her curtsy at the beginning of the folk dance. Like most of the men who had come in a suit, his jacket had been discarded. His rolled-up sleeves revealed a thick covering of coarse gold over his sun-bronzed arm. She could not help but feel his broad shoulders and narrow waist made her the envy of many young women present. At their lead to sashay, she felt like Kristen, for he nearly carried her down the aisle of clapping dancers, her feet barely touching the ground.

When the dance was over Melanie abandoned Ryan to the group gathered around Sanford Dole at the punch bowl, having had her fill of politics for one day. Idly, she compared the golden-haired captain to his darker-haired brother standing next to him.

How very alike they were, in spite of the difference in coloring and build, she thought, leaning against the riser of the masonry steps and sipping a cup of fresh lemonade. They had the same mannerisms, the same eyes. Sometimes it was difficult to tell one laugh from the other. The tenderness and sensitivity she so admired in Gilbert became more and more evident in the younger brother, once she could see beyond the protective shell heavily enforced with the boldness and aggression of a leader.

"You love him very much, *maka polu.*"

'Io's quiet observation was made so close to her ear that Melanie started. *"Kolohe!"* Rascal, Melanie accused, catching her breath. "I think you've frightened the life out of me."

"Then a quiet walk should still your beating heart." 'Io held out his hand to her and helped her up from the step.

The walkways Amanda Cummings kept swept clean were shaded by the wide-leafed branches of the tropical trees growing overhead. Interspersed between them were flowering shrubs that lent privacy to paths and made them the perfect spot for the children's game of hide and seek. Melanie picked a blossom of white ginger and twirled it in her fingers as 'Io told her of his whereabouts the past year.

"Your mother is upset that you have not written her," Melanie chided upon hearing that he had been in San Francisco a good deal of the year. "A letter wouldn't have hurt."

"She is well, is she not? My friends in Lahaina have kept me informed." 'Io looked away from the gentle chastisement in Melanie's eyes, admitting guiltily, "But she didn't know where I was, I know."

"Are you still involved with Wilcox, 'Io?" Melanie had

heard Robert Wilcox's name mentioned in contempt on many occasions by important and powerful people intent on destroying him, and she feared for 'Io by association with the man.

'Io crooked his finger under her chin. "Don't look at me like that, *maka polu*. I promise I will do nothing you would not approve of."

"But you didn't answer me."

"And I shan't," he assured her, pecking her on the forehead indulgently before changing the subject. "Your daughter is as beautiful as her mother. You remind me of the moon and Kristen of the sun, without which man cannot survive."

"Flattery will not get you out of this, 'Io Kuakini," Melanie warned, "but it is nice." 'Io had told her all he was going to. The fact that he was so evasive only confirmed her fears, and she wondered peevishly how he could possibly know what she would or would not approve of. She certainly did not approve of Wilcox's way of restoring the monarchy to power.

"Are you really as happy with him as you seem, Meilani?" The teasing glint had vanished from the dark brown eyes that looked down at her as he took her hands and held them. At her dreamy nod and smile, he requested brusquely, "Then you must tell me about this miraculous change in character . . . and do not try to hide the fact that he is the one who carried you off and fathered Kristen."

Melanie's smile broadened. "I wouldn't think of it." There was no need or desire to hide anything about Ryan Caldwell now. He had reappeared in her life and with love, righted everything he had done to her. It was something she wanted to share with 'Io, who had promised her at her darkest hour that things would work out. She led 'Io to the bench overlooking a birdbath and sat upon it, motioning for him to do the same. Even she became caught up in the incredulous tale of how Ryan and she were reunited.

"So if I had not been so impulsive in jumping to wrong conclusions, so much could have been avoided," she reflected, picking idly at the blossom. "And I know he is a scoundrel of a sort for his way of doing things, but I could not be happier now. It's really quite charming," she admitted sheepishly. "And he adores our daughter and—"

"—and his wife. Clever and bold man, I must say," 'Io commented with a touch of envy. "I must give him credit for admitting to his mistakes and protecting you."

Melanie's eyes misted. She lifted 'Io's hand and pressed it to her cheek. "You said things would work out best for me if I left. You made me see the importance of picking up the pieces of my life and going forth with them." She kissed the back of his hand with gratitude and affection. "And although I never fully believed it, you were right, 'Io. I can never thank you enough for that."

Her heart warmed with emotion when 'Io took her in his arms and held her. She loved him as the brother he believed himself to be and saw no reason to enlighten him. What was done was done and it could change nothing now. But fear for him over his involvement with the Royalists chilled her and she clung to him even harder. "Please don't do anything foolish to jeopardize your future."

"My wife speaks wisely, Mr. Kuakini."

"Ryan!" Melanie gasped, breaking away from 'Io in astonishment at the cutting sound of her husband's voice. Although she was innocent, her face grew hot with embarrassment over the compromising embrace her husband had found them in.

"You wasted no time in telling him, I see," Ryan sneered caustically. "I imagine it's quite a relief to find Melanie is not your sister after all."

"What's he talking about?" 'Io asked to the side, his eyes fixed warily on the enraged husband blocking the path. He was not afraid. Fear had nothing to do with his reluctance to quarrel with the angry captain. In truth, there was a time he would have leapt at the chance. But Melanie loved the golden devil and to hurt him would hurt her.

Melanie did not hear 'Io. She, too, stared at her husband, for she could not believe that after the months they had spent together he doubted her love for him. She did not expect Ryan and 'Io would be fast friends, but she never dreamed her husband would doubt her. Fire leapt to her eyes, foretelling the wounded anger mounting within her chest.

"I will not dignify your charge with a comment!" She hurled the words at him like rocks. With an upward jerk of her chin, she lifted her skirts and stomped toward Ryan. Upon reaching him, she glowered. "Will you step aside, sir, or shall we make a scene? I am quite prepared for either."

Ryan lowered his gaze to his wife's demanding one. Her head barely reached his shoulders and yet she stood there threatening him. In her ruffled dress, with its trim fit and high laced collar, and her neatly upswept hair, she was the picture of propriety. But her small fists that clenched her skirt up high above shapely ankles and the heaving of her breasts beneath the thin blue material were all Meilani—someone he had not seen in a while. That she meant what she said was clear. Under any other circumstances, Ryan might have laughed at the impertinent little figure challenging him, but instead, he meant to deal with her.

"Then let's get on with it," he answered, taking a deep breath and shoving his shoulder into her tiny sashed waist.

Melanie, temporarily winded by the sudden uplift, kicked in a ruffled frenzy at her husband's total loss of his senses. "Ryan!" she hissed through her teeth in an effort to keep from attracting attention. "Put me down!"

He ignored her completely, carrying her effortlessly toward 'Io. "Mr. Kuakini, my apologies for my impetuous assumption. I will admit my thinking is not always clear where Melanie is concerned."

'Io considered the couple for a moment. Caldwell's assumption was rational enough, though unfounded. And he knew from the way the captain looked at Melanie all afternoon that he was head over heels in love with her. Jealousy made fools of the best men, he thought to himself with a knowledge gained from firsthand experience. Melanie had apparently told her husband about their sibling relationship and the captain did not believe her. But that was for Melanie to work out . . . when she was in a better humor. His initial shock at Caldwell's unorthodox way of handling Melanie's explosive temper gave way to amusement.

"I can understand that," 'Io replied wryly, thinking that Melanie had perhaps met her match. He dodged a delicately tapered foot to accept Ryan Caldwell's offered hand. "And, although the scene you witnessed was innocent, I can see why you might think otherwise."

Melanie could not believe Ryan and Io were conversing as if she weren't even there. "Damn you, Ryan Caldwell, let me down!" she demanded imperiously.

"Melanie, this is a church picnic!" Ryan reprimanded dryly with a warning swat on her buttocks. "If you will excuse us, Mr. Kuakini, my wife and I have some matters best discussed in private."

" 'Io!" Melanie pleaded as Ryan pivoted so that she faced the bemused Hawaiian.

'Io shook his head. "You issued the challenge, *maka polu* . . . and if what you told me is true, you've nothing to fear but wounded ego."

Melanie swallowed her furious protest as Ryan emerged from the garden with her slung unceremoniously over his shoulder. Surely he would not march through the crowd assembled there like this, she told herself in horrified apprehension. But his long strides did not shorten as they rounded the corner of the church where couples still danced. The blood that rushed to her face made her feel faint from humiliation. To fight him, to call him all the names that came to her mind, would only draw more attention to them, so she closed her eyes to avoid the curious stares that followed them through the churchyard.

"Daddy, what on earth are you doing with Mommy?" Kristen squealed, skipping out to meet them as Ryan walked over to where Gilbert and Aunt Pet were seated with the Cummingses.

"Playing a game . . . and Mommy lost," Ryan placated his daughter. "Gilbert, will you and Pet take care of Kristen?"

"I want to play, too, Daddy," Kristen protested, tugging at Melanie's skirt. "Mommy, can I—?"

"No . . . you will stay with Uncle Gilbert and Aunt Pet," Ryan cut her off in a curt tone that left the child speechless.

Aunt Pet, however, was neither speechless nor intimidated. She drew herself up in front of the irritated captain, swelling with indignation. "Ryan Caldwell, you have pulled some horrible stunts in your time, but this . . ."

"Pet, I am in no humor for one of your windy lectures on propriety."

Melanie winced at Petula Caldwell's angry gasp and waited for her retaliation, but it did not come.

"Are you all right, dear?" Amanda Cummings asked quietly of Melanie. The older woman leaned over to see the younger one's face, but Melanie was too mortified to open her eyes. Instead, she whispered a timid, "Yes, I'm fine."

She vowed she would have her revenge for this. To think that only moments ago she had affectionately referred to her husband as a scoundrel. He was worse than that, but she dared not tell him what she thought until they were out of earshot of their fellow church members.

"Reverend, Mrs. Cummings, our best wishes on your retirement. Do come visit."

Their mumbled replies only served to further embarrass Melanie, for she could imagine what they . . . what all the people of the parish must be thinking. Kristen began to wail as Ryan started down the brick walk, her cry

271

reaching him when no one else seemed to be able to. Melanie issued a brief prayer of thanks that he had at last regained his senses as he turned abruptly and held out one arm to the little girl.

But he did not put her down as she expected. With her still hanging helplessly over his shoulder, he squatted to speak to the child. She felt Kristen's small fingers squeezing her legs through her dress as Ryan whispered to the child in a tone so low that Melanie could not catch his words. Occasionally, Kristen sniffed and made an "uh-uh" or an "uh-huh" in acknowledgment.

"Now don't forget Daddy's jacket," Ryan cautioned as his daughter hugged him and then raced around to kiss Melanie good-bye.

"I promise I'll be very good, so I can go the next time," she told Melanie enthusiastically. "How I love you, Mama!" Kristen's eager embrace loosened the comb holding Melanie's hair in place, so that when Ryan rose, it fell to the walk at the child's feet. "I'll put it with Daddy's jacket," she promised, looking after them and waving. "Have fun!"

272

Chapter Seventeen

The flatbed wagon jolted the breath out of Melanie as Ryan urged the horses forward with a click of his tongue. At her inadvertent cry, he cut a sideways glance at her, but she snapped her head about to stare in the opposite direction. She had not spoken to him since they left the King Street residence and had no intention of doing so.

When he carried her inside the front door and deposited her in a heap on the carpet in the foyer, she exhausted her vocabulary of every conceivable name and description she could think of. She stomped and ranted, incensed to unparalleled frustration by that damned mocking grin he wore even now. Surely from the way Megan and the other servants had stared they thought her the one mad, but Melanie was beyond caring by then. When she was nearly hoarse from shouting and could think of nothing else to say, he had had the audacity to order her to pack a case, as if she would go anywhere with him. And she had told him so.

"I'll see you in hell before I'll pack one petticoat to go anywhere with you, you arrogant bastard!" With a furious swish of her skirt, she stomped up the steps and hurriedly locked herself in their bedroom at the sound of his booted feet climbing the stairs.

Dear God, she never dreamed he'd kick the door through in his brother's home. She could just hear Aunt Pet when the servants told her what had happened. Melanie watched in trepidation as he reached through the broken panel and let himself in. Such was her shock that when he shouted for her to sit in the chair she had placed between them, she did so without thinking. With no regard for the delicacy of her things, he flung them into a case and, when he was finished, carried it downstairs in one hand and dragged her along with the other.

The sun made a magnificent display across the treetops as it began its rapid descent. The blinding gold orb dove through the layers of orange and scarlet clouds, seeming to drag them down with it behind the dark shadows of the forest. The tradewinds off the coast took advantage of the sun's absence to cool the island without hindrance, combing through the palms and bananas with soothing fingers. Night birds, unabashed by the presence of the wagon, began their song, swaying to the tropical melody in the branches.

Melanie rubbed her bare arms and wished for a shawl, but refused to make her need known. If Ryan Caldwell thought that he could make amends by taking her out to the plantation, he had a surprise in store for him. She'd bite her tongue off before she'd say one word to him, she vowed hotly. To humiliate her like that in front of their friends was unforgivable.

"If you can bring your eyes around to the forefront, the house is just ahead," Ryan informed her dryly.

Melanie would not have given him the satisfaction of any interest at all, but for the curiosity that had been building for weeks from his sketchy description. Exhaling with a flare of her nostrils, she grudgingly faced forward as if indulging him. A frown knitted on her brow, for this did not look at all like the house her neighbors had told her about.

The building loomed ahead, tucked among giant banyans, large and square. Campfires in front of makeshift shacks that housed the workers cast eerie shadows across the outside walls. They were made even more irregular by the boards and materials stacked against the rails of the lanai that encircled the house on the first and second floors. Instead of looking inviting it seemed ghoulish, as if a great square monster with many hollow eyes monitored their approach.

Again Melanie shivered, but this time not altogether from the night chill. Surely Ryan did not expect her to sleep in that, she thought with a wary peek to the side. She'd just as soon sleep in the wagon. Alone, she decided as he caught her glimpse and grinned. Although that thought did not sit well with her, either.

Ryan pulled the reins in, stopping the horses in front of one of the crew's shacks. A man emerged, pulling on a shirt as he walked up to the wagon. "Cap'n Caldwell. I wuzn't expectin' you afore Monday mornin'. Everythin' all right?" he asked, glancing uneasily at Melanie.

"Everything is fine Ned. Ned Ioko, this is my wife, Melanie. We'll be camping in the master bedroom for the next few days, so I'd appreciate it if you confine your work to the downstairs."

"Upstairs is all but done, anyways," Ned grinned with a nod of his head to Melanie. "Pleased to meet ya, missus."

Melanie managed a wavering smile in return. Ryan had lost his mind. Her eyes traveled to where wild vines grew up through the snaggled teeth of the balcony rails, as if consuming them from the bottom up. Some twisted around the columns of the lanai, intent on assaulting the second floor. She had been told that they were refurbishing the structure, but it appeared the trees and plants were winning the overall battle. It would be years before this place could be made livable, she groaned inwardly.

"See to the horses and have Lin Ho bring some food and wine up to the house for us," Ryan told Ned Ioko, jumping down from the wagon. "Other than that, we'll not be needing anything else this evening."

"Yessir," the man answered, taking one of the team by the harness to lead it away.

When Ryan's hand covered her own, Melanie inhaled sharply. It was all she could manage to glare at him as he lifted her out of the carriage and placed her on the ground beside him. If her displeasure affected him, he did not show it. In fact, he seemed secretly amused by her reaction. Torn between the urge to break her vow of silence and refuse to go into the house, and her stubborn determination to keep it and make him suffer, she opted for the latter. She followed quietly along a well-trodden path through knee-high grass, to what appeared to be the mouth of the monstrous dwelling.

But as she walked up the steps, she noted no telltale creaks of rotting planking, and once inside, the smell of new wood filled the air with dusty reassurance. In the dim moonlight shining in through the half-boarded windows, she could see that the rooms, accessed through the giant arches on either side of them, were large and spacious, but littered with clutter like the yard. She guessed . . . hoped . . . that it was building materials. Her suspicion was confirmed when Ryan lit a lamp.

They were in a large hall that surrounded a grand central staircase. It was made of a dark wood that seemed to roll down from the upstairs balcony like a giant tongue against the white background of the newly plastered walls. Melanie instinctively shrunk back.

"This is Kristen's bicycling room. She can ride from the front to the back of the house and around the stairwell." Melanie's uncertain glance at her husband revealed that he was having fun with her. She felt a degree of relief, but not nearly enough. "Let me have your hand," he told her. "We're not prepared for visitors. I'll come back for this," he added, setting the case at the sweeping foot of the staircase.

Melanie caught her dress up in her hands to keep her feet free of its hem and followed Ryan. Although she was intensely irritated with him, she appreciated the reassuring strength of the hand closed about her own. There was a landing halfway up large enough to furnish with a table or a bench on either side, and at the top of the steps was a large salon bathed in moonlight and crisscrossed by the mullions of the large doors opening onto the second-story lanai.

"Nursery and Megan's room," Ryan said, pointing to the doors on the right. "All the upstairs rooms have private dressing and bathing areas. Guest room and"—he tugged at her hand, stepping over a stack of moldings to reach a set of double doors—"the master suite," he announced, hooking the lantern just inside. "And now . . ."

Before Melanie knew what he was about, he swept her knees out from under her and lifted her in his arms. She opened her mouth to object but clamped it shut as she remembered her resolve not to speak to him. Emphatically, she crossed her arms to show her displeasure as he carried her inside.

"Very well," he said, as if to himself. "If the lovely mistress is unhappy with the bedroom, perhaps she'll be more satisfied with the bed."

His arms dropped out from under her suddenly. Melanie cried out and, too late, reached for his neck. But instead of the hard wooden floor she expected, a thick pad cushioned her impact. Recovering quickly, she realized he had dumped her on a mattress that had been spread on the floor, apparently for his use when he stayed at the plantation.

"Make yourself comfortable, darling. I'll get your bag."

A curse hung on the tip of her tongue but she swallowed it, refusing to let him provoke her any further. Although he had taken the lantern, the room was illuminated by the moon that, to Melanie's delight, could be seen hanging over the water beyond the trees. From the white rolling ripples of the silvery surface, she knew it was the ocean and recalled Ryan telling Kristen how near the plantation was to the shore.

Unable to resist taking a better look, she picked her way across the room. The floor was not scattered with debris like the rest of the house. She admired the palladium windows over the doors that did not swing open but slid into a hidden pocket in the wall. The balcony beyond smelled of fresh paint and Melanie was careful not to lean on it.

The back of the house did not look nearly as threatening and imposing as the front did. Perhaps it was because of the moon-bathed lawns stretching to a garden of plantings. Although they too were in need of pruning, the maze of paths cutting through them was easily made out from her vantage point. If only Ryan had told her, she thought with a degree of exasperation. She could have been working on the grounds instead of entertaining with Aunt Pet.

Melanie turned away from the balcony at the sound of Ryan reentering the room. Behind him an Oriental man, small in comparison to Ryan's towering form, brought in a tray containing what Melanie assumed to be their supper. He did not speak to either Ryan or Melanie. He merely placed the food on a small table Melanie had not noticed by a side window and, with a short bow to each of them, retreated as quietly as he had entered without answering Ryan's thanks.

"Do you suppose you can open your mouth to eat a bite, or is self-starvation part of this childish reaction?"

Melanie could tell from the sting of Ryan's voice that he was ceasing to find her silence amusing. Pleased that she had found a way to make him uncomfortable, since she could not physically or verbally intimidate him, she walked back into the room and, with a cool, lofty look, took the chair he held out for her. Since she had the only chair in the room, he made use of a small workbench for a stool.

"Wine?"

Melanie shoved the tin cup at Ryan, glaring over its rim in the lamplight. He ignored her display of irritation and proceeded to speak, unhampered, about the progress on the construction. Melanie tried to pretend she was not interested and concentrated on the runny stew the little man had brought up in a wooden bowl. It was cool and had very little taste to it, although she thought it might have been made from a chicken stock. The biscuits that accompanied it were stale, and Melanie could only manage to eat them after they soaked in the bland broth.

The poor quality of the food did not seem to diminish Ryan's appetite, however. He ate his portion, and when Melanie shoved hers aside with a sullen look, he helped himself to hers as well. If this was the fare, it was no wonder he ate so ravenously when he was home on the weekends. Without being obvious, she tried to determine if he had lost weight, glancing away when he returned her gaze curiously.

When finished, Ryan rose from the table and stretched, pulling his shirt over his head in the process without unbuttoning it. "Guess there's nothing left to do but go to bed."

Melanie snapped her eyes up at him. She wanted to tell him there was no need for those little sparks of interest in his eyes that she knew only too well. His treatment in bed would be no different than now . . . not until he apologized for doubting her and humiliating her in front of all those people.

"Need any help undressing?" he asked wickedly.

With a snort of disgust, Melanie jumped from the chair and stalked over to where he had put down her case. Kneeling on the floor, she went through the clothing, straining to identify it. She found a skirt, a blouse, a camisole, and matching pantaloons, but no nightdress. She growled in anger and stood up to undress. She supposed she could sleep in her camisole and pantaloons.

"I suppose we could sneak down to the shore and take a bath in the moonlight," Ryan suggested, running his hands along the curve of her hip as she tied the tiny satin closures of her bodice.

Melanie slapped his hands away, putting some distance between them to finish her task.

His laugh brought a flush of scarlet to her cheeks. "I told Kristen we were going to the new house to think of special games for her. This must be one of them," he remarked sarcastically. "You know, your hair is really growing. It's halfway down your back already." He jumped forward and caught her against him, his hand splayed against the silken tresses he pressed to her back.

Melanie grunted and pushed against him. She lowered her chin to her chest to avoid his playful attempt to kiss her, raising her shoulders to protect her neck. In frustration at her ineffective block, for his unerring tongue found the little places that drove her insane, she stomped the top of his foot with the ball of her own.

"Ho-ho! Am I to assume you are not of an amorous nature? It's so hard to tell with you quiet types," he mocked. "I suppose I'll just have to rely on body language." Holding her fast with one arm he forced his hand between them, gently but firmly, until his fingers found the hardening peaks of her breasts. "Well, that's encouraging," he remarked with dry satisfaction.

Melanie tightened every muscle of her body, forbidding it to react to his teasing play. How like a man to think he could make love to her and everything would be all right! Well, as much as she enjoyed his attentions, this was one time she would not give in. He needed to be taught a lesson, and so help her, even if she died of torment, she would not give in to him. The fact that he was not taking her seriously made her even more determined.

When she did not squirm under the meandering caress of his hands over the curves and hollows of her body, still maintaining her rigid guard, he released her and swung away with a muttered curse. Melanie could not help the victorious smile that played on her lips, and she smugly crossed the room to the mattress on the floor. She climbed onto it, unaware of the tempting display her lace pantaloons offered as she pulled back the sheet and snuggled against her pillow.

When Ryan picked up the wine bottle from the table and crossed the room to turn out the lamp, she paid him no mind. It would serve him right to spend the night on the lanai with his wine. Maybe then he'd take the time to think about the way he had acted and treated her. She was shocked when she heard the clink of the glass on the floor next to the bed and the sounds of her husband shedding his clothing.

Ryan never slept in his clothes, so Melanie was certain the apprehension growing in her chest had no basis. She had made her point. Still, she held her breath when the mattress sagged under his weight and released it when his movement became still. Her back to him, she presented a picture of white silken curves against the backdrop of the window that opened onto the side porch. Her hair spread black against the pillow behind her drew his fingers to it. She tensed again, waiting.

"How far are you willing to carry this little game, blue eyes?"

At her silence, he grasped her shoulder and turned her so that she stared up at him. His own eyes burned into hers as his fingers trekked down the valley between her breasts, leaving a trail of unfastened ribbons in their wake. They ended with the drawstring that held up her pantaloons, sliding under them against the satin of her flesh so that the garment slid down in a caressing motion of its own.

Melanie offered no resistance, but she clenched her legs together tightly as her husband knelt on the bed and drew off her clothing. She willed herself to think of the humiliation she had felt when Amanda Cummings had peeked around Ryan's back to ask her if she was all right, and her skin burned with that humiliation, not with the arousing contact of the male body drawing her to it.

"You are determined to fight me, aren't you? Right now your obstinate little mind is set against enjoying our night together, isn't it?" Ryan cooed in her ear, before burying his face in the hollow of her neck. At the nod of her head, he chuckled, his lean form shaking against the length of her. "My stubborn Meilani, you are still a novice when it comes to games between men and women." His fingers tickled the clamped valley between her thighs, causing her to quiver involuntarily to her dismay. "But I shall enjoy initiating you as much now as ever."

His voice was a seductive rumble in his throat that threatened and excited at the same time. Something cold touched the tip of her breast and, before she could react, a liquid poured over it, spilling into the valley between them and trickling under her arm to the mattress. "What?" she gasped, struggling up on her elbows, only to have them knocked out from under her.

"A word! That's progress." The chilling effect of Ryan's taunt was annulled by the burning sensation of his tongue licking the cool essence, which Melanie identified from its scent as wine, from her chest.

For the second time that evening she thought her husband had taken leave of his senses. A flood of warmth flushed her loins with a craving weakness, which made her clasp her legs together in a desperate attempt to thwart it. He was not only going to get her sticky with the liquor, but ruin the sheets as well. And yet it was wildly mind-boggling. She thrust her body up to meet the lapping tongue, which occasionally withdrew to let his teeth nibble at her quivering flesh. Her arms were about to smother his face in the fullness of her bosom when she caught herself. With a pitiful moan, she shoved him away and covered her aching breasts with her arms.

"Still not enjoying yourself," Ryan tutted infuriatingly.

At the soaking of her stomach and the closed trench of her legs, Melanie shrieked and sat up. "The bed!" she objected incredulously. "Have you taken leave of your senses?"

"Not yet. Care to join me when I do?" Holding her feet firmly against the mattress, Ryan began to make tiny circular motions with his tongue inside her knees.

"In hell, I will!" Melanie swore, using her hands to clamp her knees tightly together lest she lose to the compulsion to give him his way. "Get away!" she shoved at his head roughly.

"And waste all this wine? Never, blue eyes." Ryan came

back at her, pushing her against the mattress. "Besides, I offered you a bath in the ocean."

"Ryan!" she pleaded. His hands cupped around her breasts, holding her down in exquisite torture as he sipped the wine from her navel. It wasn't fair, this crazed passion, her sanity cried out under the relentless assault.

"I will never use crystal again," her husband vowed hotly against the taut skin of her stomach, which trembled against his lips.

"Nooo," Melanie protested weakly, losing track of her surroundings as her husband moved downward slowly, painstakingly, until she lost her breath from the realization of his destination.

When he touched the sensitive bud of her femininity, her whole body shuddered convulsively with shooting bolts of fire, melting all semblance of resistance. She did not hear the bottle of wine turn over at the bedside, spilling its few remains on the floor. Nor did she notice the way her husband had coaxed her thighs apart. All she knew was a white heat that engulfed her and robbed her of all consciousness, except its source.

Her senses reeled in a building current that made her cry out at her helplessness to do anything but feel. In a swoon of desire, she clawed at the sheets to keep from being swept away by it, and then at the man who could make this precious torture go away. As he took her, she rose up to accept him, climbing his muscular frame until she was suspended above the damp bed by her arms and legs that embraced him desperately. She could not hear his own groans of pleasure for the loud, guttural demands she made of him.

Carried away with the same fever, Ryan sat up, taking her with him. His body convulsed at the heated friction of her damp flesh against his own as she slid down to his thighs, as if trying to consume all of him. It was all he could do to grasp her buttocks, which wriggled in a frenzy to find relief from the insatiable fire he had fanned within.

He had tapped all the passion of Meilani, and its release was carrying them both away in a tide unlike any he had ever experienced before. He barely felt the nails that dragged down his back or the teeth that nipped at his chest. Her screams of sweet agony ran up his spine, infecting him with the same frisson of desire. Only the furious thrusting and gyration of her hips against his legs, her stomach against his, her breasts brushing lightly and then crushing, penetrated his awareness until he could maintain his restraint no longer.

He lunged upward, carrying the tigress back to the bed with a thud that temporarily winded her. He was mindless of anything but the sensation of her hot body engulfing him, writhing beneath and around him. His breath grew shorter and shorter until his lungs ached, his fever peaking with the rapturous cry of his mate. A riotous explosion racked them both and collapsed in shudders of fulfillment.

Melanie could not move beneath the dead weight that pressed her against the mattress. Through a languorous fog, she ascertained what had happened but could not believe it. It must have been a crazed hallucination, she told herself, ignoring the heavy body that still possessed her. Nothing could really be like that, she mused as she closed her eyes, too contented to question any further.

When Melanie opened her eyes the next morning, she found Ryan gone and a note lying on his pillow. A sleepy glance about the room made her blush with profuse embarrassment. The empty wine bottle lay beside the mattress, and the sheets were stained and smelled of its previous contents. Her camisole lay discarded at the foot and her pantaloons hung over the finial of the chair.

The last time something like this had happened, she had blamed the rum punch and hallucinogenic mushrooms. But this time there was no excuse. You sure showed him, she thought sarcastically. How on earth could she face him after her behavior? she wondered miserably as she picked up the note.

Her lips twitched as she read the only two words on the paper and then she laughed, hugging the missive to her as if it were the most eloquent love letter in the world. Yet all it said was "I'm sorry."

She found Ryan drinking coffee in front of the shack she had seen the night before. He and Ned Ioko were intent on a set of plans spread on a makeshift table when she rounded the corner of the big house, freshly bathed and dressed in the skirt and blouse her husband had packed for her. The light that kindled in his eyes as Ryan met her gaze warmed her from head to toe, rivaling the rays of the sun beating down on them.

"Good morning, gentlemen," Melanie greeted them, unable to keep from blushing under her husband's appraisal. Without thought to the stocky carpenter observing her, she walked up to Ryan and kissed him full on the mouth. "You're forgiven," she whispered quickly, before backing away. "Did I sleep through breakfast?"

Ryan grimaced. "More beaten biscuits," he apologized. "But Lin Ho will have a decent meal later."

"We were not expecting the cap'n until tomorrow, missus, and we heard you wuzn't comin' till we wuz done," Ned Ioko apologized.

Melanie grinned sheepishly. "It was a surprise for us both, Mr. Ioko."

Ryan and Ned Ioko went back to studying the house plans, leaving Melanie to chew on the hard biscuit as best she could and chase it with the strong coffee. It was a far cry from Karl's cooking, but in the light of the beautiful Sunday morning, it served its purpose adequately.

Graceful. That is what came to her mind as she studied the large white columned structure. Today it looked anything but monstrous. Melanie secretly apologized to the spirit of the mansion for her first impression, for she could see why Ryan had been so enthused about the project of restoring it. Why, she could swear the light reflecting in the windows that had appeared hollow and haunted the previous night danced in delight at the prospect of occupation again.

"When do I get the grand tour?" she asked as she finished the last of her coffee.

Ryan straightened, stretching his bare torso in the morning sunlight, and offered her his arm. "Today I am at my lady's disposal. Tomorrow, we go to work."

Like with the outside, Melanie had equally misjudged the inside. The central hall was actually a room perfectly designed for balls and grand entertainment. Adjoining it in the front were the parlor and dining room, and in the back were a library and servant's kitchen. Beautiful raised panels of koa and mahogany graced all the rooms, forming wainscoting in some and full walls in others.

A colonnade attached the outhouse or cooking kitchen to the warming room. There they found Lin Ho busily working over the fire on their supper. His short bows of greeting were done so hurriedly that Melanie and Ryan did not linger, knowing he was too busy to socialize. The tour finished in the garden, where the former owner, Mrs. Davidson, had planted camellia hedges to divide the matrix of plantings and walkways.

"And that, madame, is the end of the house and garden tour. You go to the barn and the beach at your own risk," Ryan added with a smug grin that again brought a rise of color to Melanie's cheeks. "I don't think I will ever tire of seeing that adorable pink . . . a maiden's blush from a lusty wench I know is no longer a maid. How do you do it?" he teased, dodging her playful slap and reaching for her waist with a threatening growl.

Melanie squealed and darted off through the maze, her skirts high over her ankles. She dodged in and out of the paths with Ryan close at her heels, laughing and tossing her loose raven locks in carefree abandon. How wonderful it felt not to have to worry about the day's tasks and errands, or whether her hair was primly pinned in place. She felt as lighthearted as her daughter as she bounded out of the garden across the lawns toward the trees, which separated the plantation from the beach.

Her heart felt as though it would burst from her chest when she finally reached the end of the wooded path and her feet sunk into the white sand. She knew Ryan had intentionally held back and herded her there, for it was impossible to outrun his long legs for any length of time. She staggered out into the sunlight and dropped to her knees with a winded giggle, for Ryan caught up with her and sprawled out facedown on the sand beside her.

"And this . . ." he gasped, rolling over on his back, "is the beach."

"Whatever will your men think of us?" Melanie sighed, brushing away the sand that stuck to his heaving chest with a wrinkle of her nose.

Ryan looked up at her, her hair tousled in disarray by the ocean breeze and her childlike face so much like Kristen's screwed up in distaste. He could not believe that after last night he could want her again so soon, but he recognized the stirrings that she could arouse with only a glance or a smile. It was no wonder he could not think clearly where Melanie was concerned, for he would kill for her, die for her. An emotion stronger than any he had ever known for any other being drove him to drag her on top of him and kiss her diminutive pug of a nose.

"They'll think we're two people in love," he answered huskily, before tasting the sweetness of her lips once more.

Chapter Eighteen

The week passed too quickly for Melanie. She missed her daughter's effervescent company, but the time she had alone with Ryan was much needed. Although she worked hard on the yard during the day, assisted by Liat, Lin Ho's sweet and ever-smiling wife, while he rode back and forth from the reddish tilled fields of pineapples to the house, she could not remember when she had felt so rested and carefree. More than once she was reminded of the abandoned day Ryan had taken her to the deserted island as they frolicked in the water and watched the sun go down in each other's arms.

The last day at the plantation before Ryan was to take Melanie home to King Street was sultry and oppressed, as if a hidden storm were brewing in the bright blue skies. Liat and Melanie gave up work early on the garden that looked more like a garden now than an overgrown weed patch. With Ryan still out in the pineapple fields overseeing the planting of the crowns he had just purchased from Sanford Dole, a new variety called Smooth Cayenne, Melanie decided to spend the afternoon on the secluded beach.

When she emerged barefoot from the shaded path carpeted with pine needles, the white sand burned the bottoms of her feet. In short hopping steps she made her way to the water's edge, where the saturated beach offered relief, and peeled off her sweat-soaked blouse. After rinsing it in the shallows so that it would be fresh when she donned it again to meet Ryan at the house for supper, she did the same with her other clothes, hanging them over some low-growing shrubs and limbs at the edge of the woods to dry.

A pang of guilt carried over from her days on Lahaina stabbed at her as she stretched toward the sun, luxuriating in its warm bath upon her naked skin. A sad smile touched her lips, for her foolishness, for not only was she a married woman and old enough to do as she pleased, but there was no one to chastise her now for her shameful pleasure. Well, almost no one. Aunt Pet's stern look of disapproval came to her mind—a look she knew would be forthcoming when her aunt saw the healthy golden glow that had surfaced on her skin in the past few days.

The water offered a cool and refreshing relief from the sunbaked land. Melanie swam for a while and then floated on her back, her dark hair fanned in waves about her head and shoulders. Occasionally, she put a foot down to find a piece of coral, doing so tentatively to avoid a serious injury. Unlike the north side of the island, the waves were gentler here. It would be the perfect place to teach her daughter all the things about the ocean that she had learned as a child growing up near Lahaina.

After a time of studying the wispy white cloud formations, determining that a small horse and innumerable puffy monsters floated overhead, Melanie swam back along the shoreline to where the gentle tide had carried her from and emerged from the water. With another lazy stretch in homage to the blinding yellow-orange god of the sky, she spread the full skirt Ryan had hurriedly packed the day of the picnic over a patch of knee-high dried grass and lay down.

The workout in the salt water was therapeutic for the aches in her arms and shoulders, which came from pulling the entrenched weeds all week long, as much so as the long, penetrating fingers of the sun that massaged them until Melanie felt so relaxed she could not move a muscle without a concentrated effort. The echoes of a thousand seashells reverberated around her with each churning wash of the mother sea against the white sand, until her eyelids grew heavy with sleep.

She had teased Ryan that he deprived her of sleep during the nights and worked her to death during the day. Whether lack of sleep was the case or not, the slumber that claimed her was deep. So much so that she did not hear the heavy footfalls of the shabbily dressed men who walked along the shoreline from the direction of the large rock formation that loomed in the east and overlooked the southern shores of the island.

The leader, a man as tall as he was round in girth, held up his hand upon seeing the delicate silk undergarments Melanie had hung out to dry. "I theenk, *mes amis*, we have some diversion."

One of the other men pointed excitedly to where Melanie lay all but hidden in the grass. "There in the grass, good gawd amighty!"

The leader's thick lips spread over yellowed teeth, one of the front ones missing. Using the shovel as a walking stick, he made his way to the sleeping figure. Leaning heavily on the handle, he knelt down beside her, his eyes roving over the pinkening curves of her slender body. With his rough hand, he cupped the firm roundness of her buttocks, his labored breath from the oppressive heat growing shorter as she began to stir.

A soft moan of pleasure escaped her full lips as she raised up on her elbows. "I thought you were out in the field," she mumbled in a voice husky with sleep.

"Who could think of farming, mademoiselle, with one so lovely as you here waiting for me?"

With a startled cry at the strange voice, Melanie clutched her skirt to her breasts and rolled up in it, instantly awake. She squinted in the bright sunlight at the giant shadow of a man squatting beside her, looking up into his lascivious grin. Instinct identified him before she recognized the scraggly black beard of the Frenchman.

"You!" she exclaimed, hardly daring to believe her eyes, for this was not Lahaina. She tried to tuck the fullness of her skirt about her body to shield it from the hungry eyes staring down at her. "How dare you trespass on private property, let alone touch me with your filthy hands!"

Somewhat taken aback at the girl's recognition and spiteful reproach, the Frenchman narrowed his eyes until they were no more than slits in the fluid-swollen sockets. Suddenly, they widened. *"Sacre bleu!* If it is not the minister's daughter from Lahaina! It has been long since my eyes have beheld your"—his eyes raked down the length of her scantily clad form—"beauty," he finished insultingly. "You are expecting someone, no? A lover perhaps?"

"My *husband!*" Melanie declared boldly, unable to help the color that flooded her skin under the lusty appraisal of the men surrounding her.

The Frenchman glanced about him uncertainly. "Take a look," he instructed his comrades. "Theese little lady and I have much to discuss." He ended his threat with a guttural purr that sent vibrations of fear up Melanie's spine. A short, pudgy finger scraped along the delicate taper of her jaw. "I have friends in the Orient who would pay dearly for your dark-haired blue-eyed beauty, leetle one."

Melanie snatched her head away defiantly, her hands too occupied with keeping her cover on to slap at him. She glared at him, willing away the bile that rose to her throat from his degrading touch. She had to keep her head. Ryan would not be back from the fields until close to sundown, and the chance of the men at the house hearing her screams for help was slim if the man hovering over her decided to satisfy the lust in his eyes or carry her off.

"I had been told theese place was abandoned, mademoiselle. Am I to theenk your husband owns it?"

Melanie rallied with false bravado. "He does, sir . . . and he has a large crew, so you might as well give up any foolish notion you might have of abduction. This is not Lahaina and you cannot pay off my husband." She swallowed dryly. "So, if you and your men would kindly be on your way, I would like to dress."

The Frenchman made disgusting snorts of amusement through his large flat nose at her lame threat. He reached out and wrapped a raven length of silk about his fingers. "I always said you were full of hellfire . . . an odd quality for a preacher's leetle girl, no?"

Melanie pulled away, wincing at the tug of her hair as it came free. "I warn you," she hissed, "if you touch me one more time, my husband—"

"—*is not here*, mademoiselle. We are quite alone."

His words were like a blade of ice, stabbing her chest with the truth. Rape was nothing new to her companion. She could not count the number of young girls he had been accused of molesting—accused, but never convicted. Abner Hammond swore he paid someone a very high price to see that he had no serious trouble with the authorities in Lahaina.

What would Ryan think? a panicked thought struck her. What would he find but her clothes? Would he assume her drowned and not come looking for her? Dear God, not now, she prayed fervently. Not when she and Kristen had finally found happiness with the captain of the *Liberty Belle*. A cutting pain lodged in her throat. Kristen! She had to get away. She couldn't leave her baby.

Melanie's eyes darted about her like that of a cornered prey, noting the distance the Frenchman's men had walked down the beach to make certain there was no one around to thwart their plans. Don't get hysterical, she cautioned herself sternly. If she could get away from the Frenchman, the others were too far away to catch up with her. Gradually, she brought her gaze back to her would-be abductor.

He was straining to maintain his awkward kneeling position. His beet-red face and the sweat soaking the stained handkerchief he'd stuffed under the brim of his hat attested to that. If she could just throw him off balance. A callused hand reached out to stroke the shapely length of her calf just as Melanie drew her knees up. His mouth curled with premature self-confidence, her assailant misreading her movement as fearful withdrawal. With a calculated kick aimed at his chest, Melanie sent his big hulk flailing backward and scrambled to her feet.

She did not bother to look behind her. Clutching her skirt to her, she raced toward the trees, spurred on by the curses of the men on the beach. She ran straight toward the plantation yard, giving up the winding footpath. Sticks and sharp cones pricked at the soft soles of her feet, but the panic that now ran rampant through her veins numbed her to the pain. Low hanging branches whipped across her face, her hands too preoccupied with her covering to sweep them aside.

Somehow, from deep within her chest, her terror found release in her voice. She screamed Ryan's name above the pounding pulse in her ears, which sounded like pursuing footsteps at her heels. "Ryan!" she screamed again at the sight of the clearing just beyond the last yards of the wooden glen. She was almost there. Surely the Frenchman would not follow her into the open in front of her husband's men. But those thumping sounds, she wondered, teetering on the verge of hysteria . . . her heart?

"Ry . . . an! His name came out in an agonized cry as her foot, landing on its side in a small depression, twisted sharply under her and threw her to the ground.

All semblance of reason left her. Tears blinded her as she tried to get up, crying in terrorized pain, but her foot would not support her weight. At the thundering blur of Ryan's sorrel stallion racing toward her, she dragged her body toward him in mindless desperation. All she could make out was the burnished gold of his hair as he bolted off the horse before it came to an earth-scattering stop in front of her, but she reached for him, forgetting her tattered skirt.

"Good God, what happened?" Ryan demanded hoarsely, gathering her shuddering body into the protection of his arm. "Get a blanket!" he shouted over his shoulder.

"He's here!" Melanie sobbed, her voice high with hysteria. "He's going to take me away and I'd never see you again!"

"Who, Melanie?" Ryan reached for the skirt and tried to wrap it about her violently trembling body. His eyes searched the woods from which she had just emerged, seeing no sign of anyone in pursuit.

Ryan bent over, trying to make out the incoherent babble she had fallen into. Her fingers dug into his shirt, clenching and clinging as though she feared he would let her go. He made out the words *Frenchman* and *Lahaina*, but they made no sense. But someone had frightened the woman in his arms out of her mind and his body steeled with rage.

"Here ya go, sir," Ned Ioko interrupted. The foreman handed Ryan a blanket, his head turned respectfully. "You want us to go have a look?"

"Yes . . . and thanks, Ned."

The men who had been working on the house filed past him hurriedly, some carrying their tools as weapons, as he wrapped Melanie in the blanket and picked her up. Her disconnected account had faded into heart-wrenching sobs that made him shake with bewildered fury. He glanced to where the crew had disappeared, torn between staying with Melanie and going after the ones who had done this to her.

From what he could gather, the Frenchman and two or three men were going to abduct her. He touched her and she was asleep. And the men had shovels. Ryan looked down at Melanie's tear-streaked face. Her eyes were squeezed shut, their wet lashes spread against the sun-pinkened ridge of her cheeks. Her lips quivered with silent words and ragged breaths, which made her body stiffen and collapse shakily with each one. Her slender fingers were white, so tight was her grasp on the material of his shirt, as if she feared he'd leave her.

"Hush, blue eyes," he rumbled softly against her forehead in reassurance, grateful for his notion to come back early and spend the remaining part of their last day at the plantation with his fetching wife. "No one is going to take you from me, not while I live and breathe. I promise."

Liat met him at the back door of the house, her almond-shaped eyes wide with alarm at the sight of Melanie in his arms. Ryan sent her for a basin to soak the ugly blue-tinged ankle that was swelling threateningly below the shapely leg that protruded from the blanket, and he carried Melanie upstairs to their room.

She did not want to let go of him when he deposited her on the floor bed. Her eyes grew round in the same terror he had witnessed as he'd urged the stallion toward her, and in a rasping voice, she begged him not to leave her. He managed to assuage her fears long enough to fetch a bottle of brandy from the trunk he lived out of during his weekly stays.

As he uncorked it, he scanned the water beyond the trees, swearing silently at the fact that the beach itself was hidden from view. All he could see was a shimmering expanse of blue water, which reminded him of Melanie's eyes when she laughed, and he turned to go back to her. But as he did so, he caught a glimpse of something strange farther down the shoreline and swung back to take a closer look.

Beyond a finger of land that jutted out into the blue water was a small ship. It was almost square, squatty and low in the water—a steamship, judging from the smokestacks amidships. At that distance, Ryan could not make out the smudge of a name on her rust-eaten hull, but he committed it to his memory with a vengeance. If he ever saw that vessel again, he would know it without question.

"What is it? Is it them?" Melanie's shaky voice made him pivot at the unexpected nearness of it.

She had climbed out of the bed and was using the back of the chair as a crutch to make her way to him. Her skin was blanched beneath the golden tan she had earned the past few days and her eyes were still frightened. But the grim set of her mouth as she struggled with her painful ankle made him smile in a combination of admiration and irritation at her spunk. His little survivor, he mused, shortening the distance between them in long, quick strides, and relieving her of her weight effortlessly.

"This time, stay put!" he admonished gently, depositing her back on the bed.

As much as he enjoyed the sight of her exquisitely proportioned body, he knew that Liat would be up shortly and that Melanie would be mortified later, if not now, over her state of undress. Again he consulted his trunk and came up with a clean shirt that served well as a nightdress. Once he had dressed her in it, he insisted she drink the burning liquor to settle the nerves that still quivered beneath her flesh.

Her black hair hung spread across his chest as she rested her head in the cradle of his arm and sipped the brandy from the bottle he held to her mouth. God, he loved her. It was so overwhelming that it was all he could do to keep from crushing her in his arms to demonstrate this helpless feeling of caring so much and not being able to avenge her hurt and fear.

So help him, he would find them, if his men did not. And if it was indeed the Frenchman, he would finish the business he should have finished years ago. He had only let it pass because, inadvertently, the swine had delivered this sweet angel into his arms. He had almost felt a certain gratitude for having been cheated of a trollop and given in her place his innocent Meilani.

And if the Frenchman was on Oahu, he knew exactly who would lead him to him. His wife's ex-sweetheart, 'Io Kuakini. The term brought a ghost of a smile to his lips, for he no longer doubted her love. He was foolish to have done so to start with, but he had never been in love before and still was not adept at handling all the emotions that went with it. As he looked down at the delicately carved features of his wife's face, now soft in liquor-induced repose, he wondered if he ever would be.

* * *

296

'Io Kuakini proved easier to find than he had anticipated, for he was a guest of Priscilla's at his brother's house the day Ryan drove Melanie back to Honolulu on the flatbed wagon. The night had been a restless one for her. Ryan had had to shake her more than once to wake her from her nightmares about the men who had found her on the beach. He considered postponing their return but thought she'd rest better in the city . . . particularly if he had to leave.

Melanie's demeanor was quiet during the meal, her eyes lacking the certain sparkle Ryan had come to adore. She smiled and answered Kristen's endless questions about the house, but there was that certain reserve that concerned him and made him impatient for the meal to be over so he could confront Kuakini about the Frenchman's whereabouts. The Hawaiian was an ardent follower of Wilcox, and everyone knew Wilcox was instigating rebellion. The fact that he had approached Ryan six years earlier only confirmed his suspicion that the Frenchman's appearance on the plantation beach was not wholly coincidental.

After the meal, Melanie retired to their bedroom, complaining of a headache. Petula Caldwell, with a disdainful sniff at Ryan, declared that no doubt it was from the exposure to the sun that had darkened the young woman's skin. But Ryan was too preoccupied with speaking to Priscilla's guest to concern himself with the affront. He was actually growing used to his sister-in-law's constant blame of anything and everything that went awry between him and Melanie, and he took exception less and less out of consideration for his brother and for Melanie.

Mellowing, Gilbert had called it. But there was nothing mellow about the way he felt when the gentlemen retired to the library for an after-dinner drink while the ladies saw to Melanie. He imagined they would question her about her behavior, but she had already vowed not to tell anyone, for fear of upsetting them. She had even tried to convince him that she had dismissed it from her mind as

297

a freak encounter, but he knew her too well to believe it.

"So how much more do you have to do to finish the new addition, Mr. Kuakini?" Gilbert asked the young Hawaiian as they entered the large room that had been converted into an office.

Already the accounting member of the team was setting up books and working projections on the new line Ryan wanted to set up between San Francisco and the South Pacific Islands. But on Sunday, the ledgers that usually covered the expensive walnut desk had been put away, and the servants had put out crystal decanters of assorted spirits, along with matching glasses.

Ryan paced the perimeter of the room lined with book-filled shelves, as if searching for a particular title, but he was actually planning his approach to the subject. Accepting the glass of Irish whiskey, a housewarming present from Amos Cobb to his brother, Ryan took a leather upholstered chair across from Kuakini and sipped his drink thoughtfully, while the Hawaiian elaborated about the work he was doing during his visit with the Cummings.

"Well, Priscilla will certainly miss you when you return to San Francisco," Gilbert observed dryly. "I'm beginning to get the idea that you have impressed my stepdaughter quite a bit."

"No, it is I who am impressed," 'Io objected modestly. "Your stepdaughter is a remarkably generous and intuitive young woman when it comes to the children, not to mention her accomplishment with a needle. I have seen her perform miracles on the children's hand-me-downs."

Gilbert smiled reflectively. "Perhaps Priscilla has at last found her calling."

"I think so," 'Io agreed.

"And what is your calling, Mr. Kuakini?" Ryan spoke up lazily. But there was nothing lazy in the alert green gaze fixed on the young man. "You are a carpenter, a teacher, a political activist," he finished pointedly. "Which career do you plan to pursue?"

'Io Kuakini turned the glass in his fingers in quiet contemplation of the unspoken challenge. "I am waiting to see what changes are in store for my people before I choose."

"Do you really think President Cleveland will recognize the new government or support the queen?" Gilbert asked, shifting his eyes uncomfortably from one young man to the other.

'Io shrugged. "I only know what I pray for."

"Is that all you are currently doing, Mr. Kuakini? Praying?" Ryan asked sharply.

'Io was nonplussed. "No. We have our delegates in Washington and other major nations' capitals, pleading the case of our queen."

"You sound like you have taken a stand, brother," Gilbert observed in surprise.

"It is one he made clear last week, Mr. Caldwell."

"Why do you suppose the Frenchman and his men from Lahaina were trespassing on my land yesterday, Mr. Kuakini?" Ryan stood up, his teeth grating with restraint. There was no point in hedging. He usually went straight to the point and had no wish to become involved in a political debate when all he cared about was catching up with Melanie's would-be abductors.

'Io's brow lifted in surprise. "I'm sure I don't know."

"They were carrying shovels and came in on a small freighter. You know what that smacks of to me?" At 'Io's silence, Ryan told him. "Treason to the current government. Your friend set me up to meet Robert Wilcox a few years ago to bring arms ashore and bury them on the beach. Sound familiar?"

Ryan had to admit the Hawaiian was a cool one. His dark face was inscrutable as he nodded. "But a lot can change in six years . . . and Bartot is no friend to anyone, Captain."

Bartot. So that was the Frenchman's name. "So you are no longer involved with Wilcox?"

"Do you think I would tell you that if I were?" 'Io laughed humorlessly. "So that you could run to Sanford

Dole or Marshal Hitchcock with the news?"

Ryan leaned over, his eyes burning into 'Io's. "I don't give a damn about Sanford Dole or your queen," he declared hotly. "I want Bartot!"

"You and more like you."

"My wife was on that beach alone when Bartot and his men discovered her," Ryan exploded, his patience expiring completely. He seized the lapels of 'Io's linen jacket and drew the young man out of his seat, so that his face was level with his own.

"Dear God in heaven, was Melanie hurt?" Gilbert asked faintly, abandoning his intention to break his brother apart from his guest.

But 'Io's reaction was a low growl. Fire leapt into the placid brown eyes that sought the answer to Gilbert's question on Ryan's face. He did not offer to break away or seem to take offense at the way the captain held him.

Ryan recognized his own fury in the Hawaiian's reaction and knew he had an ally, if not a friend. "She escaped before he could make off with her." He let go of 'Io's coat, easing the tension of the moment with the same effect of his words. "But she was hysterical when I found her. By the time I could get out of her what had happened, your friend was on his way out to sea."

"Don't *ever* call him my friend," 'Io Kuakini hissed in warning with more emotion than Ryan thought him capable of. "He is a mercenary bastard whose loyalty goes to the highest bidder." As if in desperate need of fresh air, 'Io stalked across the room to an open window and stared out at nothing in particular. "He would have taken great delight in carrying Melanie off . . . and not just because of her obvious charms. It would be the perfect revenge."

Ryan scowled in confusion. "Revenge for what?"

"Abner Hammond closed him down and ran him out of Lahaina two years ago. He's been scratching out a living on that rust-eaten barge of his in shipping . . . supposedly." 'Io turned to face Ryan, his features grave. "Their feud goes a long way back."

"So that's why he seemed so pleased with himself the night of the raid," Ryan mused aloud, his mind racing back six years. He remembered thinking that night at the police station that the Frenchman wasn't the least bit perturbed by the reverend's damnation. He had secretly outwitted the old man and used Ryan's weakness for Meilani's beauty to do it. "He wasn't selling Meilani, he was selling Abner Hammond's daughter," he echoed faintly.

"You bastard!"

Before Ryan realized what was about, 'Io was across the room, his fist clipping Ryan's chin and sending him flying backward into the armchair. The chair overturned with the impact of his weight, but his early years of barroom brawling prepared the captain for retaliation without thinking. He rolled backward out of the chair and onto his feet, crouching low for the enraged Hawaiian's charge.

"That was my sister, not some tramp you carried off!" 'Io shouted hoarsely, his fury cresting again. But before 'Io could reach him, Gilbert grabbed his arm and pinned it behind him in a quick fluid movement that checked his attack.

"Gentlemen!" he warned sharply as Ryan sprang to his feet.

Something in Gilbert's tone made him hesitate, giving reason time enough to prevail over instinct. Or perhaps it was surprise at his gentle brother's swift command of the situation. Be that as it may, Ryan rubbed his chin warily as Gilbert released 'Io, who had also managed to contain himself out of respect for his host.

'Io straightened his clothing and offered his hand to Gilbert in apology. "I am sorry, Mr. Caldwell. Old wounds never heal, and your brother dealt me a grave injury when he took Meilani."

"Are you talking about Melanie?" Gilbert's face was a mirror of confusion as he looked from the angry sun warrior to the dark-skinned Hawaiian for clarification.

"Melanie," Ryan confirmed. A light still burned in 'Io's

eyes for Melanie, a reflection of the same frustrated rage he had felt at not being able to hunt down the Frenchman. Only the old rage had been directed at him. "And you might as well know Kuakini, my wife is not your sister." He wanted to get it all out in the open and settled between them. He felt he at least owed the blank-faced young man staring back at him suspiciously that much.

"You said that before," 'Io answered flatly. "Do you not trust your wife's words?"

Gilbert let out a heavy breath and, realizing that he was for the moment being ignored, took a seat. "I assume this will all make sense if I just wait," he remarked to himself.

"Implicitly," Ryan assured Kuakini. "But it seems her mother kept a secret from all of you, including Abner Hammond. Melanie just found out a few weeks ago when I took her home upon her mother's death. A deathbed confession, if you will," he added sourly.

He wasn't exactly sure what he expected 'Io to do, but his reaction of quiet contemplation was not that at all. His shining dark eyes masked his feelings as he helped himself to another glass of liquor and poured one for Ryan as well. With a curious glance at Gilbert, who declined with a shake of his head, he handed Ryan the drink.

"I have done what I wanted to do . . . To do you more harm would not endear me to the woman whom I still consider a sister, blood tie or no." He held his glass up to Ryan's. "You and I are more alike than we realize, Captain. We have felt the same things for the same woman, but our ways of handling our emotions are different. I must accept what I cannot change. If she is happy — and I can see that she is — that is all that matters. Peace of mind is the most precious gift we can give her . . . and protection. I cannot tell you where Bartot is presently, but I can find out. To that cause, we must ally ourselves."

Ryan drank to the toast, a new respect forming in his mind for the seemingly shiftless Hawaiian whom he perceived to be anything but that now. He was not certain, had the cards of fate been reversed, that he could have accepted things so graciously. For that, he admired 'Io Kuakini. He did not agree with his politics or like the idea of waiting until the man could locate Bartot. But he had no doubt of his unexpected ally's sincerity and knew the time would come when the Frenchman would pay dearly for ever crossing their path.

Chapter Nineteen

"Daddy, hurry up! We're going to miss it all!"

Kristen Caldwell tapped her calf-slippered toe impatiently as her father descended the steps, fastening the cuffs of his starched shirt. Her golden curls were gathered under a straw bonnet adorned with fresh flowers Melanie had woven into its band. Melanie retied her dark blue sash one more time and handed her charge over to the handsome man shrugging on his coat with a grimace of distaste.

"Are you sure you won't reconsider? It's going to be quite an occasion . . . history in the making," Ryan said in a last-minute attempt to get her to change her mind.

Melanie placed her fingers to her temples, feigning the headache that was to leave her free for other pursuits she and Priscilla had discussed earlier. "I am just going to relax and enjoy the quiet of an empty house."

She helped her husband with his tie. Not that he needed her assistance. He could do quite well without it, but she enjoyed the chance to be close to him and tease him in the full company of others. Her eyes met his, twinkling mischievously as she pressed closer than required and pretended to be concentrating on the knot.

She knew from the sensual curl of his lips that he was fully aware of her little game and enjoying it. "When we return I think I can do something to take your mind off that headache of yours," he threatened with equal devilment, reaching out and bussing the tip of her nose.

As soon as the family carriage was out of sight, Melanie hurried out the door and down the street in the opposite direction. With all the traffic focusing toward the palace, there was no hope of securing a hack or tram to the outskirts of town, so she resigned herself to walking the long distance to the orphanage.

Melanie felt guilty for deceiving her husband and family, but feared Ryan would not understand her need to know that 'Io Kuakini was not anywhere near the heavily guarded palace today. How ironic that the new government that had elected Sanford Dole as its president was to be formally declared on the Fourth of July, the birthday of the United States. They still wooed President Cleveland in hopes of annexation. Worse, the newspapers boasted that the old Provisional Government that had formed the new Republic of Hawaii was going to be recognized by the United States and other world powers as the official government of Hawaii.

As she walked along the streets, she thought every *haole* family must have turned out for the grand occasion. But there were a considerable number of darker peoples among the throng, too, indicating a gaining of support among the natives and part-natives of the island. Still, many of the lanais were filled with people who, like herself, refused to take part in the beginning of the end of tradition. They waved in somber response to her nods as she passed them, reflecting the mood of those less enthused about the end of the monarchy.

The children were out in the play yard when Melanie reached the large shed that had been converted into a dormitory for the orphans. She followed the sound of hammering to the back of the building, where the framework for the new addition had been built. 'Io Kuakini was bent over a long timber with a measuring stick, a pencil in his hand.

He was stripped to the waist, his skin coated with sawdust that stuck to its clammy surface in the heat of the day. In spite of the dusting of his hair, its blue-black color glistened in the midday sun. His features were drawn in concentration as he straightened and remeasured the wood again. Then, with the agility of a cat, he leapt onto the scaffolding to check the measurement of the area the beam was to span.

"Need some help?" Melanie offered, cutting off his curse abruptly when one end of the rule fell from its mark while he was trying to read it.

The frown on the Hawaiian's face transformed into a sheepish grin at having been caught unawares. "You're too pretty to wallow in all this dust. How come you're not at the big doings?" he added with a sarcastic twist.

"I came to check on you," Melanie answered truthfully. "Priscilla and I . . . well, we were afraid you and your friends might follow through with some of the threats we've been reading about in the paper."

The newspapers had been full of editorials and warnings against the new government, written in the form of advertisements. Some mentioned overthrow, while others threatened assassination of the president and members of his cabinet.

"Those are put in there by radicals. Is that what you think I am, *maka polu*?" 'Io looked at her steadily.

"I'd think you had better sense," Melanie evaded his question and his interrogatory gaze. She lifted the hem of her dress and held out her hand for 'Io to help her up on the braced boards.

But 'Io shook his head. "I'm coming down." He landed lightly on his feet beside her. Self-consciously, he brushed off the sawdust with ineffective swats of his hands and then gave up. "How did you manage to get away from your family? Priscilla told me there was a busy day planned for all of you."

"I told them I wasn't feeling well," Melanie admitted shamefully. "And I thought you might need me more than they did." She put a hand on his arm as he picked up the saw to make his cut. " 'Io, what will happen now? Is it over?"

"Not until we hear it from Washington itself. A delegation from the queen is already on its way. Sam Parker's one of them."

"So there's nothing to this revolt scare," Melanie breathed in relief.

"Not until diplomacy fails." 'Io's words were not comforting. Ryan had told her Foreign Minister Stevens already acknowledged the new government and it was only a matter of ceremony before Cleveland did so officially. "Did Priscilla understand my not going?"

Melanie raised inquisitive eyes to her friend. "She knows what you believe and is afraid for you . . . like me."

"Then why didn't she come instead of you?"

"You know Aunt Pet. Priscilla didn't want to upset her mother by not going. It might embarrass them since most of their friends are supporters of Dole and his cabinet."

'Io's voice reflected his bitterness. "I don't think embarrassment has as much to do with it as your aunt's growing concern that her daughter is becoming involved with a dark-skinned Hawaiian."

Melanie caught her breath in surprise at 'Io's vehemence. "Why, 'Io Kuakini! Did you say *involved?*"

'Io turned away from Melanie awkwardly and studied his mark. "Did I?" He lined the saw up and began to slide it back and forth, until its sharp teeth cut a track for him to follow. Melanie watched his back muscles ripple with each jerking movement, as if he were taking his anger out on the wood.

"You really like Priscilla, don't you?"

"Well enough," came the grating answer in time with the saw. The board fell in two as the blade cleared the last of it. 'Io bent over and picked up one end of it, examining the cut. "She'd be fine if she stayed away from her mother. Your aunt just pushes her and pushes her to be something she isn't."

"Then why don't you do something about it?" Melanie challenged perceptively.

In the two days a week she spent at the orphanage, Melanie had seen her friend and cousin together, laughing and talking, but had assumed it was their common interest in the children. Her suspicion that it was developing into something more came when 'Io had left for two weeks to visit Lahaina, for Priscilla was beside herself until his return. And on the day he had promised the children he'd come back, she had worn a new dress she'd made just for the occasion. Melanie had been so wrapped up in Ryan and the new house that this budding romance had slipped by her unnoticed.

And now she felt an odd mixture of joy and disappointment at the idea that 'Io had found someone else. She was glad that he had the good sense to see past Priscilla's plain shell to the beautiful person inside and that he might have someone who could make him as happy as Ryan had made her. However, there was a selfish part of her that was reluctant to see his heart go out to someone else. But it must, she chided herself, and who better to win it than Priscilla, who had had her own share of disappointment where romance was concerned.

"What do you suggest?" 'Io answered, slinging the timber aside with a force that interrupted her reverie with a start. "Take her away from her mother? I can see it now," he sneered bitterly. "Come marry me and live with me in the back room of the orphanage, Priscilla. I'm not a shipping magnate like her father or your husband, Melanie. I can't keep her in the style she's accustomed to."

"Well, that's as poor an excuse as I ever heard!" Melanie exclaimed indignantly. "My cousin thinks you are the most wonderfully sensitive man she's ever met. She thinks you are an inspiration of kindness. She thinks you're brave for standing up for your beliefs when they are not the most popular. And until now, I agreed with her."

At 'Io's miserable look, her ire melted. "Aunt Pet doesn't dislike you because you are dark. I've heard her say you cut quite a figure in your morning coat," she cajoled, brushing away some of the sawdust from his hair. "Her only problem with you is that you are shiftless . . . you have no job like most respectable young men do. And she is strong-willed." Her lips puckered impishly. "But most of the women in our family are."

"You are not at all like your mother, nor is Pris like hers," 'Io disagreed.

"I said strong-willed. Aunt Pet is domineering, I'll admit, but she stood by me . . . even when the truth came out about Ryan and myself. I think she even loves Ryan in her own sort of way." The thought made her smile. As much as they sparred, Melanie had seen a certain respect develop between her husband and her aunt. "Compromise," she thought aloud. "That is the answer." She turned to her friend, her eyes sparkling. "Why don't you see Gilbert about a job. You're good with figures and he could show you—"

"No." His answer could not have been more emphatic had he shouted it, but it came in a quiet stubborn tone that left no room for argument. "I can't . . . not now. Things are too unsettled."

Melanie took 'Io's face between her hands, forcing the dark eyes to meet hers. " 'Io, what are you involved in? I know it has to do with Wilcox. I just know it." Her plea softened the frustration on his face, but she felt his jaw muscles tighten at her mention of Wilcox.

"Don't look at me like that, *maka polu*. I will not tell you anything that will endanger you any more than you've already endangered yourself," he told her grimly. He removed her hands from his face and turned back to his task.

"What do you mean *already?*"

"By your association with me." 'Io recovered smoothly, condemning himself for his slip of the tongue.

The Frenchman had told Wilcox's men about his encounter with Captain Caldwell's wife. If Ryan had gone after the man without saying anything to 'Io first, Melanie and her hot-blooded husband might have mysteriously disappeared by now for knowing or guessing too much. The Frenchman wanted to kidnap her before she identified him as a suspect in burying the arms that would be forthcoming if the United States did not back the queen. But 'Io had been there and had vouched for her trustworthiness. He'd told them she was his sister and a Royalist, in spite of her husband's association with Dole, and that she would not speak against the Frenchman now that she knew he was working for the supporters of the queen.

His conscience had given him a hard time over not sharing his knowledge, but he dared not tell Ryan Caldwell. Each time the golden-haired captain asked him if he had found Bartot's whereabouts, he answered negatively. Melanie's husband could ruin everything if he became involved, and 'Io did not trust him to contain his rage enough to allow more important events to take place . . . particularly events he did not endorse.

The Hawaiian was certain, given enough rope, Bartot would hang himself. If it came to armed rebellion and the Frenchman behaved as 'Io expected, he would allow Ryan the privilege of giving the swine his just desert. But he had to let it get to that point. In the meantime, Melanie was under his protection from Wilcox's men.

He looked over at her as she made circles in the sawdust with her toes, preoccupied with her own thoughts. For a moment he was reminded of earlier days when she had done the same thing in the sands of Lahaina. With the sun dancing off the crown of her raven hair that was tied back loosely with a ribbon, she looked much the same as the little girl he'd carried on his shoulders, afraid of nothing as long as she was with him. How proud she had made him feel as her protector.

And for now, she was safe. The Frenchman was on his way to San Francisco to see about the purchase of arms for the cause. And if Washington did recognize the new Republic of Hawaii in lieu of Queen Liliuokalani, there would be a need for that purchase and more.

"How about letting me clean up and I'll walk you home before you get caught hanging about subversive suspects? I can imagine your husband's reaction to paying a fine to get you out of jail," 'Io teased.

"Are you being watched?" Melanie was uncertain that he was being completely facetious.

"Anyone that was on the queen's staff is suspect, Melanie." With that, he turned and walked toward the small room he occupied when in Honolulu.

Melanie and 'Io arrived well before Ryan and the family got back from the ceremonies. Kristen bubbled on about the beautiful fireworks display, complaining only that the explosions hurt her ears. But the little girl's face was no brighter than Priscilla's when she saw 'Io. Aunt Pet and Gilbert had been invited to an inaugural party at the Thurstons and hurriedly made their excuses to leave, Gilbert promising to give Ryan and Melanie's regrets.

"I see your headache has improved," Ryan whispered to Melanie as she cut some slices of cake to serve with the tea Priscilla was fixing. Gilbert and Aunt Pet had given the servants the day off in order to attend the Fourth of July gala at the palace.

"Mmm-hmm," Melanie answered with a nod. But that doesn't mean I'm no longer interested in your earlier proposition. My mind is quite in need of distraction." She leaned into the warm body pressed lightly against her back, smiling at the familiar touch of Ryan's hands at her waist.

Kristen, who had coaxed Uncle 'Io into a game of checkers, began to whine when the game was interrupted for the tea and cake. Melanie knew from that, as well as from the way her daughter picked at the cake, that the day had been a little too long for the young lady to handle without a nap. As soon as the dishes were cleared, she insisted the child go upstairs to get ready for bed.

The silent crocodile tears that ensued made her feel absolutely wretched as she led Kristen up the stairs, but Melanie was also aware that that was exactly what they were intended to do. As she bathed the sullen child and pulled her light cotton shift over her tumble of curls, Kristen was already giving in to her exhaustion with gaping yawns between her tearful protests.

"When I have a little girl, I'm never going to be mean and make her go to bed when everybody else is having fun!" she accused defiantly as Melanie tucked her in.

"That will be your prerogative, Kristen," Melanie told her coolly. "And in spite of what you think of me right now, I love you very much."

"I don't believe you!" The sniffed challenge tried Melanie's patience.

"Kristen!"

311

"If you loved me, you and Daddy wouldn't leave me to go play games at the new house. It's all you and Daddy ever talk about."

So that's what this is about, Melanie thought in relief. She was supposed to leave with Ryan tomorrow to go back to work at the plantation and Kristen had apparently overheard her speaking to Aunt Pet about keeping her. She gathered the hiccoughing child in her arms. "Darling, we are not just playing games. We are working very hard to fix the house pretty for you to come live in."

"But I can work! I can pull weeds and pick up little pieces of wood. Ask Miss Amanda how much help I am at the orphanage. She told me I was the best helper in the whole world. And if you and Daddy keep leaving me, I might as well just go live there."

Although Kristen's sentiments were unfounded, they were very real to her. Melanie held the sobbing child, rocking her in her arms. She hadn't realized that she and Ryan had neglected Kristen. It always seemed the child was going here or there with Priscilla or her aunt . . . or even Gilbert. She kissed the top of her daughter's head and hugged her tightly.

"Darling, don't ever say that! You are the most loved little girl in the whole world. Everybody loves you."

"And I think that you are being unfair to your mother and I," Ryan said quietly from the doorway. He came in and sat down on the edge of the bed next to Melanie. "We didn't take you because that old house was not safe for a little girl to play in. There were broken steps and loose railings . . . high grass and weeds to get lost in."

"The first time I saw it, I thought it looked like a giant monster in the dark," Melanie chimed in, catching on to Ryan's train of thought.

Kristen pulled away from Melanie and looked from one to the other with wide eyes. "If it's that horrible, I don't want to live there!"

"It *was*," Ryan corrected. He scooped Kristen up in his arms like a doll. "But I daresay, if she listens very closely and goes to bed when we say, that it's safe enough now. What do you think, Mother?"

Melanie thought of all the cleaning that needed to be done and the multitude of other chores that would be made more difficult with a child underfoot. But there was no way she could say no to both of them. She floundered from blue water to green as she looked into their expectant faces. "If she listens very well," she stipulated with an indulgent smile.

"Oh!" Kristen squealed, squirming out of Ryan's lap. "How I love you, Mama!" She threw herself at Melanie, her small arms choking her in a hug. "We're going to be a hard-working family, I promise. And I'm going to go to sleep right now so I'll be fresh in the morning. I'll bet I can even plant pineapples!"

"No doubt," Ryan laughed. He dragged Kristen away from Melanie and tossed her onto the bed roughly.

Melanie watched as he tucked their daughter in, her heart swelling with love for them both. What a complex man she had married, she mused in wonder. If anyone had told her during those first few days on the *Liberty Belle* that its arrogant, bullish captain was capable of the tenderness and compassion she had come to know in him, she'd have laughed in that person's face. He had hidden his weaknesses from her so well then — weaknesses she treasured as his greatest strengths.

And she told him so later in the lazy aftermath of the distraction he had devilishly promised. "You haven't changed," she whispered, placing an affectionate kiss on the chest that served as her pillow. "You've just let me see beyond that protective armor of belligerence and bravado. Oh, how I love you, Ryan Caldwell!" she mimicked her daughter with a tight hug.

"Then why don't you trust me, blue eyes?"

The question took her back. Melanie frowned and raised up on one elbow, trying to make out her husband's expression in the moonlight. "Why do you think I don't?"

"I would have understood your need to know 'Io was safe today without your having to sneak off after we'd left the house."

His words shocked her. "How . . ."

Strong arms rolled her over so that she had to look up into the shadow of his face, her body pinned once more beneath his. "You are a terrible liar, blue eyes. At first I thought you were really ill from the pitiful way you looked when we left. But when I decided to go back and check on you, I realized it was guilt, not illness, that haunted those overly innocent eyes of yours."

"And you're not angry?"

"Disappointed," he corrected, his lips gently slipping over her own. "Don't ever let this muddle of politics come between us, Melanie. What we have is more important than whether or not a queen or a president rules the islands. Stay out of it."

"Can you, Ryan?"

"I won't let it come between us." He slid his hand over the smooth stretch of her abdomen, causing her muscles to ripple involuntarily. "No secrets, agreed?" he murmured against the sensitive bud of her breast.

"No secrets." She inhaled sharply as the contact tightened the knot of desire he had recently ignited and satisfied.

"Impartiality?" Her other breast quivered in anticipation as his warm breath promised its due.

"I'll try." Melanie refused to make a promise she might not be able to keep. Her sympathies were strong. Ryan nipped at her playfully, causing her to squeal in protest. "Ryan!"

"At least you're honest . . . for the moment," he added devilishly, shoving away from her and landing on his back at her side. "Good night, blue eyes."

Melanie lay still, stunned by his sudden retreat. "Are you going to sleep?" she asked incredulously. It was unfair of him to toy with her like that and then leave her cold.

"Actually, I have a headache." Ryan's laugh became a grunt as she drove her fist into his hard stomach.

Smiling wickedly to herself in the darkness, Melanie leaned over him and kissed the spot she had just attacked. "Then let me try to distract you, sir, so that you should not suffer all night. After all, we're going to have to be fresh to keep up with our daughter in the morning."

314

Kristen was true to her word. Her endeavor to help them at whatever the task surprised them both. She worked in the house and garden with Melanie every morning, either scrubbing or weeding. Liat delightedly dubbed her "little missy" and took the time to show her the difference between the flowers and weeds so that she could have a section of the garden for her very own. She even allowed the child to pick several plants for the special spot Kristen determined was going to be just like the bird-feeding place her Grandpa Hammond had shared with her during their visit after the death of Melanie's mother.

During the afternoon, Ryan took his daughter out to the fields with him on the big red stallion. Melanie often watched them until they were out of eyesight, before concentrating on the scraping and cleaning of the windows. She wondered which of the two enjoyed it more—the father who held the bundle of petticoats and bouncing curls that refused to stay up under the wide-brimmed straw hat she wore to protect her fair skin, or the bundle herself encased in her daddy's strong arms.

Due to that same bundle of energy, the workday was shortened in order to permit a family swim before supper. The first time she returned to the beach where the Frenchman had threatened her, Melanie was uncommonly quiet, her eyes constantly searching the horizon for any sign of movement to indicate his return. Her preoccupation upset Ryan enough to teach her how to use a small pistol he had purchased for her in Honolulu on one of his supply runs. Eventually, she was able to relax with her family and enjoy the beautiful afternoons at the ocean.

Kristen astonished Ryan by swimming over and under the waves like a little fish. She was not afraid of the breakers or of getting water in her eyes. "This is softer water than Boston waves," she declared with smug confidence, referring to the gentler wash of the ocean waves on the beach.

Although she could not stand on the board Ryan had

smoothed with his own hands to do away with harmful splinters, she loved to ride it into the beach on her stomach. Taking no chances, Melanie always waited close to the shore while Ryan held onto the youngster until she caught the wave that would take her to her mother. At high tide, Kristen had to be content to play at the water's edge building sand castles.

Her independence grew even more the day her father came home with a little grey pony named Pele. Melanie's heart was in her throat the first day Kristen rode out to the pineapple fields on her own mount, but her fears proved needless. Her daughter took to riding the pony the way she had the waves, although Ryan insisted on using a long lead line for the first few days until he was certain Kristen actually controlled the gentle beast.

After many weeks of family campouts in the large, empty house, the inside was completed. Ryan and Melanie were looking forward to occupying the master bedroom alone once more. After her initial visit, Kristen would not hear of them going to the house without her, and they hadn't had the heart to force Megan to rough it in the large, empty nursery that still smelled strongly of fresh paint. Melanie and Ryan had both worked to the point of exhaustion to meet the deadline when the *Liberty Belle* would arrive with the new furniture from Boston. Yet those weeks were among the most cherished times Melanie could remember, she thought as she stood at the sparkling window of the front parlor and looked expectantly down the well-traveled lane toward Honolulu for the first of the moving wagons.

She turned and scanned the spacious room that the painters had finished in a soft beige tone. Its lustrous planked floor was graced with a new carpet from the Orient, as were all the floors in every room except the grand hall. As Ryan had predicted, that marble tile floor was perfect for riding the tricycle Gilbert had bought for Kristen at the general store.

"Are they here yet, Mama?" her daughter questioned as she passed on the most recent of innumerable circles she'd made around the central staircase since rising that morning.

"No sign yet."

Melanie's nerves were on edge from the long days of hard work and the longer nights during which sleep could not edge in on the incessant planning of which pieces went where. She had so looked forward to this day and wanted everything to be perfect when her aunt arrived to see the house for the first time. But it was, she told herself sternly. Ryan had hired a competent staff, most of them members of Lin Ho's family who had been there when the Davidsons had owned the home.

"Missy, you come have tea. Stomach be much better . . . you see," Liat suggested upon entering the room and finding her mistress stationed at the window again, her hand pressed to her abdomen. "You not eat this morning with little missy, you be sick."

"They're here!" Melanie exclaimed upon seeing a wagon round the last bend in the road from which she had first seen her new home. "It's just butterflies, Liat," she assured the Japanese woman with a hug before skipping to the front door.

"Butterflies?" Liat echoed in bewilderment behind her.

"Aunt Pet!" Melanie raced down the newly painted steps to greet Petula Caldwell, who had commandeered the first wagon. Bedecked in an old dress, apron, and dust cap, her aunt looked prepared to go to work.

"Hello, dear!" the woman greeted Melanie with a hug, looking over her shoulder at the graceful white columned home. "My, my! No wonder you've fallen off to a wisp of a thing! Why didn't you put your foot down with that stubborn husband of yours and insist on letting us help you?"

"Where's Ryan?"

"At the ship, still unloading. This is only the beginning!" her aunt announced with a sweep of her arm toward the other three wagons bringing up the rear.

"This here's bedroom furniture, scrapper. Where do you want it?"

Melanie turned at the sound of Amos Cobb's voice. "Amos! I didn't recognize you without your beard!"

"Looks a good deal better to my notion," Aunt Pet observed

bluntly as Melanie fondly embraced the crusty seaman.

"It's so good to see you! Oh, and look, there's Sven!"

"And the rest o' the lads what ain't helpin' the cap'n," Amos informed her. "Now whereabouts do ye want this?"

"Aunt Pet, come see me ride my bicycle!" Kristen called from the lanai. "I have a whole room just for it!"

Before Melanie could answer, Aunt Pet shoved an authoritative finger at Amos. "You just sit tight, old man. I need to see the house before I can tell you where things go."

"How about some coffee or lemonade?" Melanie offered, trying to smooth over her aunt's domineering manner. "You can wet your thirst while I give Aunt Pet a tour."

Amos winked. "Might as well. S'long as it ain't where she is," he added slyly.

Kristen rode ahead of them on her bike for the tour of the first-floor rooms. The gentle earth tones Melanie had used throughout blended the wainscoting and paneling in each room with the lighter walls, and were picked up in the carpets as well. Aunt Pet examined every detail with a critical eye, giving little nods of approval.

"I think the drapes and furniture we chose will do beautifully," she decided, taking a panoramic view of the first floor from the landing of the large stairway. "Just beautifully," she thought aloud.

She loved the stenciling that Melanie and Liat's son had done in Kristen's room. They had made a border of little dolls and stuffed animals that held hands around the ceiling. And the rose-colored woodwork against the white walls made it look just like a little girl's room. Even the shutters and panels on the doors were stenciled to match.

"And I have named all the ones on this wall," Kristen told the older woman seriously. "But I'm going to have to have Soon Yin write their names under them because I keep forgetting."

It was only when Petula Caldwell saw the master bedroom that disapproval darkened her face. Her lips thinned as her eyes roamed from the mattress Ryan and Melanie had used as a bed to the smaller one they had made up for Kristen.

"The man has had you living like an animal, Melanie! Sleeping on the floor, indeed!"

"No, Aunt Pet," Melanie objected with a stubborn tilt of her chin. "Ryan has given me every consideration I would have. As much as I care for you, I will not hear you put him down. These past weeks here have been among the happiest in my life."

She could see her aunt wrestling with her reaction to Melanie's unanticipated defense of her husband. The thin line of her lips twitched undecidedly and finally settled on a stiff smile. "I understand completely, dear. You are young and in love." She sighed, the icy blue of her pale eyes melting in warmth. "I had almost forgotten . . . God, I can still see that tiny little apartment Gilbert and I rented when we were first married. It was in the attic over a store, unbearably hot in the summer and unheatable in the winter. Priscilla slept in a drawer next to the bed." She looked back at Kristen's muddle of blankets. "We were never happier." To Melanie's astonishment, when her aunt faced her again, her eyes were misted with nostalgia. "I hope someday my daughter will know that same happiness."

"I do, too." Melanie put her arm over her aunt's shoulder, her own eyes suddenly infected.

"Well! Those men are wasting away the day and there's work to be done," the older woman declared with renewed vigor. "You leave them to me, dear."

"But . . ."

"No buts! I came to help and I mean to do it."

Her aunt's recovery was swift, for as soon as her feet touched the bottom step, she took command of the group of men meandering about the first floor and set them to work. And her assistance was sorely needed, for there were more teams of men than there were women to tell them where to put the beautiful pieces they uncrated in the yard and carried inside. Before Melanie could think about where the desk went, two more men heavily burdened with a chest stood by impatiently waiting for instructions.

At one point she saw Amos Cobb assuring her aunt, with

every step he took, as he carried a heavy mahogany dresser up the steps that it had been handled with care from the day it had been handed over to him. He caught Melanie's apologetic look over the dust cloth her aunt was wiping back and forth under his nose and winked in reassurance. Why the men did not lose their patience was beyond her understanding, for some pieces had been placed against every wall in a given room before Petula finally decided she liked the original placement best.

As the temperature of the day increased with the sun beating down overhead, tempers seemed to rise accordingly. Ryan arrived with a string of curses that sent Melanie flying back to the house in retreat before anyone saw her. She was able to deduce from some of the comments she overheard that one of the lines had snapped back in his face just as he'd reached for it, cutting him across the forehead. By noon, she was near fainting from trying to steer him clear of Aunt Pet.

Priscilla and 'Io arrived last with the barrels containing the china and crystal, and a heavy crate that was stamped as being shipped from Lahaina. In addition to the dining accessories were several hampers of chicken, ham, salads, and cakes stacked behind the seat of the flatbed—a thoughtful courtesy from the women of the parish.

Leaving Gilbert to referee Aunt Pet and the men, she and Priscilla began to put out the food while 'Io unloaded the barrels. To Melanie's surprised delight, each item was wrapped in a handmade table scarf or embroidered linen that had been sent as housewarming gifts from her friends at the church.

She was overwhelmed by the consideration behind the little presents, for, unlike her cousin, who had a hope chest full of beautiful linens and domestics, Melanie had nothing of the sort with which to set up her new home. Everything she and her mother had made had gone to the needy. There had been little time for frivolities.

Such was her excitement that after all the effort to avoid setting off Ryan's temper, it was she and not Aunt Pet that did so. He was holding a heavy mirror upright while one of his men fastened it to the massive carved sideboard in the dining room, when Melanie dumped all the precious gifts on the banquet table and began to show them to him, raving about how perfectly the colors suited this room or that.

"Goddamnit, Melanie! I don't have time to look at your stupid doilies!" he swore, holding the mirror with his knee long enough to wipe the sweat from his brow where the blood had clotted from his earlier mishap. "Jesus Christ, you've ordered enough furniture to furnish the damned palace!"

Melanie shrunk at the explosive outburst, her breath lodged like a cutting blade in her throat. She had worked as long and as hard as he had, she thought, trying to keep in check the tears that stung her eyes. He had not even wanted to bother to look at the furniture or choose the drapes and carpets . . . and now he had the nerve to reprimand her! Her chin quivered as she shoved the crocheted scarf down the front of his shirt.

"Then take it all back!" she shouted furiously.

The general noise of the chaos came to a screeching halt at her high-pitched challenge. As the silence thundered in her ears, she became aware of the apprehensive stares directed at her and ran out of the room in dismay before they could see the flood of tears that started down her cheeks.

"Did Mama throw a tantrum?" she heard Kristen ask from her tricycle as she fled up the staircase to her room.

"No, dear, your father did," Aunt Pet huffed. "All right, everyone, back to work!"

Chapter Twenty

By the time the picnic-style lunch was over on the first-floor lanai, Melanie had regained her composure. She had cried until she was sick to her stomach, but after drinking the tea Liat brought up to her and washing her face and neck in cold water to fight the oppressive heat, she felt much better. The cry had done her good, for her wound-up nerves had come completely unfrayed and she was now more relaxed.

She knew she was going to have to tell Ryan of her suspicion, but now was definitely not the time. Besides, it was still too early to be sure. But she didn't think the overwhelming odor of the paint could only make her ill first thing in the morning and not bother her at all the rest of the day. Nor did it cause the familiar tenderness in her breasts that she had had when she carried Kristen.

And if her husband continued to act insufferably, he might only find out when she grew distended with the new life she suspected growing within her, for she was not inclined to speak to him at all at the moment. But just because he was acting like a braying ass was no reason to take it out on everyone else, she decided, tidying up the loose damp ends of her hair before going back downstairs.

Ryan was on his way through the front door at one end of an apricot damask loveseat when Melanie reached the bottom of the stairwell. With a cool return of his assessing gaze, she marched in the opposite direction to the kitchen. Her recent strain, however, was no match for her amusement at the sight of 'Io Kuakini clad in a ruffled apron standing over a basin of water with his sleeves rolled up. He was busily washing the china Priscilla unpacked beside him.

At her unfettered giggle, he explained wryly, "She doesn't want to ruin her hands."

"Don't you think that shade of green is his color, Melanie?" Priscilla teased, receiving a flick of water in the face in retaliation.

"The mighty hawk in ruffles!" Melanie squeezed 'Io's waist gratefully as she passed by, needing some reassurance.

"We saved that large crate from your father for you to unpack," 'Io told her. The concern showing in his eyes as he glanced around at her belied his grin.

It was all she needed. With a smile that told him she was all right, Melanie crossed the room to the crate 'Io had pried open for her. She lifted the boards and peeked inside to see several bundles wrapped in paper and rags. Carefully, she took out the first and unwrapped it. An "Oh!" of admiration escaped her lips when she recognized the hand-painted bowl and pitcher set that had been one of her parents' wedding gifts. Lydia Hammond had treasured it so much that she'd kept it only for the use of guests, for fear of chipping or breaking it.

A silver-handled brush and comb set with mother-of-pearl inlay, which had been Lydia's, and a matching hand mirror were in the next package. She emptied an old flour sack of its rag-covered contents, to discover the tea set she had played with as a child Kristen's age. It had come from Boston as a Christmas present from Aunt Pet. With a nostalgic smile, she carefully put them aside. At the bottom of the box were several large bundles that turned out to be the quilts Lydia Hammond and Nalani had made — quilts her mother had told her would be hers someday when she married.

Melanie sniffed loudly, unable to hold back the single tear that ran down her cheek. "I seem to be such a baby today," she laughed in embarrassment at the attention she drew from her companions.

Priscilla got up and walked over to her. "There's not a thing wrong with you that a good night's sleep in your own new home won't cure," she chided fondly. "For heaven's sake, I'd be hysterical if all this was going on in my house. Now, let my maid wash up this bowl and pitcher, and then you'd best get it upstairs before one of the men get hold of it and break it."

At 'Io's indignant protest, Melanie laughed. Her mood lightened by her friends, she did exactly as Priscilla suggested, then came back for the other things. After several trips, she stood back and idly traced the blue and white pattern of the bowl and pitcher set she had placed on the marble-topped washstand. She never dreamed when she'd done the same thing as a child that it would be hers one day.

And the quilts. She studied each one before folding it carefully and placing it in the blanket chest at the foot of the bed. She recognized some of the patterns from having helped sew the pieces together under the older women's supervision, but they all were equally dear to her. The last one she folded across the foot of the large oak bed.

Now this really felt like her home, she mused as she smoothed out the wrinkles tenderly. Everything until now had been new, bought with her husband's money. It bothered her that she had not contributed anything of her own, but her father's gift had changed all that. Now there was a part of her in the home as well — part of her past to take a place with all the newly purchased things that marked the beginning of her future.

A knock at the door behind her brought her out of her reverie with a start. She turned to see Ryan standing there with a handful of flowers she recognized as having come from the garden.

"I'm told by a very good authority that these will earn me forgiveness," he told her, holding the floral peace offering out in front of him. His expression was uncertain as he waited for some sign of encouragement. When none came, he took a deep breath of courage and approached her. "I am also told that if I hadn't built such a big house, Mama wouldn't have had to buy so much furniture." He chuckled tiredly and reached out to touch her face. "Makes sense to me. Besides, t's all unloaded now. The men would mutiny if I had them re-crate it and haul it back." As only he could do, Ryan looked past the surface of her eyes into her very soul for the forgive-ness he awkwardly sought.

Melanie could not stay mad at him. It wasn't Kristen's sound advice but rather his haggard look that warmed her. His hair was damp and disheveled from running exasperated hands through it, and his shirt was soaked with perspiration and clung to him. Dust and dirt smeared his face, mingled with the dried blood where the rope had cut him. The most ridiculous thought came to Melanie as she wondered how it had escaped Aunt Pet's dust cloth.

Endearingly disconcerted by her silence, he tried to compli-ment. "And everything looks kind of pretty where your aunt finally put it."

His wry *finally* was more than she could bear. A bubble of laughter, velvet in quality, erupted from her throat, bringing further confusion to the green depths of the eyes narrowing at her as if she had lost her mind. But it was warm and infec-tious. Catching on to its source, his own rich amusement blended with it, only to be muffled when he took her in his arms and kissed her.

"God, I love you! I wouldn't hurt you for the world, blue eyes."

He emphasized his feelings with a hug that nearly squeezed the breath from her lungs, then fell backward in exhausted relief on the new bed, taking her with him. The commotion that ensued made Melanie scream out in alarm, for the mat-tress went right through the frame of the bed with a crash that shook the pitcher on the washstand across the room.

"Damned tricky bastards!" Ryan cursed halfheartedly at the howls coming from the first floor. "Are you all right?"

Her cheeks grew hot as Amos Cobb's voice bellowed, "Guess we ain't got to carry it back after all, mates!"

"*Both* of us are," she answered softly. Her heart was pound-ing as she took Ryan's hand and placed it on her stomach, but not from the fright of the sudden collapse of the bed. She was apprehensive about his reaction.

For once, her very perceptive husband was thick. His face was totally absent of comprehension as he looked at her in puzzlement. But she remained quiet, letting her meaning sink in and watching it take root in his eyes. It started as a small kindling that, as it caught on, melted the lines of fatigue on his face and drained it of color simultaneously.

"A baby?" he whispered hoarsely in disbelief.

Melanie's heart froze, wondering if the fact that he looked like he might faint was a positive reaction or not.

"When?"

"Next summer, I think." It wasn't as if she had gotten this way on her own, she thought indignantly at the way he stared at her. It was an odd look that she had never seen before and it made her uneasy. After all, he was the eager tiger who took her to bed every chance he had to get her alone.

His eyes crinkled devilishly above hers. "And I thought I was just planting pineapples." His loud outburst of laughter shook the half-cocked mattress as he rolled over on his back and gave in to it.

"Ryan!" Melanie poked him spitefully. "This is not a laughing matter!"

"I know," he agreed breathlessly, his broad chest still jolting. "I've got a wife that's filling the house faster than I can build it."

Shocked at the light in which he was taking this, Melanie crawled to her knees and glared down at him. "Now I've had some *help!*" she declared pointedly.

Ryan wiped the tears from his eyes and pulled a sober face upon seeing her distress. "Indeed you have, madame . . . and more to come, if I have to hire a full-time crew of men to keep the rooms coming faster than the babies."

"You're demented!"

"Is that what it is?" her husband retorted with a quick rise of his brow. Suddenly, he reached for her and swept her under him in a rolling motion. His lips hovered just above hers as he peered earnestly into her eyes. "I thought it was love." He pecked at her mouth. "I think I caught it that day you bit me and I haven't been right since."

"So you're not upset?" Melanie asked timidly, a churn of a

326

different nature than her earlier sickness taking place in her stomach.

Ryan didn't need to answer. The tenderness in his kiss told her all she needed to know.

The week that followed brought with it a tropical storm front that washed away the oppressive humidity that had foretold its coming. Melanie took advantage of the inclement weather to see to the hanging of the drapes and other odds and ends that usually followed a move. Ryan and his men were forced to work in the downpour and gusting winds, digging trenches to drain the low-lying fields so that the newly planted pineapple shoots and crowns were not washed away.

But no matter how busy he was, Ryan managed to get away at noon to share the midday meal with Melanie and see her tucked in bed for an afternoon nap with Kristen. In fact, his concern over her condition was beginning to wear on her nerves, for if not for her insistence, he would have her remain bedridden for the full term.

And when he wasn't there to make sure she lifted nothing heavier than her petticoat, Kristen was. The little girl was so excited about the prospect of having a little brother or a sister that she had been at Melanie's heels every waking moment since she had heard her father's exuberant announcement from the head of the staircase after he had recovered from the initial shock of finding out himself.

Melanie still chuckled to herself when she recalled how he had carried her to the head of the stairs, shouting to the men below to break open the barrel of rum he had ordered for after the move because he was going to be a father again by summer. She was grateful that most of the furniture was in place, for little else was accomplished after that. Her embarrassment at the good-natured jibes directed at them by the crew was overshadowed by her husband's joyous reaction. If his hand rested on her stomach once, it rested there a thousand times, as if he were not only proud, but also amazed at what he had done.

And when Aunt Pet chastised him for his indelicate celebration of his wife's condition, he'd gathered the matron up in his arms and swung her around until she could do nothing but giggle at his reckless delight. "Quite mad," she'd pronounced him to her wryly amused husband when Ryan deposited her in Gilbert's lap.

His feet did not touch ground until the next day, when he awoke in the bed 'Io and Gilbert had had to put him in when his fatigue and consumption of rum caught up with him. Melanie felt sorry for him, for in spite of the brave front he tried to maintain, she could see he was quite hung over.

"Won't you mash the baby?" Kristen asked as Melanie drew the laces of her corset in about her tiny waist.

"It's not big enough yet," Melanie assured the concerned child. She kept her fingers crossed that no more disconcerting questions would be forthcoming, having already answered more than she ever dreamed a child could come up with. And she was only three months into her pregnancy. Hoping to distract her daughter, she pointed to the organdy gown that hung on the back of the door. "How about helping me into my dress?"

The princess-style gown skimmed Melanie's figure. Kristen tugged at the hem to smooth it over the petticoats purposefully, taking time to admire the embroidered blossoms, pale blue and roses on white, that made up the floral pattern.

"Are you going to wear the locket like mine?" the little girl asked, backing away to survey her work critically.

Ryan had given them each a locket for Christmas. They were identical except that Kristen's was a smaller version. Both contained photographs of Ryan and Melanie on one side and Kristen on the other, which brought up the question of where baby's picture was going to fit.

"I think I will," Melanie told her. Her fingers went to the gold locket at her throat as she considered it. Actually, she should wear the sapphire necklace with the gown, for the occasion was a formal one. But she, like her daughter, was so thrilled with the present that she was loath to part with it.

Ordinarily, Ryan would have declined the invitation to the

party being given in honor of the new British Commissioner, but the consultant Sanford Dole had summoned to complete a study on the new cannery the President was building was going to be there. Her husband was anxious to speak to the man about his recent findings, for he agreed with Dole. Canning was the only way to successfully grow and ship the delicious pineapple.

Kristen stood on the lanai and waved good-bye as the carriage pulled away from the house. Melanie rested against her husband's arm to enjoy the late afternoon ride into town. They would be stopping by the King Street home to pick up the other Caldwells. Melanie had not wanted to go in early. Since they had moved, she only left the house to go to the church and the orphanage. The hour's ride to and from the city gave her time to think and enjoy the scenery.

"I promise I'll try to make this as short as possible tonight," Ryan murmured, drawing her attention from the thick shadowy growth at the edge of the road.

"Oh, I'm quite up to it," Melanie protested, warming at his consideration. "In fact, I hope there will be music. We haven't danced in ages."

His lips turned up wryly at one corner. "If there isn't, we'll dance anyway, blue eyes," he told her, snuggling her closer to him.

But there was, and Ryan waltzed her around the room until she was giddy with delight. The brilliant chandeliers swirled overhead, crowning the frescoed ceiling with flickering light as they moved among the colorful sweep of dancers. Handsome officers in impressive uniforms turned the heads of the many young women present, but Melanie only had eyes for the man who smiled down at her with leonine good looks that commanded every bit as many admiring glances.

She had grown so used to seeing him in his field clothes that she found herself staring like some of the other women she had caught casting sly looks in their direction. The cut of his suit seemed to emphasize his broad shoulders and narrow hips. He looked so . . . royal, she decided wickedly, considering that word was a taboo under the recent regime.

And when Ryan was not dancing with her, Gilbert was. His sense of humor had not diminished, and Melanie found herself in stitches as he made his dry observations about this one's manner or that one's opinion. But his comments about Ryan were the funniest, for he was enjoying this new side of his younger brother's character immensely.

"Any day now, I expect to ride out to see you and find Ryan with a long white beard, knee-deep in that red soil, and you surrounded by a string of children lined up like stepping stones."

"Gilbert Caldwell, you're awful to pick on Ryan like that."

"Madame, permit me my revenge! 'T'was I that was forced to listen to his lectures on the pitfalls of matrimony. I can see his cocky grin now as he vowed no female would ever make him stay in one spot for long, let alone saddle him with squalling brats." Gilbert looked off thoughtfully and nodded. "Yes, I believe those were his exact words." He darted a glance over to where Priscilla sat by her mother, her mind anywhere but on the animated conversation his wife carried on with the woman next to her. "If only another young man I know would give in to his feelings," he sighed regretfully.

"He still hasn't written?" Melanie asked, following his gaze.

"Not a word in six weeks," Gilbert confirmed. "I really thought things were looking up for her when he asked me if he could call on her formally. She's attended all the holiday parties alone, bless her."

Wasn't that just like a man, Melanie fumed, as irritated at 'Io as her cousin was. She remembered his lack of communication with his own mother and his light concern when Melanie had told him Nalani was worried about him. Men were an odd lot, she decided, returning to the seat beside her husband at the banquet table when the dance ended. They refused to acknowledge such things as love, as if they considered it a weakness. Even when 'Io had shown his anger at being unable to support Priscilla, he had refused to admit to Melanie that he really cared for her cousin.

"Anything wrong?" Ryan asked, noting the uncharacteristic scowl on her flushed face.

"Thank heaven *you* came to your senses!" Melanie declared in aggravation.

Before he could question her further, the President stood up and announced the entertainment for the evening. He had thought it proper to welcome Captain Hawes with a traditional Hawaiian greeting and, as such, introduced one of the well-known hula troupes. Melanie could not help but give the gentleman credit for trying to incorporate tradition into the new regime. And she was not the only one, for several of the guests stood and applauded in approval as the President took his seat.

The lights were turned down, and at the same time a conch shell sounded its mournful call. Six young men entered from one end of the room to the beat of drums and gourds. They were clad in the *malo* loincloth, their magnificent bodies oiled and glistening in the light of the torches they bore. Behind them, girls wearing grass skirts over shifts, their hair and shoulders adorned with fresh *leis,* entered, keeping time with the bamboo sticks and smaller gourds. Melanie recognized the ancient chant that filled the silenced room.

It seemed ironic that they chanted of war when the corridors and streets were heavily patrolled by uniformed police and militia, due to the increased political unrest following the arrests of several rebel leaders earlier that month. Their homes had been searched as a result of a secret tip, revealing several weapons that lead to conspiracy charges. The guest of honor that night had recognized the danger enough to offer the use of his British troops from the *Hyacinth,* but Dole had politely declined, not wanting to appear overly alarmed by the increased rebel activity.

The introductory chant came to an end when the troupe had spread out so that everyone in the large square of tables could see the performance. After a brief applause, the drums began another less solemn selection than the first at the prompt of the leader. Melanie's lips moved silently to the chant, the familiar Hawaiian words bringing back a more carefree time for her people, when their fears were of the gods of nature and their needs no more than the land could provide.

"Oh my God!"

At Priscilla's gasp, Melanie followed her gaze to the male dancer only a few feet beyond and recognized 'Io Kuakini. But the Hawaiian did not seem to see them. He concentrated on his dance, his dark eyes aglow in the torchlight. His bare feet padded the floor with the palms of the musicians on the drumheads, his lithe body moving fluidly to the beat. But at the end of the dance, his eyes lit on Priscilla and kindled briefly.

Her cousin was spellbound, for all she had ever known was the fashionably attired young man who taught and worked at the orphanage. Here he was exactly what Aunt Pet muttered in astonishment under her breath. "Why, he's a savage!" But unlike her mother, Priscilla did not react in disdain but rather in awe of what she saw. There was no trace in her eyes of the irritation she had avowed on more than one occasion since 'Io's sudden disappearance, sparks of a different nature leaping to her cousin's eyes that Melanie knew only too well.

"I feel sorry for the girl. I know exactly how she feels," Ryan remarked under his breath. "A hot-blooded wench named Meilani did the same damned thing to me."

"No!" Melanie disclaimed in feigned protest as the drums stopped abruptly. The idea appealed to her greatly, and she sought her husband's hand under the table. Their exchange of glances did as much to stir Melanie as if Ryan had touched her in all those little places he knew exactly how to find. She felt shamefully sinful for the longing that stirred when she was in her condition.

"Hele mai, maka polu."

Caught up in the spell of the moment, Melanie did not hear 'Io's command until Ryan's gaze sharpened beyond her to the Hawaiian who stood holding out his hand to her. Not only were 'Io's eyes fixed on her, but also the eyes of everyone in the room.

"Come, Meilani. Show your host and his guests that our cultures can blend in beauty."

"Oh do, Melanie!" Priscilla implored at her side. Impulsively, her cousin put her hands together, stirring the startled audience into uncertain applause.

The closeness they had briefly shared was gone when Melanie returned her glance to Ryan for approval. He neither gave it nor forbade her. She wasn't sure what was going on behind the eyes that watched her warily. What wasn't he sure of? she wondered. Her love? How could he doubt her? She had given all she had to give of herself and now carried further proof of her love for him.

"Ladies and gentlemen, I give you Mrs. Ryan Caldwell. Would anyone else care to join us?" 'Io asked, his alert eyes darting about the room at the gowned ladies and tuxedoed and uniformed men. But no one volunteered. Their curious attention rested with Melanie, who kicked off her shoes and accepted the *leis* 'Io placed about her neck with a kiss on the cheek.

"I must talk to you," he told her quickly in Hawaiian, nodding to the musicians to start. "After the performance . . . outside."

When Melanie forced a smile and made a graceful sweep with her hands at the introduction to the dance, the crowd put their hands together more enthusiastically. Her voice chimed in with the others in the words to the song about the lovely maiden of the islands. It was one she had performed for Ryan when they first met, she recalled.

She moved directly in front of the man who was no longer a stranger and her smile became genuine. She blossomed in the sunshine for him, her eyes taking on the warmth of the heavenly body and casting it upon him. She was kissed by the dew, blowing the kiss to the only man in the room she was aware of. She swayed with the trade winds that brought her love home to her, her body moving with the gentle movement of the palms in the breeze as she embraced her love to her heart. And when she finished, she raised her eyes from her bowed position, looking straight into his soul with her own.

"Here! Here!" the crowd echoed above the beating of her heart for the man that rose and took her into his arms in a passionate embrace. The reaction of the audience was mixed with shock and enthusiasm as the native dancers filed out. In the background, chairs scraped and the band struck up a dance tune, but her husband did not let her go.

"Ryan, everyone is watching!" Melanie protested weakly against him.

"To hell with them! I've a right to kiss my wife when and where I please," he challenged with a devilish glint that made her sing inside. "I might even carry you out over my shoulder if you keep looking at me like that."

"Caldwell, you're a lucky man." Lem Samuels clapped Ryan on the back, forcing his congratulations between them. "You've not only got the prettiest woman in Hawaii, but the most talented. How'd that savage know you knew how to dance, Mrs. Caldwell?"

"His mother taught me as a child, Mr. Samuels," Melanie retorted stiffly, taking exception to the way the man slurred his reference to 'Io. "That savage and I are like brother and sister."

"Well, she taught you well, ma'am. Indeed she did."

Samuels was saved further embarrassment by the congratulations of Sanford Dole. "You, madame, have not only done us an honor this evening, but demonstrated there is room for the old with the new. I want this government to work . . . to make a strong united republic. The Hawaiian could not have put it more aptly . . . cultures blended in beauty. My deepest thanks. And as for you, Captain, I think Mr. Morrison has come up with an idea that will be of interest to you concerning the cannery." He smiled at Melanie. "Might I borrow your husband for a moment?"

"Of course, Mr. President." Melanie took one of the *leis* from her neck and placed it over Ryan's head with a peck on the cheek. "*Aloha,* darling. I'm going to step out on the lanai for a breath of air. I won't be far."

"Is everything all right?" Ryan asked, glancing down meaningfully.

"Wonderful."

Melanie hoped her act was convincing. She made her way through the people, who stopped her to tell her how much they enjoyed her dance. 'Io had said he needed to see her, but he didn't say where. Hoping that he would find her, she stepped out into the night.

The cool air that assaulted her made her conscious of how warm it had been in the crowded ballroom. She inhaled deeply, savoring the tropical scent of the *leis* combined with the blossoms of the flowering shrubs planted in the beds surrounding the building. The strains of a Viennese waltz floated on the air, lending a romantic quality to the starlit night. Crossing her arms in front of her, she leaned against a Florentine column and sought out the Big Dipper in the jewel-studded sky.

"Meilani!"

She looked for 'Io in the thicket beyond the railing, but all she could see was the pink bougainvillea bracts against the dark foliage.

"Come down off the lanai," the whisper came again.

Melanie walked past the guards stationed at the entrance and tried to appear nonchalant as she made her way down the steps.

"Around to the side of the building."

Following the directive, she pretended to watch the stars. Her hands were folded behind her as she meandered along the brick walk, her fingers entwining nervously about each other, for she knew the two men at the door were watching her. As she rounded the corner, a hand seized her arm and dragged her into the shadows. Melanie swallowed the cry of alarm that rose in her throat, startled by the sudden movement.

"Have you lost your mind?" she demanded upon recovery. "Is Priscilla mad?"

"Why don't you ask her yourself?" Melanie snapped impatiently. "Where have you been?"

"I haven't had a lot of choice, but I can't explain right now. Tell her — tell her it's almost over."

Ice ran through her veins at the finality of his words. "What is almost over, 'Io?"

"My commitments . . . I . . ." He glanced away, wrestling with his thoughts. "Look, if you need to reach me for any reason, contact Kela. She can get word to me."

"But . . ."

"It's all wrong, Melanie, but at least it's coming to a head. I couldn't just walk away, knowing what I know." He took her by the arms. "Tell Pris I love her and *if* things go right, I'll be back to take that job Gilbert offered me . . . but only until I finish my degree."

"What do you mean 'if things go right'? How long is she going to have to wait to know if things are going to go right? 'Io, you have put her through enough. You need to talk to her, not me!" Melanie chastised severely.

"After tomorrow night. I promise, I'll talk to her." He glanced over his shoulders cautiously. "And give her this."

He withdrew the gold cross suspended on leather from about his neck and folded it in Melanie's hand.

Melanie looked at it, sick at the revelation it brought. *He wasn't certain he was coming back.* Her father had given 'Io that cross when he'd left to go to school in Boston. Melanie had never seen him without it since . . . until now.

"You're afraid you're not coming back, aren't you?"

"I just want her to have this until I can talk to her!" 'Io evaded impatiently. "I have to go, Meilani." He turned away from her but did not leave. "I love you, too, *maka polu.* I've never stopped." His hand sought hers in the darkness, squeezing it with unspoken affection. *"Aloha."*

The rustle of the shrubs in his departing wake left her numb. " 'Io!" she called after him.

No answer came. She clutched the cross tightly in her hands and ran along the edge of the shrubbery, searching for any sign of movement, but her attempt was futile. If 'Io was still there, he had no intention of giving his position away. Kela. He had said Kela would know where he was. Was the half-witted servant of the Cummings involved in this madness, too?

"Excuse me, miss, but no one is allowed around here. Are you ill?"

She felt it but denied the sick feeling of fear that gnawed at her stomach. "I'm sorry, officer. I was just taking some air."

What could she do? Tell Ryan, she wondered, smiling at

the guard and hurrying past him to return to the ballroom. Tell him what? That 'Io had given her his cross and that she was afraid he was going to do something to endanger his life? He'd think her foolish. She weaved in and out of the clusters of guests toward the burnished gold head that stood slightly above the others across the room. Damn 'Io for this, she swore silently, tucking the medallion in the folds of her skirt as she joined the group.

"Are you absolutely certain?" Sanford Dole asked of an aide who stood nervously at his elbow.

"Positive, sir. Marshal Hitchcock told me to let you know right away."

The President turned back to his guests apologetically. "Gentlemen, forgive me, but it seems there is an urgent matter that needs attending." He lowered his voice so that his words fell on only those ears he designated to hear. "The rebels are making their move. Our informer has made one contact and is expected to let us know more as soon as he can get away from them. Those of you who will volunteer to augment the Citizen's Guard will assemble at the palace grounds within the hour. I think we've found the devils out!"

Ryan turned at the sharp dig of nails in his arm to see Melanie reaching for him. There was a desperation in her eyes that alarmed him as much as the color that had drained from her face, taking her strength with it. Her lips were moving but no sound emerged as she swayed against him, her arms limp against his chest as she began to slide to the floor in a crumble of organdy and lace.

"Melanie!" Without thinking, he grasped her shoulders to break her fall.

"Someone get some water!"

"Give them air, for God's sake!"

"Oh my God, the baby!" Petula Caldwell cried out, shoving through the onlookers to her niece's side.

Melanie heard all the voices but answered only to that of her husband. "Take me home," she whispered shakily. "Please, don't go with them."

She needed to talk to him and could not possibly do so with

all those people standing around. He mustn't go with the Citizen's Guard. She needed him to find 'Io.

"I'm not going anywhere, blue eyes," Ryan assured her, gathering her up in his arms. "Gilbert, get the carriage." He looked over his shoulder at Sanford Dole. "Mr. President . . ."

"Your place is with your wife, sir," the leader interrupted, "Go with my prayers."

Chapter Twenty-one

It was a short carriage ride to King Street, since the party was only a few blocks away. Melanie felt horrible for the concern she had caused her family but knew she had to find a way to get her husband alone. When they arrived Ryan would not let her walk, in spite of her insistence that she was quite recovered from the overwhelming heat, and he carried her up the stairs to the guest room where they were supposed to spend the night.

"I think we should send for the doctor," Petula Caldwell fretted, following them into the room.

"No!" Melanie objected, sitting up in her husband's arms as he tried to deposit her on the bed. "I am fine and if you call a doctor, I vow, I'll walk right out of here!"

"Those are mighty big words for a little scrapper like you . . . even if there are two of you," Ryan intervened with a grin.

Some of his coloring was coming back now that familiar sparks fired his wife's eyes. But when he'd seen her slumping to the floor, he had thought for a moment he might wind up beside her. He hadn't been around when Melanie had carried Kristen and he was not so sure he wasn't better off for it. He didn't think he had ever been so excited about anything in his life . . . or any more frightened.

He loved Melanie more than his life and had heard the horror stories of deaths related to childbirth. It had killed Gilbert's mother and had weakened his own to the point where she had no strength to fight the pneumonia tha[t] claimed her life at the birth of his stillborn sister. Yet, a[s] he glanced down at Melanie, he could not help but fee[l] foolish for his fears.

"I do not need a doctor, and if you'll kindly stop smoth[er]ering me with your body, I could regain my breath!"

"By all means, madame."

He complied, unable to master his open admiration fo[r] the way she drew herself to a sitting position and rear ranged the organdy and lace about her like a ruffled he[n] making a nest. His little survivor. He'd never seen he[r] look healthier. In fact, her earlier morning sickness ha[d] given way to an appetite that sometimes put his to shame gaining her back the weight she had lost during the reno vation of the house. And her skin glowed with the kiss o[f] the sun and her own special blush that never ceased t[o] stir him.

"Why don't you and Gilbert go back to the party There's still dancing. Ryan and I will be fine," Melani[e] suggested, blue eyes cutting sideways in a manner tha[t] made him fight to keep from laughing outright.

Her appetite for food was not all that had increased She'd confessed to him that in her condition she felt les[s] attractive. As if she had added an inch to her perfect fig ure. It frustrated him not to be able to find the righ[t] words to convince her she was being ridiculous. He love[d] her spirit, what she was. He didn't care if she grew t[o] twice her size. It was with their baby.

"Why don't you, Mother? I'll stay and send for you i[f] there's any need. I've some music to work out for the chil dren, anyway," Priscilla chimed in.

It was Gilbert who finally persuaded his wife to relent Aunt Pet had been the same way when Melanie arrive[d] heavy with Kristen years earlier. The way she'd fusse[d] and carried on, one would have thought Melanie he[r] daughter. And it was that that had endeared the woma[n] to Melanie. She hugged her aunt tightly, promising not t[o] overexert, then hugged Gilbert extra hard for relieving them of Petula Caldwell's overly concerned presence.

When the bedroom door closed and she was alone with Ryan, Melanie grasped 'Io's cross in her hand and got up from the bed resolutely. Ryan lifted a quizzical brow as she approached him, her face once more grim.

"Ryan, I have a favor to ask of you."

"Anything, blue eyes," he vowed, taking her in his arms. His fingers began to work at the fastens of her gown in the back.

Realizing he had misread her intent, Melanie pulled away in exasperation. "Ryan, you must warn 'Io! I know where he is . . . at least who can tell me where he is." She knew it was too much to ask to go with him. He was so protective of her.

"Tell him what, Melanie?"

"That there's a traitor in his midst! Ryan, I heard what Sanford Dole told you . . . and I know that something terrible is going to happen."

Suspicion clouded her husband's face. "You mean you feigned that little scene?" When she did not answer, he seized her shoulders but only held them, careful not to hurt her. "Damn you, Melanie. I ought to shake the life out of you!"

"Ryan," she pleaded, "he gave me this!" She held up the cross. "He thinks there's a chance he won't come back. He asked me to give this to Priscilla with his love. Kela can tell me where he is."

With a curse, Ryan released her and turned away. "You don't realize what you are asking."

Cold shock seeped through her veins at the terseness of his words. He couldn't turn her down, she thought in disbelief, stepping after him. He had told her he understood. "You asked me to trust you, Ryan. I could have sneaked off alone like I did before, but you told me you understood how I felt about 'Io." She grabbed his arm and slung him around in challenge. "I am trusting you, Ryan

341

Caldwell. I need your help to save someone I love."

"Melanie, Sanford Dole gave me his trust, too. Would you have me betray that friendship?" he asked incredulously. "Your 'Io knew what the dangers were in his involvement with Wilcox. It should not come as a surprise to him when this whole thing blows up in his face."

"Fine!" Melanie picked up her skirts, tilting her chin in that manner that had so often tempted him to strike it. Her eyes spat at him in hurt rage. "Then you stay here and keep your friend's confidence!"

"You're not going!" Ryan threatened, reaching for her as she started past him.

Melanie turned into a fighting cat when his arms caught her about the waist and hauled her toward the bed. She cursed him with every breath, raking his arms with her nails. But her strength was no match for his. The steel that she had counted on to help her held her down to the mattress in helpless despair.

"Will you come to your senses?" he demanded above her, bouncing her on the bed in a violent shake.

"I'll hate you for this for as long as I draw breath, Ryan Caldwell!" she grated through her teeth. Tears spilled from the corners of her eyes to the bed of raven hair that had come undone in the tousle, causing her even more anguish. She hated that weakness. Ryan could always make her cry with every emotion she was capable of. And as much as she loved him, she meant her words. If anything happened to 'Io because he refused to try to save him, she could never forgive him.

"You're not thinking clearly or you'd see—"

A dull thud jolted the body holding her down. Startled green eyes stared down at her before rolling up in unconsciousness. His body collapsed on her, crushing an alarmed scream from Melanie. Her wrists no longer held in the relaxed fingers wrapped about them, Melanie frantically tried to shove him aside.

"Here!" Priscilla's voice echoed beyond the leaden chest

hat pressed her face to the bed.

Still too shocked to understand what had happened, Melanie slid out from under Ryan as her cousin pulled him over on his back. She stared down at her husband's unconscious figure, her heart leaping to her throat. "Ryan!" She glared back at her cousin incredulously. "Have you lost your mind?"

"He wasn't going to let us go," Priscilla explained sharply. "Now let's tie him up before he comes around."

Melanie glanced from Ryan to her cousin again, her emotions torn. Dear God, please don't let him be hurt, she prayed fervently. Her fingers snaked around to the back of his head but could find no sign of blood.

"For heaven's sake, Melanie, he's just unconscious. I tried not to hit him too hard," Priscilla told her in an exasperated apology. "He's just hurt a little. 'Io could die if we don't get going."

A strangled moan rumbled deep in Ryan's throat, spurring Melanie into action. "Right!"

She wasn't sure how Priscilla knew what was going on, but her cousin had done what had to be done. They made ropes from ribbons and sashes, wrapping Ryan's feet and wrists securely and tying them in knots Melanie was certain had no name. But they were tight and that was all that mattered. Priscilla gagged him so that he could not alert the servants, while Melanie wet a washcloth and tenderly placed it over the swelling on the back of his head.

"You made me choose," she accused softly.

"Let's tie him to the bed so that he can't knock things around and draw someone in here."

Melanie nodded and helped her cousin turn Ryan so that his feet could be fastened to the foot rail and his wrists to the head of the bed. Thank goodness someone had a clear head, she mused miserably. When her husband was positioned so that he could not move without making any more than a cushioned creaking sound on the mattress, Melanie kissed his forehead gently and followe Priscilla down the stairs.

"Where do we find 'Io?" Priscilla asked as they hurrie out the back door of the mansion.

"Kela knows where he is." Melanie hesitated, glancir back one last time. Then, as if making up her mind, sl unwound the cross from her wrist and put it around Pri cilla's neck. "Here. He wanted you to have this with h love. And when this is over, he's going to take that jc Gilbert offered."

Priscilla's crisp, cool facade crumbled at the news. Sl embraced Melanie tightly. "I'm sorry I had to hurt Ryar I overheard you arguing and I panicked. I'll just die something happens to 'Io."

"It won't if we can help it," Melanie assured her. Sl broke away and started for the carriage house. "We'll tak the flatbed."

They hitched the horses to the wagon in the moonligl for fear of a lantern drawing attention to them. Melani was grateful for the inconvenience at the plantation dur ing the restoration, when she had had to hitch the sam team to haul out prunings and branches, for Priscilla ha never handled a team in her life.

The moon gave the empty streets an eerie presence Shadows of the mansions nestled in the trees and shar picket fences made the earlier drive in the comfortabl presence of Ryan and Gilbert seem a lark in comparisor It was as if they were watching and waiting for the rebel to make their move. Upon reaching the turn to the out skirts of the city where the Cummings had built the or phanage, they discovered a gathering of uniformed an well-dressed gentlemen lazing around a campfire near th edge of the dirt street.

Melanie slowed the wagon, apprehension growin within her chest until she thought it would explode. A sentry carrying a lantern met them, the sight of his gu alarming her further. She could feel the pinch of Priscilla'

344

fingers through the folds of her gown as she spoke to the uniformed man.

"Good evening, sir. What is happening here?" she asked innocently. Her eyes traveled over the group that had ceased their assorted conversations to appraise the two women in the wagon.

"We got orders, ma'am, that no one is to leave the city. You and your lady friend will have to go back home."

"And just who gave you those orders, sir?" Priscilla snapped, mustering her most commanding tone.

"My superior, ma'am."

"What's the problem, sir?" another gentleman called out. Melanie watched as the formally attired man handed over his tin mug of coffee to a companion and sauntered over to them with an air of authority he obviously enjoyed.

"These ladies wish to leave the city and—"

"Why, Mrs. Caldwell . . . and Miss Caldwell," Lem Samuels declared upon recognition of them. "Are you quite well enough to be out alone like this?" he asked Melanie.

Melanie held out her hand, extreme relief on her face. "Mr. Samuels, how wonderful to see you! I am very well now, thank you. I believe it was the heat."

"Where's the captain?"

"He has gone to President Dole's office, sir," Melanie answered smoothly. "And Priscilla and I . . . well, in view of the recent developments, we thought it best if we went to the orphanage to help with the children." She lowered her voice. "If there is to be any violence, we should be safe there, shouldn't we?"

"Of course you will, madame!" Samuels exclaimed wholeheartedly. "And I will personally escort you there myself. You two!" he called out to two of the men who had been lounging with him. "Come with me."

"You are a blessing indeed, sir," Priscilla told him gratefully. She exchanged an apprehensive glance with Melanie as they started off once more.

Lem Samuels did little to assuage their fears. He boasted of the additional men being assembled at the palace and the councils of war being discussed in the President's office as a result of the informant's message. But they still did not know where the rebels had gathered. They were merely preparing for when that information reached them.

The large shedlike structure of the orphanage was a welcome sight to Melanie's eyes. The building was dark, the children having been put to bed hours earlier, but a light shone from the kitchen where she was certain she would find Kela. Hopefully, Amanda and William Cummings had retired, for she was not certain how the reverend and his wife would react to their purposeful mission. However, the cottage they had taken as their residence since William Cummings's resignation from his parish showed no sign of anyone stirring within.

She thanked the members of the Citizen's Guard for their escort, while Priscilla summoned an answer to the door of the outhouse where Kela did most of the cooking for the children.

"Mrs. Caldwell, it was my honor to assist such lovely ladies in such a kind and generous endeavor as this. I know the Cummings praise the day Captain Caldwell brought you two here from Boston."

"You are too kind, sir," Melanie replied with appropriate modesty. Her eyes darted to the opening door, and with a curtsy, she bade the proud members of the guard good night.

Kela was fully dressed, an indication that she knew the night was far from ordinary. Instead of offering tea or taking part in the usual amenities, she turned her dark gaze on them, devoid of curiosity.

"You need 'Io," she stated flatly.

"It's terribly urgent, Kela," Priscilla pleaded, taking the servant's work-roughened hand between her own.

346

"Where is he?" Melanie asked.

Kela walked over to the window, watching the departing guard. "I show you when the *haole* is gone."

Her use of the word *haole* struck Melanie as odd, but she was warmed by the thought that Kela considered her and Priscilla one of them. But she knew from what 'Io had told her that the rebellion was not manned by pure Hawaiians only. There were many, both *haole* and Hawaiian alike, who supported the queen out of respect for the past and wanted to cling to the old ways.

They waited for half an hour to give the men a chance to get back to their station before taking to the wagon again. As Melanie drove the team, her heart no longer beat furiously. It was as if she had become numb with purpose. Priscilla rode silently at her side, her fingers working nervously over the medallion her love had sent to her, while Kela kept a sharp eye out for any movement in the trees that increasingly surrounded the road leading around the perimeter of the city toward Waikiki.

They passed through fields of taro and rice paddies, with an occasional palm growing in solitary dignity in their midst. Along their perimeters, one and two-room cottages that housed the plantation workers cut clean shadows in the moonlight.

"Turn there. Go slow . . . easy to miss," Kela explained, pointing to a small break in the trees that Melanie would have bypassed had the woman not made it obvious.

She shifted on the uncomfortable seat, too anxious to notice its hardness, and maneuvered the wagon around the turn. The lane was so narrow that the side boards scraped some of the bushes at the entrance, snapping off a few limbs. The sound startled the horses, so that Melanie had to rear back on the reins and soothe them with her voice to bring them in line. It was as if they, too, were as nervous as she.

"Now wait a minute," she cautioned, reining the team to a full stop. "What exactly are we looking for, Kela?"

"Old sugar farm. House not there now. Burned many years ago."

"Are the rebels there?"

Kela shook her head. " 'Io's friends digging up guns. Somebody there to find him for you."

Melanie frowned. Without 'Io to identify them, would anyone believe them? "Do they know you, Kela?" she asked hopefully.

"Kela tell them you 'Io's ladies." A hint of a smile played on the woman's lips, but only briefly. "We go."

All that remained of the plantation house in the overgrown clearing was the chimney of the kitchen and a few blackened timbers that reached up into the starlit night. But to its rear was a large barn. Although it had escaped the fire that had delivered death to the farm and its owners, it suffered the torment of the weather without their maintenance. The roof sagged ominously on one side, distorting the once-proud profile against the sky. A soft light filtered through the entrance, belying its deserted appearance.

Melanie did not know whether she was simply frightened or there was just cause for the fine hairs that rose on the back of her neck as she surveyed the desolate surroundings. Something wasn't right, instinct warned her.

"Wait!" she whispered as Kela and Priscilla started out of the cover of the trees. "I don't think we all should go. If anything should go wrong, we'd all be caught."

"Meilani, come," Kela decided, demonstrating her decision with a firm push against Priscilla's chest. "You go get help if trouble. Good idea."

Priscilla's eyes widened. "I don't want to be left alone!"

"Meilani speak Hawaiian," Kela argued simply.

Melanie shook her head. "I'll go alone first. If anything is wrong, you both go get help. If things are normal and I need Kela, I will call for you."

Melanie felt ridiculous wearing a ball gown into the barn. Her nerves were so taut that the thought almost made her laugh aloud. She wondered if she were crazy to think such odd things at such grave times as she stepped into the dim light and peered inside the structure.

"Hello! Is anyone here?" she called out in the native tongue. She repeated it in English, taking another cautious step.

There was no answer. She searched the dark corners of the room with her eyes and dared to venture farther in. A cobweb brushed across her shoulder, causing her to recoil with a startled gasp. In irritation, she brushed it away and walked straight to the lantern that hung on a large square beam. Under it was a table that had been fashioned from one of the unhinged stable doors laid over two benches.

Two hands of cards lay scattered on it as if the game had been abandoned hurriedly. Sniffing the dry, dusty air, she picked up the scent of cigar smoke and glanced down to see the smoldering source at her feet, where a retreating foot had failed to stomp it out completely.

"I know you are here," Melanie challenged. She turned as she spoke, seeking any sign of movement. "Please come out of hiding. You must take me to 'Io Kuakini. I have news that is urgent to your plans."

"And I had thought you dressed so just for me! Are you always to disappoint me, madame?"

In a whirl of organdy, Melanie faced the large man emerging from the shadows. Her heart thumped madly as she drew herself to her full height and demanded, "I must find 'Io Kuakini. Can you help?"

"Ah, yes, your brother," the Frenchman reflected aloud in a toying manner. "Would that I had such sisterly affection."

"Damn you, Bartot, your own hide is in danger as well! Now take me to him!" She prayed Kela and Priscilla would not come out of hiding now. If she had to go anywhere with Bartot, she wanted them to know where.

She could barely see the glint in his eyes through the

narrow slits he made of them. "What is thees you spea
of, madame?"

"I won't tell you. I will only tell 'Io."

His giant figure was made larger by the shadow cast i
the lamplight. He shuffled over to her, his booted fee
dragging in the dust, but Melanie did not retreat thi
time. If the Frenchman was 'Io's contact, then she woul
do what she must to get past him to her friend.

"But I theenk you will, madame." He tutted at her i
disapproval and dug something out of his coat pocket. I
was the same coat he always wore, reeking of cigar smok
and body odor, which stirred her offensively. "You see
madame, you have caused us much trouble this evenin
by not being at your home."

Melanie was distracted by the emergence of two mor
men from the shadows, one of them shoving a pistol i
his belt as if realizing she posed no threat to them. It wa
the gentle click of metal that drew her attention back t
the man in front of her.

"So we were forced to take your daughter in you
stead."

A tiny gold locket hung from a delicate chain, opene
to show the pictures that matched those in the one abou
her own neck. "Kristen . . ." Melanie reached in disbelie
for the necklace, only to have it snatched back and hun
tauntingly over her head.

Anger unlike any she had ever felt surged through he
veins at the man's mocking smile. But instead of sendin
her off in a furious temper, it calmed her icily. "Where i
my daughter?"

"On my ship." He shrugged in feigned apology. "It wa
a precaution, should you remember who was walking
down the beach a few months ago when the authoritie
find out that the rebels have dug up all the arms they'l
need for their pitiful rebellion. But in truth, *mon cherie,* i
was you I intended to take." A stained grin spread acros
his mouth as his rough hand accosted the satin skin of he

shoulder. "And if you cooperate with me, I shall leave her on the beach. My tastes are varied but do not include children. I prefer their mamas instead." It slid down the vee of her neckline, tracing over the swell of her breasts . . . testing. "Now what is this urgent news?"

"How do I know I can trust you?"

The grin widened. "You do not."

Kristen! This vermin had her baby on his ship. Surely she must be frightened out of her mind by these cutthroats. All the little girl had ever known was love. And if it was in her power to do so, this nightmare for her daughter would be brought to an end at any cost.

"There is a traitor among you." Melanie did not withdraw from the lascivious touch. She met his superior gaze equally. "We must find 'Io and warn him."

"Who else knows of this traitor?"

"The President and his officials."

"So they have a spy among them as well," he laughed gratingly. "And the rebels' spy is so much more beautiful than I."

A sinking feeling invaded her senses as his admission registered. She had walked right into the traitor's hands and ruined her chances of helping 'Io . . . maybe. She found her voice. "What are you doing to do with me?"

"Now, madame, or later?"

Melanie flinched at the pinch of her breast through the thin material of her bodice. She could well imagine his plans for later. But she would deal with that when it came. Now she had to let her friends know she was in trouble. "For now, monsieur."

"I am taking you to Waikiki Beach to meet my ship as soon as the rebels come back with my money. It was them I expected to enter the barn, not a vision in lace."

The Frenchman was enjoying himself too much to realize the steel warning of her fury. She shoved against him with all her might, counting on his loss of footing over one of the half barrels upended for use as a chair. "You traitorous bastard!" she shouted at the top of her voice. She knew she couldn't get away, but that was not her intention. Out of the corner of her eye, she saw her captor catch himself on a supporting beam, and Melanie ran that much faster. "Traitor," she screamed again, hoping that Prisclla and Kela would understand what was happening.

"Ye ain't gittin' away so easy this time, gal!"

"Take your hands off me, you traitorous dog! 'Io will kill you when he finds you've betrayed him!"

"Who the hell's 'Io?" the man who nearly strangled her with his arm across her neck laughed as the Frenchman came out of the barn.

"Her brother? Her sweetheart? Who cares, *mon ami?* Bring her back inside."

"No!" Melanie twisted and kicked into the air. "I won't go to Waikiki with you. To hell with your boat!" Her message delivered, she bit viciously into the sweaty arm that had slipped down from her neck.

"Bitch!" the man swore vehemently, throwing her away with such force that she was winded when she struck the ground.

"Joe!" the Frenchman snapped angrily. His rolls of flesh jolted with each hurried step toward the spot where Melanie lay, trying to assemble her wits.

"She bit me!"

Melanie tried to get up but a heavy foot crushed her wrist against the dirt, causing her to cry out in pain.

"Madame, I truly look forward to turning that passion to other directions, but if you do not behave yourself, I might be forced to hurt you more than this."

The grind of his sole against her skin would have broken her wrist had it not been for the give of the ground beneath it. The pain ripped through her like a searing bullet exploding in her mind, so intense that she nearly lost consciousness. She whimpered involuntarily as the foot was lifted, replaced by a rough hand that yanked her to her feet. The sharp protest of the crushed muscles and bruised bones was more than her conscious state would bear. As the Frenchman gave the injury another impatient jerk toward the barn, Melanie fainted, falling outstretched on the dirt yard.

Ryan fretted alternately between cursing his wife to worrying about her as he rode away from the orphanage. He had wrenched and twisted until the silk ribbons she and her cousin had tied him with cut into his flesh. He swore again, under his breath, at his addle-brained niece for endangering Melanie. If only he could have gathered his senses from the blow, but it was as if he were half conscious—aware of what was going on yet helpless to stop it.

If it hadn't been for the messenger who arrived shortly after they left, he'd still be bound and gagged on the bed. The man had insisted his message was urgent. Because of that, Gilbert's servant finally opened the bedroom door after what seemed to Ryan like hours of knocking. He had barely taken time to read the missive, but the small Oriental had followed him to the stable, shoving it in his face stubbornly.

Thank God he had, Ryan thought, noting the lather on the animal that strained beneath him in its running fervor to please. It was the news 'Io Kuakini had promised him . . . the whereabouts of the Frenchman. With nothing to go on but that, Ryan had little choice but to leave the Cummings bewildered and head for Waikiki Beach.

His fingers went to the pistols he had taken from Gilbert's office, pistols that had belonged to their father. His brother kept them in mint condition. Now they were loaded and tucked snugly in his sash, ready to deal with anyone who came between him and his wife.

Melanie. His hands gripped the leather reins tighter. Leaning over the horse's neck, he urged him on in a strained command that conveyed to the animal his rider's urgency. He would have capitulated. The hurt and fear in her eyes was more than he could stand. Even as he'd tried to calm her, he was trying to think how he could handle Kuakini without betraying Dole's confidence. And then the lights had gone out.

He rounded the turn in the road in time to see a wagon in the distance, racing across the fields of taro. It waved from side to side out of control as the team galloped toward him. Without slowing his mount, he watched as the flatbed jolted on a turn, the wheels clearing the ground and tipping it precariously. A woman's scream broke the pounding drum of the horses' hooves, piercing the still of night.

The team suddenly struck out across the taro patch, with the slapping sounds of its wheels striking down the large wide leaves of the plants. With little choice but to abandon his race for the moment, Ryan whipped the nose of his mount toward the runaway wagon.

It wasn't until he seized the harness of the team that Ryan recognized the matched greys he had purchased with the plantation. He swallowed the cry of relief he felt, coaxing the spooked animals into a trot and, finally, to a halt. He slid off his own mount and ran his hands along the flanks of the team, easing their nerves with gentle commands until he reached the flatbed, where two women huddled together behind the seat in a hysterical pile of skirts.

"Melanie?" He vaulted over the side of the wagon and crawled over to them, but his wife's name hung on his lips when he coaxed them apart, discovering only Priscilla and Kela.

"Ryan!" Priscilla sobbed, reaching for him. "Dear God, we didn't want to leave her, but they had guns!"

A sickness washed over him, but he fought it. He grabbed Priscilla and shook her roughly. "Who has her? Where?"

"That awful man! He was horrible. He's the traitor and he has Melanie!" Tears streamed down the woman's face. The wild strands of hair that had once been braided prettily in a chignon stuck to her damp cheeks.

"Where, Priscilla? Where?" he demanded fiercely.

"I didn't mean to hurt you. I swear, I—"

"I show you." Kela gave Ryan the same suspicious appraisal he always received from her. He never understood what he had done to deserve her dislike. Whenever he had been around her he'd treated her politely. But it was always there . . . wary and accusing.

"Nooo!" Priscilla cried, grabbing him in panic as he pulled away from her and clinging desperately. "Don't leave me alone. Pleee . . . . ease!"

"Damn it," Ryan swore, slapping her cheek with the palm of his hand. Priscilla screamed higher and higher, and he slapped her again. "Get a hold on yourself, Priscilla!"

"You touch again, I cut open your throat."

Ryan jerked back involuntarily at the cold press of steel against his throat, shifting his gaze to Kela's glare beside him. She held a kitchen knife against him, her eyes filled with such hatred that he did not doubt she meant her threat.

"Make her stop crying, Kela. We can't help Melanie until she stops crying," he pleaded hoarsely. A cold sweat soaked the starched shirt Melanie had playfully fastened earlier, bestowing a kiss with each button until he had seriously considered canceling the affair. Would to God he had, he thought as he watched the native considering his words. They would have all been safe at the plantation, unaware of this damned travesty of rebellion, instead of being at the mercy of these two—one hysteric and one madwoman.

Chapter Twenty-two

The lowered voices of the men, the clink of coins—gold, she had heard them say—all swam around in Melanie's consciousness. She'd hoped against all hope that it would be 'Io who came to pay the Frenchman for his delivery. But the voice of the paymaster was not that of her friend. 'Io was probably hauling the guns from the beach to one of the two assigned destinations she had overheard them talking about.

She shifted, wincing at the throbbing pain in her wrist. They had bound her hands behind her, and now her wrist was so swollen that the rope cut her viciously. Her hand felt as if it were going to burst. Ignoring the dried sticks of moldy hay that pricked her skin where it did not cling and itch, she tried to sit up, inadvertently drawing the attention of the guard Bartot had left with her.

"Down, ye bloodthirsty bitch!"

Melanie crashed back into the musty bed with the impact of his foot against her shoulder. "My wrist, sir. It's swollen about the bonds."

"Ye've been nothin' but trouble since we come acrossed ye. It'd serve ye right if it fell off, it would."

"Loosen the ropes, idiot. She'll bring a higher price alive with both hands."

The seaman approached Melanie, leery of her teeth, and worked at the knots behind her. She rubbed her wrist tenderly, flexing her fingers to pump pinpricking circulation into them.

"Do you think you can behave like a lady, madame? For if so, we can do away with those uncomfortable ropes." Melanie flinched at the Frenchman's touch as he lifted her to her feet by the shoulders. "What is your answer, minister's daughter?"

"You give me little choice, sir."

"Mon dieu, but you are a sight to stir a man's blood!" he murmured, picking a piece of hay from the hair that fell in disheveled layers of curls past her shoulders. It tickled as he dragged it lightly down the taper of her neck and into the valley of her breasts, his lips twisted in sardonic pleasure.

"Pua'a!" Melanie muttered in contempt. She stiffened as her insult struck home. In a flash, she was forced against him, his wet lips smearing a fetid kiss that gagged her as she tried to push away with her good hand. Every muscle in her body tensed to conceal the dreadful shudder that swept through her.

"Even pigs need love, madame," he threatened her, yanking her head back so that she inhaled his hot breath. "And you will please this one before the night is out, if I have to keep my little insurance aboard to see that you do."

"No!" Melanie protested, her defense shattered by his threat to her daughter. "I . . . I'll do anything you say. Just keep your promise."

"That's much better, *mon cherie.* Much better." He contemplated the prospect, his tongue sliding from one corner of his mouth to the other as he raked his gaze over her once more and then turned to his man. "Get the horses. Madame?" he said expectantly, offering Melanie his arm.

Her shoulders sagged in defeat as she put her uninjured hand on the tattered sleeve of the jacket and walked out with her abductor. Everyone she loved was in danger except Ryan. And he would never forgive her for this. She

357

swallowed the sob that rose in her throat, choking her with despair. Priscilla and Kela might be able to help 'Io by getting a message through to the rebels, but she would be on the Frenchman's ship before anyone could help her. The deep breath she took ached in her lungs. At least they would find Kristen.

They waited outside for the Frenchman's henchmen to bring out the horses they kept in the back stalls of the barn. Bartot's interest in tormenting Melanie dwindled as the minutes passed and his orders were not promptly followed. With a growl of irritation, he pulled her toward the barn entrance.

"What the hell is the holdup?"

"I can't find Joe."

"He's probably taking a leak," the leader remarked sarcastically. "You stand right here in the moonlight where I can see you," he ordered Melanie with a pinch of her cheek. "You know better than to try to run away."

Leaning against the edge of the barn door, Melanie closed her eyes in miserable helplessness. She dared not run. As long as they had Kristen, she was at their mercy . . . unless 'Io came for her. If Kela and Priscilla found him close by, he might help. She blinked hard at the pain in her wrist and lifted her hand to examine it. She wasn't going to cry. She wouldn't give Bartot that satisfaction. She'd sooner spit on him.

A loud grunt and a pistol shot interrupted her vindictive thought with a start. A violent commotion erupted in the back of the barn, with horses neighing and stomping frantically. Melanie tried to see in the darkness, drawn in apprehension toward the barn. A horse bolted from the shadows, screaming in panic, its saddle slipping where the girth had not been tightened.

She reached for the lantern and held it higher as the man who couldn't find Joe staggered out, a gaping red hole in his forehead spewing blood. He stared blindly at Melanie, his eyes bulging in death, and pitched forward, landing at her feet. No, she thought frantically. Nothing must happen to the Frenchman! His men had Kristen.

Charging into the dark stable, the lantern swinging in her hand, Melanie made out the figures of two men wrestling in the hay. The horrible blows of fists against flesh resounded in the confines of the area as the larger of the two rolled to the top. Melanie recognized the Frenchman as he slammed a heavy blow at his opponent. The momentum carried him forward, the thud of the impact muted by his curse and the dirt it struck, for the smaller man had twisted under him, avoiding the offense. Long, lean legs scissored, propelling him over as Bartot fell to his side. In a matter of seconds, the Frenchman's opponent was on him, striking sickening blows to his face like a madman.

"Ryan!" Melanie cried out in recognition of the golden hair embedded with straw and dirt. "No!" She dropped the lantern and grabbed her husband's shoulders, pulling until the pain of her wrist made her cry out in agony. "Stop it! He has Kristen!"

The shock of her action and words afforded the Frenchman the opportunity he needed. With a tremendous upward punch, he caught the enraged captain under the chin, clipping him backward in a stunned sprawl against his wife's skirts. Ryan struggled to keep the thousands of tiny lights swirling between him and the grotesquely large shadow rising in front of him from obliterating his consciousness totally.

He was going to kill him. He burned with a white heat that would be satisfied with nothing less than the blood of the man who had so familiarly taunted his wife. But her words confused him, her pleas to spare the vermin. He shook them away, flinching at the sharp agony in his jaw. Kill, he thought obsessively, willing away the tempting lights of unconsciousness.

But it was difficult to think with such hostility, when the sweet scent of hibiscus infiltrated his senses and the soft touch of organdy caressed his cheek. A hand softer than the material spread on his chest and lips sought his swollen ones tenderly. This wasn't Bartot, part of him sneered at his bloodthirsty side. He shook his head again, trying to clear the muddled images from his mind.

His eyes rolled as he blinked them and focused on the pained face above his. It was a beautiful face, with delicately formed features he knew by heart. Dark hair he loved to run his fingers through framed it and fell forward, brushing his face. For an unguarded moment, he yearned to do just that, but reason reminded him of the danger. Where the hell was Bartot?

"Get out of the way, Melanie," he groaned, shoving awkwardly in his stunned state at the gowned figure between him and his enemy. He hadn't seen his gluttonous face, but he knew he was there. "Bartot!" he challenged, dragging himself to his feet unsteadily and trying to make out the blurred shadow in the dim light.

"Very clever, *mon capitan*," Bartot's voice answered only a few feet away. "You have managed to kill two of my men and nearly overpowered me. That would have been a horrible mistake, eh, *mon cherie?*"

His laughing endearment curled the anger in Ryan's stomach, launching him forward, only to be halted by the frantic restraint of the woman at his side. Ryan turned to look down at Melanie in bewilderment.

"He has Kristen!"

"Where?" he forced out, the news more staggering than his opponent's blow. That explained the way his wife had permitted her captor to paw her without protest. Ryan had wanted to charge into them right then, but he had been outnumbered. Only by eliminating them one at a time had he had a chance of saving Melanie. Or so he'd thought.

"Where you are going to take me, *mon ami* . . . to my ship," the Frenchman answered smugly. "But I only intend to keep your wife. You may keep the little girl, provided

360

you do exactly as I say." Bartot snapped his fingers at Melanie. "You, madame, come to me while your husband rounds up the horses he has frightened off."

Ryan considered the pistol that was now aimed at him, which he had lost in the scuffle, and laughed bitterly at the irony. The big oaf did not need a weapon with Melanie and Kristen in his control. Patience, he cautioned himself. He would have to wait his chance and play the game by the Frenchman's rules for the moment. Somehow, he thought, looking away as Bartot pulled Melanie against him, flaunting his hold over them both with his familiarity.

Only two of the horses remained at bay in the stableyard. Ryan managed to grab their reins and bring them to the hitching post to secure their tack. His mind raced as he thought through their situation. Kela and Priscilla would be close to Honolulu by now . . . if they hadn't lost control of the wagon again. They were to tell the authorities his wife had been kidnapped by the rebels who were escaping from Waikiki by ship.

But he could not count on that. The police stood a chance of heading them off at the beach by taking the more direct route along the shore, but it was slim. Bartot held all the cards and he knew it. Ryan looked at the dejected way Melanie stared at the ground, suffering the Frenchman's rough caresses, and he ached to take her into his arms and comfort her. By God, he'd see Bartot dead for this!

"Now, put your wife on one of them, *capitan*."

"He has Kristen," was all Melanie said as he drew her away from Bartot and gathered her in his embrace. But her arms sought his neck and she buried her face in his chest, hugging him in silent desperation. Without a word, she told him she understood his quandary and shared it.

"It's going to be all right, blue eyes. We'll get her back."

He could almost laugh with Bartot at the foolishness of his words, but they were the best he had to offer her. But for Kristen, he could tear the man apart with his bare hands, he swore to himself, condemning their captor with the smoldering hatred in his eyes. God, had he ever been so helpless?

"I know," Melanie assured him with a parting squeeze. Suddenly, she whimpered and drew her arm to her stomach in a grimace of pain.

Ryan reached for her wrist, his face going whiter yet with unvented rage. It was hard to tell where her arm ended and her hand began, for the bluish-black swelling around it. A vile curse rumbled in his throat, catching out of respect for the woman looking at him with stark fear in her eyes that he might jeopardize their daughter's safety.

"Your wife did not heed my warnings about crossing me, monsieur. You, too, would do well to take heed, lest she suffer worse."

In spite of his hold over him, Bartot did not trust Ryan. He tied Ryan's hands behind his back and forced him to walk alongside the animals as they made their way across the patches of taro and rice that separated them from Waikiki Beach. With each step he took, Ryan's rage grew, until his body agonized in its inability to release it.

Because he had killed Bartot's henchmen, there was no one at the beachhead to row the Frenchman and Melanie to the ship anchored off the shore. Once again, with a great show of satisfaction at Ryan's helpless predicament, Bartot cut him loose and pointed to the longboat his men had beached earlier.

"You will take me and theese lovely lady to my ship, *mon capitan*, and provided you offer no trouble, I will hand over the little girl for you to take back."

"You might as well kill me, Bartot, because there will be no place you can hide from me," Ryan growled as he shoved the boat into the water and swung over the side. He took Melanie from the Frenchman and settled her next to him.

"The thought has occurred to me, but what better way to exact revenge than to leave you alive to wonder what has become of your lovely wife?" Bartot nearly overturned the vessel as he heaved his cumbersome frame over the side. Once he regained his breath, he commanded Melanie to his side, continuing his torment of both of them. Ryan's knuckles were bloodless about the handles of the oars as he dwelled on the pleasure it would be to bash in his companion's head with one of them.

"If I do not appear hale and hearty to my mates, monsieur, the little golden doll baby will be tossed over the side to the sharks without thought. Those were my orders. So give up those wicked thoughts you are having."

The boat rode high in the water, attesting to an empty hold. Bartot's men had tossed a rope ladder over the side to assist their obese captain and his hostage in boarding. Perspiration formed on Ryan's brow as the longboat drifted against the metal side of the freighter. The next few minutes were critical as to whether he'd ever see his wife and daughter together again on the little beach where they had shared many memorable afternoons. He had to get Kristen into the boat first. What he would not give for Amos Cobb to be at his side now, he mused, for he still could not count on saving them both.

"Well, whadda ya have there?" the first mate called out to Bartot, peering over the rail at the odd trio.

"Take up my lady friend, *mon ami*, and bring the little girl to the rail," the Frenchman ordered. *"Capitan,"* if you will, pleese turn your back and put together your hands."

Ryan stared at the rope the leader held out with a rebellious jut of his jaw. His hatred boiled, tempting him to charge his tormentor, but his daughter's cry reined him into submission.

"Mama!" Kristen sobbed upon seeing her mother trying to climb the ropes. Small arms reached toward Melanie, her fingers opening and clenching as if clawing their frantic way to comfort. The heart-wrenching sobs shook the small body being held effortlessly over the rail. She wore her pink and white nightdress, her hair a tangle of curls hanging about a face streaked red from crying. "Mama, mama, mama, mamaaaaa . . ."

Melanie tore out of the wiry arms that hauled her over the side of the ship and rushed to the man who held her daughter so precariously, forcing him back from the rail and grabbing at the child at the same time. The seaman let Kristen go under the mother's scorching glare before he even heard Bartot's command to do so. But as the gowned fury dropped her gaze to the little girl who tried to crawl up her dress, the fire was extinguished with a tenderness that astonished the man.

"It's all right, darling," Melanie shushed against the topmost layer of curls that were soft as down and damp from the night air. "Mama's here."

"I . . . want . . . t . . . to . . . g . . . go . . . home," Kristen gasped raggedly, her frail chest shuddering with each word. "They put m . . . me in a hole and r . . . rats are there!"

"That's just where Daddy is going to take you, darling. You'll be safe there and no one will ever bother you again." Melanie was so grateful to have the child safe in her arms, if only momentarily, that she paid no need to the pain it cost to hug her tightly. Kristen was frightened, but she wasn't hurt.

"A touching reunion, no, *capitan?*"

Ryan clenched his teeth at the bite of the rope against the raw places he had rubbed trying to get out of the ribbons Melanie and Priscilla had used earlier to subdue him.

"You had best hope your little one does not fall overboard until you drift ashore . . . or find a way out of these bonds." Bartot shoved him forward roughly.

His knees catching on the seat in front of him, Ryan pitched headlong into the bottom of the boat. He twisted as he struck, saving his head from hitting the other seat and jarring his shoulder instead. He grunted with the impact and struggled to get up, only to be downed again with a vicious kick in the ribs.

"Hand down the girl!"

Ryan heard Kristen's shrieks as they dragged her out of her mother's arms. Melanie called after her in tremulous reassurance that her daddy was going to take care of her. The words cut at him worse than the bonds ripping his flesh or the pain that stabbed his side with each breath he took.

He forced his eyes open in time to see Kristen being handed over the side, kicking and screaming in panic for her mother. The Frenchman nearly lost his grip on the wisp of child, catching a handful of her ruffled nightdress and lowering her into the longboat.

"Now stay still, leetle brat, or the sharks'll have you for supper!" he shouted above her hysterics.

"Mama!" Kristen's face was upturned, seeking out the pale face that stared at her from the rail above.

"Damn you, Bartot!" Ryan swore hoarsely, throwing his weight forward to catch the heavy man behind the knees as he turned to climb the rope ladder. A warning came from above and a boot exploded against his temple, followed by a laugh that etched itself in his memory forever as he collapsed in a daze.

"Daddy!"

Ryan clutched to consciousness long enough to see an oar cutting through the air to strike the back of the Frenchman's head, before it splashed into the growing gap of the water between the small boat and the freighter. The heavy man swung precariously on the ladder, then clawed his unsteady way topside with a string of curses that faded in the darkness that claimed him.

"I should have drowned the little nit!" Bartot ranted as his men helped steady him from the blow the child had delivered. "But to grow up without her mother will have to do," he sneered, jerking his head toward the woman straining over the rail to see the small craft carrying her crying daughter and unconscious husband away from them with each lap of the tide. "Let us leave this place, *mes amis,* and take her to my cabin."

If Melanie lived to be as old as the ancient ones in the chants, she would never forget Kristen's pitiful wail as the child huddled over Ryan in the prow of the boat. It would haunt her every night of her life. She prayed in the dim light of the unkempt cabin that the tide would carry them in to shore. It was an incoming tide, she consoled herself in a futile attempt to assuage her fears for her loved ones.

She lifted her hand out of the cool salt water Bartot had ordered for her wrist once his humor had improved over Kristen's unexpected attack. "A leetle theeng like that!" he had laughed, smacking his first mate on the back in amusement. "She has her mama's spirit, that one!" Then he'd seen Melanie's drawn face contorted in pain and sent her below to soak the injury he'd cruelly inflicted upon her.

And he'd sent a bath. If she weren't so despondent, she might have laughed, for surely the man had never used the tub himself. Not that it could actually be called a bathtub in the same sense as the one Ryan had provided for her long ago. It was a large round washtub filled with offensively strong perfume, which permeated the musty odor of the cabin nauseatingly with the mingle of stale cigars. Melanie had to open a portal to air it out.

Not only had he made his plans for her, but he'd also made them clear to his men. Each time one came in with a bucket of water, he leered at her knowingly in such a way that gooseflesh crawled on her skin. It was only a matter of time, she supposed, before he turned the ship over to his men and sought her out.

But he would not take her without a fight, she vowed, all the outrage of the evening flowing through her veins with a vengeance. Kristen was no longer in danger from him. All he could do was threaten her, and she would rather die than give in to him willingly. However, she was not foolish enough to think she could overpower him, particularly with her injured wrist. No. She would use his own blind lust against him.

She waited until the tub could hold no more, certain the men had taken turns getting a good look at her with each bucketful of water they brought in. A spare one for rinsing sat beside the tub, along with a dingy towel. Melanie slipped out of her gown and petticoats as quickly as she could manage the fastens, then stepped into the water.

She allowed herself no more time than it took to soak completely in the cheap perfume, then got out to don her silk and lace bodice and pantaloons. With a comb that was missing several teeth, she was able to comb out the straw that had embedded itself in her hair and make some order of the raven locks that spread about her shoulders in dark array. Then, with a purposeful set to her mouth, she climbed onto the bunk, her hand seeking the weapon that she had found earlier and hidden under the pillows.

She had no more than forced herself to relax to the familiar vibration of the steam engines when the door opened to admit the slovenly captain of the vessel to his domain. Through narrow slits in her eyes, she watched him as he looked from the pile of abandoned clothing to the bath and then to her. He was so intent on following the generous curves of her body that he did not realize she was awake.

She was afraid, as he began to undress, that he could hear the thunderous pounding of her heart and suspect her intentions. A cold, clammy sweat enveloped her body. It required an effort not to tense, to clench the small knife she had discovered in a box of miscellaneous fishing gear. It was the type used for opening shellfish, dull but sharp enough to do what needed to be done.

The mattress sagged as he leaned on it and whispered against her ear, "Wake up, *mon cherie*. It is time for you to please me." To Melanie's surprise, he gently lifted her injured hand and kissed it. "It is only a sprain, no?"

"You could have broken it."

"I had meant to, madame. Such a handicap can be useful in persuasion." His eyes swept over the rise and fall of her breasts beneath the thin silk cover. "But I can see that I have misjudged your ability to see reason."

Melanie locked gazes with him as he untied the laces to her bodice one by one and spread it to expose each breast, taking time to cup each firm mound possessively. She wanted to be sick but swallowed her pride for revenge. There were no second thoughts about her intent, no pangs of conscience. She was going to kill him.

"Do you ever take off that jacket and shirt, monsieur?"

"I am usually in too much of a hurry," he grinned, bending over to suckle the breasts he grasped in his hands.

Melanie arched a fine black brow at her prospective lover. "I thought we had all night," she suggested softly.

"All night, *mon cherie*," he confirmed, one hand sliding down the flat surface of her stomach to the waistband of her pantaloons. "My men will not disturb us."

Melanie could not help her involuntary retreat against the wall, no matter how much she tried to accept the man's touch. No man but her husband had ever known her with such intimacy and Bartot revolted her.

"So, you are not as brave as you would have me think, eh?" Melanie pressed against the cold wall as he climbed into the bunk and took up all the space between them. A hand slipped behind her, forcing her hips against his stomach. "Well, I am going to show you how it feels to be made love to by a pig, minister's daughter."

Her hand gripped the handle of the knife as he covered her mouth with his lips, licking and probing with his tongue until she thought she would gag from his fetid breath. With all her strength, she lifted it and stabbed into his side. The Frenchman's face registered astonishment above her own. Melanie waited for him to collapse, but instead the hands that had stroked her hips and buttocks flew to her throat.

Wildly, she withdrew the blade and stabbed again, feeling the give of his ample flesh beneath it, but the choking force about her neck only wavered with the blow. The bulging eyes above her were filled with murderous rage. Melanie tried to scream for help, but only a strangled croak escaped the death grip.

Her hand was sticky with his blood this time as she tried again. The blade glanced off him ineffectively, her strength failing with the lack of air that was gradually claiming her awareness. Ryan, she thought, clinging to the image of her husband that came to her mind. Would he know? Damn Bartot! She tried with one last thrust, burying the blade to its hilt between the Frenchman's ribs before her body went limp from lack of oxygen.

He was so heavy, she thought, her hands moving on their own to weakly disengage the thick biting fingers at her neck. She closed her eyes and pushed in a desperate fight for survival, and to her stunned amazement, her assailant rolled away, falling with a terrible crash to the floor.

Melanie moaned with relief, unable to do more than drink in the air she had been denied. She shook, so much so that it hurt her wrist just lying against her stomach. Another thud and a grunt echoed beside her. Groping for the knife that had gone off the bunk with Bartot, she opened her eyes to face her murderer again and cried out in disbelief.

"Hush, *maka polu!* He's dead," 'Io Kuakini soothed her.

Melanie blinked her eyes, certain that she was hallucinating and not really seeing the half-naked Hawaiian who wore only the *malo* of the ancient ones. A hunting knife, larger than the one she had used, was sheathed at his waist, fresh blood staining the leather insert. "How?" she asked, unable to assemble the many questions that came to mind.

"Later, Meilani. We must get over the side quickly." He helped her to her feet, drawing tight the laces that exposed her and tying them as if dressing a bewildered child. "Can you swim?" At Melanie's nod, he took her hand and led her away from the inert body of the Frenchman toward the door. "All we have to do is make it to the water undetected, *maka polu*."

He tried to sound as though it would be no problem, but 'Io knew that with every passing moment their chances of escaping the vessel alive diminished. With a forced smile and a reassuring hug, he checked the corridor and stepped out of the cabin, drawing Melanie behind him.

Chapter Twenty-three

"Daddeee . . ." Kristen's voice cracked close to Ryan's ear. He had to give up the haven of darkness and face the pain that hovered on its edge. Even as his muddled consciousness cleared he forced himself up, assisted by small hands that pinched as they tugged on him. Kristen's face was red and puffy from crying, her dimpled chin quivering. She looked at him in a mixture of relief and misery. Her sobs had robbed her of any more voice than a whisper.

"Are you hurt bad, Daddy?" She touched the dried blood where the heel of Bartot's boot had cut his temple.

The tenderness reminded him of her mother's and he winced in mental anguish, his eyes scanning the shimmering moonlit surface for the freighter. It was just a speck in the distance, its billowing smoke clouding the clear sky.

"They t . . . took Mama."

"We'll get her back, Kristen." If he had to search every port in the Orient, he'd find Melanie and kill Bartot. "Now look down in Daddy's boot and you'll find a knife."

Under other circumstances, her quizzical look would have been comical, for it was clear that she wondered what her father was doing with a knife in his boot. A kitchen knife at that.

Ryan had managed to convince Kela he meant no harm to Priscilla and insisted the native accompany her friend after telling him of Melanie's whereabouts. It puzzled him how she could be so perceptive about some things and so damnably simple about others, for she'd lucidly told him how many men were there and had given him accurate directions after her spell of madness in threatening to kill him. Then she'd given him the knife she'd held at his throat and wished him God's speed.

Not that he'd gotten the chance to use it, he reflected bitterly. "Now, carefully cut this rope away from my hands," he instructed when Kristen had removed the knife from his boot. "Make sure the sharp part is away from my skin."

"I hit that fat man for what he did." Kristen made small grunting sounds as she sawed away determinedly at the jute.

Ryan found himself holding his breath. The slide of the dull edge of the blade rubbed his broken skin with each slice, but his daughter was as careful as she was stubborn. "You're a brave little girl," he complimented sincerely. Like her mother.

Again his eyes went to the retreating silhouette. He noted the direction the ship was heading, realizing that it could change. But it was something to go on. As soon as he was free, he would get Kristen ashore and back to Honolulu. While he wished Amos and the crew of the *Belle* were in port, he would have to make do with the new crew he was assembling for the turbine steamer he had just purchased from the Boston shipyard. She was fast, and speed was what he would need to catch up with Bartot.

As he rowed feverishly toward the shore with the one oar left, Kristen's revenge having lost him the other in the water, he saw approaching horses. Reluctant to be too quick to rejoice, he instructed his daughter to get down in the boat. The little girl obeyed without question, her eyes rolled up at him in complete trust.

"Hold there!" the leader shouted, reining in his horse so sharply that it reared beneath him. "This is the police! Identify yourself, sir!"

"Ryan Caldwell!" Ryan answered, recovering quickly from the rejoicing crack of emotion in his voice. "It's all right, sunshine."

Kristen would not be separated from him when they reached the beach and he had to go through the ordeal of telling the police the details of what had happened. Ryan kept to the story that Melanie had been kidnapped by rebels. It was true to an extent.

"Why would they kidnap your wife, sir?"

"Her father put Bartot out of business in Lahaina. She's a beautiful woman . . . goddamnit, you're wasting time while they're getting away, Lieutenant!" Ryan cursed impatiently. The steamer was making its way toward Diamond Head and would soon be out of sight.

"Well, these horses can't catch it, Captain," the officer replied sardonically. "How do you know they were rebels?"

Kristen's arms about his neck were the only thing that kept him from striking the obstinate official. "Actually, Bartot is not a rebel. He accepted payment for delivery of arms to the rebels. I witnessed the exchange when I tried to get my wife back."

"And you didn't notify officials when you discovered her missing?"

Ryan now wished he could have gotten away before becoming entangled with the authorities. He glanced at the diminishing spectacle of the freighter and glared at the lieutenant. "I'm going to Honolulu, sir. I'll answer your questions later."

"I'm going too," Kristen told him as he started past the officer toward the horses they had abandoned earlier. Her grip about his neck tightened. "I want to get Mama."

"Captain, we have to report—"

The lieutenant's words were obliterated by a horrendous explosion that illuminated the black rise of Diamond Head across the water. Another and another ripped through the night. Ryan could not believe the splintering vision that had been the freighter as it flew apart in balls of flaming debris. He froze, denying his eyes with an agonized "Nooo!" that ripped from his chest.

"Maaaa . . . maaaa . . ." Kristen screamed, her arms and legs crawling desperately against Ryan, seeking refuge from the fiery horror across the orange-glazed water.

"Dear God in heaven!" someone in the group behind them echoed in prayer.

Ryan's knees buckled beneath him as he stared at the floating inferno. He held the hoarsely sobbing child to him, clinging to her in equal desperation. He'd failed her and her mother. His chest swelled with sobs of frustration that would not erupt. They just kept growing in number until he thought he could not bear any more.

It couldn't be, he agonized, shaking his head in refusal to accept the terrible truth. Melanie was a survivor. Even now she was swimming ashore, he told himself.

"Captain . . ." the lieutenant interrupted his frantic grasp for sanity. "I am terribly sorry."

"Good God, man, let's ride to the shore There may be survivors!" Ryan exclaimed, clinging to hope. "Mama may be swimming to the shore right now, sunshine. You know how your mother can swim. We have to go to her."

He knew by the looks the men around him exchanged that they thought he was mad with grief, realizing no one aboard could have survived the explosions and if anyone had, that person would be too injured to swim to safety. Ignoring their grim pity, Ryan swung into the saddle of his horse, sliding behind it to allow room for Kristen in front of him, and rode off in lead of the dubious group.

But they didn't know Melanie, he argued silently at their reason. He didn't want to think of her injured arm or the fact that she was with child and tired more easily than usual. He didn't want to dwell on the fact that by the time they reached the rim of Diamond Head, the Frenchman had surely had her in his cabin. Nor did he want to think beyond that, purposely avoiding recalling the way the swine had fondled her, unable to keep his hands away from her delectable body.

* * *

Melanie floated on her back in the cool water, too exhausted to do more than keep her head above the surface. Surely they had been swimming for hours. Her cheeks grew hot with the heat of the fire that burned on the floating debris that was left of the Frenchman's ship. She now understood the reason for 'Io's urgency to go over the side.

"You must try again, *maka polu*," 'Io encouraged her. "We have gone farther than this many times."

He treaded water at her side, his face somber as he considered her. Her features were ghostly white in the brilliant glow of the fire, her lashes fanned against her cheeks dark in stark comparison. Her breaths were short and rapid, almost trembling under the thin silk that clung to her like a second skin in milky translucence. The wrist that had given her such trouble during their frantic swim to escape the undertow of the ship floated limply to her side.

If only he could find something for her to cling to, he could pull her to shore. But he was afraid to leave her. The large, dark presence of Diamond Head never seemed more ominous as he gauged the distance between them and the rocky shore they had yet to reach.

"I can't," she sighed so softly that he had to ask her to repeat her words.

"You have no choice, Meilani. You have a husband and a daughter who need you."

It had been a close brush with death. He'd discovered Bartot's treachery and had been prepared to bring the traitor the justice he deserved for selling out his friends. 'Io was about to go over the side after planting the explosive charges when he had heard a child crying.

He knew before he ever saw the little girl that it was Kristen. That instinct that had led him to send Ryan Caldwell the message warning him to keep Melanie at his brother's home and revealing to him Bartot's whereabouts told him so. But he never believed Bartot would have stooped to kidnapping the child.

Then they had exchanged Kristen for Melanie. He had hidden in the shadows with no weapon other than the hunting knife at his waist, helpless to assist them. But the child was relatively safe with her father. 'Io had seen the kick that had knocked Caldwell out and counted on the fact that he would recover quickly. And Kristen showed no signs of panic. The way she attended to her father had brought a proud smile to the Hawaiian's lips. She was every bit Meilani's daughter.

But it was Meilani who needed him. She had been locked in Bartot's cabin. The constant stream of sailors who were in and out of the compartment carrying bathwater had made it impossible for 'Io to slip in undetected. So he had had to wait for what seemed an eternity, the fuse on the charges burning dangerously along, before Bartot came in and dismissed the lot of them. The fool had been so cocky with his success that he'd not bothered to lock the door. And that had been his undoing.

'Io had never killed a man before. He had argued with his fellow compatriots against the use of violence. He had given up hope of their success when Wilcox finally won his way and kept in touch only to find the source of the damaging information leaking out to Marshal Hitchcock's men.

But when he saw Bartot violating Meilani, his hatred was such that he felt no compunction as he plunged the knife into the bastard's back, severing his spinal cord with a twist. It was only then that he had seen that the Frenchman was actually strangling her. And he had stabbed him again, thrusting his rage into the body already convulsing in the throes of death.

Had time permitted, he would have cradled Melanie and soothed the aftermath of nerves that shook her violently. He would have kissed away her fears as he had when she was a child. Time, however, was no more on his side than fate had been in the past. Every moment spent on the ship risked discovery and fiery death.

And Meilani was not his, nor would she ever be. Besides,

he had discovered someone else who could share his love. She was not Meilani, but she held a place in his heart—a heart he'd thought would never have room for anyone but his *maka polu*.

The splash in the water beside him dragged him back to his current crisis. Melanie had flipped over, inspired by his mention of her family, and was struggling ahead again. Her injured hand cut through the water, gaining her little headway, but with every other stroke she moved smoothly. Still her handicapped pace made it difficult for him to hold back for her. He would have to let her rest again before they braved the white water breaking along the ragged shoreline.

He kept up with words of encouragement as Melanie fell behind, often swimming back to her to assist her until she could regain her breath. When the crash of the breakers only yards away from them roared in his ears, he nearly shouted for joy but conserved his energy for the treacherous swim to shore.

"We're almost there, Meilani," he called to his companion, turning on his back until she closed the few feet he had kept between them. Every muscle in his body tensed, for he did not see the girl who had been with him only a moment earlier. "Meilani!" 'Io cried out, plunging into the water where he had just seen her.

His foot contacted something solid beneath the surface as he kicked to return in the direction they had just come from. 'Io pivoted and dove for it in the murky, breathless darkness. Frantically, he reached and grabbed at nothing, knowing it was his companion his foot had touched. And then his hands became entangled in the silken strands of her hair.

He wound it about his fingers and propelled himself to the surface with powerful kicks of legs long accustomed to the ocean depths. He broke through the surface that was growing dimmer as the vessel in the distance sought the cool respite of its ocean grave and tugged Meilani's head out of the water. He turned her and, treading water furiously with his legs, tightened his arms about her waist with a terrible thrust.

The limp body in his arms went rigid with a cough. He jerked his arms about her again, forcing the water she had swallowed out of her stomach. She coughed again, gagging and spitting spasmodically. Swimming on his back with her body resting atop his own, 'Io felt the rise and fall of her breathing resume between fits of coughing and offered a grateful prayer.

A few yards more, he thought, his lungs bursting from exertion as he pulled his unconscious charge toward the small rock barely visible in the swells rolling toward shore. His hand slipped on its slimy surface at first but managed to secure a firm grip the second time around. Heaving with his last ounce of strength, he shoved Melanie up on the sloped surface and braced himself against her to keep her from slipping off into the water.

She was breathing, he assured himself, putting his ear close to her mouth. Her breath was shallow, but nonetheless it was there. He condemned himself for expecting her to be able to make it to shore in her condition. If she didn't drown, he feared she'd lose the baby. He should have taken a life ring with them, but that would have meant risking exposure to the lantern light.

" 'Io . . ."

'Io lifted his eyes to the half-lidded ones staring down at him. "You're safe, *maka polu.*"

"I—" her body shuddered weakly, "I can't make it to shore. I tried." Her arms cradled the conical point of the sloped rock as if she held onto a pillow, and she sobbed in quiet defeat.

"Can you stay here then?" 'Io asked, lifting himself out of the water as a larger swell washed by.

He could make it alone, but he knew he could not swim ashore and carry her with him. He judged the incoming tide and decided that he could get ashore and back before it swelled over the rock. Sometimes the natives left their ca-

378

noes along the banks. If he could not find a boat, a log or anything that would float would do. She could keep her head above water and he could pull her in.

"I can't swim it, 'Io," Melanie sniffed, trying to face her circumstances as bravely as her fatigue would allow.

"Listen to me, Meilani!" 'Io commanded sharply. "I am going to swim in and get a boat. You hold on to this rock until I get back. Can you do that?"

Melanie ran her hands over the smooth surface of the rock thoughtfully as the idea caught on. "I think so."

"Just keep to this rock, *maka polu*. If you are washed off, swim back to it, do you hear me?" Her face was like ice to his hand. He wavered in his decision for a moment, but the delicate hand that closed over his issued a gentle strength that surprised him.

"I won't go anywhere," Melanie assured him. "I promise." As if to show him she meant what she said, she hauled herself further out of the water until only her feet dangled below the surface. She was going to make it, she vowed with the smile she forced for her brave companion. She wasn't going to let 'Io or her family down.

She leaned down to accept 'Io's kiss of encouragement, collapsing against the cold wet stone as he shot out across the water toward the breaking point of the swells rolling past her. Her bravado faltered with each powerful stroke that carried him away from her, and the fear that had eaten at her before she lost consciousness and slipped under the surface sprang up again to gnaw at her weary mind.

All she had to do was hold on to this rock, she argued sternly against the doubts that reared unbidden in her thoughts. 'Io could easily make it to the shore. He was part fish. She laughed at the memory of her actually believing that he was the son of a mermaid his uncle had caught in his net. The things he had told her when she was small. And she had believed them . . . just as she believed in him now.

The struggle to put her fears to rest took its toll on her

strength. The water around the rock rose gently with each wave that swept past her, and her eyelids grew too heavy to keep open. She thought she had seen a figure emerge from the crashing breakers to the shore before she became lost in a dream world, drugged by the lullaby of the sea lapping around her.

How long she lay in the deathlike slumber, her body draped limp across the hard seabed, she did not know. The loud report of wood scraping the side of her rock island failed to do more than stir her to a moan of protest. Hands, warm against her cold body, seemed to latch on to her. They lifted her free, so that the air hitting her underside where the rock had stored her body heat chilled her.

She opened her eyes in irritation, determined to will away the unwelcome intrusion. "Don't . . ." Her eyes grew wider at the sight of Ryan's face peering down at her. "Ryan?"

"Don't snap those blue eyes at me after all you've put me through, blue eyes," he chided tenderly as she was hauled into a boat. He tucked a wool blanket about her, folding her in his arms with it. "How are you both doing?"

"I don't know about him, but I'm cold." Melanie wanted to pinch herself to see if this were some wonderful dream, but Ryan had so much blanket about her that her hands were encased in wool. His hand managed to find her stomach, pressing against it gently.

"My little survivors," he whispered with a warmth that spread comfortably through her.

Melanie started, remembering 'Io's swim to the shore. " 'Io!"

"Eia, maka polu," 'Io Kuakini acknowledged from the opposite end of the canoe, drawing her attention. "Somebody has to row," he teased. "The captain got the easy job."

"And Kristen?" she asked Ryan, her heart beginning to pump with joy at what was happening . . . if she dared believe it.

"On the shore, waiting very anxiously for her mother."

"The only way she could be pried from Ryan was to convince her the canoe only had room for three people and we'd have to leave you until we could get a bigger boat," 'Io interjected, adding softly, "I told you they needed you, *maka polu.*"

"She's the bravest five-year-old I've ever come across," Ryan told her. He kept stroking Melanie's hair with his hand as if he weren't any surer than Melanie that their reunion was real. "Just like her mother."

The final piece of her puzzle in place, the how and why of it no longer important, Melanie snuggled in his embrace. The nightmare was over, its heavy shadow lifting like a massive weight washed away by the aura of the sun rising behind Diamond Head. She strained anxiously toward the shore, spotting a small ruffled figure scampering up and down the beach, waving wildly. Above the roar of the breakers that shot the canoe toward the beach, she heard Kristen's high-pitched "Mama!"

As 'Io jumped out of the canoe and pulled it up on the sand, Melanie disengaged herself from Ryan's arms with renewed strength and climbed out of the boat. Blinded with happy tears, she held out her arms to receive the bolting youngster who nearly bowled her over on the sand but for Ryan's strong brace behind her. Her own tears mingled with her daughter's as she was covered with hundreds of enthusiastic kisses interrupted by strangling hugs, Kristen's golden curls tickling her nose with each one.

"Mrs. Caldwell, I can't believe you and Mr. Kuakini survived that explosion!"

Melanie cuddled Kristen in her arms and looked up in surprise at the uniformed official, too overcome to acknowledge him with more than a nod.

"Would you mind answering a few questions?. . ."

"She would, Lieutenant," Ryan swore emphatically, cutting him off. "My wife and family are going home, and to hell with you and your damned questions."

"Then perhaps Mr. Kuakini—"

"—is family, Lieutenant," Ryan insisted. "He's going with

us." Glancing at 'Io expectantly, he asked, "Uncle 'Io, can you take Kristen on your horse?"

'Io's inscrutable eyes held Ryan's for what seemed to Melanie to be an eternity before he nodded solemnly and took Kristen up in his arms. Melanie could have kissed them both for the first hint of friendship between them.

"I must object . . ." the disconcerted officer started, but before he could finish his objection, Ryan's fist shot out, knocking him backward to the sand.

"But hell! If you've any further objections, take them to my business partner. I'm sure Sanford Dole will be interested in your badgering me and my family after the ordeal we've been through, you by-the-book bastard." Her husband turned and offered Melanie his hand, the belligerence gone from his voice. "Let's go home, blue eyes."

Once out of earshot of the officials, 'Io Kuakini pulled his horse up alongside Ryan's and Melanie's, one eyebrow arched curiously. "Whose side are you on, anyway?"

Melanie felt the shake of Ryan's chuckle against her back and leaned into it. "Hers," he answered wryly, "and hers," he added, pointing to Kristen. "And if you have one lick of sense in that hot head of yours, you'll make a similar commitment to my niece. She certainly risked her neck for you tonight . . . at the expense of my aching head."

'Io was astounded by the account Ryan gave him of the women's effort to warn him. Melanie listened, so tired that her husband's account of Kela threatening him with a knife made her giggle.

"I'm sorry," she gurgled in apology at Ryan's annoyed look. "I'm just slaphappy." She sighed heavily, regaining her composure. "I guess I'm just silly with happiness."

Ryan let the horse follow the dirt road on its own, his attention fixed on the blue eyes dancing up at him. Her lips moved with just the slightest hint of a pucker, and he did what he had longed to since he and 'Io had pulled her into the boat. His lips closed gently over hers, conveying all that had gone through his tormented mind in the past few

382

hours—his anguish at having lost her, his love and concern for her and the child she carried, and his joy that he had her in his arms.

Everything fading from focus except the two of them, Melanie surrendered to his ardent message. There was no pain in her arm, only a quiet, comfortable feeling spreading through her, lasting and promising. Hawaii would struggle in its growth, but their love was as long and as lasting as the great banyans that shaded the road from the early morning sunrise. And together they would grow with it.

THE BEST IN HISTORICAL ROMANCES